White Hot Holidays

Ellora's Cave
Romantica Publishing

Tell Us What You Think

We appreciate hearing reader opinions about our books. You can email us at Comments@EllorasCave.com.

An Ellora's Cave Romantica Publication

www.ellorascave.com

White Hot Holidays Volume 1
ISBN 1419956000, 9781419956003

Cover art by Syneca.

This book printed in the U.S.A. by Jasmine-Jade Enterprises, LLC

Electronic book Publication December 2005
Trade paperback Publication October 2006

Content Advisory:

S - ENSUOUS
E - ROTIC
X - TREME

Ellora's Cave Publishing offers three levels of Romantica™ reading entertainment: S (S-ensuous), E (E-rotic), and X (X-treme).

The following material contains graphic sexual content meant for mature readers. This story has been rated E–rotic.

S-*ensuous* love scenes are explicit and leave nothing to the imagination.

E-*rotic* love scenes are explicit, leave nothing to the imagination, and are high in volume per the overall word count. E-rated titles might contain material that some readers find objectionable—in other words, almost anything goes, sexually. E-rated titles are the most graphic titles we carry in terms of both sexual language and descriptiveness in these works of literature.

X-*treme* titles differ from E-rated titles only in plot premise and storyline execution. Stories designated with the letter X tend to contain difficult or controversial subject matter not for the faint of heart.

WHITE HOT HOLIDAYS
VOLUME 1

SEALED WITH A WISH

By Lora Leigh

Dedication

To my readers and the Ladies of my forum.

May all your Christmas wishes come true.

Prologue

"If you could have anything you wish for, Cara, what would it be? Riches and power, the world at your feet. Whisper it to me, and it would be yours for this service you have given unto my people."

The voice whispered through Cara Montgomery's dream. She felt the warmth that surrounded her, a healing, mending warmth that eased the vicious pain tearing at her, brought comfort, peace and filled her with hunger.

"Come, Cara. Whisper to me this wish. I would give you whatever would be your greatest desire."

She twisted against the sheets, her bruised body protesting the movement as she searched for a way to draw closer, to fill her senses with the sound. It was deep, rasping over her like dark velvet, pulling to the surface of her subconscious every sexually erotic act she had ever imagined. It was a caress in and of itself, stroking over her from head to toe, pulling her from the darkness that held her as she fought to draw closer. Just a little closer and she would have it, that greatest dream. Something to call her own.

A voice shouldn't pull a woman's darkest desires from her deepest imaginings. It was painful, saddening. Especially for Cara Montgomery who had never known anyone to call her own. An orphan from birth, raised amid the cold disinterest and mercenary homes her foster families had provided. She had learned to hide, physically and mentally, even from herself. She couldn't afford to wish, because she couldn't bear the loss.

"Cara." Sensuality laced the tone. It was rich with amusement, with warmth. It was so gentle it awoke the

sleeping sensualist inside her and made her scream out in horror at the barren landscape of her life.

Cara squirmed to get closer, fought to fill the emptiness with this warmth, this voice, only to whimper in pain.

The pain brought the memories. The child. It flashed before her again, the little boy, so small, laughter giggling from his cherub lips as he stepped in front of the car. The car was going too fast. The driver had to have seen the child, but it wasn't slowing down. It wasn't swerving.

"Move!" Her scream was lost within her own terror.

She raced from the curb, knowing she couldn't make it in time, there was no way she could make it. The car was going too fast. Her heart was racing, her muscles straining as she pushed herself, stretched her legs, screaming in fury as her arm hooked around the frail little body and she threw him forward.

But she hadn't escaped unscathed. The breath knocked from her body as she was thrown to the pavement as the child's screams had her battling the darkness threatening to cover her. She could feel her own blood, shattered bones, and the certainty that if she died, there would be no one to miss the woman she was.

Weak, disoriented, she had tried to get closer to the little boy, to pull him to her, to assure him everything was okay. But just as quickly he was gone. People moved around her, rushed, anxious voices. But where was the child? Was it safe?

"The child is safe, Cara," the voice whispered. *"So brave, so gentle. Sweet Cara. Whisper to me your wish, allow me to repay you for your strength and your bravery."*

"Find the baby." She could ignore the pain, she fought the more primal needs rising inside her, the demand that she wish for herself. Just once, for herself. Just a touch, a single touch.

"The child lives, Cara. Come, sweet one, surely there is something you wish for the pain you have endured? I will give you whatever you request."

Touch her. That was her request. Just one touch, one kiss, one moment in time to call her own. But she had learned long ago, time and time again, that some things were not meant to be hers.

"Find the baby." Someone had to find the child. Why else would she throw herself in front of a car, risk her own life in such a manner?

A sigh whispered over her brow. *"I will find your heart's desire, little one. I will find it, and by all that I hold dear, I swear that it will be yours…"*

Hers.

The voice. The gentleness within. The promise of passion.

That could never be hers.

"Find the baby," she whispered tearfully instead. "Save the baby…"

Because she couldn't whisper her true wish. Her deepest desire. In that moment she knew the only thing she wanted, even more than life, was to be held in this man's arms. Always.

Kheelan Mattero stared down at the young woman, her cheek dark with the livid bruises that discolored it, her eyes swollen. Wayward strands of short black hair, so soft it put First Earth's silk to shame, flowed around her face in tangled strands before falling barely to her shoulders in a waterfall of midnight color.

She was beautiful. Delicate and small, unlike the warrior women of First Earth, but all the more beautiful for it. Like the pixies Jhemar had told him about. Kheelan believed the stories to be nonsense until he came here to this primitive hospital to assess the injuries of the young woman who had saved his ward.

Jhemar had slipped from the prince's safe house, determined to find adventure within the crowd of children who had gathered in the park across from the house. His Highness had made a mistake in choosing such a locale to hide his family within. Jhemar craved adventure, excitement. He was a warrior in a child's body.

The vehicle that had nearly crushed his little body in the hit and run had, of course, been driven by one of their enemies. Kheelan had taken great pleasure in the death of the coward who would kill a child. Who had nearly killed the glowing life and spirit of this brave young woman.

He touched her brow, sending the healing heat of a warrior's touch to ease her pain and heal the potentially fatal wounds. Without true healing, she would not live past this night, and that he could not have.

When he finished, he brushed his fingers through her hair one last time. Drawing back, he frowned down at her. He had felt her heart's desire for the briefest moment. She was deserving of whatever she wished, and the prince would gladly have it bestowed it to her. Yet, her only concern had been for Jhemar. For the child she had fought to save.

His lips quirked as he trailed the backs of his fingers down the other side of her face, unbruised, unblemished. Perfect satin and silk, it warmed his fingertips, drew him. Made him wont to linger.

He sighed deeply as he drew back from her.

"I will gift you, precious one, one way or the other, for the life of my ward. Had I been close neither of you would have suffered so."

Jhemar would forever be scarred by his actions after slipping from the house. He had been frantic when he called Kheelan, near hysterical as he cried over the pixie who had surely been killed saving him. His own pixie, he had wailed, and now she was gone forever.

But she wasn't and he would see to it that whatever this precious pixie wished, would be laid at her feet.

"Soon, precious," he whispered again. "Think on your payment for such a selfless act. For soon I will know it, and that payment shall be yours."

Her lashes fluttered. For a moment they opened and shock coursed through his veins. Eyes the color of a summer rain. The deep blooming violet of the mountain storms that filled the land of First Earth with its fertile, life-giving moisture. A color that had not been known to the Tarrans for millennia and came even more rarely to those of this Earth as well.

She stared back at him, bemused, certain she dreamed. He could feel that certainty whipping through her with a touch of remorse. And amazingly, with a surfeit of arousal. On the heels of the heat in her eyes whipping around him, his gaze fell in amazement to the binding bands that circled his left wrist. They heated. Glowed. The gold bands, one thick, one more slender, were for one purpose only—the identification of his true mate. This woman, brave, courageous, and so very delicate, was his true mate.

To seal the bond only one requirement was left. Her wish to seal him to her forever. To bind her heart, her soul, and her beautiful body to his own, the words must pass her lips, and the desire must fill her soul. And only her deepest most heartfelt wish would bind her to him.

Chapter One

The club was hopping and the golden sex god was back.

Cara Montgomery watched him enter, decked out in black leather pants that worshipped powerful legs and muscular thighs and lovingly cupped an impressive bulge between them. They rode low on his hips, emphasizing the masculine stride that wasn't a swagger but should have been.

He was head and shoulders above most of the men at the club. He had to be at least six feet five and every inch of his body was proportional to his height. Now, if that bulge matched…

Her face flamed as she jerked her eyes from him, refusing to track the rest of his body. It was forever imprinted in her mind's eye though. The black silk shirt that covered his wide shoulders, emphasized the golden blond hair pulled back from a sculpted masculine face and tied at his nape. She rarely liked blond men, especially men so tall, powerful and confident.

He could have any woman he wanted, but she had yet to see him leave the club with one. He arrived alone, he always left alone. And he always spoke to her. Smiled at her. Made her wet and ready to come. He never failed to rouse a hunger and a heat inside her that grew deeper, stronger, each time she saw him. And she saw him often. Too often.

And she felt him. She knew the minute he headed toward her, everyone at the table went silent. The girls she worked with at the insurance office, their eyes were wide, their lips open, gasping for air like damned fish.

But she could feel him. The closer he came, the warmer she got. Her womb tightened, her sex flooded with moisture and she could feel her nipples hardening, growing hot, pressing against the light chemise she wore.

"Cara." His deep voice was a weapon, one she couldn't defend herself again. God help her if he ever decided to really turn the charm on her.

Ignoring the lusty sighs of the women around her, she turned her head, gazing up…oh Lord, that bulge…up, until she met the blue-gray depths of his eyes.

"Kheelan." His name slipped past her lips, drying them out, sending a flush of need whipping through her body.

Cara felt the flush that washed over her face then through her bloodstream. It wasn't fair that a man should look so sexy, so tempting. Surely he had some kind of horrible habit. Bad breath? With a mouth like that she doubted it. Sensual lips, perfect white teeth. He had to be a lousy lover.

He smiled then, a slow, wicked curve of his lips that forced her to breathe in deep to keep from panting like the women around her.

"You are looking especially lovely tonight." He bent, balancing his weight on bent knees between her chair and her best friend's.

"You're looking pretty good yourself." Yeah. Right. He looked good enough to make a meal out of. For a couple of years. Yeah, she could do without food for a steady diet of Kheelan.

His head tilted in acknowledgement of the compliment.

"I had hoped to see you tonight," he murmured, the sound barely carrying past her own ears as one long finger stroked around the dip of the chemise material at her back.

Oh shit. He was touching her?

"You did?" She blinked back at him. "Why?"

The twitters of nervous laughter around her reminded her that she wasn't alone with Kheelan. That every word, every look would be dissected later. This was what she got for having friends.

He smiled again. That crooked little curve of his lips that made her want to eat him right up.

"I missed you." His finger was drawing designs on her upper back that were driving her crazy.

"I was out of town." She ducked her head, wishing her hair were longer, to hide the guilt on her face. Wishing she could lie to him, to her friends.

She was supposed to give up her insane search, but she couldn't. Her accident the year before hadn't been a mistake, it hadn't been a figment of her imagination. There had been a child. She would not have rushed in front of a speeding, oncoming vehicle for the hell of it.

"Again?" His fingers paused on her back before resuming the caress. "Your boss sends you out of town too often."

"Uh yeah. She's a real slave driver." Cara ignored the disgusted snorts that came from her friends.

What the hell did he think he was doing? Didn't he know the questions she was going to have to answer if he didn't stop this insanity. Teasing lonely spinsters wasn't very nice of him, anyway. Especially lonely, virginal spinsters.

"Perhaps I should discuss this with her," he suggested teasingly. "You need time to play, pretty Cara. You cannot play here with me if you are out of town."

The sudden silence was nothing compared to the shock that sizzled through her system.

"Excuse me?" She nearly choked.

"I miss you when you are not here." His blue eyes twinkled. "How am I to have fun if you are not here?"

Cara licked her lips nervously. Okay now, this was getting out of hand.

"I'm sure you have plenty of other friends, Kheelan." She kept her voice gentle, despite the certainty that he was playing with her now. "I doubt you've even missed me."

He was tired of playing games with this woman, with his true mate. Kheelan narrowed his eyes on the delicate little beauty, and fought to hide his determination to have her in his bed, behind the fall of his lashes.

She was stubborn, this Cara. For a year he had tempted her, come to her dreams and teased her with his touch, and for a year she had denied him. She did not come to him, but rather made him seek her out, made him all but go to his knees to plead for her attention.

A woman of First Earth would have never done such a thing. They were certain of their ability to draw their true mate, and made no excuses for their sexual natures. They tempted their warriors, drew them, used their exquisitely honed bodies to ensure the mating held firm. As with any bonding, neglect could weaken the binding bands and leave a couple forever distant, unable to enter each other's souls. It could literally be the death of a warrior or a warrioress.

"I have few friends, Cara." This was no more than the truth, a warrior made few friends out of necessity. The lands of First Earth were still wide-open, and other than small sections, unpopulated. A warrior's travels could take years, and unless he was mated, such travels were made alone.

Suspicion glittered in her eyes then. She was an intelligent little thing, his Cara. She took no one at face value though, trusted no one, loved no one. From his investigation of her, other than a few friends, she had been alone most of her life.

What made her wish such an existence?

"Then go find your other friends, Kheelan." Her voice was gentle, her eyes, though suspicious, were kind.

"Oh Cara…"

"She's lost her mind…"

"Where's the straightjacket, she needs to be committed."

He watched the frown that flitted over her face at her friends' muttered comments, as well as the heat that intensified in her face. And such an intriguing little face. Like a curious little cat, especially when those unusual eyes narrowed on him and she pushed her chair back.

Ahh, success.

Kheelan straightened, staring down at her as she rose to her feet and grabbed his hand.

"Come here."

That did not sound like an invitation to the nearest bed. Her voice snapped with ire as she tugged at his hand, leading him through the club at what he was certain she thought was a quick pace. It was a leisurely stroll for his much longer legs.

But he liked the way her small hand attempted to circle his wrist. Her fingers lacked quite a bit of space before meeting, but her hold was firm, strong for a woman so delicate.

"I cannot believe you." Amazement colored her voice as she drew him into the crisp late December air of the balcony attached to the restaurant and connected club.

The woodlands surrounded the balcony, providing an intimacy in the area that Kheelan reveled in. It wasn't like home, but it reminded him much of the wildeforests of First Earth. The trees grew huge there, the streams ran deep and wide and the mountain lakes were a mystery all their own.

"I have not yet said anything for you to disbelieve." He noticed the chill bumps that covered her arms, the way she hugged herself against the cold.

Shaking his head, he drew his leather jacket from his shoulders and laid it over hers. Her reaction was breathtaking. Her eyes widened further as his body heat surrounded her then sank into her, just as he had intended. He did not like to think of his woman being cold.

"What are you trying to do, Kheelan?" she asked, confused. "Why are you teasing me like this?"

Kheelan stared down at her in surprise. For a year he had chased her, doing everything he could to draw her into his arms, and still she fought him. And she believed he was only teasing her? Playing a game with her?

"Have you ever wanted anything so deeply, with such hunger, that you thought of nothing else? Dreamed of nothing else?" he asked her, staring intently into her perplexed gaze as his hands touched her hips, drawing her slowly toward him. "I do *not* tease you, pretty Cara. I ache for you. I hunger for you. Perhaps it is you who teases me?"

Damn her, but he was hard. His cock was pressing against his pants with such insistence that he had to grit his teeth to keep from giving it freedom. For surely if he did he would lift her from her feet, wrap those silky thighs around his hips and show her why all women should wear such short, tempting little skirts as the one she wore.

Because it would make it easy for their men to push it to their hips and lift them easily as they sheathed their cocks in soft, heated pussies. Sweet mercy, he needed to fuck her. He thought of nothing else. Hungered for nothing else.

"No..." She shook her head, her tongue peeking out to lick at her lips.

"Yes. You tease me with your soft tongue, licking your very kissable lips each time I am near. You tease me with the soft mounds of your breasts, which become ripe and heavy, their hard little nipples straining toward me the minute you sense my presence. You tease me much, little one, and I am not a man known for his ability to withstand such tempting promises."

His hands slid from her hips to lift her small hands from where they gripped the front of his jacket.

"Here." He pushed them into the large sleeves then raised them to his shoulders. "Hold on to me, precious, allow me to show you the many ways you tease me."

He turned her, pressing her against the wood siding of the restaurant as his hands gripped her waist then slowly slid beneath the camisole top. Flesh so silky it made his hands ache, warm, delicate.

"Kheelan, why are you doing this?" Her voice was thin, a needy little whimper that raced through his bloodstream and sliced through his scrotum.

He could feel her against him, feel her need burning inside her.

"Are you wet for me, Cara? Are you as wet as these pretty little nipples are hard?"

His hands covered her breasts as a shaky moan left her lips. Then his head lowered, his lips nudging at hers as his thumbs raked over her nipples. Her lips parted on a soft gasp of pleasure.

"Shhh." He kissed at her lips, refusing the very enticing invitation of the parted curves as he rolled his thumbs over the tight points of her breasts. "I have only the need to bring you pleasure, Cara. Do I bring you pleasure?"

Her head fell back against the building as his lips nudged at hers again, stroked over them, felt them quiver against his.

"Kheelan." The feel of his name being spoken against his own lips sent blood racing to his cock as he groaned roughly.

"Come with me, Cara," he whispered then. "Come to my home, to my bed. Lie against me and feel my pleasure in you."

Kheelan could feel the fever burning in his veins now. The sweet taste of her, the feel of her body finally pressed against his, conforming to him, as heated and filled with hunger as his was. He had dreamed of this for a year. Ached for it, ached for her.

Finding a true mate was never an easy accomplishment. The children of First Earth had been flung far and wide as they seeded other planets, brought life to them, and watched over them. A warrior traveled often, to many planets, over the course of his long lifetime. Kheelan himself was rarely in one place for more than a few years, and he had given up hope of finding the woman destined to fill the life he lived with happiness.

"Why are you doing this?" She was panting against his lips, reaching for that first kiss with the same desperate hunger that filled him to give it to her. Her lips were soft beneath his, warm and silken. The feel of them was like summer's heat, impossible to deny, to not find joy in. And he needed more.

He caught the upper curve between his, kissing it gently as his tongue swiped over it before pulling back. It would be so easy to forget where they were, who he was, in her arms. Arms that twined around his neck and tightened as she arched closer to him.

"Because I hunger for you," he whispered, his eyes staring into hers as his hands shaped and caressed the swollen mounds of her breasts, feeling his chest tighten with emotion at her response to him. "I ache for you, Cara. I have ached for you since that first meeting, and the hunger only grows."

Confusion filled her gaze as he lifted his head, staring down at her. Her lips were parted and damp, the soft curves reddened from his caress, his kiss. But she wasn't convinced. Naked vulnerability and distrust shadowed her gaze. Tenderness overwhelmed him, weakened his knees as he saw the need to believe, and yet the fear of pain.

Stubborn, hardheaded woman. He would have growled in frustration if he weren't certain the sound would send her running. Enough of this. Enough of chasing after her as a callow youth would do.

His head lowered, swooping down before she could protest, to steal her lips in the kiss he hungered for, ached for as one hand slid from her breasts and moved territorially down her curvy little body. She belonged to him and none other. Her body, her sweet kisses, her cries of pleasure, they were his, forever his, and this he would begin to show her tonight.

Chapter Two

She was going up in flames.

A part of Cara stood back in shock to watch as she melted beneath Kheelan Mattero's kiss, his touch, in a way she had sworn she would never do. But there she was, her arms locked around his shoulders, her lips opened to him, her tongue licking at his as she surrendered beneath the driving pleasure. Nothing mattered but this. Nothing mattered except the driving whiplash of pleasure tearing through her body and bending her to him.

One large hand held a breast captive, his thumb and forefinger doing things to her that stole her objections, her will. Pinching, pulling at the straining bud, sending a lash of burning pleasure-pain to sear her senses as fingers of sensation raced from the tortured tip to convulse her womb.

And if that weren't enough to burn through any objections she might have, then his hand at her thigh, pushing beneath the soft hem of her skirt, blazed through them. She shuddered at the feel of his calloused palm sliding over her skin, his fingers moving ever closer to the saturated folds of flesh hidden beneath her panties.

Oh God, this couldn't actually be happening to her? She was not standing on the restaurant's balcony, pressed against the siding, her thighs opening for this incredible man's hands. But she was. She was following his direction as his hand lifted her thigh until her foot touched the seat of the small metal chair beside them, spreading her open, leaving her vulnerable, defenseless against his touch.

She couldn't protest, her lips were too enthralled with his taste, with the pleasure, with the blinding heat he filled her with. She could only tremble as the hand gripping her breast moved around her back, anchoring her to him. She shouldn't want like this, she told herself. She had forced herself to hold back from him, tried to protect her heart. But there was no protection against this gentle seduction. A year of fighting her attraction to him, her feelings for him, and still she was sinking into his touch.

She knew what was coming. She knew if she allowed it, then she was lost. Her heart raged in denial though. It pounded in fierce demand as hopes, dreams, need coalesced inside her.

Those diabolical, knowing fingers slid to the center of her body, nudging beneath the silk triangle that covered her pussy.

Cara couldn't hold back the strangled cry she fed into his kiss as his fingers rasped over the sensitive flesh. She lifted to him, desperate to draw closer, her pussy weeping her slick juices as it begged for his touch.

His fingers sank into the narrow slit, easing up, parting the swollen lips to find the engorged bud of her clitoris as she felt the pleasure tightening in her womb. It was agonizing, the pleasure bordering pain as she fought the rising tide of insanity threatening to take her over. Oh God, she needed him. His touch, his smiles, the hard male groans of his pleasure.

As his finger rasped around her clit, she jerked against him, feeling the spiraling tentacles of sensation that tore through the oversensitized little bud. She'd had no other man's touch there, only her own. She had never been able to force herself to allow a man to touch her there, until now. And this was excruciating. A pleasure she swore would be her downfall as she fought to throw herself into the flames.

She needed more. She craved more. She needed all of him.

"Easy, precious," he breathed against her lips, his voice immeasurably gentle, coaxing, as he rubbed around her clit, stroking her, building the growing fury of hunger tearing through her. "So wet and wild. Your little clit is throbbing to the touch of my fingers, Cara…" His lips slid along her jaw as he bent to her, moving to her ear as he licked and nipped at the flesh.

There was too much pleasure. Too many sensations.

"I want to lay you beneath me and crawl between your pretty thighs. I would spread you before me and lick all that sweet juice from you. Taste you. Fill my senses with the heat and sweetness that flows for me."

Oh God. Would she survive it?

His fingers continued to stroke around her clit, never with enough pressure to send her over the edge. Just enough to push her higher, then higher still, until the only way to keep from screaming in need was to lower her head to his shoulder.

She meant only to muffle her cries against the broad expanse of muscle. She swore she didn't mean to bite him. She didn't. But as her lips pressed against the cloth-covered flesh, his finger rasped over her clit. A shower of sparks filled her mind, blinding, so hot she thought she would melt then and there. Her lips opened on a scream only to clench instead. They pressed into the rippling power of his shoulder, tightening as the strangled scream tore from her.

Then his teeth were doing the same. The growl that came from his throat should have terrified her, instead it stoked the flames higher, hotter, throwing her deeper into the maelstrom destroying her.

So close. She arched into his touch. So close…

And then it was gone.

Just as quickly as it had risen to overtake her, the tidal wave of sensation shrieked through her nerve endings with the lack of friction, and his fingers were easing from her cunt as his hand hurriedly moved her leg from the chair.

"Cara, I asked if you were ready to go." Milly's voice echoed with ire from the balcony doors, no more than a few feet from them. "I understand Mr. Sexgod there is pretty interesting, but I have to get home to the kids."

Jealousy rang in Milly's voice, as did a hard core of anger.

Cara stared up at Kheelan, seeing the lust glittering in his eyes, feeling the demand in the hard proof of his arousal pressing into her stomach.

"Cara will be inside in a moment, Ms. Blanchard," he was saying softly, his voice rasping, almost frightening in its command that Milly leave. "Please await her there."

"For how long? It's nearly eight, and as much fun as I'm certain you are, no one else is willing to leave until she returns. I should have known to drive myself."

Cara shook her head, fighting to force the drugged passion from her mind at the sound of her friend's snappish voice.

"I'm coming…"

"I'm sure you are, darling," Milly drawled. "But I need you leaving."

Embarrassment raced through her system at the knowledge that Milly was very well aware of what had been going on. The other woman was the most caustic of the group of women who worked at the insurance agency. Mocking and sarcastic, she rarely let a chance to snap at anyone pass her by.

Cara pushed against Kheelan's chest. "I need to leave."

"Come with me, Cara." He ignored Milly's mocking snort. "I promise you, you will not regret it."

"So they all say," Milly answered snidely. "Come on, Cara, you really don't believe him, do you? Look at him. He only wants you because you've fought him for a year…"

"You will leave immediately." Kheelan's voice hardened as he turned to the other woman. "Your vicious tongue pays a disservice to your gentle looks, madam, and shows you for the shrew you are. I will not have your tongue wounding her in this manner."

Cara's chest tightened at his tone, but not in fear. Offense drew his body tight, furrowed his brow and caused his eyes to gleam with anger. He was insulted on her behalf? Trying to protect her? When had anyone ever tried to protect her?

"Where the hell is he from anyway?" Milly mocked, her voice cold. "The Middle Ages? Let's go, Cara. I'm getting cold and I've had enough of his alpha wannabe bullshit. If you're going to leave with Mr. Studly here, at least come in and let the others know so they'll stop giving me grief over wanting to go home."

Milly turned and stomped back into the restaurant, her head high, her flaxen hair spilling over her shoulders as she tossed her head with a sniff of anger. Great. Now she was pissed off. The next week was going to suck. Milly was capable of making everyone's life hell when she was pissed off.

"I feel sorry for her babes," Kheelan muttered then. "To have such a coldhearted shrew for a mother must be torture indeed."

"I have to go." Cara shook her head, fighting to balance herself, to make sense of the emotions, the sensations tearing through her body.

She had never reacted in this way to a man before. One touch of his lips and she had been open, eager for him. She hadn't fought him, hadn't wanted to fight him. Even now her body was pulsing, her pussy convulsing in a wave of need that nearly stole her breath.

"Come with me, Cara," he whispered again, his hand touching her cheek, whispering along her jawline. "Do you truly wish to throw away what you feel in my arms?"

No. She didn't. She was twenty-five and other than those five women waiting on her inside, she had no one. A once-a-week dinner with friends didn't make up for the loneliness, or the demons that chased through her dreams. She could have one night, she told herself. A Christmas gift to herself that someone else would bestow. A far cry from the tiny, empty tree that graced her living room.

For a year she had dreamed of him. Ached for him. The tall, handsome stranger who had made himself a part of her life for one night each week. She didn't know, and for once she didn't care, why.

"My house," she whispered. In her bed, where she could feel the memory once he was gone and hug it close to her.

His dark eyes gleamed with sudden pleasure. Not satisfaction. Not cold triumph, but pleasure, as though her answer meant more than a one-night stand. Yeah. Right. But the illusion was there, and she found herself suddenly desperate to believe in it.

"Come, my car is outside," he whispered, drawing her close to his side as he led her to the automatic doors that led back into the restaurant. "We will say goodnight to your friends."

Would a serial killer be worried about letting her friends know she was safe? Cara felt a near-hysterical spurt of laughter at that one. She was putting her life in someone else's hands at a time when she knew she couldn't afford it. But something else raged inside her, something stronger than the fear. The need. The hungry blinding need this man had fed into her for nearly a year. A need Cara knew she couldn't deny any longer.

* * * * *

She couldn't believe what she was doing. Cara unlocked her front door, feeling the heat and power of Kheelan's hard body behind her, even as his jacket still covered her. The scent of him filled her senses, drew her, and only built her arousal.

She stepped into her small living room, ignoring the sight of her pitiful attempt at a Christmas in the corner of the room. The fake pine sat on the end table, lights twinkling around it, its base empty of presents. Maybe the girls at the office would amend their policy of no gift giving this year. It was her only hope of gaining a present from anyone but herself. And what was the point of buying for herself?

The door clicked closed as Kheelan stepped in behind her. He towered over her, making her feel at once weak, and protected. His jacket hung on her, falling well past her thighs as she felt his hands settle on her shoulders.

"Look at me, Cara." His voice echoed around her, so much like her dreams, filled with arousal and power.

She lifted her eyes, staring into the warm reaches of his blue-gray gaze as she felt the jacket sliding from her shoulders, along her arms, until a shiver raced over her when it no longer enfolded her. He tossed it to the nearby chair before reaching up to smooth her hair from her cheek.

"I have waited forever to touch you," he whispered as his hand trailed down her arm. "To feel you soft and warm against me."

"Why?" He wasn't like any man she knew. This man was strong, sure, and obviously way out of her league.

"Because you shine with purity," he whispered. "With strength and courage. Because in your beautiful violet eyes, I see a hunger that matches mine. A hunger to belong, to be a part of something…of someone. The same as I feel, Cara."

She shook her head firmly, pulling away from him as she pushed her fingers through her hair. God, this was such a mistake.

"You are so far out of my league," she muttered before turning back to him. "I'm a nobody, Kheelan—"

The fierce frown that wrinkled his brow stopped the words in her throat.

"I will show you differently," he growled, his voice thick with feeling. How could he sound so sincere? "You are much to me, Cara."

"You don't even know me," she protested, confused. "A year, a few dances. Kheelan, I'm not a fool. You want sex. A nice little one-night stand from a woman who has been out of reach. Admit it. I have."

He tilted his head, staring back at her as though confused.

"How were you out of reach, Cara?" he asked. "At any time I knew where you were. You told me where you worked, where you lived. The few dances you allowed me, you melted into me, allowing me to lead you through the steps, your body as perfectly fitted to my mine as your passions fit with my body. This is not out of reach, little one."

Okay, so she had been easy more than once.

"I wasn't exactly throwing myself at you," she pouted.

"This is true." He nodded sadly. "Despite my wishes that you would."

He moved to her, his hand reaching out to her, drawing her close to his big, hard body once again. He was so warm, secure. His arms wrapped around her as though they were meant to be there, sending spikes of pleasure, of fear racing through her. She hadn't known how much she had come to care for him, how much his presence at that damned club had come to mean to her each week.

"You wanted me to?"

"I dreamed of it, Cara," he whispered, his lips moving to her brow, caressing over it. "Each night as I gripped my cock in my hand and found what little satisfaction there is to be found there, I dreamed of you coming to me."

Heat flooded her face. "You're very blunt," she whispered breathlessly, feeling the clench of muscles in her stomach at the explicit words.

"I'm very hungry for you, Cara," he growled, his hands smoothing down her back. "A year of waiting, of needing your touch, has created a man who knows no other desire, no other need. It is my greatest wish…" The words jostled through her. "You are my greatest wish, Cara. My greatest desire."

Whisper to me your greatest wish... She hadn't thought of that dream in a year, or the voice that whispered through her mind.

As his head lifted, he stared down at her, his look gentle, yet blazing with arousal.

"Would you prefer me in your bed, precious, or on your living room floor?" It took a moment for the question to process.

"Would you prefer a drink first, something to eat..." Anything to give her a chance to think.

"I would drink from your kiss, I would make a meal of your sweet flesh and find sustenance in the soft cream to be found between your lovely thighs," he murmured, his voice an aroused growl as his hands gripped her hips and pulled her to him. "Make your choice, Cara. I am a man nearing the edge of his control."

Cara turned from him, feeling his hands slide from her hips as she glanced back over her shoulder.

"My bedroom..." The choice was incredibly easy.

It wasn't everyday a woman was given a chance to be with a man like Kheelan. He looked like a throwback Viking—his voice was dark velvet, his touch sure and confident. She might regret it in the morning, but tonight...tonight she would find the pleasure she had only dreamed of in the past year.

Cara led the way into her bedroom, more proud of this room than she was the pitifully decorated living room. Here, every inch of the room was comfort. From the thick throw rugs on the hardwood floor, to the queen-sized, thickly mattressed bed and its dark forest green comforter turned back to reveal exceptionally soft, lighter green sheets.

It looked warm, inviting. A room to share with the lover she only dreamed of having. Unfortunately, Kheelan was the only man she had ever dreamed of in this bed. And Lord, how she had dreamed of him, ached for him. She felt as though the foreplay had been going on for a year now, and she was ready for the promise it had written across her dreams.

She paused by the bed before turning to him, seeing the passionate flush to his high cheekbones, the sultry fullness of his lips. He was sex personified and yet, she knew he was more than sex. More than just physical. He was the one thing she couldn't wish for, no matter how much she dreamed of it. There wasn't a chance in hell he was all hers. Nothing in life ever had been.

"How beautiful you are, Cara."

Her breath caught in her throat as he stopped before her, staring down at her with those incredible blue eyes. Eyes that glittered with hunger and with emotion.

"Don't." She shook her head. She couldn't afford to believe him.

"I will convince you, Cara." Her breath caught in her throat as he gripped the hem of her chemise top, drawing it slowly upward. "I will show you the beauty of your body, of your spirit. I will show you your greatest dream..."

The rasp of the material sliding over her nipples sent a wave of heat coursing through her body, but the look on his face as he tossed the top away broke through any misgivings she might have attempted to listen to. His eyes glowed with approval. It was too much. A woman could only be so strong.

As he undressed her, he drew her hands to his shirt, encouraging her to touch in kind. Encouraging her to lose herself within him. How easy that would be, too easy. And fighting it grew harder by the second.

"Feel us together, Cara. This is not for me alone, nor for you alone. It is to be shared. Share with me, baby."

She needed no further coaxing. She forgot her lack of experience, her misgivings, her certainty that there was suddenly more to this than a one-night stand. That Kheelan was more than she had even suspected, was washed away by a pleasure she had waited a lifetime for. Her fingers moved on the cool buttons of his shirt, fumbling a bit at the stubborn discs, only to shiver and try again as his voice whispered over her senses.

"Easy, precious. We have all the time you need. I promise you this. There is no need to rush."

But there was. She needed him now before life had the chance to reach in and snatch the moment from her.

She pushed the shirt from his shoulders, whimpering as his hands fell away from her to allow the material to pass over them. But his chest was revealed. She stared in fascination at the tattoo there, the star trail that blazed from the center of his chest diagonally to his hip. The lush gleaming color was a splash of cream, silver, hues of stormy grays and glittering gold against his dark flesh, and incredibly erotic.

She bent her head, placing her lips where the trail began and licking her tongue over the rich gold color that began the spiraling rainbow as her hands smoothed down his powerful arms.

She was lost and she knew it. The whispered voice that asked to reveal her greatest dream, her greatest wish for a year now… The man she longed to call her own.

Chapter Three

Sweet mercy how could her touch alone brand him more deeply than her spirit, his need for her, already had?

The feel of Cara's lips against the warrior mark that blazed across his chest nearly broke Kheelan's control. Highly sensitive, the sweet touch of his mate's lips caressing it, accepting him for the warrior he was, shot straight to his cock. It strained beneath his leathers, throbbing in delicious need as his hands smoothed up her back to the small, lacy bra she wore.

The clip came loose easily, allowing him to reach to her shoulders, to draw the tiny straps down her arms as his lips followed the path. She tasted of sunshine, the remembrance of summer's heat in the midst of winter. She filled his soul as only such warmth could.

The small responding shivers that raced through her had his body tightening in anticipation. Her lips were licking lower, following the path of the blazing star. Soon, she would reach the point where it dipped beneath his leather pants—where then would she go? Would she follow the mark to his upper thigh, or would she detour to more responsive flesh to answer her siren's call?

Clenching his jaw against the pleasure ravaging his nerve endings, Kheelan moved to the small hook closure of her skirt at her hip. Flipping it open, he lowered the zipper to her acquiescent moan, and allowed the material to slip from her body.

As his gaze lifted from the sight of her, his eyes narrowed in surprise to see the large, freestanding mirror to the side of the bed. Tall enough to send back to him the full view of every delectable inch her body.

Curvy hips, rounded buttocks bisected by the black material of her silky thong, the slender line of her back marred only by the tiny mole in the center of her spine. She was exquisite. Completely gorgeous. And her lips were making him insane. Her head moved lower down his chest as her hands moved to the clasp of his pants, causing him to hold his breath as it slowly came undone.

Encouragement. All she needed was encouragement, he reminded himself as lust burned through his senses. His hands moved to her hair, tangling in the short strands as he held her to him. She was virginal, he knew this from his research of her. Alone. Her childhood and her life marked by those who had left her. She would need his caring, his sheltering of her as she became the woman he knew she was. Confident, secure. She needed only the chance to realize the depths of her own heart.

"You're lips are like silk, burning into my flesh," he growled. "I have dreamed of this, Cara. Your lips on my flesh, your hunger burning into my body. Burn for me, precious one. As bright and hot as you fuel the flames within me."

Her hands tightened on the material of his pants as she parted it. He could feel the indecision whipping through her as he allowed one hand to move from her hair, to caress over her shoulder, beneath her arm, to the firm breasts, swollen and heated for his touch.

With thumb and forefinger he captured the stiff peak, working it slowly, feeling it harden further beneath his fingers as she whimpered her surrender. Her hands hooked in the waistband of his pants and lowered them slowly. He could feel her melting into him further, her soft flesh softening to his touch, her tender emotions coming to life.

Kheelan's gaze was caught again by the mirror. His abdomen flexed at the power of the wave of lust that tore through him, ripping through his bloodstream until it centered in his scrotum and sent heat pouring into his cock.

That stiffened flesh came quickly into view as she shifted, allowing him a full side view of his rising shaft and the delicate, passion-flushed profile of his mate. His pants went no further than his thighs as he watched her expression soften further, her lips part to allow her tongue to dampen it with a moist swipe.

He was panting now, fighting desperately to breathe as anticipation crawled over his skin, licking over it with a phantom touch similar to the feel of her breath on the oversensitive crest of his erection.

"Cara, sweet love," he whispered, the need to feel her lips on him making him insane.

"I've never…" Her voice was thready, filled with a need that thrummed through him as well.

"Your touch is enough to bring a man to his knees," he whispered as her head raised, her eyes staring up at him with such vulnerability it broke his heart. "Come to me, love, and I will pleasure you this time. There is time for all things."

Denial flashed in her eyes. A denial that at first he thought extended to him, until her head lowered, her soft little tongue emerged and nearly did bring him to his knees.

One delicate soft hand cupped his scrotum as her lips parted, then sank over the head of his cock. Her eyes lifted then, glittering with her pleasure as he felt the heat of her mouth engulf him. Felt his cock sinking further, further inside her mouth. Blazing, fiery, damp flames shot through his body as a growl wrenched from his throat. He lowered one hand to circle and hold the rampant erection, to create a barrier between her lips and his helplessly thrusting hips. He needed to fuck her. Her mouth. Her sweet pussy, her hot little ass. He had to mark her, to make her dream, to need as she had never needed anything in her life. Only her wish could seal their bonding. A wish that grew as deep, as strong as his had over the past year.

But for now, her mouth was everything. Her mouth and those inquisitive little fingers that learned the shape and texture of his scrotum as she began to suck at the rampantly engorged head of his cock. Sweet little fingers that moved lower, shifting behind the sac as she cupped it in her warm palms, and the pads of her fingers stroked, caressed flesh so sensitive his eyes blurred.

Even he was unaware the sensations to be found behind his scrotum. But she somehow knew. Her lips slid from his cock, only to lick, to turn and suckle the side of the hard flesh as she brushed his fingers away and tongued the hard, blood-engorged vein that ran to the base of his cock. There, she licked, tempted, tormented. Then, she became evil, wicked, so innocently carnal with her hum of pleasure as she bent lower, nuzzled beneath the sac and began to lick, to nibble and suck erotically at the violently sensitized area she found.

Her low, hungry moans had his teeth clenching around the strangled groan that tore from his throat. The vibration of the sound on his cock, the smell of her sweet arousal, the touch of her hands, like hot silk, were ripping past his control.

"Sweet love." He fought to breath through the pleasure. "You will bring me to my knees."

Kheelan held her head to him, unable to pull her away, unable to deny her whatever she wished. No matter the torment to his own body, he would give her the freedom she sought. The torture of it was agonizing. The fight for control lost before it began. He could feel the pre-come leaking from the damp head of his cock and had no desire to find his own release before she found hers. She was his mate. Her pleasure came before his own.

His hands moved beneath her arms as he lifted her, ignoring her protesting moan before he stepped to the bed and pushed her back. Her legs dangled over the side. Before she could fight, or roll aside, he had the pretty lips spread wide and his mouth buried in the hot, luscious depths of her pussy. And here was the ultimate sweetness, nature's honey, spilling from her clenching pussy, taken eagerly by his waiting tongue. Here, Kheelan found his own version of paradise.

She could still taste him on her lips. The earthy tang of the pre-come that had leaked from the head of his cock as she covered it with her lips. It had exploded against her taste buds in a taste that sent pleasure shooting through her body. She had wanted nothing more than to feel him, to know every inch of his flesh, to taste it, lick it. To feel him tighten, his muscles bunching at each new pleasure she triggered with her touch. The low, primal moans that fell from his lips with each new touch she had given him only pushed her own arousal higher, hotter. His cock had seemed to harden further at her touch, if that were possible. Flexing and throbbing in approval of her caresses.

It was addictive, intoxicating. He had given his body to her for a few precious seconds, allowing her to explore him, to pleasure him. But it was nothing compared to the feeling of his mouth suddenly taking her. His lips covering the folds of her pussy as his tongue stroked, licked, set fire to the entrance to her vagina. She could feel her juices flowing, hear his groan of pleasure at her taste.

"So beautiful," he moaned as his head lifted, but only to spread her legs further as he caught her hands. "Come, sweetheart. Help me pleasure your sweet body."

Shock tore through her as her fingers covered her own clit. He wanted her to? She flushed in mingled embarrassment and arousal as she felt her own thick juices and the heat radiating from her pussy.

"Show me, love," his husky voice washed over her senses. "Show me what pleases you. I would know so I can always give you what you wish."

Always? She whimpered at the promise. He couldn't mean always, like in *always*, could he?

His fingers were moving hers though as he knelt by the bed, his head returning to the saturated folds of her cunt as he moved her fingers against her clit. Oh yes, it was so good. So good.

Cara fought to breathe as she moved her fingers, catching the rhythm she knew would at least bring ease. But the sensations gathering in the swollen bud were more intense, brighter, hotter, flaring deeper inside her womb than ever before as his tongue flickered over the entrance to her vagina. She could feel her orgasm building as his devilish tongue slipped inside her, pulled back, only to return once more. He was humming his pleasure against her hot flesh, one hand holding her thigh in place as the other—

"Kheelan." She tried to scream his name, but the sensations that exploded through her body left her breathless, shaking, not just at the pleasure, but the emotion unleashing inside her. Possessiveness, despair, joy. One night she had promised herself, but she wanted so much more.

He had spread her juices back slowly, lubricating the tiny hole of her anus. Now his finger filled her. It was buried inside her, thick and hot, moving with shallow thrusts inside the forbidden depths of her ass. She clenched against the invading fingers in shock, her eyes abruptly widening as she stared back at him in surprise.

"Kheelan, what—" Was he doing? Making her feel? A shimmering wildness exploded inside her at the knowledge that he was making no allowances for innocence, he was asking for nothing, allowing her to feel, to know everything she had missed in the cold years she had been alone.

His eyes blazed at her from between her thighs, his long hair spread around his face like a shimmer of light as the sun-darkened flesh tightened over his cheekbones. His expression was carnal, wicked, warm. Naked lust mixed with an emotion she was terrified to believe in.

"Easy, love," he groaned, licking at her again, moving to her fingers that had stilled against her clit. "Feel how tight, how hot you are there. I would prepare you easily for what I need, Cara. Soft and easy, baby, trust me."

His finger slid free, but only for a second. When it returned, it was slicker, a cool gel spreading through her as he worked his finger inside her again. In, out, preparing her, spreading the cooling lubrication until not one but two fingers were taking her. Her head tossed on the mattress as his lips worked over her clit then, sucking it into his mouth as he rasped the delicate bud with flickering licks of his tongue as his fingers raided her rear.

It shouldn't feel so good, but her legs were lifting of their own accord, her knees bending as she braced her feet on the edge of the mattress and lifted closer, driving his fingers deeper inside her.

She couldn't process the sensations tearing through her. Her ass, never touched sexually before, even by herself, was suddenly invaded, impaled, his fingers fucking into her with slow, easy strokes as his thumb tucked against her vaginal opening and slid marginally inside.

"Kheelan..." Her keening cry rasped from her throat as she felt talons of ecstasy raking through her. Her womb spasmed with enough force to draw her upright, to widen her eyes in unseeing rapture as the explosion tore through her.

It didn't ripple. It didn't explode. It tore through her spirit with the power to steal her breath, her senses, her heart, and leave her gasping. She was lost within him, certain that nothing about her life would ever be the same without him now.

Kheelan was teetering on a total loss of control and he knew it. His muscles were tight with the battle that waged within him, the need to dominate, to overtake versus the need to cherish, to love. The possessive gentleness that filled him was nearly more than his warrior's senses could process at once. A man should be either/or. Not both at the same time.

Yet, as he stripped his clothes from his body and lifted her supine body further over the bed, sliding between her damp, quivering thighs, he knew the battle would not end any time soon. With the hard length of his cock poised at the soft, saturated folds of her cunt, he could feel himself trembling with the need to fill her. To take her. Now. He should not be waiting. He should not be staring into her slumberous violet eyes and feeling his heart clench.

"What do you wish?" His voice was strangled, his throat tight with the effort to hold back, just a moment longer.

He had to touch her though. His hands slipped from her hips to her swollen, hard-tipped breasts as his erection docked at the tender portal between her thighs. Heated cream caressed the tip of his penis as she shifted against him, rubbing him into the hot little pussy he was dying to fill as his hands cupped and caressed her breasts.

"I wish for you." Her hands lifted from her sides, her fingers curling as her nails raked over his hard abdomen.

Kheelan sucked in his breath at her answer, as well as her touch.

"How much of me do you wish?" His hands moved to hers, his fingers twining with her more slender ones as the binding bands heated on his wrist.

"All of you..."

Lightning forks of sensation seared through his body as her words broke the last fragile threads of his control. His left hand held hers captive as the bands heated further, while the other clasped her hip, lifting her to him as his hips flexed, pressing the head of his cock past the tender entrance. Heat enveloped it. Searing.

Overwhelming.

The soul fire of her creamy juices washed around the crest of his erection, causing his teeth to grit, though the effort to control himself was gone. He surged inside her, feeling the fragile shield of her innocence give way to the steady impalement of his erection.

Her voice echoed in his ear, the call of his name, her gasping cries of pleasure as he came over her, holding her body close as he felt the binding band release his wrist, slip over their entwined fingers before tightening to fit her more fragile wrist.

Kheelan stared down at her, his cock buried in her to the hilt, feeling the virginal sheath rippling around him, tightening, flexing as she stared back at him with dazed, uncomprehending eyes.

Could she feel the heat of the binding moving through her? The bracelets amplified the need, the thirst for touch, taste, a lust that fed from the emotions of the soul, binding them together in ways they would never be free of.

There it was. He felt their souls connect, saw the knowledge of it in her face as she stared back at him, nearly uncomprehending in her pleasure and the fierce thrust of his pleasure added to her own.

Kheelan fought to breathe, to hold onto that last measure of sanity as he slowly withdrew his cock from the fist-tight grip clenched around him. As the silken tissue caressed the oversensitive flesh, he wondered if he could bear the pleasure now surging through him in a racing, overwhelming tide of sensation.

Cara was certain she had to have imagined the glow of the band that had somehow moved to her wrist. The heat, the wicked forks of renewed pleasure striking at her womb, couldn't be normal. She knew it wasn't normal. Kheelan wasn't normal.

But how had she expected him to be? He was the stuff of fantasies. Sex personified. She had always known he couldn't be normal, but she hadn't expected this. This connected. She could *feel* him. Not just his body invading hers, but his heart, his soul, his emotions. His love for her.

Kheelan loved her?

She hadn't expected pleasure like this.

Her thighs opened wide as his gaze held hers, the dark depths shattered with feeling. He slid inside her in a long, slow thrust that had her gasping, panting, her hips lifting as she arched closer to him, driving him deeper. The feel of his cock stretching her, burning as it slid inside, possessing her, caressing nerve endings she couldn't have imagined she had. The feel of her heart opening, her soul easing… She was going to cry. Oh God, she hated to cry, but the surfeit of emotion was close to breaking her. He needed her. Really needed her.

"So sweet…" he whispered as he broke the eye contact, coming over, his lips caressing her brow, smoothing to her neck before nipping erotically at the flesh. But the emotional connection only grew. A wild, pulsing ecstasy began to throb through her system then, spurred by his touch, his possession.

The little nips along her neck blended in with the pleasure-pain tearing through her as her hands moved to his shoulders, holding tight to him as her nails bit into skin and her legs rose, opening herself further to him as she wrapped them around his waist. He sank in deeper, groaning, a sound of tortured pleasure that enflamed her.

"Kheelan…" His name was a tormented wail falling from her lips as she felt the pleasure growing in her womb, tightening through her muscles. Every cell was sensitized, her blood racing through her veins as she fought for release.

"So sweet and tight, wrap around me, sweetheart, give to me. Give all of yourself to me, precious."

A grimace of hunger transformed his features as he thrust inside her, the thick, rock-hard length of his cock moving faster, deeper, stroking nerve endings so violently sensitive she was shuddering beneath him with each penetration, writhing, twisting in his grip as she fought for release.

"Beautiful. Sweet precious Cara," he growled, his voice hoarse, his muscles bunching, tightening as his thrusts began to gain in speed.

Cara arched her neck as his lips slid further down it, placing stinging kisses along her collarbone before moving to her heaving breasts. Her nipples were spike-hard, sensitive to even the air in the room as perspiration dampened her flesh. Then his lips covered one firm tip, sending her senses reeling as her orgasm ripped through her.

She felt herself trying to scream, but all she could do was gasp for air. Sensation tore through her body like a rocket, exploding, fragmenting, tossing her through space and time as waves of ecstasy pounded around her, in her.

"Kheelan... Oh God. Yes... Oh God...it's too good...too good..." She felt him moving harder, plunging inside her, fucking with frantic driving thrusts until she felt his release rock him.

She felt his come jetting into her, fierce pulses of heat searing her, sending another orgasm rocking through her system as she felt the heat slowly ease from the bracelet, but felt something more destructive, more shattering than any event that had transpired so far.

Cara blinked up at Kheelan, staring into his face, his eyes, and she knew in a moment of clarity, of knowledge, why he wasn't normal. Why he had chased her the past year, why his hunger for her was matched only by his gentleness.

"Oh my God," she whispered as his eyelids lifted, his gaze connecting with hers.

"Not yet," he growled, his expression fierce, dominant. "You will give me this night at least before I must battle your disbelief and your anger. You will give me what you have demanded of me, Cara. All of yourself."

Chapter Four

Cara whimpered at the loss as she felt Kheelan withdraw, felt the slow, velvet slide of his cock easing from her pussy as his eyes still blazed with hunger. They needed to talk. She needed to make sense of the thoughts, feelings, the sensations tearing through her as the bracelet circling her wrist heated once again.

"What…?"

"Not yet." His voice was tormented, tortured.

Before she knew what he intended, he turned her, his hands possessive, demanding as he pressed her to the bed, her cheek resting against the perspiration-damp sheets.

"Kheelan, what are you doing?" Mingled fear and excitement raced through her as she felt his hands on her back, then his lips.

His teeth raked over her shoulder as a primal groan tore from his chest.

"You are mine," he whispered, his lips moving across her shoulders, his tongue licking against her flesh as she felt his still hard cock lying along the crease of her ass. "I claim you, Cara. By the stars, by the warrior rite, I claim you as my own. Whispered from my heart, sealed by your wish, belonging only to you."

Shock blazed through her mind as she trembled beneath him. No one had ever been hers, not in any way. How could this man, this extraordinary man, belong to someone as ordinary as she? And why would he want to claim her?

"I cannot get enough of you," he groaned, pressing her to the bed as he moved behind her, pressing her legs apart as he lifted himself from her, spreading her legs and easing her knees beneath her. "I need all of you, sweet Cara. I need this," he growled, his hand smoothing over the sweet curves of her ass. "Give to me, precious, even as I have given to you."

She shuddered, her hips twitching, lifting to him. She knew what he wanted. No—what he needed. The same as she needed.

"Kheelan, what's happening to me?" she moaned as the ache for this possession began to grow within her. "What have you done to me?"

"I have claimed you..."

Kheelan parted the curves of her rear, staring at the little pucker hidden within it, the soft pink flesh surrounding it. It was so tiny, a tight little haven for his cock, a dark, heated portal to spend the hunger consuming him.

"It will hurt at first," he warned her then, knowing he couldn't let the erotic pain surprise her. "You'll have to relax, press. Press out to me. You cannot fight me, even for a minute."

He lifted the small tube of lubrication he had brought with him, dribbling the heated slickness along the narrow cleft as his fingers caught it and began to work it against the flexing entrance. It was of First Earth, created to lubricate, to ease the sweet muscles and allow the most intimate of invasions.

Cara was whimpering now, exciting little growls of demand leaving her throat as he worked the finger into her, watching the little hole part for him before pulling back, adding more oil, then joining that finger with the second.

She flinched, a startled cry leaving her lips as he pressed both fingers in and worked them in small screwing motions inside her. The hot little cries spilling from her lips were filled with pleasure though, rather than denial. He pulled free, added more of the slick oil before beginning to work the third finger in with the first two.

She pressed back, opening for him as her buttocks trembled. But she took him, clenching around his fingers as he fucked them inside her, slow and easy, scissoring them in and out, stretching the snug muscles as his chest tightened and his breathing became harsh. The oil was perfectly balanced for her sweet body, creating a fire for possession as it eased the snug muscles.

He pulled free seconds later, coated his cock with the oil then pressed the engorged head against the flushed entrance. She could hear his breathing, harsh, desperate, the tension in his body and the sense of incredible need filling her. It wasn't her need alone, but his. And it rocked her to her soul.

"Breathe in, baby," he crooned as he parted the cheeks wide and began to stretch the tight little hole. "Now out, breathe out and take me, Cara. Give me your pretty ass, precious."

She gave. Screaming in pleasure, her pussy weeping against the fingers he placed over it to be certain it was pleasure rather than agony he was giving her. He watched his cock sink inside her, one slow, torturous inch at a time as every muscle in his body strained to hold back.

He was sweating furiously, blinking back the moisture dripping into his eyes as he watched the tiny entrance open wide for the length of steel-hard cock impaling it. Breathing hurt, because the pleasure was so good. Because her cries were filled with shocked arousal and pleas for more and her pussy was drenched with the juices flowing from her.

He swore he would take her slow and easy. That he would ease her into this new experience, show her all the gentleness he could rake from his soul. He was taking the final bit of virginity she possessed. His cock had now taken every portal possible and there wasn't a doubt in his mind she belonged to him, body and soul. He could afford to go slow. To slide his cock in as he watched her clench around it. To ease back, watching the oil-slick flesh as it stretched her, penetrated her, until he could ease back in. That lasted for all of a minute before his hips jerked and he watched in amazement as his body jerked control from his mind and his cock slammed inside her. The bands heated at their wrists, connecting their pleasure, the sensations racing through both of them, as well as the emotions.

He felt her surprise, her shocked pleasure.

She jerked, a strangled scream leaving her throat.

"God yes," she cried, pushing back, impaling her ass harder on the spike-hard flesh invading it. "Harder, Kheelan. Oh God yes, fuck me, fuck me harder."

Kheelan heard his own growls, groans, animalistic and fierce as he pounded inside her. He could feel her acceptance of him and it filled him with strength, with purpose.

"Mine!" The possessiveness, the hoarse demand that erupted from his lips would have shocked him had he the ability to stop and consider his own emotions. "Give to me, precious. All of you. Everything." His spirit tangled with hers as he thrust inside her harder, deeper. Taking all of her.

He was possessed. Out of control. One hand gripped her hip as the other speared two fingers deep inside her pussy as he came over her. His cock began to thrust hard and fast inside her, his hips pumping into the soft cheeks of her ass as he reamed her with delicious abandon. There were no pleas to stop, to go easy.

"Yes," her cries echoed around him. "Harder, Kheelan..." Her hips pumped harshly beneath him, pushing him harder up her ass as his fingers fucked her cunt. "Ah yes. It's so thick. Oh God, Kheelan, you're killing me... So hard... Harder...fuck me harder...harder..."

He growled, a demented sound of lust as he drove them both over the edge, feeling her pussy clench, convulse, erupt as the muscles of her ass clamped down on his cock, milking the seed from his balls and sending him careening into a bliss that had a strangled cry spilling from his own lips as he pumped his seed deep inside her hot little rear.

Cara was in shock. She lay beneath Kheelan's body, shuddering in the aftereffects of a blinding orgasm, feeling his cock twitching as it filled her rear, spurting stream after stream of semen inside her, heating her anus with each spurt as he shuddered above her.

She couldn't believe… Pleasure and pain, in equal force had torn through her as he impaled her ass, filling her until she was certain she couldn't take more, and yet she had, taken more, begged for more, screamed for it.

"Precious." She trembled as he crooned the words, his lips stroking her shoulder as he moved, pulling his cock free of the tight hold she had on it.

Cara whimpered as he popped free of her ass, feeling the heated slide of his semen as it followed his exit. Exhaustion swamped her as his emotions, his need, his…adoration of her, slowly receded from her mind. How strange. How completely intimate. As he moved to her side, collapsing against her, she allowed a smile to tip her lips. He thought he had tricked her into this mating, or whatever it was. That the truth of him would shock her. She wondered if he was even aware of exactly how much she did know now.

Chapter Five

ᘓ

She knew what he was. Human, but not human. A warrior who traveled the stars and oversaw the fledgling growth of the planet his people had seeded millions of years before. They were considered gods at one time, until they had slowly receded and allowed man to grow without them.

She knew his loneliness, his exile from his own people because of his duties. His determination, his dedication and his love.

He loved her.

Cara stared at the wall as her back rested against his chest, feeling the strength of him behind her, protective, secure, warm. But even more, she felt the strength of his soul and his commitment to her.

Had anyone ever been committed to her?

She frowned as she thought of that. She had been isolated for so long, even when she hadn't wanted to be, as though a part of her knew something or someone waited. Or was it just the shock? It wasn't every day a woman realized she had just spent the most incredible hour of her life being fucked into exhaustion by an alien.

Her gaze shifted from the wall to the gold bracelet that now bound her wrist. Not tight, but definitely not removable.

"You know, you're supposed to ask first." She winced at the tight, hoarse sound of her own voice.

Behind her, Kheelan flinched slightly as she felt his worry surface within her own mind. Now that was strange. Cool, in a very odd, adventurous sort of way. But damned strange.

He cleared his throat, searching for an explanation. Cara wanted to smile at the male consternation she could feel.

"I fear rejection. It is a sad thing, Cara." She could hear the smile in his voice, feel the worry in his heart. Could he feel her? Did he feel the confusion, the wariness, the uncertainty.

"I hadn't rejected you," she said softly.

"You ran from me every chance you were given," he snorted, a flaring sense of anger drifting to her. "I would chase and you would run, twitching that little tail like a doe in season as you flitted from me."

Arrogance slid over her, not the impossible, "kill the asshole feigning it", arrogance. The arrogance of a man who knew what he wanted, knew what belonged to him.

Did she belong to him?

"You belonged to me the moment you stepped in front of that car to save the life of our prince," he whispered at her ear. "From that moment on, I would have moved both our Earths to possess you, precious."

Cara jackknifed up in the bed, turning to stare at him, wondering why she even bothered to be shocked now. It *was* his voice. She thought she had only imagined it, only wished it had been him.

"Jhemar is safe, as I assured you." He stared back at her, his eyes somber, his expression saddened. "It broke my heart that you had no proof of your sacrifice. We had to shield Jhemar, his life is most precious to our people, and in much danger."

"I didn't imagine it." She swallowed tightly, her hands fisting around the sheet she held to her breasts. "There was a child?"

"A most inconsolable child," he whispered as he reached up, brushing her hair from her face, tenderness swamping her as his dark eyes gazed back at her with a hint of adoration.

Surely it couldn't be this easy? Finding love. Finding the magic she had always believed life should hold?

"You call this easy?" He snorted, a mocking frown creasing his brow as he obviously read her thoughts. "I nearly lost you to Jhemar's assassins, only to be forced to chase after you, to woo you in a most disturbing manner until I was your greatest wish. Courtship on this planet is a trifle problematic, my love. The women in those clubs you inhabit are downright scary."

And to him, they were.

Cara felt as though her heart would burst. Right there, sitting in her bed, her eyes filling with tears as so much emotion, hers and Kheelan's, threatened to overwhelm her.

"It is the same for me, precious," he whispered, his hand cupping her cheek as he drew her to him. "Finally, love. Finally belonging. I feel these things as well, Cara. You were my wish long before I met you. One I never knew I had."

Her fingers smoothed over the band of gold at his wrist. The thick, engraved gold was warm, filled with a comforting heat, a connection she knew she would take time to accustom herself to.

"I lived for love. And adventure," she finally admitted, risking a glance up at him, knowing all her Christmas wishes had come in the form of this man. "I have a feeling you'll give me both."

"Forever, my love. Your wish is my greatest desire." His lips touched hers, filled with need, passion, and all the love her wishes had held.

She had sealed him to her with a wish. But he had sealed her with his heart.

Also by Lora Leigh

A Wish, A Kiss, A Dream (*anthology)*
B.O.B.'s Fall (with Veronica Chadwick)
Bound Hearts 1: Surrender
Bound Hearts 2: Submission
Bound Hearts 3: Seduction
Bound Hearts 4: Wicked Intent
Bound Hearts 5: Sacrifice
Bound Hearts 6: Embraced
Bound Hearts 7: Shameless
Cowboy & the Captive
Coyote Breeds 1: Soul Deep
Elemental Desires (*anthology*)
Feline Breeds 1: Tempting the Beast
Feline Breeds 2: The Man Within
Feline Breeds 3: Kiss of Heat
Moving Violations (with Veronica Chadwick)
Legacies 1: Shattered Legacy
Legacies 2: Shadowed Legacy
Manaconda (*anthology)*
Men of August 1: Marly's Choice
Men of August 2: Sarah's Seduction
Men of August 3: Heather's Gift
Men of August 4: August Heat (12 Quickies of Christmas)
Wizard Twins 1: Ménage a Magick
Wizard Twins 2: When Wizards Rule
Wolf Breeds 1: Wolfe's Hope
Wolf Breeds 2: Jacob's Faith
Wolf Breeds 3: Aiden's Charity
Wolf Breeds 4: Elizabeth's Wolf

About the Author

Lora Leigh is a wife and mother living in Kentucky. She dreams in bright, vivid images of the characters intent on taking over her writing life, and fights a constant battle to put them on the hard drive of her computer before they can disappear as fast as they appeared.

Lora's family and her writing life co-exist, if not in harmony, in relative peace with each other. An understanding husband is the key to late nights with difficult scenes and stubborn characters. His insights into human nature and the workings of the male psyche provide her hours of laughter, and innumerable romantic ideas that she works tirelessly to put into effect.

Lora welcomes comments from readers. You can find her website and email address on her author bio page at www.ellorascave.com.

ICE ON HER WINGS

By Leda Swann

Chapter One

Bonny Eagle, Beagle to her friends, smoothed her hands down her black leggings to wipe off the slippery film of sweat. Her black gym shoes squeaked as she stepped forward and she winced at the loudness of the noise in the night. To her hypersensitive ears, it was as loud as a gunshot. She knew she should have broken them in a bit before she went off to play cat burglar.

Taking another step forward she suddenly found herself bathed in a harsh yellow light as all around her automatic security lights flickered to life.

Instantly she froze, hardly daring to breathe, expecting every second to be challenged, to be ordered off the grounds, or worse, to be held until police arrived to arrest her.

Damn it all. Why on earth had she forgotten about the risk of such a basic security measure? A man like Robert Barron was unlikely to leave his castle completely undefended, especially in his absence.

She moved carefully on the balls of her feet, ready to take off running as fast as she could. As an ex-champion sprinter, that was pretty damn fast when the occasion demanded.

Nobody came to confront her, no burly security guard with a gun holstered at his side and a mean temper to match came storming up to her demanding to know what she was doing on Robert Barron's estate in the middle of the night. Dressed as she was, in black from head to toe, with her black hair tied up in a ponytail, she could hardly pretend she was here on business. Or on entertainment, either.

Maybe she should have worn a cocktail dress and a pair of high heels instead, slip-on heels that she could have kicked off if she needed to run. That way she wouldn't look quite so obviously like a thief, but like someone who'd just left a Christmas party. And if she got caught, she could have made up some story about being a friend of Robert's and that he was expecting her. She was good at reporting stories. After all, that's what she did for a living.

If she got caught breaking and entering, she'd have to come up with a pretty damn good story, or her job was history for sure. No editor of a respectable daily paper would tolerate one of his junior reporters getting into trouble with the cops for burglary.

Although the motto of the paper was to get the story come hell or high water, if you got caught, it was well known that you were on your own. The paper washed its hands of you.

Getting away with murder, the editor had always said, was the mark of a truly great reporter.

Her breath slowly returned to normal as she realized that no one was coming to challenge her. Slowly she crept into the shadows by the side of the wall, moving out of range of the security lights, needing to get inside before someone decided they were worth investigating after all.

An unlocked door or window was all she needed, and she would be inside.

Before she had crept more than partway around the house she found exactly what she had been looking for. High up on one wall was a partly open window, small enough and set high enough off the ground to deter the casual intruder, but not her. Lean, lithe and athletic, she could get through such a window with ease.

Well, maybe not with ease, she admitted fifteen minutes later when, exhausted, sweating and scratched to pieces, she finally wriggled through the window and found herself in a tiled bathroom. She knew it was a bathroom even without the lights on—she'd damn near fallen head first into the toilet on her first attempt to get through the window. And the tiles made her gym shoes squeak even louder than before.

At least it was warmer inside out of the cold. Flicking on the flashlight she carried, she stole through the bathroom and into the adjoining bedroom. With any luck she would find the papers she needed right away and be out of there, the tantalizing prospect of a promotion to senior reporter measurably closer, before Robert Barron or any of his staff were any the wiser.

Robert Barron brought his red sports car to a growling halt in the basement garage. Not in the mood for celebrations, he'd left the Christmas party given by one of his business associates as early as he decently could. Though it had been five years ago now, the death of his wife, Lisa, seemed to hurt twice as badly at Christmastime as at any other time of the year. He was tired of drinking endless Christmas toasts with businessmen he barely knew, and with pretty women whose baby blue eyes could not hide the avarice in their hearts.

He took the stairs two at a time, not bothering with the lights. He knew his house so well that he didn't need them to know where he was going.

Reaching his bedroom, he flicked the lights on and headed for his dressing room, eager to throw off his formal attire and sit back down in front of the computer in his study. One of the spreadsheets from the financial analyst this morning hadn't looked quite right and he wanted to go through the figures himself…

A startled gasp sounded in the silence, breaking his train of thought completely.

He whirled around, his hands still fumbling with the knot of his tie. Who the hell was in his bedroom?

A figure in black, a woman by the shape of her, stood bent over guiltily at his desk, a sheaf of papers in her hands.

He stalked towards her, his natural sense of caution giving way to anger. "What the hell are you doing here?"

The figure in black did not stop to answer. Dropping the papers she was rifling though, she darted to the side, making a surprisingly fast run for the bedroom door and for her freedom.

Acting on instinct rather than on thought, he made a wild grab for her.

His wild grab was more successful than he had expected. His fist tangled around her swinging ponytail, stopping her dead with a jerk.

"Owwww," she yelped, dancing up and down on her black-sneakered feet. "Let go off my hair, you…you caveman."

Her tone of offended dignity struck him as so ludicrous he very nearly laughed out loud. Here he was, half expecting to have a gun thrust against his temple for his rashness in tackling her, and instead she was complaining about having her hair pulled.

Gun or no gun, he wasn't going to let her go now that he had caught her. She'd had the temerity to break into his house. No one, but no one, messed with Robert Barron and got away scot-free. Not even a young woman with silky black hair and the lithe, lean body of a dancer. Or of a professional thief. "So you can escape down the stairs and make off with whatever of mine you have stolen?" he inquired silkily, leaving his fist tangled in her hair. It seemed the easiest way of keeping hold of her. "It may be nearly Christmas, but I'm not feeling that generous."

"I haven't stolen anything." When she wasn't squealing in indignation, her voice matched her body—slightly husky and naturally seductive.

"I interrupted you too soon, did I?" It was just as well he'd left that blasted party early, or he would have come home to a burgled house and missed the satisfaction of catching the thief. "My apologies, but you will forgive me if I check before I let you go."

"You are going to let me go?" The surprise in her voice was a dead giveaway. Whether or not she had stolen anything yet, she had come here to make mischief. Her clothing alone would have told him that much. No one paid social calls wearing skintight black leggings. Even though they certainly showed off a woman's legs to advantage.

"Is there any reason why I shouldn't?" He was not above tormenting the little thief with a sense of false hope. "After all, you claim not to have stolen anything."

She started to shake her head vigorously, and then stopped, wincing with pain, as she realized her hair was still tangled around his hand. "No reason at all. It's just that I thought…" Her voice trailed off into silence.

"You thought what?"

"I thought you would, uh, want to talk to me or something," she finished lamely. "But seeing that you don't," she continued in a determinedly chirpy voice, "I'll just have my hair back, if I may, and I shall be on my way."

She was way too naïve to be a professional thief. There was so little cynicism, so few hard edges on her. Which simply raised another question—what the hell had she been doing in his house rifling through his papers? "I don't think so."

"What do you mean?" That startled look again, like a frightened sparrow.

"I intend to let you go. Eventually. Once I have called the police and informed them that I caught an intruder in my bedroom and they have come to take you away. I will be perfectly happy to let you go into their custody." He felt like a complete heel threatening her with the police, but he wanted to get to the bottom of the story.

"The police?" Her eyes widened with horror. They were, he noted, rather beautiful deep brown eyes fringed with long, dark eyelashes. Gorgeous eyes, in fact. The sort of eyes a man would lose his head over. "You can't call the police."

"It's the customary thing to do when you discover a burglar in your house."

"I swear I haven't stolen anything." Her voice was high, almost panicked, whether it was from fear of the police or fear of being caught in her lies, he couldn't tell.

"Ah, yes. The body search. Thank you for reminding me." He pulled her over to the door, closed it and stood with his back against it. He wasn't going to let her get away without first making sure she hadn't swiped anything that mattered.

Now that there was no way out except through him, he released her hair.

She stepped back a few paces and shook it free with an exclamation of relief. That done, he saw her eyes flicker around the room, clearly looking for an alternate escape route. He saw her hesitate for a fraction of a second as she looked towards the bathroom and then dismiss her momentary thought with a tiny shake of her head. There was no other way out.

He eyed her slim silhouette. Not many possible hiding places that he could see. "Turn out your pockets."

"I don't have any pockets to turn out," she said defiantly, her hands on her hips.

"Come here and let me check."

She shook her head. "I don't think so."

"Fine." Reaching into his pocket, he dug out his mobile phone. "I'll just call the police right away and give them the pleasure of searching you."

Her face visibly paled. "Not the police. Please."

"You have a problem with the police? A prior record, by any chance?"

"I already told you, I'm not a damn burglar."

"Then come here and prove it to me."

She inched a step closer.

"I don't have all night."

Swallowing her nerves, she stalked up to him and stood nose to nose. "Fine then," she spat at him. "Search me all you like. A deviant like you would no doubt enjoy humiliating me like that. I don't care. As long as you promise to let me go when you're finished."

"A deviant?" Her accusation touched his pride. "I am not a deviant." He was simply defending his property, nothing more.

She shrugged. "Whatever."

A sudden suspicion crossed his mind. "This wasn't an accident, you being here in my bedroom. You know who I am, don't you?"

"Who doesn't?" Her defiance was back again in full swing. "Your face is on the cover of every sleazy tabloid in town."

"You knew this was my house."

"It's hardly a state secret that you live here."

"You knew I'd be at that Christmas party tonight."

"A lucky guess."

So he wasn't imagining things. He *had* been deliberately targeted. "Who sent you?"

"Nobody sent me. I came here on my own." She sounded decidedly miffed that he thought she had been sent by someone else. Interesting.

"What were you looking for?"

She shrugged again, refusing to answer.

"I can see I will just have to look for myself." He was really angry now. Angry that she thought she could break into his house and use her gorgeous body and the promise in her deep brown eyes to get away with it. "Take off your sweater."

Stretching her arms above her head, she pulled off her sweater, revealing a tight black T-shirt underneath. Really, the woman ought to buy clothes that were big enough for her, not T-shirts that strained over her breasts like that. It wasn't even that her breasts were particularly large, the T-shirt was definitely too small. "You like black?"

"It doesn't show the dirt," she replied, in an offhand manner.

"Give me your sweater."

She tossed it to him. "Catch."

The warmth of her body lingered in the soft wool and he had to resist the temptation to take it to his face and inhale the scent of her. She would definitely think he was a deviant if he did that. Instead he gave it a brief inspection to make sure nothing was hiding in its folds and then tossed it in the corner.

"Now your shoes."

With a glare of irritation, she kicked off both her trainers. "Nothing in them but my feet."

"And your socks."

Hands on her hips, she simply looked at him. "Aren't you taking this a bit far?"

"I can always call the cops instead if you prefer."

"What on earth do you think I would be hiding in my socks?"

"Beats me. I don't know what you've stolen."

"For the third time already, I am not a thief." Her fists were clenched at her sides as if she was ready to strike him for the insult.

"I beg your pardon," he said with mock courtesy. "I don't know what you were trying to borrow then."

She heaved an irritated sigh. "Nothing that I would be able to slip into my socks, that's for sure." Bending over at the waist she pulled off first one sock and then the other and tossed them on top of her shoes.

They weren't the sort of socks he would expect a cat burglar to wear. Not that he had much idea what the run-of-the-mill cat burglar wore on her feet, but it sure wasn't these. "Glittery Christmas tree socks?"

"I happen to like Christmas trees. And they were hidden by my leggings anyway so nobody was going to see them. Have you finished humiliating me yet?"

"Humiliating you? Yes. Searching you? No."

"I'm not taking off any more of my clothes, so don't even think of asking me to," she warned. "I haven't got anything of yours on me. I swear."

"Do you really think I would take the word of a cat burglar? Come over here."

She stepped a fraction closer.

It was close enough for his purposes. Kneeling down in front of her, he ran his hands first over one ankle and then the other.

"What are you doing?" she asked, trying to shuffle backwards out of his way.

He held her ankles so she could not move away. "Patting you down." Finding nothing out of the ordinary on her ankles or calves, he moved his hands to her knees. "What does it feel like to you?"

"It feels like you're groping me," she said in an accusatory tone.

He shot a glance up at her face, which had started to redden around the edges. "Now then, why would I do that?"

"Because you're a deviant."

"For a cat burglar who has been caught red-handed, you're not very polite. Shouldn't you be on your knees in front of me, instead of the other way around? Shouldn't you be begging for mercy right now, promising me whatever it takes to let you go?" He wouldn't at all mind having this little cat burglar on her knees in front of him.

That thought brought an image to his brain of her kneeling in front of him, sucking his cock in exchange for him letting her go. His cock leapt to life at the thought of her soft black hair falling over him as she suckled him with her mouth and tongue.

He tamped down the inappropriate image, doing his best to encourage his cock to behave more circumspectly. Hell, she'd never believe he was innocently patting her down if he got a huge erection.

"You've already said you would let me go if you didn't find anything. And you won't find anything," she added confidently.

"I won't if I don't look," he replied, moving his hands to her thighs. The leggings were so tight on her that they left no room for any contraband, but he was going to make damn sure of that. Not because he wanted to run his hands over her tightly muscled thighs—that was merely a side benefit. He did not like being robbed, not at all. He just wished he knew what she had been after.

"Excuse me. Do you mind?" Her voice was choked.

He came to with a start, realizing exactly where his hands had been. He had been caressing her like a lover not like a body searcher. And hell, her panties were damp under his fingers. So damp her juices had leaked right through her leggings while he had been touching her.

His face burning he snatched his hands away as if he had been stung. "Sorry," he muttered. "I wasn't thinking."

"On automatic pilot, huh?" she asked rather nastily. "Find your hands on a woman's pussy and start stroking it without thinking?"

That was exactly what had happened, but he was damned if he was going to admit it. His search had made one thing clear to him—she was certainly not hiding anything in her panties. Nothing bar a hot, wet pussy that he would love to get his hands on. And into. He got to his feet again, standing eye to eye with her. "Take off your bra," he ordered her brusquely, to hide his discomfiture.

"My bra?" Her face was as red as his felt.

"I was married once. I know that women hide things in their bra when they want to keep them safe."

"No. I won't."

"Then take off your T-shirt if you prefer. I don't mind either way. In fact," he said with an exaggerated leer, "I'd rather you took off your T-shirt."

"My T-shirt? You have got to be joking."

"Nope. Either your T-shirt or your bra has got to go. Your choice."

Her glare was colder than the howling wind outside. She reached under her T-shirt, unhooked her bra and drew the straps awkwardly over her shoulders. With an evil look at him, she tossed it on top of the rest of her clothes. "See. Nothing in it."

Christmas trees on her socks, and a plain white sports bra under her black cat burglar clothes. An odd mix. She certainly hadn't come here with seduction on her mind. A pity that. He would have enjoyed being seduced by her. "Not even a set of car keys?"

"I walked."

His brain barely registered her answer. If her T-shirt with her bra on was tempting enough, her T-shirt without her bra on was way worse. It was hard not to stare openly at her breasts. Pert and full, they tempted his gaze. Only the sure prospect of being called a deviant yet again forced him to look away.

What to do with her now? She hadn't stolen anything—yet. Clearly from lack of opportunity than from lack of motive. She had broken into his house when she had no business being here. Yet he was reluctant to call the police on her. After all, what harm has she done to him? And it was nearly Christmas, after all, a time that should be about peace and goodwill to all mankind. All womankind, too, even if they were cat burglars.

"So, now what?" she asked, mirroring his thoughts.

"Now," he said, surprising even himself with the words that came out of his mouth, "you will come over here and kiss me."

Bonny gasped. Of all the deviant ideas she had ever heard, this one took first prize. "K…kiss you? What on earth for?"

"So that I don't call the police and ask them to take you away."

"You said you would let me go if I hadn't stolen anything. And I haven't." She crossed her arms over her breasts, feeling uncomfortably vulnerable without her bra under her T-shirt. Even if she could make a run for it at this last stage, she'd never be able to run far with her boobs bouncing around all over the place. If he called the cops, she'd have to chance it though, bare feet and all. Being a journalist was her life—she wasn't going to have her dreams ruined by Robert Barron, of all people.

"You broke into my house. God knows how much the damage will be—"

"I didn't break anything," she protested. No way was Barron going to stick her with some fictitious bill for some nonexistent damage she hadn't done to his precious damned house. "You left a window open."

His eyes narrowed. "Which window?"

"The one in the bathroom next door."

"You crawled through that tiny window without breaking anything?" His eyebrows rose. "You must be an impressive contortionist."

"Gymnast," she clarified. Ten years of gymnastic lessons hadn't been entirely wasted on her. Of course, her mother would turn in her grave if she saw what use she was putting them to.

"You broke into my house," he repeated. "I figure I deserve some compensation for that."

"How about if I offer to leave right now and never come back again." It was hopeful, she knew, but she couldn't resist trying it. For whatever reason, he didn't really want to call the cops on her or he would have done it long ago. Maybe Mr. Barron had a few secrets of his own hidden around his house that he didn't want the cops to find. She would be sure to pay him another visit to see what she could find—only she would make sure he was out of the country at the time, not just supposed to be at some damned fancy Christmas party. It was typical of her bad luck. If only he had stayed there for another half hour or so, she would have been gone before he had caught her.

"Not good enough."

"So what do you want, then?"

"A kiss."

She turned her head on its side and looked at him. Really looked at him. He wasn't too bad, if you went for rumpled Italian suits and funky eyeglasses. His hands had certainly known what to do around a woman's body. Her pussy was still wet from when he'd been groping her earlier. She should've stopped him earlier, she knew, but it had just felt so damn good. No man had gotten that close to her for months—not since Murray had run out on her with the blonde bimbo he worked with.

She'd like to bet that Barron was dynamite in the sack. Any man who could just about make her cream in her panties with a few distracted fondles, not even on her bare skin, had to be worth getting to know a little better. Especially when she shouldn't have been standing there letting him touch her in the first place, but kneeing him in the groin and leaping down the stairs and out the front door instead.

"A kiss, huh?" She crossed her arms more firmly across her breasts to hide the peaking of her nipples. Damn it all, she wanted to kiss him. "How do I know you won't kiss me and then turn around and call the cops after all?"

"You don't." His grin was as bright as a lit-up Christmas tree. "That adds to the spice of the deal."

What the heck. She was young and single and trapped in the bedroom of a very hunky man, whatever his morals were like. And it was nearly Christmas. Mistletoe and all that. She might as well take her kisses where she could get them. They hadn't exactly been thick on the ground since Murray had left. He'd been a lousy kisser anyway. A pretty lousy fuck, too, though that was beside the point. She wasn't going to sleep with Barron—just kiss him and leave again.

"What the heck. It's only a kiss." Moving closer to him, she leaned into his body and reached up to his mouth with her own.

He smelled good. Better than good. Absolutely wonderful, in fact. He smelled like peppermint sticks and cinnamon cookies, like fruitcake with almond icing, like Christmas pudding soaked in brandy. It must've been some Christmas party he'd abandoned.

He even tasted like Christmas.

Better than Christmas.

His mouth was firm against hers as he kissed her softly, gently. She'd thought he would kiss her roughly, demand more from her than she wanted to give. Just the opposite. She wanted more than he was giving her. Deliberately she deepened the kiss, opening her mouth wide and inviting his tongue inside to explore her.

With a moan in the back of his throat he accepted her wordless invitation, exploring her mouth with growing confidence. Her own tongue fought back against the invasion, dueling with his, the touch making her shiver with desire. Damn, but it had been a long time since she'd been kissed like this, by a man who knew what a woman wanted and cared enough to try to please her. Murray had kissed like a dog in comparison—all teeth and slobber.

She leaned into him, her braless breasts pressing against his shirt. Her nipples were standing to attention for real now, so hard and sensitized that the slightest bit of friction sent waves of pleasure shooting through her whole body.

His hands were on her hips, drawing her body closer to his. Her T-shirt rode up, leaving a patch of bare skin at her waist, and his hands slid up to her waist, and then higher, under her T-shirt, until they were on her rib cage, just below her breasts.

He stayed there, hesitating. "Do you want me to touch your breasts?"

She should not want Robert Barron's hands on her breasts, but she did. "Please," she begged him, humiliated that she had to ask, but wanting his touch so badly she was willing to humble herself in front of him. Thrusting her breasts forward, she did not give him a chance to back away.

Her nipples were so hard that the brush of his knuckles against them made her jump.

"Do you like that?"

His hands moved to cup her breasts, squeezing them until she thought she would faint with pleasure. With no breath to answer him, all she could do was moan her acceptance.

She wanted more. A whole lot more. She wanted his hands back where they first had been when she started thinking naughty thoughts about him. Taking hold of one of his wrists, she tugged at it, moving it down off her breast.

Misunderstanding her at first, he took both his hands away and stepped back with an apology. "Hell, I'm sorry. I don't know what came over me."

"Don't apologize," she said, moving his hand still lower and slipping it inside her leggings, inside her panties, until it was resting on her mound. "And don't stop."

He swallowed audibly. "Your pussy is bare. Shaved."

"Waxed. Do you like it?"

"God, yes. I more than like it. You want me to keep touching you?"

His hand was warm against her skin. "Yes. I want you to keep touching me." She wriggled against him, urging him to explore her between the legs, to touch her clit and stroke her pussy, to put his fingers into her and feel how wet she was for him. "I want you to take all my clothes off and strip-search me from top to toe. And then…" Her voice trailed off. Even with her eyes closed so she could not see his face, she wasn't brave enough to put her fantasies into words. How could she possibly tell Robert Barron, multimillionaire property developer and darling of society, that she badly wanted him to fuck her?

"And then what?" he prompted her.

She couldn't tell him. But maybe he could tell her. "What would you want then?" she asked slyly, stroking his chest through his white dress shirt. His chest was hard and muscled. Robert Barron was no soft-bodied, soft-living pussycat, but a panther on the prowl.

"Then I would want to lay you on my bed and kiss you all over. Every inch of you."

His voice, combined with the soft strokes he was giving her clit, sent wave after wave of desire roiling through her body. Just a single lick of his tongue on her clit would be enough to make her come, she was so turned on. "That would be a good start," she agreed breathlessly.

"Then when I have had enough of tasting your sweet body, I would like to take my cock and thrust it into your warm, wet pussy." Pushing her panties out of the way, he thrust the tip of one finger inside her as he spoke.

His finger was nice enough, but she wanted his cock. She moved her hands down to his hips and stroked them over his groin. His cock was standing up thick and stiff inside his trousers, as hard as her pussy was wet. "It keeps getting better and better."

"And thrust into you over and over again until we both can't last another minute. Do you want that, too?"

She wanted to come in her panties just at the thought of it. "Yes, I want that, too," she said, as she gave his cock a gentle squeeze through his pants.

He pushed first her leggings and then her panties over her hips until she was standing before him, wearing nothing but her little T-shirt.

His hands nudged her thighs apart. "Open your legs for me."

Helpless to resist, she spread her legs wider until her cunt was on display for him.

Then he knelt in front of her and began to lick her naked pussy.

His tongue was magic. In and out he thrust his finger into her cunt as he licked and sucked at her clit until it was throbbing with desire.

"Robert, please, I can't take any more."

His head rose for a second. "Surprise yourself." And then he was back again at her pussy, licking her again.

"I'm going to come. I can't take it any longer."

"Come then." His voice was muffled in her cunt. "I'll catch you."

Her hands wound in his hair, tugging at it. If he kept licking her like that, he was going to make her come. Clenching her pussy muscles tightly together, she tried to stop the inevitable, but one last hard thrust of his finger and she was undone.

Waves of orgasm rode over her, leaving her gasping and helpless in the aftermath of pleasure.

"Did you like that?" His voice was the voice of a man who thoroughly expected to be complimented on his lovemaking abilities.

What had she done? Not only was she gasping and helpless, she was also thoroughly embarrassed. She'd just let a perfect stranger lick her clit and fuck her with his finger until she orgasmed right in front of him. And he hadn't even taken off his clothes. "I can't believe I just did that."

He stood up and clasped her to him, grinding her wet pussy against his erection, leaving damp patches of her cunt juice on his expensive Italian suit. "That was just an appetizer. The rest of the meal is still to come."

"The rest of the meal?" she asked weakly. Her knees were close to buckling under her. She hadn't had a powerful orgasm like that since goodness knows when. "I don't think I could take much more."

"Surprise yourself again," he said, throwing off his jacket and tie, kicking off his socks and shoes and stepping out of his trousers. "I intend to see just how much you can take and how far you can go. I'll push you to your limit tonight. And then beyond it."

Standing before her in nothing but his shirt and his boxers, he looked like he meant business. Though she had just been completely satisfied, she felt her pussy respond to him again. She wanted to taste him as he had just tasted her and make him wild for her.

"You're wearing a few too many clothes still," she said, her hands on the waistband of his boxers. "Can I take these off for you?"

"Please."

She pushed them over his hips and stood back to admire his cock, proud in the night. "Mmmm, nice," she murmured, running her hands over its silky softness. "Naughty and nice." She went down to her knees, her face close to his groin. "Can I taste you?" she asked, her words a caress of breath against him.

"Yes." His voice sounded slightly strangled.

She reached out with her tongue and placed the very tip of it on the head of his cock, teasing him. "You taste good."

"Take me into your mouth and suck me."

His cock was long and so thick she had to open her mouth wide to fit him inside.

Wanting at first only to give him a taste of the pleasure he had given her, she sucked on the head and licked him up and down the shaft of his cock.

His groans of pleasure egged her on. Her pussy was getting hotter as she sucked on him. His obvious pleasure was turning her on all over again.

"Enough," he finally ground out between clenched teeth. Wanting to give him a taste of his own medicine, she kept on sucking at him, until he pulled back from her and helped her to her feet.

"Too much more of that and I'll come in your mouth."

"Surprise yourself," she teased him. "Let yourself go."

"I want to come in your pussy tonight," he growled, as he steered her towards the bed.

There would be no complaints from her. Her pussy was aching to have his cock inside thrusting into her.

Together they tumbled on to the bed. He pulled her T-shirt over her head as she wrestled open the buttons on his shirt and dragged it over his shoulders.

Finally they were both naked.

"You don't have to fuck me."

She paused in the act of kissing down his breastbone. "What?"

"You don't have to fuck me if you don't want to. I won't turn you in."

"I know you won't. If you wanted me arrested, you'd have called them as soon as you saw me."

"You haven't come to bed with me just to get away with whatever you were trying to steal?"

"I'm not a damned thief. I have come to bed with you, Robert Barron, because you made me cream just by licking me. Nobody, and I mean nobody, has ever made me do that before. Now I want the good hard fuck that you have been promising me. So don't disappoint me now."

That seemed to deal with his scruples. Pausing only to grab a condom out of his bedside drawer and pull it on, he came to lie over her, his cock nestled between her legs.

Positioning herself so he was at the entrance to her cunt, she spread her legs wide and then nudged him inside her.

He continued the thrust, pushing inside her until he was buried to the hilt in her cunt.

God, it felt good to have a man inside her. She clenched her pussy muscles around him as he withdrew, not wanting him to leave her, and then opened up again in welcome as he thrust back inside her.

Her orgasm was building up inside her again, stronger than before.

His cock pounded into her, faster and faster, taking her with him.

His breath was coming fast and shallow. "Your cunt is so hot and wet for me," he grunted as he thrust deeply into her, "I can't hold on much longer."

Her pussy was tingling, as she felt herself on the verge of coming again. Grabbing his hips, she urged him to plunge deeper into her, wanting to feel him explode inside her. "Come inside me."

One last guttural moan and his face contorted as his cock throbbed and pulsed deep in her cunt.

Feeling his orgasm pushed her over the edge. She exploded into a million tiny tremors, each one more intense than the one before, until she could only lay, limp and exhausted, under him.

Finally he rolled off her and took her into his arms. "I'm sorry. I couldn't hold out any longer."

"It was plenty long enough for me," she murmured back sleepily. Two orgasms in one night and she was more than content.

"That was the first time I've made love with a woman since my wife died."

Her sleepiness suddenly dissipated, replaced with surprise. "But that was—"

"That was Christmastime five years ago. I know."

"And you have never had a lover since?" A man like Robert would surely have dozens of women panting after him. How many men were there in the world who had what he had? Oodles of money, a hot body and a touch that could melt an ice queen.

"Since Lisa died, I never met a woman I wanted to take to bed. Until you came along."

She was silent, not knowing what to say to a man who had just unburdened his soul to her. How little she knew about Robert Barron.

The awkward silence was broken with a chuckle. "How could I resist a woman who creamed her panties when I was strip-searching her?"

His words only reminded her of the tenuous nature of her position. Sooner or later, he would want answers from her. And she would not want to give him any. "I should go."

His arms tightened around her. "Stay the night."

She hesitated. The bed was warm and Robert Barron was warmer. Outside was nothing but a cold wind and a long, cold walk back to her empty apartment. The temptation to stay curled up with him was great.

He wasn't such a bad sort of man. Anyone who fucked like that couldn't be all bad. Especially someone who had seen to her pleasure—twice—even though it had been five years since his last fuck.

"Please."

The wistfulness in his voice settled it. Relaxing into his embrace, she stayed.

Chapter Two

Bonny awoke with the wintry sun filtering through the bare trees outside the window. The white sheets around her were disheveled with the gymnastics of the night before, and the comforter was all bunched up on one side.

She looked over at Robert, sleeping peacefully on his side. God, he had a nice body. She was surprised that a business mogul like him had the time to keep himself so well toned. Maybe he'd had nothing better to do since he lost his wife. He sure hadn't spent his time picking up women. She was his first fuck in five years. Small wonder he'd exploded as soon as he'd thrust into her pussy. Not that she could complain. She'd exploded pretty damned fast too, and she didn't even have the same excuse.

Her eyes were drawn to his cock hiding under the sheet, also sleeping peacefully, so different to the vibrant and rigid member it had been last night.

Just the memory of that wonderful cock in her cunt made her nipples harden and her pussy moisten.

He'd liked her Brazilian, too. She liked a man who appreciated a naked pussy.

And yet, despite the tingling in her pussy, she worried about the situation she had allowed herself to get into. How had breaking into his house ended up with them fucking each other senseless and then her sleeping all night in his bed?

So, what now, Beagle? she thought to herself. Sneak out before he wakes? Wake him up and leave? Stay for breakfast? *Well, Beagle, you dumbass, you've put yourself into this, you can damn well get yourself out again.*

Her musing was interrupted when she noticed Robert's eyes were open, watching her. He hadn't moved, but he was awake. How long had he been like that?

"Good morning. Sleep well?" His voice was husky with contentment.

"Mmmmm," she said noncommittally. "And you?" She should have gone home last night after all. Mornings after were impossibly awkward.

"Like a baby. You were so responsive, so exciting, you wore me out." He gently stroked her smooth mound. "And this, this is a delight."

The discussion had caused his cock to stir to a semierect state, and was now quite clearly outside the sheet.

Maybe it wouldn't hurt to stay for a while longer. To stay for just one more taste of his cock before she left. "I'm glad you like it."

"I more than like it. It's exquisitely sexy. And great for kissing." To prove the point Robert flung back the remaining sheet and kissed at the top of her hairless pussy, his tongue questing for her clit, but not quite being able to reach.

Her good sense made one last play to be heard. "Do you think this is wise?"

Robert looked up at her, resting his head on her upper thighs. "You smell nice." He glanced down at her cunt, just inches from his nose. "Look, it's Christmas, goodwill to all men and women, and all that. I'm not going to turn you in to the cops, and you're clearly not going to rob me and run, or you would have done so already."

"You don't know anything about me. Not even my name."

"Maybe not, but I do know that I like you, and that you turn me on."

"It's Bonny, by the way."

"Bonny. A pretty name." He spoke to her pussy rather than to her face. "Speaking for myself, I'd rather we let go of the past and concentrate on the future. Friends now, not enemies."

To reinforce the point he nuzzled up to her pussy again, and despite her misgivings about climbing into bed with Robert Barron, Bonny couldn't help but open her legs to afford him better access to her clit.

Robert took the hint and the initiative and wriggled around so that he knelt between her legs. There was no resistance when he lifted her knees and spread her legs wider.

"Pass me a pillow," he ordered her, his face muffled in her pussy.

His breath tickled her. She giggled and passed him one of his big feather pillows.

He placed it under her ass and pushed it up to the small of her back, lifting her ass and legs into the air. With the pillow under her, she was completely exposed and open to his gaze and to whatever else he might wish. Grabbing the back of her knees she pulled back even further, causing her pussy to gape in pink anticipation.

After a moment's pause to enjoy the view, Robert bent down and gave her a long lingering lick with a flat tongue from her asshole, up over her cunt, to her engorged clit. Encouraged by her moan of pleasure he gave her several more laps before probing her pussy with the point of his tongue. As he fucked her with his tongue he lightly rubbed her easily accessible asshole with his finger. He felt her shiver as he gently slipped in the tip of his finger. "Is that okay?" He needed to prove to her that there was more to his bedroom style than what he had shown her already. He wanted to give her something a little different to make up for his speed in coming the previous night. Something fun and sexy at the same time. And a little bit daring.

"Mmmm, I like it." The reply was husky. The increasing wetness of her pussy confirmed her words.

He continued to lap at her pussy with short strokes of her clit. Sensing when the effect was bringing her to the brink, he moved to taste the wet opening just below. All the while his finger moved effortlessly in short strokes in her ass.

He looked up from her pussy, wondering how far she would want to go and what would turn her on. "Would you like to try something a bit different?"

Bonny, eyes glazed with lust and the pleasure he was giving her, nodded.

Reaching across to his bedside drawers, he rummaged around for a minute. Ah, there it was. God, he hadn't used any of this stuff for years. He hoped it was still all there.

Yep—just as he'd left it. A soft rubber butt plug. Tapered at the point, it fattened to a reasonable diameter at its middle then narrowed again at the base. As a touch of fun it was colored with bright blue and red swirls.

Applying a generous amount of lube he eased it into her accommodating ass.

She panted at the feeling as it reached its widest point, a moan of pleasure escaping her throat as it slipped all the way to its disc-like base.

A look of concern crossed his face. "Is that okay?"

She couldn't help but rub her clit. "Better than okay. Move it in and out a bit."

He pulled gently until the plug reached its widest point, then allowed it to slip back in. Repeating the movement several times, he watched her approach her orgasm.

Leaving her teetering on the brink of an orgasm, he stopped and brought his cock to the entrance of her pussy. After rubbing the head over her wet entrance a few times, he slid into her hot pussy.

Her position with the pillow in the small of her back allowed for complete penetration, and his cock was angled to rub at her G-spot. She clutched at the pillow by her head, barely able to breathe. She had never felt so full, the butt plug in her ass and the large cock sliding in and out of her cunt. Too soon her climax came, and she cried out in absolute pleasure as his cock made short strokes over the sensitive entrance of her pussy.

Robert removed his still hard cock and moved around to her side.

"I saw you come. You look liked you saw heaven." As he spoke he stroked his cock, slick with her juices and wiggled the butt plug a bit. "Did you like this?"

She looked at him dreamily. At first her eyes focused on his cock, only inches from her face. And he was stroking himself without the least bit of embarrassment. She'd never had a lover do that in front of her before. It was turning her on all over again.

"I've never done anything like that before. I would have thought having that thing stuffed in my ass would hurt but it didn't. It felt good going in, and once it was in I felt really full. Like your cock was really huge. Porn star huge."

Throughout her monologue he continued to massage his cock, a grin spreading across his face. "You sound like a blasted reporter," he said with a laugh. "Now, play with your clit while I come across your gorgeous tits with their pointy dark pink nipples. I want to make them sticky with my cum."

She looked into his eyes, then at his cock, while he rubbed his hand over the purplish head. Without too much conscious thought she teased her clit as instructed.

With one hand Robert massaged his cock with full firm strokes, while the other toyed with the butt plug, still buried deep in her ass.

Incredibly, so it seemed to Bonny, she was about to come again, even though his cock had brought her to such a peak barely minutes ago.

She could see by the fierce grimace on his face that he was about to come. Her own rubbing increased in tempo, as she watched Robert stroking his cock furiously until with a strained cry his cum splattered with some force across her breasts.

Seeing him come with such intensity brought on her own climax, and just as she cried out in pleasure he slowly pulled the plug from her ass, tripling the power of the ecstasy flooding her brain. The butt plug spread her ass wide, her clit was on fire, flooding her brain with unimagined pleasure, paralyzing her body with the exquisite sensations coursing through her.

She lay there, quite simply unable to move, breath coming in short pants. He lay beside her, his own breathing heavy with exertion. He pulled the sheet over her, keeping the cold away.

Slowly her body came back to life, and she rolled to her side to snuggle up to the man beside her. Outside the dull sun had risen in the gray sky, the dormant tree silhouetted in the window.

* * * * *

She wouldn't have gone looking for it. Not deliberately. Not after she had shared his bed.

But there it was on his desk, the proof that she had been looking for, that Robert Barron, so generous to her, had the soul of a miserly Scrooge. There was nothing else she could do but stop and read it. She was a journalist, after all.

There it was in black and white. Signed contracts for the property development that would dispossess the poorest of the poor. Everything she needed and more. Her stomach felt sick at the thought that she had shared her body with a man who could thrust the poor and the helpless out into the streets just before Christmas.

She would make up for what she had done. By presenting his vileness to the world she could make up for having thought, for one glorious night, that maybe, just maybe, Robert Barron was a man who deserved her love.

Just a few moments ago she had been flying high. Now she had ice on her wings and was ready to crash.

The shower was still running in the bathroom. Moving quietly, she picked up her shoes in one hand and the incriminating papers in the other and moved off down the stairs.

The front door was soon unbolted. Without even pausing to put on her shoes, she took off down the street, running as if all the hounds of Hell were after her.

* * * * *

She was gone. He sat at the kitchen table, a cup of strong black coffee at his elbow, the Sunday newspaper rolled up next to his empty plate and forced himself to face facts. There was no point hoping for a Christmas miracle. She was gone and she wasn't coming back. This holiday season was shaping up to be as lonely as the last four had been.

Hell, if she wanted to find him, she knew who he was and where he lived. That was more than he knew about her. Bonny. That was all. No surname, no phone number, nothing else that could identify her. Not even enough to get a private investigator on the case. He'd tried, but the dick had just laughed him off the phone. Wouldn't even take the retainer he offered.

Bonny. He rolled the name around on his tongue. Even the sound of it was like a caress.

If she had wanted to see him again, she'd be able to manage it. She'd already shown him that locks couldn't stop her.

He'd hardly left the house in the last week just in case she decided to drop by again, but he was out of luck. There wasn't a cat burglar to be found.

He sipped at his coffee and unrolled the Sunday paper, and for the first time in a week he forgot all about Bonny.

The headline blazed out at him. "Robert Barron—the latest Scrooge". With growing disbelief he read the front-page article. A lead article lambasting him for his latest property development, a development that would, according to the article, raze several blocks of inner city slums and turf the inhabitants out on the streets in the middle of winter, just before Christmas, to freeze and to starve. He, Robert Barron, was being publicly accused, on the front page of a respectable Sunday newspaper, of callous, savage, premeditated murder.

It was a travesty of justice. A complete travesty. Righteous indignation swelled in his chest until it threatened to explode right out of him. The reporter clearly had a personal grievance against him to misrepresent the truth so blatantly, though what it was, he had no idea. The reporter hadn't even had the courage to sign his whole name to the litany of lies that he printed. The byline simply read "B. Eagle".

He pushed aside his coffee cup and got to his feet, his depression forgotten on the instant. Bonny was a mystery he still had to solve, but she would have to wait until he had first unmasked B. Eagle and forced a public apology for the scurrilous and utterly unjustified attack on his business dealings. Such lies could ruin a man's reputation and his credit rating if they gained credence.

B. Eagle would eat his words publicly or he would sue the little muckraker and the paper that printed his lies and ruin them both.

Newspaper companies were famed for their deep pockets, but his were deeper. And he'd spend every last penny to keep his good name intact. As it deserved to be.

His red sports car smoked the distance to the newspaper offices downtown. Sunday or no Sunday, they could damn well answer to him right now.

He stalked into the newspaper offices, ignoring the frightened-looking receptionist on the front desk and striding straight into the offices of the editor behind her. Tossing his paper down on the desk, he glared at the small man sitting behind the desk. "This is a bunch of lies. I want a retraction and I want it now. Front page of tomorrow's newspaper, or I sue you and your paper for defamation."

"Robert Barron, I presume."

"Damn right I'm Robert Barron."

The editor steepled his hands in front of his face. "I can't print a retraction just because you dislike the story, Mr. Barron," he said in a snooty voice. "I need rather more to go on than your complaint."

Robert tossed a handful of papers onto the desk in front of the man. "Here is all the proof you need. Call my lawyer if you have any further questions."

The editor picked up the papers and looked through them.

Robert Barron waited.

"Hmm, I see. This does put a rather different light on the matter."

"Damn right it does. And one more thing. I want you to fire the reporter who made up those lies. Call him in right here and now and fire him."

For the first time since he'd walked into the man's office, the editor looked irritated. Worried even. "You want me to fire Beagle?"

"Damn right I do."

The editor tossed the papers into a heap on his desk. "I expect it's all a misunderstanding. Beagle is one of the best cubs I've got. Just about ready for a promotion to senior, too."

"Misunderstanding, my ass." He wasn't going to be placated with such rubbish. "Call him in right here. Now."

The editor sighed. "If you insist." He picked up the phone on his desk and buzzed the receptionist. "Send Beagle in here, will you."

Robert waited, his fury mounting against the weasel of a reporter who had written such lies about him.

By the time he had finished with him, Beagle would rue the day he made up such scurrilous lies.

Bonny opened the door to the editor's office with no more than the usual trepidation she felt when summoned by the boss. She'd done a great job on the Barron story, even the editor had said so. Maybe this was payback time. Promotion time. Her insides did a little dance thinking about it. She'd been waiting for it for so long.

Ruthlessly she squelched the memory of Robert Barron's face, the touch of his hands on her, the feel of his body against hers. So what if her promotion was gained at the cost of his reputation? He did not deserve to be remembered fondly.

The door was shut behind her before she registered the presence of another man in the room.

"Bonny." The voice was Robert Barron's. Incredibly, he sounded happy to see her.

She felt the blood drain from her face and her knees started to buckle under her. He had found her. This couldn't be happening. Not to her.

"Beagle? You know Mr. Barron?" The nasal whine in her boss's voice had never grated on her so badly before.

"You're Beagle?" His face visibly whitened. "You're the reporter?"

She nodded. "Bonny Eagle. Beagle to my friends."

Robert Barron was looking at her as if she had just crawled out from under a rock. "I guess I hardly qualify as one of those anymore."

She would not feel guilty for exposing him as he deserved. She would not. "I guess not."

"You wrote those lies about me. Even after…?" His voice trailed off as if he could not bear to finish.

"There were not lies. They were the truth."

"You need to check your sources better, Bonny. Though I guess that is exactly what you were trying to do that night I found you."

"I'm a reporter. I don't write lies."

"They were all lies, Bonny." He took the papers from the editor's desk and handed them to her. "If you had hung around a bit, maybe you would have gotten around to reading these papers, too. They weren't hidden. You would've found them if you'd looked. But I guess once you had the dirt on me, there was no point in staying any longer."

Then, with a sorry shake of his head, he turned on his heel and walked out.

"What was that all about?" her boss asked, as the door closed behind him.

"Nothing," Bonny replied abstractedly, ruffling through the papers he'd handed her. She backed out of the door and into an empty meeting room, shutting the door behind her.

Ten minutes later she was still there, her head in her hands, kicking herself for the worst mistake she had made in the whole of her messed-up life.

Robert Barron was no Scrooge. Far from it. Sure, he was knocking down one of the slums and rebuilding it, but no one was going homeless. Not only was he housing all the old tenants in temporary accommodations while the rebuilding was taking place, but every old tenant had the promise of a brand-new townhouse when they were finished.

It was a Christmas gift to the city. His Christmas gift to those who needed it most.

And she had publicly pilloried him as a greedy, grasping tycoon, out for what he could get.

Her sense of shame completely enveloped her. In her ignorance and arrogance, she had done him a huge wrong. Only the burning necessity she felt for setting it right again could get her back on to her feet.

Feeling lower than a worm, she crawled back to her desk and started tapping away. It was three o'clock in the afternoon before she was finally finished to her satisfaction.

"Publish it tomorrow morning," she said, dumping the sheaf of papers on her boss's desk as she walked out the door.

He let them lie there, not even glancing in their direction. "What is it?"

"A full retraction. A chance to set things right."

* * * * *

It was the night before Christmas and Bonny still felt like a louse. A complete and total louse.

The retraction had been printed earlier in the week, exactly as she had written it, and Robert Barron's reputation was more glowing than ever before.

But she hadn't been able to get over the look in his eyes when he'd realized she had written that story about him. It was the look of a man who had taken a chance for the first time in five years and had sand kicked in his face for it.

A retraction and a public apology wasn't enough for the hurt she had caused him. She still owed him compensation, and she would never be able to enjoy her Christmas with that hanging over her.

Nervously she slithered into her black leggings and tied the laces on her black sneakers. It was time to go cat burgling again.

*****

Robert poured himself another brandy and swirled it around the glass. Christmas Eve. A night just like any of the other three hundred and sixty-four nights of the year. Only it was different. It was worse.

Christmas had been a difficult time of year for him since Lisa had died. It was almost unbearable this year.

This year he had taken a chance of getting to know another woman, the first woman who had heated his blood in years, and she had been nothing but a journalist after a story. She'd fucked him senseless for a scoop and the chance of a promotion, leaving him feel used and dirty.

He took a swig of brandy, feeling it burn its way down his throat. He'd learned his lesson there. No woman would get through his defenses so easily again.

A slight rustle behind him was all that warned him. Before he could even put the brandy glass down, there she was in front of him just as she had been the first night, dressed all in black with her glorious black hair tied up in a ponytail.

Another swig of brandy to settle his nerves and disguise the shaking in his hands. "Do you need another story?" He waved an expansive arm around at the papers on the desk. "Go ahead. Help yourself. Whatever you write it can't be any worse than your first one."

"I didn't come to take anything. I came to apologize. And to give you something." She handed him last Monday's copy of the newspaper.

He brushed it away. "I've seen it." Not that he'd read it. It was enough to know that his demands had been met and his reputation was still salvageable. It didn't take away the hurt. Nothing could take that away.

"I meant every word that I wrote. I am truly sorry. When I found the paper that confirmed my worst suspicions, I was heartbroken. I thought you deserved to be pilloried. I had no idea there was so much more to the story than that."

"Whatever." Even now, knowing that she had wanted nothing from him but a story, his body could not help but react to her closeness. He yearned to take hold of her and draw her into his arms, to slip his hands under her T-shirt to feel the warmth of her body, to hold her close to him.

"Please, forgive me. I wronged you terribly." Kneeling in front of him, she looked up into his eyes. "Is there nothing I can do to make things right between us again?"

He shrugged. There were no words to describe how badly she had hurt him. Wounds like that did not heal over with a mere apology.

"You told me that first night that I ought to be on my knees in front of you asking what I could do for you. I'm on my knees now."

Weariness suddenly overcame him. There was no use prolonging the pain of seeing her. "There is nothing I want from you."

Her hand reached out and touched his cock, hard in his pants with the nearness of her. "Your cock wants something from me."

"So I want to fuck you," he said crudely. "That hardly makes you unique among women."

"So fuck me then."

"What?"

"You want to fuck me. So fuck me."

He shut his eyes so he could not see the temptation that lingered in front of him. "Go away, Bonny."

"I'll still respect you in the morning."

"Go away and leave me alone before I do something I'll regret."

"If I leave now, I'll always regret it." The words were a mere whisper.

And then came the touch that he both craved and feared—the touch of her hands on the fastenings of his trousers.

"Bonny." He didn't know if he was warning her off or egging her on.

"Shh." She had his trousers open now, his cock springing forth at her touch. "Let me do this for you. Just sit back and enjoy yourself."

Then she took him into her mouth and he was lost. Glued to the chair, he could only moan as she sucked on him, licking up and down the base of his shaft and around his balls.

A boy of sixteen would have lasted longer than he could. When she took him in her hands and started to pump the base of his cock while she sucked on the head, he could not hold back. Though he tried to stop himself, he came with a rush into her mouth, his cum shooting out of him forcefully.

Still she sucked on him, milking every last drop of cum from his cock until he was totally limp.

"You didn't have to do that," he said, as soon as he had regained his breath enough to speak again.

Her head was on his knees as she looked up into his face. "Of course I didn't have to. I did it because I wanted to."

His orgasm had only taken off the edge of his hunger for her. Already his cock was stirring again, wanting to lose itself inside her pussy. Damn it, he would take what she was offering and worry about the consequences later. Standing up, he took her by the arm. "Come to bed with me."

"I thought you'd never ask."

In no time at all, they were both naked. "Lie on your back," he instructed her. He wanted to appreciate every inch of her in case it was the last time he had the opportunity.

She lay there as he explored her body with his mouth and tongue, laving her breasts and licking her nipples to hard peaks.

By the time his mouth made its way to her naked pussy, she was already soaking wet and her breath was coming in short pants. That was one thing she couldn't fake—the evidence of her desire for him. Her cunt was dripping juice on to the sheets beneath them even before he started to lick her there.

His cock was as hard as nails again at this evidence of her desire. He licked her until he could tell by the tiny tremors in her clit that she was close to coming.

All of a sudden he rolled away from her and lay on his back on the bed. "Come and sit on my cock. Ride me like you would ride a horse."

Straddling herself above him, she slowly lowered herself on to his cock, taking her time about enveloping him completely. Impatient, he grabbed her hips and thrust up into her, burying himself deeply into her.

Up and down she rode him, each stroke with her pussy making his cock harder.

Hands on her hips he urged her on faster and deeper, until there was nothing in his world but the feeling of her pussy sliding up and down on his cock.

He wanted her to keep riding him forever, fucking him with her pussy until he died of it.

All too soon, the tension built up to an unbearable pitch. She gave a cry and he felt her pussy muscles convulse around him as she came. He held himself deep inside her as she came, letting her milk every last drop of pleasure from his hard cock. Then, with a last thrust, he shot his second load of cum for the evening deep into her pussy.

Bonny clambered out of the bed she had shared with Robert Barron. He had forgiven her, she was sure of that now. He was too much of a gentleman to hold a grudge.

But she was only Bonny Eagle, an investigative journalist even further than ever from a promotion to senior reporter after this last debacle, and he was Robert Barron, multimillionaire property developer and darling of society. What on earth would he want with her?

Still, she would not leave him on Christmas morning without a word. Life was nothing without hope.

Grabbing a pen and paper from his desk she scribbled a short note and left it on his pillow. Then, with one last kiss to his sleeping forehead, she sneaked away.

As soon as the door closed softly behind her, Robert reached for the note she had left on his pillow. Please God he hoped that she felt something for him. His heart might not survive being ripped out of his chest one more time.

A name. A phone number. An address. And an offer of Christmas dinner that evening if he was hungry and had nothing better to do.

A smile broke out across his face. He would be there with bells on and an appetite that had little to do with roast turkey with all the trimmings and a lot to do with the woman who had invited him.

Wild reindeer wouldn't drag him away from Bonny's place tonight. Together, they would make this Christmas one to remember.

Epilogue

One year later

Bonny snuggled up next to Robert Barron on the couch as they gazed with satisfaction at the Christmas tree they had just finished decorating. "We got that done just in time," she said with a sigh of relief. "Santa Claus comes down the chimney tomorrow."

He hugged her closer to him. "Santa Claus gave me everything I wanted for Christmas last year. There's nothing else I need."

"As I remember it, you didn't get much besides a Christmas turkey with all the trimmings." And even then, they hadn't spent much time on eating their Christmas dinner. Not when they had each other.

"It was the trimmings I was referring to," he said with a grin. "The trimmings were spectacular."

"Mmmm, they were." The memory of that night made her wet just thinking about it. "I think we should have exactly the same trimmings for dinner this year."

"Your father is coming over," he reminded her.

"Maybe we'll have to keep the trimmings for later on," she conceded. "For dessert."

He fell silent for a while, fidgeting slightly as if he had something on his mind. "We've had a good year, haven't we?"

"The very best," she agreed. It *had* been a wonderful year for her. She'd earned a promotion to senior reporter for an exposé of exploitative labor practices in the city's factories. And throughout the year Robert Barron had been in her bed and in her heart. When she had fallen in love with him she didn't quite know, but he was now so firmly lodged in her heart that she couldn't dislodge him if she tried.

Taking courage from her words, he fumbled in his pocket and brought out a small box which he offered to her with a shamefaced air. "I know I ought to wait until Santa brought this down the chimney for you, but I couldn't."

Her heart stopped as she accepted the box. Her fingers were shaking so much she could hardly open it. A large solitaire diamond winked back at her from its nest of velvet. Her mouth opened and she looked at him for clarification. Was this really what she thought it was?

"I love you, Bonny Eagle. I think I've loved you since you first broke into my house dressed in your ridiculous cat burglar outfit."

"You do?" Happiness threatened to overwhelm her. "You really do?" She could not muster anything else to say.

Taking the jewelry box from her limp hands, he took out the ring and slipped it on to her third finger. "Will you marry me, Bonny?"

Was she dreaming? "You really want to marry me?"

"Absolutely I do."

She launched herself at him, hugging him tightly so he could not see the tears that welled up in her eyes. "Then yes. A thousand times yes."

"You have made me the happiest man in the world tonight." Slipping his hand under her shirt, he fondled her breasts until her nipples were tight little pebbles of desire. Knowing the answer, he asked innocently, "Any chance of getting the Christmas trimmings a day early?"

Also by Leda Swann

Rainlashed

School for Virgins

Sunlit

About the Author

Leda Swann is a senior executive in a large corporate, the mother of four young children, and partner of a wonderful man. She likes scuba diving, swimming, and any other sport that involves getting cold and wet on a regular basis. She is also the author of outrageously sexy romances, keeps fur-lined handcuffs in her bedside drawers, and fights hard to remember to remove the silk ties off her bed head whenever her parents come to visit.

Leda welcomes comments from readers. You can find her website and email address on her author bio page at www.ellorascave.com.

GHOSTS OF CHRISTMAS PAST

By Cricket Starr

Chapter One

It was cold on the rooftop. Calla stepped out of the shelter of the stairwell and felt the bite of the icy breeze through the threadbare coat she wore over her fast-food uniform. Thirty stories up, there was nothing to stop the wind.

Of course, the unprotected nature of the roof and its height were what had drawn her in the first place. It might be cold, but there was no way she'd survive a fall from here…a fall she planned to take in the next few moments.

Calla shivered as she crept to the edge. With the full moon it was easy to see the sidewalk far below. The view would have been pretty with the lights from the buildings around, but some of those lights were colored red and green. Christmas lights.

Another kind of shiver went through her. She hated Christmas…that was one of the reasons she was here on the roof.

She swallowed a hard breath. Was this really her only option? No, but it was the only one she wanted to pursue. She stepped onto the low wall that edged the roof.

Oblivion beckoned. She'd never feel the cold again, or pain. She'd never be alone anymore. No one would miss her…

She tried not to imagine what it would feel like to land on the concrete from this high. She expected it would hurt when her body shattered on impact, but perhaps the fall wouldn't be so bad. Possibly it would feel like flying and she'd always wanted to fly.

Even so, she hesitated. Maybe this wasn't such a good idea…

A sudden gust of wind hit her, and then she was teetering on the edge…

And then there was no longer any decision to make. She wasn't on the roof but falling, the glass side of the building a blur of light and dark bands as it swept past.

Terror grabbed her as the ground grew closer and Calla opened her mouth to scream.

But before she could, warm arms wrapped themselves around her and then her downward progress slowed until she was merely floating next to the building.

Floating in midair, in the arms of someone large and solid. Calla turned her head and saw his face—handsome, pale, with dark hair and compelling black eyes.

Those eyes compelled her now. *Sleep…*came an insidious whisper into her mind.

But she fought that. "Who are you?" She looked down at the expanse of space below their feet. They hovered at just about the fifth floor and now began to rise slowly. "You an angel, or some kind of Superman?" No wings were on his back, nor did he have a cape.

He smiled with large, evenly spaced teeth that gleamed in the moonlight. "Not even close," he told her in a dark sensuous growl, and a third kind of shiver hit her, that of long-unexpressed sexual need. When was the last time she'd had that reaction to a man?

"But we've a ways to go and you should sleep." Again there was that compulsion in her mind, stronger than before, and this time he gave her no choice. Calla's mind went dark and she knew nothing more.

She came back to consciousness surrounded by warmth and water and…bubbles?

Calla opened her eyes to see and smell the unmistakable sensations of a bubble bath in a very large tub with a man sitting in the water behind her. His hands massaged her scalp, working shampoo into her hair.

She knew it was a man because of the large erection poking her backside.

Calla tried to pull away, but his arm went around her waist, clutching her close. "Hold still. You'll get soap in your eyes."

Soap in her eyes. Was he kidding?

No, I'm not. You needed a bath so I decided to give you one. She heard him sniff her scalp. *You smell much better now. Hold your breath*!

With a quick jerk he pushed her under the water and then let her sit up, wet hair streaming into her eyes.

With extreme annoyance, Calla shoved the hair off her face, twisted in his arms and glared at him. Of course she hadn't had a bath…the flophouse she'd called home these past few months didn't boast a working shower. Half the time the toilet hadn't been operational, but it was all she could afford on her Burger Barn salary.

So she'd smelled a little—that didn't give him permission to strip her and take her into his bathtub. She liked to pick whom she got naked with.

Even so, his intrusion into her mind bothered her more. "What are you doing inside my head?"

He grinned at her and again she was struck by how perfect his teeth were. "Not to worry. You are a psi with strong mental powers. My being able to touch your mind is not only normal, but under the circumstances quite useful."

In spite of how gorgeous he was, Calla's uneasiness grew. "What do you mean 'circumstances'?"

"The ones we are in. What I am…why you are here." He stared at her long and hard then gave a heartfelt sigh. "I guess we might as well get this over with."

He put two fingers into his mouth and with a jerk dislodged the teeth she'd been admiring, pulling and revealing an artificial upper plate. The teeth underneath—the real teeth—weren't at all even, but shorter than normal except for the incisors on either side, which were long and pointed.

He had fangs like a vampire and as she looked, his dark eyes briefly glowed red.

Oh my God…fangs, glowing eyes, and he could fly—he was *a vampire*!

Shock and fear battling within her, Calla tried to get out of the tub, her feet slipping on the bottom. "It's been very nice meeting you…thanks for the bath…"

He leaned back and watched her, "And saving your life."

Calla reached for a towel off the pile by the side of the tub. "Uh, yeah. That too."

"Is that the best you can do? You value your life so little that you can't even thank me for saving it?"

"No…that is…"

He grabbed her shoulders and pulled her back into the tub, still clutching the towel to her as if it were a lifeline. She held it to her chest even though it was sopping wet.

"I would think that the least you could do is kiss me."

"Kiss you? But you're a vampire!"

He actually looked hurt. "Actually, I use the term 'nightwalker'. The 'v' word isn't socially correct. And what does that have to do with kissing?"

"I don't kiss dead things."

"Nightwalkers are not dead things!" He sat higher in the tub, revealing the long hard line of his erection. "Do I look dead to you?"

Uh, well, no. Her first sight of his cock made her dumb with appreciation. It had been a long time since she'd been with a man, and never someone built like this.

He smirked knowingly. "Like what you see?"

Now Calla blushed, knowing she'd been caught staring. "What do you want with me?"

He crossed his arms and wiggled his eyebrows. "Are you not woman enough to know?"

Calla rolled her eyes. "Oh, please. But why do you want me of all people?"

He hesitated then shrugged. "I picked you when I saw you leave the homeless shelter without getting any food. You ran when you saw the Christmas tree and I read in your mind such desperation—I wanted to stop what you were thinking about doing."

She shivered, knowing what he was talking about. With little money from her part-time job available for food, Calla had gone for the traditional holiday feast served at the shelter, but as always the simple holiday decorations had paralyzed her and she'd run instead. She didn't remember thinking about ending her life at that time, but maybe she had.

"So since you thought I was willing to kill myself, you thought I'd let you bite me and die that way?"

The nightwalker frowned at her. "I am not a monster and I don't kill people by drinking their blood. I only take enough to survive and you can spare that much." He ran his gaze up and down her frame and she clutched the towel tighter across her breasts. "Even skinny as you are. I'll have to get more food in to feed you right."

"I'm not skinny."

"Aren't you?" With gentle, but firm pressure he pulled the towel from her and let it drop into the tub. His gaze turned admiring. "You do have very nice breasts."

"Do you always grab women off the streets to have sex with?"

"In your case it was more a matter of grabbing you in midair after you jumped. You wouldn't have been much good to me once you'd reached the street."

Calla shuddered, remembering her near miss. "I didn't jump, I was blown off the roof. It was an accident."

"Really." He didn't sound as if he believed her. "It is a good thing there's a full moon out tonight so I can fly. And no, I only do this once a year. It is a kind of Christmas tradition I have."

"I don't understand."

He shrugged his shoulders. "Every year I bring someone into my home to celebrate the holidays with. Usually a woman, sometimes a man…it depends on who I feel needs my help the most at the time. That's why I go to the homeless shelter to find someone. After Christmas day I let them go with enough money to live on for a long time."

He planned to set her free and give her money? That didn't sound so bad. He'd said he'd done this before, many times. Maybe she could trust him.

"You sleep with men?"

This time he didn't look affronted but just amused. "I don't object to homosexuality, but I don't practice it myself. If my guest is a man I don't have sex with him. In fact, I don't always make love to the women, but in your case I want to. Very much." He said the last with an emphasis she felt right to the center of her beginning arousal.

"I don't go to bed with strange men."

"Then I should introduce myself. Daniel Wilder. And you are?"

If there was an odder situation to be in than sitting in a pool-sized bathtub with a naked nightwalker who'd saved her life, Calla wasn't sure she wanted to know about it. It was even odd enough to make her willing to discard some of her normal wariness. "I'm Calla Douglas."

He seized her hand and shook it briefly, then drew her into his arms. "Happy to meet you, Calla. Let's get dried off and go to the bedroom."

She wasn't sure why she went with him, except for the fact that he was handsome and charming, and the size of his cock promised a rare treat for her body. Maybe he was casting a spell over her to ensure her cooperation, but at the moment, she was willing to be bespelled.

Very willing.

Chapter Two

Daniel tugged his guest into his bedroom and anticipated just how enjoyable the next few hours would be. Calla was perfect for him...just curvy enough to make his body happy, just strong enough mentally to engage his mind. Perhaps too strong mentally—twice now she'd been able to slip past his control over her, once in the air, and then again in the bath. He'd wanted her completely aroused before she'd regained control of herself and instead she'd woken while he was still washing her hair.

Fortunately she found him attractive, so it wasn't any problem convincing her to go to bed with him. He hardly had to exert his will on her at all. And she felt so good in his arms. He pulled her close and felt the press of her breasts against his chest, the tips of her nipples hard with arousal and awareness of him. As he'd said before, she had virtually no fat on her, but there was still a comforting roundness to her hips that he knew would welcome him when he thrust deep into the valley between her thighs. Her long slender legs would feel great wrapped around him.

When he'd gotten her back to his apartment and stripped her clothes off, he'd been more than pleased with what he'd found. It had been just like opening up a drably wrapped present to find something glorious within.

Already his cock was so hard he could barely stand it.

But he would have to be patient and not just toss her on the bed and have his way. Yes, she'd accept that from him now, but later she'd resent him and that wasn't how he wanted to begin their relationship, short as it was going to be.

Better to seduce her and win her loyalty for the next couple of days.

Calla's feet slowed as they neared the bed and her face turned troubled. "I'm not so sure this is a good idea."

"Why not?" Daniel breathed in her sweet citrusy scent, the one he'd detected even before he'd bathed her.

"I don't do meaningless sex."

He turned her face to stare into her eyes. "Then we will make it meaningful, Calla. Something to remember all our lives." He stroked her soft cheek. "Don't worry about what future we have right now. That will sort out."

And it would, as it always had in the past. He wouldn't get too attached to her, even if she did have hair the color of an evening sunset and her eyes were as blue as the midday sky he barely remembered. He wanted her for the here and now, not for always. But that was all right, he knew she wouldn't want him for longer either. Most of his previous holiday guests had been happy to take the money he'd given them at the end of their stay and leave. Calla wouldn't be any different.

In the meantime, she felt wonderful in his arms, as if she really belonged there. Daniel drew her closer and let his lips gently press against hers, carefully avoiding piercing her with his fangs. Soon enough he'd taste her blood but he was afraid to do it before she was ready. It could frighten her.

He wanted her aroused and willing, not frightened. Fortunately she didn't seem the least bit frightened of him as she gave up first her lips to him, and then her mouth fell open, giving him access. His tongue swept in of its own accord, as if it knew its welcome even before he did.

Her whole body seemed to accept him as its lover, as if they'd already made love a dozen times before. She felt new and soft against him, but there was still a familiarity…not a commonplace feeling, but more like that of coming home.

She tasted of sweetness and passion and caring. She tasted wonderful, of sunshine and a world that no longer belonged to him. And yet he felt welcome when kissing her.

Again he had to fight the urge to throw her onto the bed and cover her with his body, plunge his cock in her pussy, taking instead of asking for her favor. Again he had to fight himself to take it slow…he might feel she belonged to him, but she undoubtedly did not share his opinion.

Instead he let his hand cup the back of her head and hold her gently to him. There was no pressure on her—she could pull away from him if she wanted. But she didn't want to now. He read her acceptance in her body as much as in her mind.

He felt a question in her and pulled back to give her the opportunity to speak. Her eyes looked puzzled. "Why am I not saying no to you?"

Daniel had to admit to being impressed. He was letting his own passion for her flood her senses through a minimal link and for her to question what she felt took greater mental strength than he'd expected. She'd seemed so dragged down by life when he'd first seen her that he hadn't expected such spirit.

"Do you wish to say 'no'?"

The puzzlement grew. "Not really. But I don't want to say 'yes', either."

"Then say nothing and just let things progress. We want and need each other. Let that be reason enough tonight."

A shy smile caressed her lips. "Reason enough tonight. I like that."

He let his finger trace the route of that smile, her lips soft beneath his fingertip. "I like you. I'm happy to have you here with me."

The fleeting smile returned in earnest. "I guess…I'm happy to be here."

Daniel smiled back but lost his smile when she faltered, and he realized that she'd again caught sight of his fangs and been reminded of what he was. He had to make her forget that, at least for a little while, so he drew her closer and kissed her on the forehead, pressing his cock against her soft belly. That, at least, was humanly normal.

The press of her nipples against his chest drew his attention and he reached to stroke them gently. Calla moaned as he did and her expression of concern faded. Again she was caught in the sensual spell he wove around her.

Carefully hiding his fangs, Daniel slipped to his knees and closed his mouth around one of those tempting maroon buds. Up close her skin was like many redheads', the color of cream flecked with freckles, tiny and barely distinct from each other. Freckles on top of freckles until they blended together, even on her breasts, which he knew must rarely see the sun.

She was a sun-kissed woman, a woman of day in his world of night—something rare and precious. He'd chosen wisely this year and was again glad that he'd spotted her at the shelter.

He was even gladder that he'd been concerned about her and had followed her and been there when she'd fallen. He'd made light of it before, but it had taken several years off his long life when she'd slipped off the roof. He'd needed all his speed to get to her in time.

Now she moaned as he worshipped her breasts, sweet altars of softness. He'd spoken the truth when he said she had lovely breasts. They were pale, full and round, the tips and areolas deep maroon in contrast.

Lovely. Between his lips her nipple was as textured and sweet as a berry. It grew harder under his ministrations, in contrast to the softness of the rest of her breast. That softness seemed to beg for his hand's caress, and he kneaded it with careful fingers.

Calla responded by placing her hands on his shoulders, pulling him just a little closer—a signal of acceptance that he noted with pleasure. He opened his mind more to her and read her desire, a reaction in part to his caresses but even more to his need for her.

She needed and wanted him. He saw that in her, and in her reaction to him. It was just what he'd hoped for and it was all he could do not to shout with pleasure.

Her hands came up to cup the back of his head, and she took a stance with her legs further apart. She moaned and her head went back and he sensed an orgasm coming, just from the effect of his mouth on her breasts. Her open stance gave him access and he reached for her pussy, slipped his hand between the narrow cleft of her folds and unerringly found her clit.

At the first caress of his fingers she came apart, her legs shaking, and he had to grab her waist to keep her from collapsing to the floor. Jumping to his feet, Daniel swept her into his arms. She clung to him as he crossed the short distance to the bed, her body still shaking from what must have been an extraordinarily intense climax.

He wished he'd mentally linked with her so he could have experienced it himself, and then he realized how odd that was.

Daniel usually didn't allow that deep a link with his annual holiday guest. As he'd told her, it wasn't all that often that he found someone who both interested him and aroused him, but almost never did he try for the kind of link he now found himself wanting to create with her.

He was treating her like a real companion, someone to keep for far longer than a few days.

"Daniel." She said his name quietly but with appreciation, and he halted in mid stride, simply enjoying the way she felt in his arms. She felt as if she belonged there. She belonged to him.

Well, she did, after all. He'd saved her life and in some cultures that would mean he owned her. Not that he intended anything of the sort, but there was a brief visceral thrill at the thought of someone like her belonging to him.

Belonging with him.

His to be with, to take care of. *His to care for.*

Disturbed by his wayward and unfamiliar thoughts, Daniel completed the journey to the bed and laid her gently crosswise on it. She stared up at him with such trust in her eyes that for a moment it took his breath away.

Sure, she was partially reacting to his manipulation of her senses, the almost link that existed between them, as well as the fact that he'd just given her what had to have been one hell of an orgasm. The lady would have to be made of stone to not want him.

But he could feel that there was more than that to her reaction, not to mention his own. Something disturbing was happening between them and his mind wasn't so sure it liked it…even though his body and soul were more than happy about it.

Daniel shoved those disturbing thoughts to the back of his mind. Calla was a woman to seduce and a companion to secure for a few days. He kissed her again and enjoyed the sweetness of her breath against his mouth. He laid a line of kisses along her face, down her chin and to her neck, where he felt the throb of her arterial pulse just below his teeth.

A strong pulse, young and healthy. Deep within him came the urge to sink his teeth in her, drink her blood and leave his mark. It was nearly as strong as his impulse to sink his cock inside her pussy. He had to pull back. Time would come for that and soon, but not quite yet. He'd mark her when the time was right.

Instead he used his hands to stroke her body and used his mouth on her breasts until she was squirming again, seeking another orgasm, but this time he didn't give her the satisfaction she wanted. This time he wanted to be inside her when she climaxed, and feel her slick tightness grip his cock. That was the goal now.

Daniel ran his hand down her belly to where the soft hair that guarded her clitoris grew, the same red as her hair—a natural redhead was his Calla, just as her breasts were natural, something almost rare in Hollywood. But there was no mistaking her soft curves for anything enhanced.

He parted the hair with a gentle finger and found her clit and massaged it. Again he only wanted to bring her close to orgasm, not past it. Calla's eyes were wild by the time he slid two fingers inside her pussy. He stroked a few times and she moaned, her hands clutching first at his chest then on his back. She reached for his cock, hard and weeping for her, and gave it tentative pulls. Not an experienced move, but he didn't mind.

By the time she left him, she'd know much more about making love…he'd see to that. He'd told her the truth—that he didn't always take his once-a-year Christmas guests to bed, but with her there was no question about it. They were going to make love several times before he let her go.

Starting right now. Calla's untutored stroking of him had pushed him beyond reason and he couldn't hold off possessing her any longer. He rolled her onto her back and held her shoulders down as his knees slid between her thighs, opening her to him. He fit his cock to her just as Calla seemed to catch on to what they were about to do.

"Protection," she whispered.

He appreciated her concern, but she had to understand that she wasn't dealing with an ordinary man. He bespoke her to emphasize that point. *I can't make you pregnant and you cannot make me ill. There need be nothing between us.*

*Oh…*was her mental reply, and it was laced with traces of fear. Daniel kissed her until her mind was quiet and accepting, but as soon as it was, his cock was again at the entrance to her pussy.

He entered slowly. She was tighter than he'd imagined…not a virgin, but as he'd suspected, more innocent than most. Certainly not familiar with someone of his size.

She gasped aloud as he sheathed himself in her pussy and he covered her mouth with his, absorbing her soft cry. For a moment he simply lay on top of her, letting her body learn to accommodate him. He wove a thread into their link, making it stronger and easier for him to share his thoughts with her. Once she was marked it would become simple for their minds to touch.

Calla's hands found his back and raked across it gently. Daniel raised his head to stare into her face. A look in her eyes, of wonder, and something a little deeper, greeted him. Daniel pulled out, almost to his length and then reentered her, achingly slow. Calla's eyes closed and she whispered something unintelligible. He repeated the action, this time faster, and she cried aloud.

Now it was all he could do to stay in control. He moved in her with a push of his hips that sank her into the bed and her legs came up to wrap around his. He barely had the presence of mind to recognize how good those legs felt. Barely holding onto his sanity, he drove his cock deeper into her, fucking her hard, putting aside all thoughts of her inexperience. All she'd known before was irrelevant—now she was his.

And she knew it too, her body meeting each of his thrusts with raised hips, moving with him, their bodies intimately joined. His mind reached for hers and wrapped around it. Pink…her mind had a distinct pink color, which blended oddly into his silver thoughts.

Mine, mine, mine… Daniel wasn't sure if they were his thoughts or hers, but for the moment the sentiment seemed appropriate. He thrust and thrust until his mind couldn't hold back any longer, until there was only one thing left…

His mouth found her neck, and the now wild pulsing of her artery. With unerring accuracy he bit down and almost groaned as the first taste of her blood filled his mouth. He'd never tasted anyone like her. He swallowed and took another deep sip. Calla didn't cry out or jerk away as others had, but kept her head still, even as she continued to meet each drive of his cock.

He continued to drink deep until he felt her weaken, forcing him back to his senses. He pulled his mouth away and sealed the small wounds on her neck, but left them, leaving his mark. Now Calla moaned with oncoming passion, no longer passive, but crying with each thrust.

More, Daniel…please!

Through the link he sensed her climax before it started and he no longer tried to hold back his own orgasm. Calla cried out, her mind swirling with hot-pink passion and when it crested it swept him away as well. He'd barely noted how tight her pussy clenched his cock before it seemed to explode deep within her.

When Daniel came back into himself, he was lying over her on shaking arms, his body quivering as much as hers. Calla's face showed the same astonishment he felt through their link. Slowly he lowered until he could not see her face any longer but only feel her tremble beneath him.

Had he *ever* had sex like this before? Granted it had been a couple of years since the last time he'd taken a woman to bed, but even so, this was profound in a whole new way. It had been wonderful…but a little scary as well.

Even so, he tried not to let her know just how affected he'd been. Instead he rolled to the side and held her against him.

When he caught his breath, he put two fingers over the holes he'd left in her neck. Even if their situation was temporary, he never failed to give the oath.

"I take you to be my companion, to serve me as long as you wear my mark. In exchange you have my support and protection."

Calla had a funny smile on her face as he finished. She licked her lips. "That was…odd. When you bit me, it was almost as if I could taste my own blood."

He blinked at her and it was all he could do to keep his jaw from dropping. It was a rare companion who could link deep enough to share tastes and there was no way an unlinked psi could do it. She must be mistaken.

"Don't worry about it, Calla."

"I'm not worried." Replete, she lay dozing on the bed next to him and for a moment Daniel was content to watch her. But he'd taken too much blood and she needed nourishment, now more than ever. He shook her shoulders.

"Wake up, Calla. We need to get you fed."

She perked up. "Food?"

He couldn't help smiling at the interest in her eyes. "Yes…a feast fit for a queen…or at least a nightwalker's companion, waits for you."

Daniel dressed her in one of his robes, which hung loosely on her. He took mental measurements and determined what he needed to order so that she would have proper clothes. He had no intention of letting her wear her original clothes, with the deep-fat fry smell embedded in them, again. Ordering a new wardrobe would be a project for later tonight, after she'd gone to sleep, since she wasn't adjusted to staying awake to dawn the way he was.

Not that Calla seemed to notice how poorly the robe he gave her fit. She was still yawning as he took her hand and pulled her toward the kitchen.

Chapter Three

Hand in hand, Calla let him lead her from the bedroom. They traveled down a plush carpeted hall, with open doors revealing an office on one side and a second modern-styled bedroom as well as a guest bathroom on the other, neither of which looked like they received much use. They passed a window and she realized that her host lived in an apartment high in a building that faced Sunset Boulevard. So much for her first idea, that he lived in a gothic home in a dark corner of the Hollywood Hills.

When they reached the living room she scented the distinctive smell of pine and pulled away from him. Sure enough, there it was, an undecorated Christmas tree fully seven feet tall in the corner of the room. Daniel started as she pulled away, old terror gnawing at her and preventing her advancing.

It was the same terror that had struck her on entering the homeless shelter earlier that evening.

Daniel noticed. "What is it, Calla? Surely you aren't really afraid of a Christmas tree."

"I'm not afraid..." she started to say, but Daniel took her arm and turned her toward him. He put two fingers on the marks on her neck and his gaze grew serious.

"You bear my mark, Calla. This means there is a link between us and I know the fear you feel. What ghost haunts you?"

The whimsy of the question caught her attention. "Ghost?"

He smiled slightly, relieving the sharp lines of his face. "Memories, ghosts. Experiences that haunt us, we all have such things. Like in the book by Charles Dickens where a man is visited by the ghost of Christmas past to make him realize why he was the way he was. Scrooge was the result of the unpleasant things that happened to him at Christmastime. They'd turned him into a bitter man."

Something in his face—or was it the link he kept talking about—made her realize that he was speaking about more than just her. "You have ghosts?"

His smile tightened and he dropped his hand from her neck. "We all do. Perhaps we'll share them later." He pushed her through the living room and toward the kitchen. "Yours at least we should banish...I can't have you going around being afraid of a harmless evergreen. At the moment think of it as a big green houseplant until we decorate it."

"Decorate? You want me to..." Calla started to say, but broke off as soon as the smells in the kitchen caught her attention.

Like everything else in the apartment, the kitchen was modern and well appointed, with shiny pots and pans on display and beautiful china resting behind glass doors. It also looked distinctly underused. She supposed it wasn't often that a nightwalker had to cook. Most of Daniel's meals probably came in on their own two feet, or maybe he made withdrawals from the local blood bank like a vampire in a movie she saw once.

Daniel pulled a china place setting from a cabinet and silverware, which she could tell from its weight was real silver, and placed both on a place mat sitting on a table in the cozy breakfast nook. The source of the smell turned out to be the oven, set on low, from which Daniel pulled a number of individual delivery boxes from a restaurant she'd only seen the front of when passing by on the bus.

"You ordered a meal from Spumani's...for me?" she managed to squeak.

"As I said, a meal fit for a companion." In addition to what was in the oven, Daniel drew clear plastic boxes from the refrigerator, which included a salad and a dish of whole strawberries.

Daniel looked at the latter then replaced it. "Those are for dessert. There is plenty of variety, so pick what you want."

He poured her a glass of white wine as she dug into the food, and then a second wineglass with a liquid the color of straw. Sipping from it, he sat opposite her and smiled as he watched her eat.

Calla loved the delicate flavor of the scallop appetizer and tried to offer him one. "Can't you at least taste them?"

With a grimace, Daniel shook his head. "I'm afraid most food disagrees with me. I can't digest it and it is unseemly to try and chew it without swallowing."

"That's so sad." Calla took another bite and thought about it. She distinctly remembered the taste of blood in her mouth through the link when he'd bitten her. Maybe it would work in reverse?

Unsure of what she was doing, Calla imagined opening the link between them, and bit into the scallop. Daniel's head shot up and he stared at her. "What did you do?"

She chewed and swallowed. "Tastes good, doesn't it?"

Clearly disconcerted, Daniel nodded. "You did that through the link…but you're untrained."

"I learn fast." Calla shared the rest of her meal with him the same way, and with each bite, Daniel seemed to grow more uneasy…not that he stopped her from sending to him. He clearly enjoyed what he "tasted".

Finally all that was left was dessert.

"Don't get up," she told him. Calla got out the strawberries, and a dish of microwavable chocolate fondue. In moments she was dipping the strawberries into the heated chocolate.

Daniel moaned at the first taste of chocolate-covered strawberry she shared with him. "It has been years since I've tasted chocolate."

"How about strawberries?"

He hesitated then grinned. "That I've been able to taste…sort of."

She wasn't sure of the sudden look of mischief on his face. Daniel came around the table and knelt on the floor in front of her. He took one of the strawberries and held it to her lips. "Bite the end off."

Wondering what he was up to, she did, then was surprised when he opened her robe and placed the juicy, dripping berry against her nipple. The chilled fruit sensitized her skin, and her nipple pebbled almost painfully. Calla gasped, then moaned as Daniel's lips closed around the tender bud.

"This is how I like my strawberries," he told her, giving her a final lick.

Calla's laugh was cut off when he gave her second nipple the same treatment. She leaned back in the chair and let herself appreciate his tender assault. She knew he could be strong when he wanted to be, but right now he was so gentle. Even the occasional brush of his fangs against her flesh didn't bother her. So he had odd teeth and an odder diet—Daniel was also a wonderful lover.

Right now he was teasing her, so she decided to play too. She grabbed the dish of chocolate and as he squeezed more strawberry juice on her nipples, she took a finger full of the fondue. Just as he leaned over to lick it, she put the finger into her mouth and shot the taste through their link.

Daniel sat upright and stared at her. Calla sucked her finger and smiled around it. "Like a little chocolate with that?"

He took the bowl of fondue from her and put it aside, along with the strawberry. "On second thought, I'd rather taste your flavor."

"Are you sure?"

He responded by grabbing her ankles and draping them over his shoulders, opening her up to him. Thrown off balance, Calla squealed and grabbed the chair seat, but Daniel took hold of her waist and secured her.

"Don't worry, little companion. I've got you." He then buried his head between her thighs and Calla didn't dare let go of the chair. He might hold her but she knew she'd collapse without him.

Scratch what she'd thought about Daniel being a wonderful lover…he was an exceptional lover. She'd rarely met a man willing to go down on her, and Daniel not only didn't need to be asked, but seemed to take absolute pleasure with each lick and nibble.

In fact, she knew just how much he enjoyed it. Through their link she felt his delight in her taste. She also realized how every one of her gasps of pleasure gave him a sense of accomplishment. He liked making a woman feel good.

No…it wasn't that exactly. He liked making her feel good. She was special to him.

If she hadn't been overwhelmed by passion she might have started crying. It had been a long time since she'd been special to anyone. Without even trying hard she could imagine falling a little bit in love with this nightwalker.

Of course she couldn't admit it, and should even keep it quiet within her own mind, since Daniel could read at least some of her outward thoughts. Nothing spooked a man faster than a woman getting serious about him.

She was safe enough at the moment. Daniel had a one-track mind and was intent on making her come with his mouth. It wasn't at all hard to oblige him. She felt the touch of his mind, which she saw as a silver haze, attach to hers just before she climaxed.

As she recovered, she saw his look of self-satisfaction and resolved to do something about it. Turnabout was fair play after all. Calla sank to the floor before him and before he could do a thing to stop her, she had his robe open and her hands around his erection.

It was as long and as wide as she'd remembered and it took effort to stretch her lips around the tip. Daniel breathed out an appreciative sigh as her mouth closed over his cock. "This isn't necessary..." he started to say, but she interrupted him with her mind.

This would be my pleasure, Daniel.

He didn't argue further with her, just cupped the back of her head with his hands in tacit permission. He was too big to fit entirely in her mouth so Calla used her hand to stroke his shaft, while focusing her lips and tongue on the more sensitive tip of him.

Calla hadn't given many blowjobs in the past, but she knew the basics and soon realized that being able to tap into the way Daniel felt made it much easier to find out what he liked.

For example, he had this one spot just below the head of his cock that he loved to have nibbled. She used her tongue to play with that very sensitive place until Daniel's breathing grew hard.

"That's so good...so good..." and then he lost the ability to speak at all. All he could do was gasp as she took hold of his heavy balls and fondled them carefully.

Like it? she asked mentally.

Fuck, yes!

She touched his mind the way he'd done with her when she'd approached orgasm and found herself swept along as well. He bucked under her hands and mouth and then cried out as his cock erupted in her mouth. She had to swallow quickly as his semen poured out of him.

He was shaking when it was over, and then he grabbed her shoulders and pulled her up into his arms. "Thank you, little companion," he whispered into her ear.

"My pleasure." Calla licked her lips. "You know, you were right, you taste good…even without chocolate."

Chapter Four

Calla woke the next evening to blackness. For a moment she couldn't remember just where she was or how she'd gotten there, although she had to admit to being comfortable. Unlike her flophouse bed, this mattress was soft and the covers warm.

The hard body behind her was warm as well, if far more still than she'd expect a man to be in his sleep. She sat up to realize that the dream she'd had of a handsome stranger taking her into his home hadn't been a dream after all. The stranger lay next to her, apparently dead to the world.

Then she remembered who and what he was, and the dead part no longer seemed so much of a joke, even though he'd assured her he was quite alive. The way he lay with eyes closed and not breathing, she could have sworn he wasn't amongst the living.

After the incident in the kitchen, Daniel had hauled her back to the bedroom for another bath and a round of lovemaking that now had her aching from tits to crotch. She'd fallen asleep until he'd joined her just about dawn. She'd roused only to have him whisper something into her mind that put her back to sleep. Her last memory had been the sound of heavy shutters sliding closed over the bedroom windows.

The shutters were still closed and from the clock she realized it was still an hour or so before sunset. She wasn't sleepy any longer, but hungry and the idea of investigating the leftovers from her feast the night before sounded good. Unwilling to re-dress in her smelly uniform, she found a large T-shirt and a pair of sweatpants that were only a couple sizes too large for her.

She was enjoying reheated pasta in the shuttered kitchen when the apartment door buzzed once. Calla peered through the doorway just in time to see the bolt slide back and two people enter, a woman and a man, the latter heavily loaded down with packages.

"Just put them down over there, Albert," Calla heard the woman say. "I'll put the rest in the kitchen."

Not knowing what to do, Calla ducked back into the kitchen and hid behind the counter, hoping not to be noticed when the woman put a bag into the refrigerator.

Her hopes were dashed though. "Come out, come out wherever you are," the newcomer said humorously. "We know you're in here. Albert can hear you breathing."

Slowly Calla rose to her feet. The woman she faced was attractive, in her middle years, and had an amused expression on her face. She looked Calla up and down and nodded approvingly.

"What did I tell you, Albert? Daniel picked up another winner. I knew it the minute I saw the order that she'd be something special."

The man, a somewhat brutish fellow with a surprising amount of facial and body hair, sniffed the air then grinned. "She sure smells like nightwalker. He's been all over her. Can't say I blame him, she's choice."

Calla blushed, but the woman shook her head at the man. "Albert, how crude! The young lady will think we have no manners at all." She stepped forward and held out her hand. "I'm Mira Anton, dear, and this is my business partner, Albert Lupas. We handle special orders for the parafolk world."

She took the proffered hand. "I'm Calla Douglas."

"You can call me Al," he said. "In fact, you can call me anything you want."

Mira gave him an annoyed glance. "Please, pay no attention to my shapeshifter friend. This close to the full moon, he's quite impossible."

Shapeshifter? "You mean like a werewolf?"

"Now who's being crude," Al said. "We don't use that word."

"Oh, I'm sorry. I'm still learning all this."

"I'm sure you are." Suddenly Calla felt a strong voice in her mind and Mira's hand gripped hers more strongly. *But I think maybe you are a quick student.*

Shocked, Calla pulled away. Mira nodded smirking. "Oh, yes. Definitely a strong psi, even if untrained. I knew it the minute I saw that you were awake before dusk. Daniel won't like it that you were able to break free from him."

"I couldn't sleep any longer…"

"Oh, you don't need to explain it to me." Mira nodded. "Yes, yes. You'll do very well."

"I'm sorry…but what are you talking about?"

"As soon as Daniel lets you go I want you to come see me. I'll find you a new position, right away. There are plenty of nightwalkers who would give their right fang for an appetizing companion like you."

"But he and I…" Daniel was her lover now…wasn't he? He'd said the future would work out. Didn't that mean she had a chance of winning a longer place by his side?

"I told you his smell was all over her."

A sudden look of sympathy covered the woman's face. She played with a small gold star pendant she wore around her neck. "You and he. I know how that goes. But Daniel does this every year…he told you that didn't he?"

Calla had to nod.

Mira looked relieved. "He never keeps a companion very long. The good part is that he almost always finds some poor lost soul with psi talent and brings them to the parafolk. So everyone benefits in the end." She patted Calla's shoulder. "It will work out all right, you'll see."

The sound of a well-tuned motor started up and the shutters over the windows began to slide open. "It's dusk. We better get going." Mira pulled a card from her pocket and pressed it into Calla's hand. "You call this number, day or night, and I'll see that you're taken care of.

She headed for the door, but Al lingered behind. "You can call me, too, if you ever decide you want to step onto the wild side."

"But I'm not a shapeshifter..."

"Hey, I'm not prejudiced—I like a little norm meat now and then. You like it doggy style? I'm the original bad dog."

Al was so good-natured that Calla found she couldn't be offended. Instead she had to smile. "I'll keep it in mind."

He grinned at her. "That's all I ask."

"Time to go, Albert," Mira said impatiently from the door.

He joined her and they left, but just before the door closed he poked his head back in. "Enjoy the presents," he said then closed the door. The bolt slid shut again.

"Presents?" Calla slowly turned to examine the pile of bags and boxes they'd left behind. A moment later she squealed with delight.

* * * * *

When Daniel woke at dusk, he anticipated having his new companion in his bed, available for a quick cuddle...and bite. He reached for her, only to find the bed empty.

Annoyed, he sat up. He distinctly remembered putting her to bed last night and putting the compulsion into her mind to stay next to him. As he looked around, the shutters that automatically opened and closed with the fall and rise of the sun slowly slid back, revealing the twilight sky outside and reinforcing how empty his bed was.

Twilight on Christmas Eve...his least favorite night of the year. He'd told Calla that everyone had ghostly memories to haunt them and that he was no different. By tomorrow night he'd no longer need someone around, but on Christmas Eve he found it easier to keep distracted.

Taking a companion banished his annual holiday ghost and this year he'd even found a bonus, a woman of incredible sensuality who heated his blood unlike anyone he'd met in the past hundred years.

Trouble was, his coping mechanism seemed to have overcome the compulsion to stay put and had removed herself from his bed. Her mind was far stronger than he'd given her credit for, particularly given that she was untrained.

Of course, there was the way she'd shared the taste of her food last night. That had also been unexpected, but a pleasant surprise. His sister had been able to do that sometimes...he'd missed that.

Disconcerted by his wayward thought of Abigail, he got up and dressed in his usual black slacks and a black shirt before hunting down his missing companion. At least he felt her nearby in the apartment.

A sudden cry from the living room made him drop his shoes and run.

Her antipathy for the undecorated Christmas tree in the corner apparently forgotten, Calla sat in the midst of cheerful chaos. Around her clothes were scattered, obviously pulled from the pile of boxes and bags to one side. She was holding a pair of short-heeled boots to her feet, her face alive with sheer delight.

"I see my order arrived," he said with amusement.

Calla leapt to her feet and dashed over to him, throwing her arms around his neck and kissing him wildly. "Thank you so much!"

He meant to disentangle himself, but somehow his arms went around her waist instead and he just held her close. "It was my pleasure, Calla. After all, I have to have you properly dressed.

"Oh, Daniel, you bought more than enough for that!" She gestured to the dozen or so outfits littering the couch, tables and floor. "Look at all this! I've never seen such beautiful clothes. I can't wait to wear them."

Originally he'd planned to stay in tonight but now he wanted to take her out and show her off. He kissed her gently on the forehead. "Pick out something pretty and get dressed, Calla. I'm taking you out for dinner."

She didn't need to be told twice. Arms loaded with clothes, Calla disappeared toward the bedroom.

* * * * *

It was far later when they returned to the apartment. Daniel tossed his car keys onto the small entryway table angrily. Behind him Calla entered, a slight smile on her face. He turned to face her and her smile disappeared.

"I can't believe that miserable nightwalking jerk came on to you that way in front of me." Daniel said.

"I'm sure that Mr. Harper didn't mean any disrespect. He was just being friendly."

Too friendly! Daniel shot at her. "It is beyond rude to ask someone else's companion to dance."

Calla hung up the warm coat that had come with the rest of her new wardrobe on the entryway hooks. "He only asked if I was going to be at the parafolk Christmas party tomorrow night, and if so to save a dance for him." She turned to face him. "You told me yourself that you don't keep companions beyond Christmas day, so by then I won't have your mark."

Daniel's chin lifted. "The mark is there tonight and I won't have anyone behaving as if it isn't."

Calla put her hands on his chest. "I haven't forgotten it's there." She decided to change the subject. "I had no idea there were so many nightwalkers and shapeshifters in Los Angeles. That nightclub was full of them."

"The Dark Water Tavern specializes in providing for parafolk of all kinds. It's owned by the city chief, Jonathan Knottman. He and his lady host the party tomorrow night as well."

"Will you be there, Daniel?"

"I don't normally go. I…like to be alone."

She wasn't so sure of that, but didn't argue. There was something about Christmas that haunted her nightwalker and she wondered if she'd ever find out what it was.

"So what should we do now?"

Daniel cheered up. "Now we listen to old Christmas albums and we decorate the tree."

Chapter Five

"Decorate?" Calla turned to face the evergreen tree she'd been attempting to ignore since last night. Old, familiar dread filled her and she backed several steps away.

Daniel acted as if he hadn't noticed and went to where several plastic crates were stacked against the wall. He opened one up and pulled out a carefully wrapped bundle of lights. He tossed it to her and without thinking Calla caught it. She stared at the unlit lights while he pulled out two more bundles.

"First we have to test them." He plugged the bundles into the wall, and smiled approvingly when they all lit up. "These are good. What about the one you have?"

Calla dropped it onto the couch. "I don't think I can do this."

Daniel caught her before she could run from the living room. "Time to banish that ghost, Calla. What it is about Christmas trees that upsets you?"

She shook her head, but he didn't give up.

"Don't tell me you've always hated Christmas. I haven't met a little kid yet who didn't love the holiday."

Calla stilled and a rough sob slipped out. "Oh, when I was little, I loved it. I loved the lights, and the decorations." She stared up at him and saw the sympathy in his eyes. He really wanted to know what was wrong.

"I loved them so much, I'd beg my mother to take me to the stores so I could see them. We didn't have anything at home…my mother always said we were too poor to waste money on stuff we didn't need, but I would stare at the decorations when we went out. And so, one Christmas Eve she took me to see the best display in the biggest department store in the city. It took us three buses to get there, but I'd never seen anything so beautiful..." Her voice trailed off, remembering that night.

Daniel's arm slipped around her shoulders and he hugged her to his chest. "What happened, Calla?"

For a moment she had trouble finding the words. "The tree looked like it was a hundred feet tall and there were huge presents and a sleigh underneath. It glowed with lights, glittery balls and shiny tinsel. I stared at it for what seemed like hours...and when I looked around, I realized my mother wasn't there."

Daniel went very still. "What do you mean she wasn't there?"

"She'd left me. I looked for her everywhere, but she was gone."

Daniel's flash of anger felt like fire through their link. "Your mother abandoned you on Christmas Eve in a department store?"

"I was afraid but I thought she'd come back and be angry if I wasn't there so I hid in the sleigh until everyone was gone. I was only about four..."

For the first time in years, Calla burst into tears. Daniel held her close and stroked her back, but said nothing and she sensed he was waiting for her to finish her story, which she told through her sobs.

"I waited but she didn't come back...I spent the night under the Christmas tree with the lights still glowing. In the morning a security guard found me and called the police. By then my mother had disappeared...there was no way to track her... I never saw her again. Since then even the glimpse of a tree terrifies me."

Daniel continued to hold her until her sobs finally subsided. By then she could sense his thoughts, his anger over what her mother had done, his understanding why colored lights on a tree held bad memories for her.

"You were poor and she probably thought you'd be better off without her. Abandoning you where you were happy probably made it easier for her to walk away."

She hadn't thought of it that way before. They had been so poor…maybe her mother had loved her and it had been desperation that made her leave. "I suppose you're right…and in a way my trying to commit suicide was just as much running away."

"I thought you said it was an accident that you fell off the roof."

"I did…but I was thinking of jumping at the time." It was the first time she'd admitted it aloud. "But as soon as I fell, I knew it wasn't the answer to my problems."

"I'm glad that's true. Suicide is a permanent solution when problems are almost always temporary. Even so, I have to admit, Calla, that's one pretty big ghost to get rid of."

"I'm sorry, Daniel. I don't want to spoil your night."

"You aren't going to spoil my night, Calla. We're going to deal with this, you and I."

She looked up at him and saw determination in his face. "How's that?"

"We're going to make decorating this tree so much fun that the memory of this Christmas Eve will banish that old one of yours like the moldy ghost it is."

Calla looked dubiously at him. "How?"

Daniel smiled confidently. "Oh, I'll think of something. At least tonight I intend to fulfill every sensual fantasy you've ever had. You willing to try it, Calla?"

She eyed the still undecorated tree, and then him. What harm could it do her? She nodded slowly and Daniel handed her the bundle of lights she'd dropped. "First thing is to test the lights. You do that while I get the music started."

Feeling as if she was stepping into deep water, Calla took the string of lights over to the electrical socket and tentatively plugged it in. Every light glowed bright and she found herself smiling at the colors. From behind her soft music began playing, a holiday album by some musician who'd been dead for a long time, but somehow the music seemed to fit the mood.

Calla turned to see Daniel watching her, his gaze cautious. She held out the bundle of glowing lights. "It works, Daniel."

Daniel smiled slowly. "Yeah, I guess it does."

Turning to face the tree, Calla approached it with the strand of lights, Daniel by her side. He put one strand on and all she had to do was plug hers into the end and drape it over the branches. Simple to think about doing.

Not so simple to do. Her old feelings of loss and abandonment rose inside her and she stopped a few feet away.

A sob rose in her. "I can't do this."

Yes you can. In her head Daniel's voice beckoned and coaxed. Warmth slid through her as well, like a hand moving up her back. It seemed to press her forward, and Calla stumbled toward the tree. *Just put it onto the tree.*

She reached forward and plugged it in and the strand lit up. Calla stared at it, mesmerized by the colors. The invisible hand came back, stroking her back then sliding around to her breasts. Calla gasped as she felt fingers tweak her nipple. She spun to face Daniel, his hands filled with lights and a mischievous look on his face.

"How are you doing that?"

He stared at her breast and the fingers settled into a soft stroking motion. "We're linked. I think of something I want to do to you and you feel it. Do you like it?"

Calla licked her lips. The teasing massage of her nipple was making her crazy. "Yes."

Then put the lights on the tree!

Too distracted to think of anything but compliance, Calla quickly draped the strand over the branches under the first set of lights. Before she could turn she felt Daniel's body pressed against her. His breath was hot on the back of her neck. He ran a line of line of kisses along her neck, his fangs sharp but not breaking the skin.

Another set of lights was pressed into her hand. *Do the same with these.*

His smell and warmth supporting her, Calla did as she was told. She gasped as they lit up, but it was easier to hang them. As soon at she finished that set of lights, he gave her another, and then another. In the meantime he stayed behind her with his lips on her neck. The phantom fingers kept up their massage of her nipples and Calla's fears slid away.

Daniel pulled her back from the tree and engaged her in a deep kiss. "That's all the lights," he murmured.

"So what do we do now?"

His real fingers began working the buttons on her green silk blouse. "I have something in mind," he whispered softly in her ear, his voice loaded with sensual promise. She shuddered as the silk fell from her shoulders, revealing the black lacy bra that had been amongst his purchases. She'd never seen underwear as beautiful as what he'd bought…and he'd even gotten her size correct.

Daniel seemed pleased as well. He cupped his hand around the delicate lace. "Now that's what I call proper packaging."

Calla couldn't help teasing him. "Wait until you see the panties that go with it." Daniel's eyes glowed briefly and Calla glowed as well.

Close your eyes, Calla.

She did as she was told, then gasped as something cool and smooth was slid along the upper curve of her breast. Opening her eyes, she saw a pair of red glass balls in Daniel's hand. In a sudden move he hooked them through the lace of her bra cup, the hooks cold against her sensitized nipples. Calla looked down to see the pair dangling from her breasts.

He grinned at her. "Time to put the balls on."

Reaching for his shirt, Calla toyed with the top button. "Only if we stay dressed the same."

Making no move to stop her, Daniel let her undo his shirt and toss it on top of hers on the couch. He gave her a smile full of fangs. "I've never decorated a tree without clothes on…could be a new trend. Remove an article with each new set of ornaments."

"I thought you said you had fun before."

Some of his humor faded. "With my sisters—not quite the same kind of fun."

"I imagine not. Well, we'll just have to make up the rules for ourselves."

Daniel picked up a pair of green balls and eyed her lacy bra. "Where should I hang these, I wonder?"

Calla unhooked the balls on her bra. "Let's put them on the tree," she said, and did, and then stepped back to realize, "That was so easy."

Behind her Daniel slipped an arm around her and handed her another ornament. He slid an arm around her waist and nuzzled her neck and through the fabric of their pants she felt the solid rod of his cock harden.

The phantom fingers returned, this time moving down her backside and into the cleft of her ass. Calla almost dropped a ball.

"I think you're right," Daniel murmured. "Let's put the balls on the tree."

With shaky fingers she hung the one in her hand, and then the next several he gave her. He stayed close to her, handing her ornaments, more often than not standing behind her, his chest smooth satin against her bared back. Even when he wasn't right next to her, she felt his presence in the phantom fingers that moved over her body, tweaking her nipples, stroking her clit, and paying special attention to her anus, something she'd never really experienced before. She wasn't sure she liked it…but it was…*interesting*.

She hung one ball high, and in its shining surface saw her face and Daniel's behind her, his eyes glowing, mouth nibbling at her neck.

"I can see us…" she pointed to the reflective surface.

Daniel turned her to face him. "It's an old tale that nightwalkers don't cast reflections. They said it was because we lack souls…but my soul is right where it belongs, here with you."

And then he kissed her and she knew he was right because she felt his soul wrap itself around her. He slid her bra off her shoulders and undid the catch, letting her breasts spill into his hands. Again he worshipped the tips, sucking hard on her nipples.

She tried to grab for his crotch, but he stopped her. "I'm set to go off like a rocket if you play games with that tonight." Then he grabbed a length of garland and wrapped it around her wrists, tying them in front.

"Time to lose another layer of clothes, Calla." He tugged on her pants, pulling them off her. He had to take her boots off as well, and now all she wore was her underwear, black lace that as much highlighted as hid her private places.

Calla eyed his pants and tugged on the garland around her wrists. "I wonder if I could get those off with my teeth?"

"No need." He stripped out of them and Calla couldn't help but smile at his totally naked body.

"Don't you believe in underwear, Daniel?"

"Only when it looks like it does on you."

She lifted her bound hands. "So what do we do now?"

"Now you hold still while I make you come a few times."

He lifted her onto the couch and spread her legs. Closing his mouth over the crotch of her panties, he sucked hard. *You've been getting very excited, Calla. You're dripping wet.*

That surprises you?

He leaned back and licked his lips. "Not really. But I haven't made you come yet." Daniel did something with his teeth and tongue that made her legs twitch and her body scream for release and just before it did, he reached behind her and teased her anus with his real finger this time. That sent her over the edge and she screamed as the first crest of pleasure hit her.

Carefully Daniel pulled her underwear off and held it up so she could see how wet the crotch was. "I think you really want me, Calla."

"Maybe."

"Oh I think more than maybe. You want me, and no other nightwalker."

He really was jealous of the attention she'd gotten at the club. Hope rose in Calla…maybe he really would rather keep her than let her go to another man. She knew she didn't want to leave him.

"I want you…anyone else will have to wait unless you give me up."

She felt that he didn't like her answer but he didn't say anything. Instead he pulled her arms over her head and covered her with his body, teasing her pussy with his cock but not penetrating her. He did not smile but stared into her eyes.

You are mine, and no other's tonight!

And tonight that was true no matter what happened tomorrow, or the next day, and that Calla readily agreed to.

Now he imprisoned her with his body, hers taut beneath him, her hands bound, her legs held fast by his. She couldn't move unless he let her. Calla felt his will bear down on her. This was not the coaxing, gentle lover from last night but a man intent on getting his way. He wanted her to acknowledge what he was to her…her nightwalker, who rescued and saved her. A man who pushed her into facing her deepest fear and vanquishing it.

She surrendered to him. *I belong to you and no other. I swear, Daniel.*

Just the hint of a smile touched his face. He leaned down to ravage her lips with the kiss of a conqueror. Callas' mouth opened wide and she accepted his tongue delving deep within her mouth, tasting her.

Through the link she sensed her own taste, sweet and spicy. It fired her senses further and she spread her legs wide. *I need you.*

Daniel grabbed her wrists with both hands, stretching her against the couch. She couldn't have moved if she wanted to. He pushed his cock again into her aching pussy and entered her slowly, inch by agonizing inch, taking possession with strength and caution, like an invading army, on guard, uncertain of its welcome. He was so large…as big as last night, but then there had been the novelty of having sex compounding the experience. Now she knew him…and yet he felt even larger. He felt huge and she felt nearly split apart by his entry.

She felt split by what she felt for him as well. She wanted him…she needed him in her life as well as her body. But he wasn't really hers, in spite of his words. He needed to believe that she would look to him only, but she knew in her heart their relationship had no future.

It was hell to know this and feel the heaven of his entry at the same time.

But then he finally reached the deepest part of her. With one last push he completed his entry and Calla lay panting beneath him. A hint of red glowed in the blankness of Daniel's eyes.

Mine now. The silver of his mind covered her and she let her mind join with his, pink and silver together.

Yours…

He moved, thrusting in and out and Calla cried out. "Yours!"

Mine.

Yes, yours.

And then there were no words possible. He thrust and thrust and Calla lifted her hips to meet each one. He picked a rhythm that she felt in her bones, and they didn't stop. Calla reached climax and shrieked, but he didn't show signs of finishing.

Eventually he slowed. "I'm not ready to come yet."

She'd come twice, at least. "What are you waiting for?"

He lifted and pulled out of her completely and Calla moaned at his absence. Daniel pulled her onto the rug, soft under her. "Turn over," he said.

She did, with his help, her hands still fastened together. He positioned her so she was facing the tree, her rear end high in the air. Two of Daniel's fingers found their way into her pussy while his thumb played elaborate games with her clit. Calla leaned back into his hand, again aware that his other hand was again teasing her anus, this time with serious intent.

What do you have in mind, nightwalker?

Going where no man has gone before…

Certain of that?

He slapped her rear lightly. "I know you better than that, Calla. No one has ever fucked you in the ass."

"I'm not so sure this will work."

"I am." One finger was inside her, then two, then three. He was in her mind, testing her readiness. She wasn't so sure of the third finger.

Wait here…

And then Daniel was gone and she was alone, facing the tree. For an instant Calla felt her old fear, but then she knew he'd be back. He hadn't abandoned her.

Miss me? And he'd returned, stroking her back gently. Then something warm and smooth was being spread into the tight muscle that guarded her backside. *Just a little lubricant. I don't want to hurt you.*

He was serious. "Daniel," she said, and she wanted to protest, but there was something so erotic about where his hands were. Her body relaxed into his control.

Then it wasn't his fingers anymore. Something large was pushing its way into her anus. He took it slow, pushing then easing off. Again, then again. Then he pushed and didn't stop and she felt the tight muscle blossom open, letting him inside. She'd expected pain, but he'd prepared her well enough and all she felt was pressure and a delicious fullness she hadn't experienced before.

He seated his cock completely inside her and spread himself along her back, supporting his weight with his hands on the floor. "Are you all right?"

Was she? "I guess."

He pulled out and entered again, his heavy balls slapping unexpectedly against her pussy. Well, maybe she was a little better than all right. "That's…interesting…"

Calla, you are soooo fucking tight, I can barely stand it. I know you aren't used to this, but I had to have all of you tonight.

And she knew that was true.

His mouth was on her neck, licking, nibbling, tasting. She knew what he wanted. *Take what you need, nightwalker mine. Drink deep as you want.*

She felt his fangs against her skin, then the sharp near pain of them piercing the skin over her vein. Again she tasted what he tasted, blood, sweet and satisfying. He sucked and stroked and Calla again felt her body succumb to yet another orgasm, bigger than any before. The phantom fingers she'd felt before returned and were suddenly everywhere at once, on her clit, her nipples, and deep in her pussy, enhancing the sensation as Daniel's cock burrowed into her ass.

She was fixed in place, hands bound, Daniel holding her to the floor. All she could do was surrender into climax...so surrender she did. Calla cried out, again and again, each orgasm bigger than the one before.

Daniel stiffened and stopped feeding, licking clean her neck. *Now Calla, NOW*!

They came together this time, in a crash of pleasure that drove away all haunting thoughts of the past, the present, or even the future. Daniel groaned and shouted Calla's name before collapsing on top of her, his elbows supporting his weight and keeping her from being crushed.

Afterward Calla lay in his arms, her hands unbound, the garland a pile of glittering gold on the floor beside her. She gazed up at the Christmas tree, bright with lights and gleaming ornaments.

"It really is pretty, isn't it?" she said softly.

Daniel turned her so he was staring into her face. He stroked her cheek. "It's beautiful, Calla. Just like you."

* * * * *

The tree was finished, bright with lights and balls and garlands and topped with a golden star. Nestled in a blanket on the couch, Calla lay in Daniel's arms, half asleep, watching what he'd called one of his favorite Christmas movies on the television.

She couldn't remember ever feeling so warm and contented before. Or loved.

The movie ended and Daniel rose to shut off the TV. He stretched and looked at the window. "Day is coming. I hate to say it, but we're going to have to go to bed."

Calla's happiness faded a little. "So soon?"

"I don't control the sunrise and wherever I am I fall asleep when it comes up. I'd rather be in my own bed."

He went to the tree and pulled a small, decorated box out from beneath the branches. "This is for you."

Calla sat up. "But you already gave me the clothes…and I haven't given you anything."

Daniel smiled but she thought it was a sad one. "You've given me a wonderful holiday, Calla."

She opened the box. Inside was a small golden star-shaped pendant on a gold chain. It struck her as familiar and then she remembered where she'd seen it before. The memory chilled her. "Mira has one of these. You give these to your companions."

His face turned guarded. "You met Mira? I thought I'd smelled Albert earlier."

"They delivered the clothes and she gave me her card. She said I should call her once you were through with me."

He winced at her wording. "Mira was my guest about thirty years ago."

She simply stared at him. "You've been doing this that long, having a companion only for a few days a year? That's your ghost, isn't it? That you don't like to be alone this one night. Why?"

For a moment she wasn't sure he was going to answer her. "My sister died Christmas Eve."

"Your sister?"

"Most of the time our families don't accept it when a loved one converts, or the nightwalker hides it from them, but that only works for so long…eventually they realize you aren't aging. My sisters were different. They accepted my change…my youngest sister, Abigail, even insisted that the family move all of the celebrating to the night of Christmas Eve. We decorated the tree that night and opened presents after midnight. She did it so I could enjoy the holiday with them."

"How wonderful, Daniel."

He looked away. "Yes, it was. I loved them so much, especially Abigail."

"What happened to them?"

"They were mortal, Calla. One by one they grew old and died. Abigail was the last. I offered to make her like me I don't know how many times but she said she preferred to live the way she did. She wouldn't even let me make her a companion. She lived in this apartment with me until she died…I think people thought I was her grandson. We still celebrated Christmas though, until she died…it was her favorite holiday. That's why I find it better to have a guest that night, someone I just met."

"You celebrate it with a stranger every year. Why not be with someone who loves you?"

"Only to see them die? Nightwalkers live a long time, Calla and it is so hard to see the ones you care about pass on. I've been through it many times already."

Calla stared at the necklace in her hand. It was true then, he intended to let her go. "So you simply stopped caring, or wanting anyone to love you?"

Daniel looked at her. "We just met last night, Calla. We've shared some special moments but that's far too short a time to really fall in love."

"Is it?" She faced the tree, the lights dazzling her eyes…or was it tears making the miniature lights dance? "Are you so sure? I know that I love you."

"Don't say that Calla," he said, his voice hushed.

"Is it really that hard for you to hear?"

Daniel took hold of her arms. "Calla, I don't want to hurt you. Tomorrow, when I take the marks off, you'll go on with your life."

She was quiet, her heart breaking. "Why wait until then?"

"What?"

Calla stared at him. "Why not do it now? That way I'll be gone before you wake up and you won't have to face me at all."

"But I thought…"

Suddenly she was angrier than she'd ever been. "You thought I'd let you fuck me tomorrow, drink from me, then discard me like you have all the others? If you're going to remove the marks, do it now. You're right—I should get on with my life."

Daniel's eyes narrowed and his jaw clenched. "Very well." He bent his head to her neck, sinking his fangs into the marks he'd left on her neck. She flinched, but he held her firmly to him. He didn't take much, just enough to open the wounds to clear them. Then he licked them clean, leaving no trace that there had ever been marks on her neck.

Once they were gone Calla felt the link between them dissipate. He whispered. "You are no longer my companion. Go with my blessing."

He rose from the couch. "There's a suitcase in the spare bedroom to pack your clothes in. You said Mira gave you her number. Go ahead and call her now and she'll set up whatever you need."

"That's it then?"

For a moment she thought he wouldn't answer her.

"Goodbye, Calla. I'll always remember you," he said, but the words sounded bitter and he didn't look back as he exited the room.

Chapter Six

Daniel woke with the sunset, and the sound of the automatic lightproof shutters in his room slowly sliding apart. The twilight sky greeted him, but his bed felt cold and empty. Empty because Calla wasn't in it and hadn't been at all.

Odd how he missed her even though she'd only shared his bed once. He'd never even had a chance to wake up with her and now she was gone. By now Mira would have collected her and Calla was probably far across town.

Daniel pulled on sweatpants and made his way to the kitchen. Most likely his serum supply had been replenished, as well as his weekly staples of bagged blood. He'd get some living blood later tonight to supplement it, but a glass of O positive would be fine for now.

He warmed the blood in the microwave to just body temperature, took a tentative sip and couldn't resist a sigh. There just wasn't any comparison with the taste of Calla, but it was nutrition.

Sitting in the breakfast nook, he wondered what she was doing, but the phone interrupted his dinner.

"Daniel, is Calla there?" Mira's voice sounded concerned. "She called this morning and said she'd call again when she was ready to be picked up, but I haven't heard from her."

"No…I thought she'd gone with you. Maybe she's still asleep." Carrying the handset, Daniel moved through the apartment to the guest bedroom. A suitcase sat on the bed, partially filled with Calla's new clothes, but the bed was made.

The box with her necklace sat on the top, next to the green blouse she'd worn last night. Without thinking, Daniel picked it up and sniffed her delicate scent on the fabric. "Her clothes are still here."

"Then she's probably still there somewhere." Mira paused. "Daniel, she didn't sound right last night when she called. If she is there, you should find her."

Daniel turned off the phone and returned to the living room. It was as he'd left it last night, miniature lights glowing and shining off the ornaments and garlands. No sign of Calla, although her scent lingered in the room, and the couch and throw were still warm from where she'd probably spent the day.

He took in the scene and alarm sped through him. Just like her mother, he'd abandoned her in a room full of Christmas cheer—the long-ago painful experience that had plagued her all her life. What effect would his thoughtlessness have? Surely she wasn't suicidal anymore, but…

He reached out with his mind, hoping even without the link he'd somehow find her but there was no trace of her in the apartment. Even so, maybe she was still somewhere in the building.

Daniel went back to get the green blouse and sniffed it hard, filling his nose with her scent. Perhaps he wasn't quite a bloodhound, but he had a far better sense of smell than any norm. He didn't bother with shoes but grabbed his jacket before leaving. Walking around his building bare-chested would get him talked about.

Leaving the apartment, he discovered her smell was fresh and strong near the door to the stairwell that led to the roof, and terror gripped him.

The roof? Fifteen stories above the street, a long enough drop if oblivion was what she was looking for. Oblivion for her—a lifetime alone for him.

Daniel took the stairs three steps at a time, a silent prayer in his mind. *Help me find her in time…* It was too far past the full moon for him to fly to her rescue this time.

When he arrived, he breathed a sigh of relief, then concern. Calla was there, alive and well, but she sat on the low wall that edged the roofline, her feet dangling over the street below.

Daniel froze, afraid any move he made might send her off. He couldn't stand that, if he were the reason for her death. Not now, not when…

His heart ached with sudden knowledge of the truth. Somehow in the past two days he'd fallen in love with her. If Calla died, it would be like losing Abigail again and that ghost would haunt him forever, worse because he knew he was responsible.

The air was chilly, but she wore the warm jacket he'd purchased for her. Daniel clutched his own closer around him. As a nightwalker he didn't feel the cold as much as a normal human, but he still felt the bitterness and it was more than the air that chilled him.

He couldn't lose Calla now, not to death—or to anything else he realized. It was more than just Christmas that haunted him. He didn't want to be alone anymore at all.

Daniel took a cautious step forward. Maybe he could grab her and pull her back?

Are you going to stand there all night, or are you going to come sit with me? Calla's gentle mental voice broke his thoughts. It surprised him to know how strong she'd gotten, to bespeak him without the link, but then again many things surprised him about Calla.

Daniel moved to the wall, sitting gingerly on the edge as she did. Calla glanced at his bare feet dangling next to her boots and he felt her amusement. *Didn't have time to dress*?

I wanted to find you…

You were afraid I was going to jump off the roof. Calla sighed and spoke aloud. "I told you before that suicide wasn't the answer."

"I know…but I thought maybe…"

It's all right, Daniel. I can live with myself now.

She lapsed into silence. As the sky darkened, lights twinkled to life along the rooflines and balconies of the nearby buildings.

"Why are you up here?"

"I wanted to see the lights, Daniel. They are beautiful, aren't they?"

"Yes." He had to know what she was thinking. "Why didn't you go to Mira?"

"After I talked to her I realized I didn't really want another nightwalker taking care of me. Being with you has taught me I'd rather stand on my own two feet—I don't need rescuing anymore. I wanted to tell you that before I left and I didn't want to leave things the way they were between us."

How strong she'd become—it took his breath away. "I've been thinking too. You were right… I was afraid to let someone get close. But somehow you've gotten to me anyway. I want you to be my companion again."

She glanced at him cautiously. "Until when—Christmas next year?"

"I was thinking more about Christmas in 2205."

Calla turned to face him and he rejoiced at the hope in her eyes. "Two hundred years from now? Do you think that's long enough?"

She laughed and Daniel laughed briefly with her. "In a way, I've been running away as well…from love and what it would mean."

"You lost your loved one on Christmas."

"And now I've found someone else to love, and to love me back."

Calla watched him steadily. "I'll still be mortal."

"I understand that. But companions live a very long time."

"Two hundred years?"

"Sometimes." Daniel reached for her cheek and stroked it. "But it doesn't matter how much time we have so long as we're together."

Very well. I'll stay. She swung herself back over the wall, and mock glared at his bare feet. "And as my first act as your soon-to-be companion, I insist you get into the bathtub and warm up."

"Only if you come with me and let me mark you again. This time for good."

Calla smiled, and it was the best Christmas present Daniel had ever been given. He stood and pulled her into his arms and their lips met in a kiss that left him too breathless for speech.

Fortunately he could still talk mentally. *After that I'm taking you to that parafolk party tonight and making it clear to everyone that you belong to me and me alone.*

She laughed. *Now that sounds like fun*!

"Merry Christmas, Calla!"

"Merry Christmas to you too, my nightwalker love."

Also by Cricket Starr

Divine Interventions 1: Violet Among the Roses
Divine Interventions 2: Echo In the Hall
Divine Interventions 3: Nemesis of the Garden
Ellora's Cavemen: Legendary Tails I *(anthology)*
Hollywood After Dark: Fangs for the Memories
Hollywood After Dark: Ghosts of Christmas Past
Holiday Reflections *(anthology)*
Memories To Come
Rogues with Liddy Midnight
The Doll
Two Men and a Lady *(anthology)*

If you are a fan of Cricket's Hollywood After Dark vampire stories, be sure to see the first in the series, *All Night Inn*, at Cerridwen Press (www.cerridwenpress.com), written under the name Janet Miller.

About the Author

Cricket Starr lives in the San Francisco Bay area with her husband of more years than she chooses to count. She loves fantasies, particularly sexual fantasies, and sees her writing as an opportunity to test boundaries. Her driving ambition is to have more fun than anyone should or could have. While published in other venues under her own name, she's found a home for her erotica writing here at Ellora's Cave.

Cricket welcomes comments from readers. You can find her website and email address on her author bio page at www.ellorascave.com.

HOLIDAY LOVE LESSONS

By Trista Ann Michaels

Trademarks Acknowledgement

The author acknowledges the trademarked status and trademark owners of the following wordmarks mentioned in this work of fiction:

Drakkar Noir: Parfums Guy Laroche Corporation

Durango: Daimler Chrysler Corporation

Jell-O: General Foods Corporation

Starbucks: Starbucks U.S. Brands, LLC

Chapter One

"I can't believe I'm actually going to do this," Caitlin whispered as she made her way down the hall toward Jonathan and Tim Trelain's offices.

Jonathan Trelain, Caitlin thought with a grin. Gay or not, if there was one man she wanted to give her sex lessons it was him and his sexy bisexual brother, Tim.

She, Tim and Jonathan had worked together for about eight months now. Jonathan was gorgeous, and she'd had the most unbelievable crush on him until she found out from her coworkers that the man was gay.

At first she didn't believe it. How could someone as gorgeous and masculine as him be gay? But the rumors continued and he never did anything to deny it. She had heard he'd dated women in the past, before coming out of the closet, so to speak.

Eventually, she got over her crush and moved on. She just moved on with the wrong man.

Her mind wandered back to one month ago when her boyfriend, Colin, had broken up with her. The things he'd said had devastated her and she'd sought refuge in her office, burying herself in her work. That's where Jonathan had found her, crying her eyes out. He didn't push her to explain. He just held her, silently letting her know he was there for her.

That was Jonathan. He was nice, easy to talk to and always there for her. Especially at work. He'd helped her to talk her way through more than one artistic block in her time at Morgan Publishing. The latest had been the cover for the newest erotic ménage that was due to be released next month.

Working on the cover had been where she got the idea for her plan.

Staring at the woman and two men entwined together had made her realize just how lacking her sex life had been. She'd never experienced mind-blowing orgasms or passion that could make you lose control. She barely even got excited, much less lost control. And she wanted to.

She wanted to learn how to be sexy and seductive. She wanted to experiment and see just how far she could go and what would turn her on beyond reason. What better two men to teach her than the two most gorgeous men in town? And the fact that they were bisexual—well, that just made them safer than a straight man she might end up giving her heart to. The three of them were friends, so there would be no emotional attachment other than that friendship, which meant no expectations and no worries. It was perfect.

But which one did she approach first? Tim, she decided. He was much less intimidating than Jonathan and when it came to propositioning a man for sex, less intimidating was definitely better.

Taking a deep breath, she headed down the hall toward Tim's office. Raising her hand, she fingered the gold lettering across the wood. *Timothy Trelain, Co-Executive Vice-President*. He and Jonathan shared the position but Jonathan worked more with the cover artists and advertising, where Timothy handled the marketing and money side of the business.

"You can do this, Caitlin," she mumbled to herself then knocked softly.

"It's open," Tim called from inside.

Trying to still her shaking hands, she took one final calming breath for courage then opened the door. "Hey, Timmy," she said with a smile.

Tim stared at her over the top of his glasses, his amber-colored eyes shining in amusement. "So it's Timmy, is it? What do you want, darlin'?"

Caitlin shrugged and stepped farther into the room. "Nothing major."

He removed his glasses and set them on his desk. Sitting back in his chair, he brushed his shaggy, dark blond hair from his brow and smiled up at her. "Whenever someone says it's nothing major, it usually is. Spill it, doll."

"Well," she began and chewed at her lip, trying to decide just how to broach the subject. "I have a request."

"Oh god," Tim sighed in mock exaggeration. "When do you need it and how much is it going to cost me?"

Caitlin laughed. "It's not something you can buy. I want to spend the weekend with you and your brother. I want the three of us to have a ménage."

Tim's eyes widened, and he choked, coughing loudly. "I'm sorry. You want to what?"

* * * * *

"She wants to what?"

Jonathan stared at his brother in a mixture of shock and pure excitement. Had he really heard him correctly? Caitlin? The adorable redhead he'd been fantasizing about for months wanted to have a ménage?

"I told her that I would broach the subject with you. So, brother," he added with a snicker. "Think you can step away from your gay lifestyle and help me accommodate the girl?"

Jonathan frowned. "You know damn good and well I'm not gay."

"I can't for the life of me figure out why you let these rumors continue."

"You know why. It keeps the money-grubbing women away."

Tim snorted. "Squat good it did. Now they just want to convert you."

Jonathan shrugged, a sideways grin lifting his lips. "They try. Some succeed, then after we have sex, I give them the 'I just can't do this straight relationship thing' speech and that's that."

Tim dropped his tall, broad frame into one of the leather chairs flanking Jonathan's desk. "Man, you're cold. Are you sure you're not gay?"

Jonathan scrunched his nose. "Ha-ha. So what the hell brought this on anyway?"

"You mean with Caitlin?" Tim asked.

Jonathan nodded and closed the file he'd been looking through.

"I don't know. She approached me early yesterday evening with the idea."

"And you're just now bringing it to my attention? Why didn't you call me last night?"

"Well, I was going to, but I got busy," Tim replied as he studied his nails. "Carlos popped in for a nightcap and well…stayed a little longer."

Jonathan groaned and rolled his eyes toward the ceiling. "Please, spare me the details."

"You're supposed to be gay, remember? You should be clamoring for the details."

Jonathan pinned him with a narrowed stare, making Tim chuckle. "Well?" Tim asked. "You never gave me your answer on the ménage weekend with Caitlin. Yes or no?"

"Like I'm going to pass this up."

* * * * *

Caitlin walked into her office and threw her purse down on the desk. She hadn't heard from Tim last night like she thought she would and disappointment had made her irritable. Had they decided not to go through with it? Had she asked too much?

With a sigh, she dropped into her chair and booted up her computer. She couldn't spend too much time thinking about it. She had covers she had to do. Her hand bumped into the small Christmas tree on the corner of her desk. The tiny glass decorations clinked against one another and she grabbed one that was about to fall off. As she secured it more firmly, she fingered the bright red ball and watched the office light reflected in the glass.

Normally she loved this time of year. The first snow of the season, although a little late, had fallen last night, blanketing the streets of Boston in a thin layer of white. Decorations hung from street lamps and front doors. Santas stood outside shops ringing their bells while carolers strolled the streets, their voices raised in song.

She just couldn't seem to get into the spirit this year. Maybe it had to do with the fact she still hadn't gotten over her latest breakup. The one that had finally pushed her to make such a drastic request.

She frowned at the tree. Was she as cold as he said she was?

A knock sounded at her door and she glanced up to see Jonathan smiling down at her, a cup of Starbucks coffee in each hand. Her heart flipped in her chest. He was so gorgeous, with the same dark blond hair as Tim, only Jonathan's was just a tad shorter. Long, thick lashes framed chocolate-brown eyes that almost always sparkled with humor.

His wide shoulders and trim waist fairly dominated the doorway as he leaned against the jamb. Six-feet three-inches tall and well muscled, he made quite an intimidating presence. "Morning. I thought we could discuss your request over coffee."

"Tim talked to you?" she asked and walked over to take one of the cups from his hands. Her stomach fluttered with nerves as she took a sip. She was so uptight the taste of the strong coffee she normally savored didn't even register.

"Yes. This morning." He stepped inside and shut the door behind him with a click. "Coffee good?" he asked.

Caitlin wondered if he was trying to break the ice and relieve some of the tension that had filled the small room. "It's great. Thank you."

Normally they weren't this stiff around each other. They were good friends. She just hoped her request hadn't ruined that. Suddenly, she regretted her impulsive action. "Jonathan, if you don't want to do this, I understand. We can just forget I said anything."

"No way," he grinned. "I just want to know one thing."

"What?" she asked as she sat in her chair, relief swimming through her.

"Why?"

"Why?" she asked, surprised.

Jonathan nodded and leaned his hip against her desk. Her gaze strayed to his hard thighs and ass, but then quickly averted. Noticing the password prompt on her computer screen, she busied herself typing it in to buy some time and compose her thoughts.

"Well," she said with a sigh. "I haven't had the best luck with men, you know that. I just want to experience something wild and completely uninhibited for once in my life without any worry of commitment or fear of someone getting hurt. Especially me. I want you guys to teach me how to be sexy, how to seduce and let go."

She chanced a look at him over her computer screen. He watched her thoughtfully, as though mulling over what she'd said in his mind.

"There's more to it that you're not telling me," he said quietly.

With a sigh, she rearranged the files on her desk. "When Colin broke up with me he said I was cold, that I wouldn't know passion and good sex if it hit me in the face. I want to see if he's right."

Jonathan snorted and she frowned up at him. "It was probably Colin that didn't know passion, honey, not you."

"Have you ever been with a woman?" she asked, although she was sure he had.

"A few." His lips twitched—adorable. "Purely experimental, you understand."

"Oh, I do," she said, returning his grin.

"This weekend? The Trelain cabin at the lake?"

"You're taking me up on this?" she asked, her heart racing wildly.

"I believe I am."

"Tim, too?"

He nodded, his eyes crinkling as he smiled.

"You guys are okay with sharing?"

"Oh, yeah. Tim and I have shared before. Occasionally he gets a wild hair and shows up on my doorstep with a woman."

He rolled his eyes toward the ceiling and Caitlin giggled. "Wild hair, huh?"

Jonathan stood and began to walk to the door. "Be prepared. Tim can get some pretty wild hairs." He smiled at her over his shoulder. "We leave at noon on Friday. Come to the office packed. We'll take my Durango."

"What should I pack?" she asked.

He grinned wickedly and a slight tremor ran under her flesh. "Doesn't matter. You're going to be naked the majority of the time."

"Oh," Caitlin sighed as she watched him stroll from her office, a very pleased-with-himself expression on his face.

Chapter Two

Friday arrived and her stomach fluttered with nerves, so much so that when Jonathan knocked on her door at noon, she almost backed out.

"Ready?" he asked, a teasing glint in his brown eyes.

"I think so," she sighed.

Her fingers suddenly felt ice-cold, and she held her hands together, trying to warm them. Jonathan noticed her pensive frown and stepped into the room, shutting the door behind him. "You look a little nervous, Caitlin."

"I guess I am," she said with a soft smile. "Never done this before."

He came to stand in front of her, the warmth from his body flooding over hers in waves. She caught a whiff of his cologne. Inhaling deeply, she sighed. "I love that cologne. What is it?"

"Drakkar Noir. Relax, Caitlin. You'll have more fun."

She hummed and smiled slightly, agreeing with him. But for some reason her stomach just wouldn't listen. Jonathan stepped closer, pinning her against her desk. With a startled gasp, she glanced up at his face and watched helplessly as it lowered to hers.

The brown of his eyes practically smoldered, causing her heart to jump against her ribs. Every pore on her flesh tingled as his hands came up to frame her face. Softly, tentatively, his lips brushed across hers, sending a jolt of fire to her belly that startled her. With a whimper, she opened her lips and welcomed the gentle invasion of his tongue.

He tasted of coffee, and she sucked at his tongue as it came further into her mouth. A soft moan rumbled through his chest, vibrating against her own, and he pressed her tighter against the desk. Her hands lifted to settle at his waist, balling the soft fabric of his sweater with her fingers.

All too soon the kiss ended. She moaned as he pulled his lips away and leaned forward slightly, seeking their warm touch again. Slowly, she opened her eyes and stared up into his smiling ones. "There. That's better," he said.

A little shell-shocked, she watched him step away and grab the suitcase she'd placed by the door.

Wow. What the hell was that?

"You coming?" he asked over his shoulder as he left her office. "Tim's waiting for us in the parking garage."

"Yeah, coming," she squeaked. On legs that wobbled like Jell-O, she followed him out to the car.

* * * * *

Tim followed them to the cabin in his jeep, which had surprised Caitlin. She'd assumed they would all be going up in the same car. Stepping out of Jonathan's Durango, she gaped at the log cabin.

This isn't a cabin. It's a damn lodge.

The massive three-story house stood on a slight hill, the back sloping to the lakeshore behind it. A porch went all the way across the front, with Christmas lights blinking in the setting sunlight. A huge pine wreath decorated with red and gold ribbon hung from the massive oak door. It was beautiful. Like something in a painting.

"Jonathan, this place is huge," Caitlin gaped.

"Yeah," he sighed as his gaze took in the house. "Thirty-six hundred square feet of Trelain Christmas cheer."

Caitlin giggled. "So do we have it all to ourselves?"

He turned to her with a grin. "Every last foot. Including the oversize bathtub." He wiggled his eyebrows.

Caitlin's mind went ninety miles per second with lots of sexy and wild images. Her hands shook slightly and she gripped them before her silently, convincing herself she could go through with this. Jonathan must have sensed her unease for he stepped forward and covered her shaking hands with his. "Still nervous?" he asked.

She licked at her suddenly dry lips. "A little. But I'll be okay. I want to do this." She smiled slightly. "I need to do this."

Jonathan brought his lips close to hers. His warm breath turned to fog as it hit the cold air between them. She couldn't stop gazing at his eyes. They were gorgeous and full of hunger and passion. "Good," he murmured against her lips.

Tim came up behind her and brushed her hair away from her neck. His hot breath blew across her flesh, making her shiver in a mixture of excitement and apprehension. "Starting without me?" he whispered. "Shame on you."

Caitlin smiled slightly, letting out a rush of nervous air. "We would never dream of starting without you, Timmy," she sighed as his lips touched the sensitive spot behind her ear.

Jonathan's lips nipped at her jaw and her head fell back, offering him her throat. Two men, both gorgeous and sexy, both making her body melt like butter. It was surprisingly erotic and she tried to relax a little and let herself fall into the moment. A cold breeze blew, cutting through her skin like a knife and she shivered.

"Cold?" Jonathan asked as he gazed down at her and brushed a stray hair from her forehead.

She nodded.

"We should get you inside and warmed up," Tim whispered as his teeth bit at her earlobe, sending a tremor down her spine.

"One of these first," Jonathan mumbled just as his lips captured hers in a kiss that sent her reeling. It was so different than the one in her office—so much more passionate. She groaned as her tongue twined with his, twirling and stroking. Oh god. He could keep kissing her right here in the snow if he wanted. She didn't care.

Breaking off the kiss, he stared down at her with that same lazy, sexy smile. "Caitlin, honey. If you're cold, I'm Cher."

"Who said you were cold?" Tim asked in surprise as he stepped around her and lifted her chin with his finger.

"Her old boyfriend."

Tim looked at her for a second in surprise then actually laughed as he grabbed her hand and pulled her behind him to the house. "Cold, my ass."

Her chest swelled with warmth and a tiny grin touched her lips as she followed them up the porch steps.

This is it, no turning back, she thought as she hesitated before stepping through the front door. Jonathan stopped in the doorway and turned to face her. With an understanding smile, he held his hand out. *I can't believe I'm going to do this.* After only a second's hesitation, she placed her hand into his and returned his grin as he pulled her into the house.

*****

"Wine?" Jonathan asked as he handed Caitlin a glass.

"Thank you." She raised the glass to her lips and took a large sip, downing half the contents at once.

"Careful, Caitlin. We want you relaxed, not drunk."

She giggled nervously and lifted the glass slightly in acknowledgment. He couldn't stop staring at her. She was so beautiful. Her blue eyes sparkled with excitement and more than just a hint of nerves. Dark red curls hung over her shoulders, and he brushed his fingers through them, feeling the silky texture as it wrapped around his knuckles.

He hadn't been able to think of anything but this all week. He'd known for a while how he felt about her, but past hurts had kept him silent. This weekend would be the start for them. The beginning of a long and, he was sure, happy relationship. He wanted all of her…forever.

Tim stoked the fire, filling the downstairs den with warmth. The wood popped and cracked and the smell of burning embers filled the room.

"I love that smell," Caitlin said as she inhaled deeply, pushing her breasts out further. Jonathan's eyes strayed to the nipples that stood proud beneath the snug fabric. "It smells like Christmas now. The decorated pine tree over by the bar and now the fire. It's perfect."

Jonathan smiled. She was perfect.

"Turn on some music, Tim," Jonathan suggested.

"Anything in particular?" he asked.

"Something sexy," Caitlin offered as she downed the rest of the wine and swayed her hips slowly. "Something that we can dance to."

"Feeling that wine, are you, darlin'?" Tim teased.

"I'm feeling something," she replied with a giggle.

Tim raised an eyebrow in interest and glanced at Jonathan. "Damn," he mouthed silently and Jonathan lifted his glass of wine in answer.

"No more wine for you, Katie dear," Jonathan said with a chuckle and removed the now empty glass from her fingers. Apparently Caitlin didn't drink very often.

Turning on the stereo, Tim picked out a CD. Music soon filled the room and Caitlin began to dance around them to the soft guitar.

"Take off your sweater, Caitlin," Jonathan ordered.

Caitlin stopped her dance and stared at him in uncertainty. Jonathan placed his glass on the bar and moved to stand next to her. He didn't want her afraid and was going to try and make her relax a little more. Taking one of her hands in his, he placed the other on her waist and began to move them to the music. Slowly, she began to loosen up, inching her body closer to his. Leaning down, he whispered in her ear. "Strip for us, Katie. I want to see how beautiful you are."

She hesitated for a moment then her hands moved to grab the hem of her sweater. Jonathan's hands moved with hers, helping her tug it over her head. The light of the flames flickered against her tan flesh and he stared in rapture at the cleavage her red lace bra created.

"You're beautiful, Katie," he whispered and brushed his fingers along the lace edge of her bra.

She drew in air sharply and lifted her hands above her head, gently swaying her hips to the soft music. His hands moved to gently cup her breasts and she closed her eyes, sighing softly.

"Keep dancing for me, Katie. Strip to the music and let us see how beautiful the rest of you is."

Tim remained silent as he watched her slowly move around the floor, her hips swaying seductively. Her hands still shook a little and her eyes still held a hint of unease, but Jonathan continued to encourage her and she became more comfortable and a little more bold in her movement, which was driving him crazy.

The woman was a vision, and he watched in spellbound attention as she sauntered toward the fireplace, her fingers slowly undoing her slacks. For a second, she hesitated, glancing at Jonathan, then Tim.

"Take them off, darlin'," Tim whispered. "Let me see if those panties match that bra."

Finally, she put her back to them and inch by excruciating inch lowered her slacks over her hips. Her ass was firm, round and the panties indeed matched the bra. An adorable red lace thong separated her ass cheeks and his breathing hitched as her hands slowly moved over the mounds and back up to her waist. Her movements were slow and uncertain. Her innocence was more of an aphrodisiac than the wine.

Jonathan's hands burned to touch that ass, to feel his cock sink into the warmth of her pussy. A sudden thought occurred to him and his gaze shot back to hers. "Have you ever had anal sex, Caitlin?" Jonathan asked.

"No." She stopped dancing and shook her head. Her shaking hands fluttered to her stomach. She'd never done that, but had always been intrigued with the idea. Unfortunately, she'd never had the nerve to give it a try.

"Then come here, darlin'," Tim said with a crook of his finger. "We need to prepare you."

Her gaze glanced toward Jonathan, and he nodded his encouragement. Licking her lips, she walked over to Tim, who now stood by the bar. Jonathan joined them. Standing behind her, his fingers skimmed over the warm flesh of her shoulders.

Caitlin's insides felt like mush. Prepare her? She had an idea what he had in mind, but still her stomach jumped with nerves.

"Don't worry, Caitlin." Tim brushed his finger along her jawline. "We won't do anything that hurts you. If we do, just say so and we'll stop. Okay?"

She nodded and swallowed down the last of her nervousness. These guys were her friends. She could trust them.

"We're also clean. We've both been checked, so you have nothing to worry about. Just relax and enjoy yourself," Jonathan whispered as his hands moved to her back and worked loose the clasp of her bra. Tim lifted her chin, bringing her lips to his. His kiss was soft, seeking, and she melted, her body swaying toward his.

Jonathan removed her bra and dropped it to the floor. His warm palms cupped her breasts from behind, squeezing them and pinching her nipples between his thumb and forefinger. She moaned as her juices flowed to coat her panties. His lips moved to nibble along her neck, and she reached behind her with one hand to bury her fingers in his hair. She was so hot. Never in her life had she thought fooling around with two men could be this arousing.

Breaking the kiss, Tim turned her to Jonathan, who took his turn at claiming her mouth. His hands moved lower, pushing her thong down around her ankles. She gripped his strong arms and kicked the scrap of red lace away, sending it flying somewhere across the room.

Jonathan's fingers moved between her thighs, sliding along her slit. Her legs trembled as Tim added his touch from behind, gently pushing two fingers within her wet depths. She groaned and spread her legs wider. Her whole body burned and it had happened so damn fast.

Jonathan's tongue continued to plunder her mouth while his fingers fondled her clit, circling and teasing to the point she was ready to burst. And Tim. Oh god. He was fucking her with his fingers while his teeth nipped at her ass. It was so wild and hot, so unbelievably erotic.

Caitlin moaned into Jonathan's mouth as Tim removed his fingers and replaced them with a dildo. "Oh, yes," she sighed. In and out he moved it, then pushed it deep and held it in place. "More," she moaned, surprised at her wantonness.

"In time, darlin'," Tim drawled as he separated the cheeks of her ass. Sliding one finger into her ass, he groaned against the small of her back. "Damn, she's tight."

Gently, he added a second and Caitlin had to grab onto Jonathan's shoulders to remain upright. In her ear, Jonathan whispered soft words of encouragement as he continued to play with her slit then moved to take control of the dildo, gently moving it to stroke the pulsing walls of her vagina.

"Oh god," she sighed as her legs became weaker.

Jonathan bent down and captured a pert nipple within his mouth. She sighed, throwing her head back and thrusting her breast more fully into his mouth. She wanted them to fuck her. Now. She needed it so badly her body burned with it.

She gasped as Tim removed the dildo from her pussy and slowly inserted it into her ass. The fullness took her by surprise and she stiffened. "Shhh," Jonathan crooned in her ear. "Relax, Katie."

Slowly, she did and once again melted beneath the dual set of lips and hands turning her to mush. Once she was used to the sensation, others began to intensify.

"Oh god. One of you, please. Fuck me."

Jonathan let out a growl as he turned her toward Tim and pushed her to her knees. She watched as Tim removed his clothes, revealing a well-muscled torso and long, thick cock. Wanting to see what Jonathan looked like as well, she turned to watch him. He stood behind her and removed his sweater, revealing a hard chest that was much more muscled than Tim's. He even had a sprinkling of hair, where Tim did not. Lowering her gaze, she stared at his cock, only slightly longer than Tim's and just as thick.

She swallowed, wondering how both of them would fit at the same time.

Reaching out, she wrapped her trembling fingers around both of their cocks, gently squeezing them. Jonathan groaned, his head falling back. Tim hissed and moved to stand directly in front of her.

"Take me in your mouth, Caitlin," he said.

Without any hesitation this time, she did as he asked, finally losing all her inhibitions and enjoying the moment. Jonathan moved behind her and pushed her shoulders forward slightly. Tim dropped to his knees, putting his cock more fully in front of her face. Bracing one hand on the floor, she licked at Tim's cock while Jonathan sheathed himself with a condom.

Holding Tim's cock at the base, she enveloped him in her mouth, her teeth nipping at the head. Jonathan's hands brushed along her hip, massaging her flesh. She moaned and wiggled her hips in silent invitation. She wanted him to ram that big cock into her, to fill her to the womb.

Tim moaned and buried a hand in her hair as she relaxed her throat and sucked him deeper. She'd never dreamed she could do this. She was wild and couldn't get enough of his cock in her mouth. She wanted to taste his cum. Feel him fill her mouth with it.

"Jonathan, please," she moaned around Tim's shaft.

"I like watching you, Caitlin. I like seeing you swallow him and imagining you doing that to me," he whispered and then bit softly at her hip.

Finally, he rose up and positioned the head of his shaft at her aching pussy. Pushing back, she tried to take him inside her, but he continued to tease, circling the tip around her clit. With a growl, he repositioned himself and pushed inside. She moaned as her body strained to accommodate his girth.

"Fuck," Jonathan groaned as he pushed deeper, sheathing himself balls-deep.

Caitlin screamed, for the moment removing Tim's cock from her mouth. She gaped in wonder as he began to move the dildo and his cock together, their movement one fluid motion. The duel sensation sent shivers of pleasure to every muscle in her body.

"Oh, fuck, she feels good," Jonathan sighed as his thrusts increased, becoming harder.

Once again grasping Tim's cock, she sucked him back into her mouth, her rhythm matching Jonathan's assault on her pussy. It felt so good she could hardly concentrate on what she was doing and she used his thrusts to help push Tim's cock deeper down her throat.

"Oh, yeah. That's it, darlin'. Suck my cock."

Tim's moans soon overrode hers as his seed spewed forth, filling her mouth.

Caitlin quickly joined him as her release gripped her with a vengeance. Every nerve in her body erupted into a mass of light and sensation. The walls of her pussy and anus quivered and pulsed around the two invading rods, sending little quakes of pleasure and pain down her spine. Jonathan fell with them a second later, his body tensing behind her with one final, deep thrust.

Gently, Caitlin continued to lick away the remaining semen from Tim's cock, before closing her eyes with a sigh. What had she been so nervous about? It had been incredible, more than incredible and she wanted to experience it again. Over and over. She could feel passion and she wanted more. "Can we do that again?" she asked.

Jonathan and Tim both chuckled. "As many times as you want, darlin'," Tim sighed. "But give us a second first."

Caitlin giggled. "Just a second?"

"Well," Jonathan drawled with amusement as he slid his cock from her pussy. "Maybe more like a minute."

The three of them laughed.

* * * * *

Caitlin reclined against the soft brushed leather sofa and slowly sipped at her wine. They'd dined on a quick dinner of fruit and cheese earlier, and she'd eaten like she hadn't eaten all day. Which in truth, she really hadn't. She'd been too nervous to eat lunch and most of it had remained back at the restaurant they'd stopped at on their way here.

They were all still nude and to her surprise, completely comfortable with one another. Her gaze strayed more to Jonathan than Tim. They were both very handsome and sexy, but for some reason there was something more to Jonathan. Something she couldn't quite explain.

As though sensing her stare, he turned to look at her, his eyes shining with a mixture of amusement and desire. He stood by the bar, refilling his wineglass. His tight ass and thick, firm thighs flexed as he turned to fully face her and let his brown eyes roam over her body, heating her flesh. Even the way he looked at her set her body on fire. Tim's stare set her heart fluttering, but what Jonathan did to her went deeper.

Oh, dear, she thought to herself and quickly downed the last of her wine. *He's gay, Caitlin. You can't fall in love with him.*

She frowned. He certainly didn't act gay. Jonathan was strong and masculine, sexy and hot. Just looking at him turned her on. Her pussy began to pulse between her legs and she shifted, striking what she hoped was a more sexy pose.

"Minute's up, boys."

"Boys?" Tim snickered from his position by the fireplace. "I see no boys here."

The orange flames reflected on his tan skin, making it appear golden. She smiled at him and stretched her arms over her head, thrusting her breasts out. "Neither do I, actually," she purred.

Tim's lips lifted in a slight grin. "I think we've created a monster."

"I agree," Jonathan mumbled as he walked over to Caitlin and stood over her. "And I like it."

His cock thickened before her eyes and she licked her lips in anticipation. Her gaze skimmed back up his chest, past the washboard abs and the bulging pecs, and her hands fisted above her head, wanting to sift through the light dusting of hair. God, he looked so good.

"Do you like that I'm brazen?" she purred, surprised with the way she was behaving. Surprised at how her body reacted to two gorgeous men staring at her like she was water and they were dying of thirst.

"That I do," he murmured. A muscle in his cheek jerked as his gaze slid to her splayed thighs. "Spread them wider, Caitlin. Let me see your pretty pussy."

A thrill shimmied down her spine and she used her hands to push her legs wider. Slowly, she slid her fingers up the inside of her thighs and brushed lightly across her labia.

Jonathan glanced over at Tim, who looked just as entranced as he was. Damn, the woman was hot. Juices glistened in the hair just above her pussy. Her bright pink nails scratched lightly at her flesh, and he practically dropped to his knees right then. No doubt about it. She was going to be the death of him.

"You are one hot little piece of ass, Caitlin. And I've got to taste you."

Her eyes moved to Tim's bulging cock and her adorable lips spread into a saucy little grin. "Then what are you waiting for?" she purred and undulated her hips.

Tim settled between her splayed thighs and bent down to lick his tongue along her slit. She moaned and lifted her hips against his face. Jonathan's heart was about to jump free of his chest. Whoever the hell told this woman she was cold didn't have a fucking clue. He'd never met a sexier woman. Or a woman who had more quickly wormed her way into his heart.

"God, she tastes good, Jonathan," Tim sighed as he continued to lick away her juices.

It was a hot picture, and when Caitlin's hands moved to massage her breasts it was even hotter. Jonathan's cock throbbed with the need to feel her mouth wrapped around him, sucking him dry. Climbing onto the couch, he braced his knees on either side of her hips. Her questioning gaze shot up to his and he smiled down at her as he braced his hands against the wall over her head. "It's my turn now, Katie. Suck me," he said as he positioned his cock before her lips.

Chapter Three

Caitlin was on fire. Tim's tongue was driving her mad as he licked and fucked her with his mouth. It felt so good. She used to not like oral sex, but apparently her jerk of an ex-boyfriend hadn't been doing it right. This was incredible! Her whole body convulsed in pleasure.

Reaching up, she ran her finger along Jonathan's length. It twitched and she smiled, leaning forward to lick her tongue around the purple head. She watched as Jonathan's eyes closed on a sigh. It made her feel powerful, sexy. Opening her lips, she sucked him into her mouth, wanting to please him as he'd pleased her earlier.

She felt Tim leave her pussy and she groaned around Jonathan's cock, wanting the feel of his tongue against her clit again. "Tim," she growled. "Don't stop."

"I'm here, darlin'. Just getting a condom." Tim purred as he lifted her legs over his shoulders. "I'm gonna fuck her, Jonathan."

Jonathan groaned an answer as her teeth moved to nip at his tight balls. She yelled her pleasure as Tim pushed his thick cock into her. Over and over he fucked her, hard and deep, his balls slapping against her ass. Her mouth matched his movements on Jonathan's cock while her hand squeezed at his balls.

The three of them moaned in unison, each lost in what the other was doing. "Oh god. I'm so close," she sighed and nipped at the head of Jonathan's cock with her teeth.

Jonathan gasped as she opened her lips wide and swallowed him deep, her cheeks hollowed out as she sucked harder. "Oh, yeah, baby. Just like that," he growled and moved his hips, pumping his cock in and out of her hungry mouth at the same time Tim pumped her hungry pussy.

"Oh god, she's got one hot little pussy," Tim sighed. "Just like lava, Caitlin."

Pushing deeper, he ground his hips against her clit and she exploded. The muscles of her pussy squeezed at Tim's cock, pulsing and pulling him deeper. She sucked harder at Jonathan's cock, just like her pussy milked Tim's. She wanted them to come with her.

With a shout, they both tensed almost simultaneously, and she hungrily swallowed every hot drop Jonathan spewed forth until there was nothing left. Opening her eyes, she met Jonathan's startled stare. Emotions she wasn't expecting flashed across his eyes before he closed them, preventing her from seeing any more. His and Tim's sighs faded and their bodies relaxed. Hers continued to tingle and pulse. Amazingly, she still wanted more and she moved to slowly drag her tongue along Jonathan's shaft from his balls to the tip.

He shuddered and grinned down at her. "My greedy little wench," he purred.

"The two of you make me crazy," she sighed with a smile.

Tim dropped onto the couch next to her and smiled. "No crazier than you make us, darlin'."

She grinned back at him and touched his cheek with her palm. Jonathan dropped to the other side of her and turned her face to his, placing a gentle kiss against her lips. "How about a bath?"

"That sounds wonderful."

Jonathan stood and picked her up. With a squeal, she wrapped her arms around his neck and held tight. The muscles of his chest bunched and flexed against her, and she marveled at just how gorgeous and strong he was. She was so glad she'd done this. Glancing over his shoulder, she grinned at Tim and he winked back, making her giggle softly.

*****

Tim returned to the den for their wine while Jonathan ran the water and filled it full of lavender-scented bubbles. He glanced at her over his shoulder as he replaced the bottle on the shelf. "Can you believe the bubble bath is Tim's?"

Caitlin smiled. "Well, lavender is very relaxing. Maybe it helps him sleep," she offered.

Jonathan raised an eyebrow. "I don't think that's it," he chuckled and held a hand out to her. "Careful going over the side, it's kind of high."

She held tight to his hand as she slipped her foot into the warm water. It felt heavenly and she quickly immersed the rest of her into the water. Jonathan settled behind her, pulling her back against his hard chest.

The tub sat within a bay window that overlooked the lake behind the house. He'd kept the lights out, only lighting one candle, so that they could see the snow-covered mountains outside. The snow hung from tree branches, blanketing everything, and she sighed at the beauty of the scenery. "It's so peaceful here."

"Especially with all the snow," Jonathan added.

His fingers massaged her shoulders then smoothed down her arms, relaxing her. It felt right sitting here in the tub with him. She gave herself a mental shake and reminded herself this was only physical. A weekend interlude between friends—nothing more.

Tim walked in carrying a bottle and three glasses. "Is there room for one more or did the two of you hog the whole thing?"

"There's room," Caitlin said with a smile.

"Down there," Jonathan pointed to the other end of the oversized tub.

"Figures," Tim drawled as he handed Caitlin her wine.

"All right, you two. Play nice…or I'll have to spank you."

"Ooh," Tim crooned. "A woman after my own heart. Will you spank me hard, darlin', and make my ass red?"

"Would you shut the hell up and get in the tub if you're going to?" Jonathan said in exasperation, making Caitlin grin.

Tim laughed and raised his foot to step over the side when a cell phone rang in the bedroom, stopping him. "Who the hell is that?" he snapped.

"I turned mine off," Jonathan drawled. "Let voice mail get it."

"It might be Jake with those figures I need. You guys stay here, I'll go handle this."

Grumbling about rotten timing, Tim left the room, shutting the door behind him. Jonathan reached toward the counter and grabbed her hair clip. With gentle hands he piled her hair on her head and secured it with the clip. "With it up," he murmured against her neck, "it makes it easier for me to do this."

His teeth nipped at the sensitive spot behind her ear, sending her senses reeling. "That's nice," she sighed and rested her head back against his chest.

"How are you doing, Katie? Is it what you expected?"

"It's much more than I expected. But I'm a little worried."

"About?" he asked, his fingers trailing softly across her shoulder.

How did she explain it? How did she tell him the crush she had on him when they first met was coming back full force? She couldn't let herself do this. He was gay. This had been fun, but a real relationship would be out of the question with him.

"Katie?" he questioned.

Placing her wineglass on the tub ledge, she sat up and turned partway to look down at him. Instead of what was really bothering her, she chose a different concern. "I've never felt anything like I've felt today. You and Tim...you're amazing. But I'm starting to get concerned that I can only feel like this with two men. That one man alone couldn't satisfy me."

"That's silly, Katie. Of course you can feel these things with just one man."

He brushed her bangs from her eyes with such a gentle touch it made her heart ache. "Can I?" she whispered.

A small smile touched his lips as he put his hand behind her head and tugged her down to him. "Why don't we test it and see," he whispered against her lips.

His kiss was slow and gentle, his tongue leisurely exploring. He was such a good kisser and she mimicked what he did as she kissed him back. Her arms wrapped around his neck as she repositioned herself and straddled his thighs. His palms gripped her ass and moved her up, settling her over his hard cock.

She moaned and rubbed along his length causing the water to ripple around them. The motion sent little shocks of pleasure through her stomach, and she moaned into his kiss. She'd been so wrong. She could feel these things with one man. Jonathan. Now what the hell did she do come Monday?

"Jonathan," she sighed.

"Shhh."

Cupping her face, he pushed her upward, sitting them up straight. Her clit pressed into his stomach and the pressure against the sensitive nub made her gasp in sheer pleasure. Everything about his touch and the atmosphere around them seemed to move in slow motion. He was so tender, much different than the passionate, wild side of him from earlier. Her chest tightened with longing for something she knew she couldn't have—something she shouldn't even want.

His lips sipped at hers. Soft, teasing little nips that left her whimpering for more. She wanted him to kiss her. Really kiss her. Plunder her mouth with his tongue. This might be their only time alone and she wanted it to be memorable. Something she could keep in her heart.

Finally, his tongue licked into her mouth, giving her exactly what she wanted and she groaned, grinding her pussy against his growing length. With a growl of his own, he bent her backward over his arm. Brushing the foaming bubbles from her breasts, he suckled one aching nipple while palming the other one. He was driving her insane. She needed him so bad her pussy pulsed and quivered. It had gone beyond tender and turned hot, fast.

His fingers pinched her nipple then moved lower between their bodies and through the water, toward her dripping sex. "Oh, yes," she sighed as he slid two fingers deep within her clenching pussy.

"You're so wet, Katie," he whispered in her ear. "You want me, baby?"

"Yes," she moaned, rocking her hips with the movement of his fingers. "Please, Jonathan."

Removing his fingers, he lifted her hips and positioned her over his bulging shaft. Very slowly, she lowered herself until all of him was embedded deep. He was so big, so thick he stretched her to the point of pain, but at the same time it felt incredible. Closing her eyes, she groaned deep in her chest and began to move back and forth, each motion taking him deeper. She wanted—no needed—to get as close to him as she could. She wanted to make this so great that neither of them would ever forget it.

Jonathan threw his head back, his eyes held tightly closed. "Damn, Katie. You feel so good."

He hadn't put on a condom and the feel of her hot, tight walls encasing his shaft with nothing between them felt like heaven. He shouldn't have done it, but he couldn't stop long enough to get one. He wanted her too badly. They were alone, just the two of them for the first time and he didn't want to break the spell that surrounded them. The undeniable need that held them both in its grip.

He loved her and wanted desperately to shout it at the top of his lungs, but not yet. He wanted to wait until after Tim left. They'd worked it out already and he'd stick to the plan.

"Still worried, Katie?" he whispered against her lips. She tasted of wine and mint, a combination that was distinctly her, and he couldn't get enough.

"Oh, no," she sighed, shaking her head. "You feel so good."

Her walls tightened and pulsed around him as she screamed her release. He gritted his teeth, concentrating on her, on prolonging her pleasure. His balls ached and his cock swelled to bursting until finally he couldn't hold it back any longer.

With a growl, he lifted her from his lap, ignoring the large amount of water that sloshed over the side and onto the floor. Caitlin's hand gripped his cock in a firm hold. He lifted his hips out of the water and placed his hand over hers as she quickly pumped his shaft. Closing his eyes, he groaned and spewed his seed onto his chest.

"Oh god," he sighed, suddenly missing the warmth of her pussy surrounding him.

"You didn't have to do that, Jonathan," she whispered. "I'm on the Pill."

He cupped the back of her head and pulled her back into his arms. "I'll remember that next time."

With a sigh, she rested her cheek on his shoulder, her face nestled within his neck. Her warm breath fanned his skin and he wrapped his arms around her more tightly silently praying to himself that his plan would work and he could make her fall in love with him.

I love you, Katie.

* * * * *

Jonathan settled Caitlin in the middle of the king-size bed and climbed under the covers with her. It felt so right sleeping here with her in his arms. The bedroom door opened quietly and he looked up just as Tim climbed in behind Caitlin.

"That was a long phone call," Jonathan whispered.

"It actually ended a while ago. I just thought I'd give you guys some time alone. Did you tell her?"

"No. I'm waiting until you leave, remember?"

Tim nodded. "Do you want me to leave now?"

"No. She still hasn't experienced both of us yet." At Tim's raised eyebrow, Jonathan added, "At the same time."

Raising up on his elbow, Tim looked down at Caitlin with a worried expression. "Her ass is pretty tight, Jon. Think she can handle it?"

"She'll be fine."

Tim nodded and brushed a stray hair away from her face. "How long has she been asleep?"

"Not long."

"Just thinking about sinking my cock into that tight ass of hers has me hard as a damn rock."

Jonathan chuckled. "I know the feeling."

A slow grin spread across Tim's face. "I think we should wake her up."

"You're going to wear the poor woman out. Not to mention me."

Tim snorted as he pushed the sheet down, exposing one smooth tan shoulder. "You love it and you know it."

Bending, he placed a soft kiss on the exposed flesh, then moved to nibble on her neck. Caitlin moaned, shifting slightly to allow him better access. Jonathan joined in the seduction and took a nipple into his mouth, his tongue gently flicking back and forth across the hard pebble.

With a gentle shove, Tim pushed her to her back and took the other nipple in his mouth. Caitlin moaned, arching her back as both he and his brother paid homage to her breasts.

Am I dreaming? Caitlin thought as white-hot lust shot throughout her body. Opening her eyes, she glanced down and saw Jonathan and Tim's dark blond heads. Tim licked and nipped at her breasts while Jonathan slowly worked a path down her stomach.

She lightly touched Jonathan's head and let her fingers sift through his hair. He lifted his head and smiled slightly. Her heart soared at the tender look in his eyes, then pounded furiously as they darkened in passion. His fingers moved to sift through the hair at the juncture of her thighs and she parted them, anxious for his touch where she ached the most.

Moving between her splayed thighs, his tongue slowly slid along her slit and her hips bucked upward. "Yes," she sighed as juices flowed from her core to soak the mattress beneath her.

"Mmm," Jonathan moaned, his voice vibrating against her clit. "You taste good, baby."

His tongue tormented her, licking away her juices and sinking deep within her pussy as he searched for more. Tim continued to play with her breasts, and she screamed as he bit down on a nipple. The shot of pleasure mixed with a little pain sent her senses into a tailspin, desperate for more.

"Change position, Tim. Get on your back," Jonathan ordered.

Tim moved to his back while Jonathan helped Caitlin to straddle his face. Bending forward, she grasped the base of Tim's cock and slowly pumped it with her palm. He was hard and soft, like velvet over pure steel, and she watched in fascination as it grew even thicker.

Tim's tongue resumed the exploration of her pussy and she gasped, intrigued with this new position and the feel of Jonathan sliding his fingers into her pussy. After a few deep strokes, he removed them and moved to the tight puckered hole of her anus. At the tender invasion of his two thick fingers, she gasped, shocked at the burning need that gripped her there.

"Am I hurting you, Katie?" Jonathan asked.

"No," she gasped, shaking her head. It felt strange, but good at the same time.

"Tim, where's the lubrication?" Jonathan asked.

"Top drawer, beside you," he mumbled.

Jonathan gave the side of her hip a pat. "Don't move."

She couldn't move if she wanted to. What Tim was doing felt too good. Using the tip of her tongue, she flicked across the head of Tim's cock to lick away a small drop of pre-cum. His hips jerked upward and she did it again, this time making him growl low in his throat. "Oh, fuck. Don't stop there, darlin'. Take it all."

Opening her lips, she drew his cock deep into her mouth just as he slid two fingers into her vagina. She moaned around his girth, moving her hips in time with his thrusts. Jonathan returned to his position behind her and spread a cold substance around her passage. With two fingers he worked it deeper, stretching and loosening her muscles.

She braced herself, trying her best to relax and accept the impending invasion of Jonathan's cock into her ass. He was much bigger than the dildo they'd used earlier, and she couldn't stop the sudden flutter of nerves.

Tim removed his fingers and moved then to toy with her clit. Closing her eyes, she concentrated on what Tim was doing as Jonathan slowly pushed his way in. At first it was overwhelming, and she stiffened. But the wilder side of her—the one that wanted this more than anything—pushed against him.

Jonathan pulled back and took a deep breath before sliding forward again, seating himself almost balls-deep.

"Oh my god," he ground out as he held himself still.

Caitlin was beyond turned on. She felt full and so hot, so consumed she didn't want him to stop. Didn't want him to be gentle. Tim's tongue returned to her clit and his fingers moved back to her pussy, gently fucking her with the same rhythm Jonathan used. Slow and steady.

She didn't want slow, damn it. With a growl, she ground her hips, taking both of them deeper. "Fuck, Caitlin. You're killing me," Jonathan gasped. "I'm trying to take it easy on you, baby."

She shook her head, almost beyond words. "I don't want easy. I want it hard. Deep. Jonathan, fuck me," she begged.

He gave her what she wanted. Hard, deep thrusts that almost had her falling forward. Tim's fingers kept the same tempo then curved inward to hit her g-spot. She whimpered, her lips opening to once again suckle Tim's cock. They worked together, the three of them pleasing each other. Caitlin went first, her body exploding around Jonathan's cock and Tim's fingers. Never in her life did she imagine it could be like this. This erotic and wild. This good.

Sucking harder, she brought Tim to climax, licking away the semen that escaped her mouth and ran back down his cock. Jonathan followed, his growl of satisfaction following the feel of his hot semen filling her.

Slowly, he pulled out, and she fell over to her back, her breathing erratic and shallow, her body totally sated. Every muscle shook and tingled with little aftershocks of pleasure. So much so she could hardly move.

Jonathan braced himself on his hands above her and claimed her lips in a kiss she felt clear to her toes. When the kiss ended, Tim rolled over and gave her one of his own—one that was much sweeter and not quite as possessive. His was nice, where Jonathan's had left her breathless.

"Don't move, darlin'. I'll be back in a sec to clean you up. I think brother dear is beyond the ability."

Caitlin grinned and turned to look at Jonathan, who had fallen onto the bed next to her. His eyes were closed as his breathing slowly returned to normal. With the back of her fingers she brushed his cheek, wondering how in the hell she was going to get over him. She was in love with him. She knew it now. The only problem was she didn't have a clue what to do about it.

His hand captured hers and brought the back of her fingers to his lips. He placed a soft kiss against them then held them entwined with his own on his chest. With a sigh, she rolled over, resting her head on his shoulder. She could hear his steady heartbeat in her ear and realized with surprise that it beat in time with her own. With a smile, she snuggled closer and waited for Tim to return and clean her up.

Chapter Four

Caitlin stepped out of the shower and towel dried her unruly curls. She didn't want to take the time to blow-dry it straight so she picked at it, fluffing the curls so that they could dry naturally. Jonathan had told her once he liked her hair when she left it curly.

With a sigh, she stared at herself in the mirror. *What am I doing? He's just a friend. That's it. I can't fall in love with him.*

"But I already am," she whined out loud. "What the hell was I thinking?"

With a growl of aggravation, she grabbed her makeup case and applied a little blush and mascara then headed to the kitchen to see what the men were up to. As she strolled down the hall, she rubbed her hand along the tongue-and-grove paneling that covered the walls. This was such a beautiful house and so big. It had six bedrooms, four bathrooms, a den, a media room, a gourmet kitchen and an oak table that could seat as many as thirty people.

Jonathan had told her his mother had the house built when he and Tim were teenagers. She'd wanted a place where the whole family could get together for the holidays. And in two days, on Christmas Eve, the house would be bursting at the seams with Trelains.

She would be out of here by then and on her way to see her own family—her mother in Florida. As an only child, she sometimes longed for the house full of family and friends that Jonathan and Tim experienced every year. Maybe one day, when she had her own family…

As she came down the stairs to the main level the smell of bacon and eggs caught her attention. She inhaled deeply of the wonderful scents and her stomach growled in response. She was starving.

With a smile, she stepped into the kitchen and surveyed the scene before her. Jonathan stood at the stove, spatula in hand. Tim stood at the sink, sipping coffee. The two of them talked to one another in hushed tones. Both of them still wore their pajama pants, their chests bare. Jonathan's muscles flexed as he moved, making her stomach flutter with hunger for more than just food.

"Wow," she said as she walked over and poured herself a cup of coffee. "The two of you can cook?"

"Well, Jonathan can cook," Tim replied, his lips spreading into a grin behind his coffee cup.

Caitlin stared at Jonathan in surprise. "I didn't know that about you."

"There's a lot you don't know about me, darlin'," he drawled, mimicking Tim.

"Like what?" She stepped closer and stood next to him as he stirred the scrambled eggs.

"You'll find out soon enough, my dear. I promise. But for now, how about we eat? Hand me that bowl, would you?"

"Sure." She handed him the bowl and studied him as he scooped the eggs from the pan. What didn't she know about him?

"Curiosity killed the cat," Jonathan purred without looking at her, his lips quirked as though fighting a smile.

"Well, after a comment like that, what do you expect? That I wouldn't try to figure it out?"

Tim chuckled and set the small kitchen table. The morning sunlight streamed through the tall windows, heating the wooden floor. He looked good, the morning sun highlighting the blond in his hair and giving his tan body a more golden hue. "Knock it off, wildcat," Tim drawled.

"What?" she asked with mock innocence.

"Looking at me like that."

"Or what?"

"Or you'll find yourself bent over that table and I'll have you for breakfast instead of the eggs."

"Oh, you think I'm afraid of that threat?" she teased.

"I would be," Jonathan drawled, making Caitlin laugh.

"Kiss my ass," Tim replied with a grin.

"You wish."

"Okay," Caitlin yelled. "Behave yourselves."

"Where's the fun in that?" Tim chuckled.

"Exactly," Jonathan replied with a lazy grin.

Caitlin shook her head as she listened to the two of them. They were definitely brothers. Sitting at the table, she grabbed some bacon and sausage. "I think it's great how close the two of you are."

"We're as close as two twins can be," Jonathan said with a grin.

"Twins?" she asked in surprise. Moving her gaze between the two of them, she studied their faces more closely.

"We're not identical," Tim said with a sideways grin.

"Well, obviously," she replied dryly. "I just had no idea."

"I thought I'd told you that," Jonathan said, his brow creasing in a frown.

Caitlin shook her head. "I don't think so. If you did, I forgot."

"You just didn't listen," Jonathan teased.

"I'm sorry. What were you saying? I wasn't listening."

Tim laughed. "She's a spunky little thing, isn't she?"

"Yeah, which is going to make later all the more fun."

Caitlin raised an eyebrow at the devilish expression on Jonathan's face. Just what did he mean by that? "What are you up to?"

"It's a surprise." Taking a bite of egg, he sat back in his chair and chewed thoughtfully.

"Think she can handle it?" Tim asked.

"Oh, I'm sure she can." Jonathan never took his eyes off her as he spoke, and prickles of a mixture of delight and trepidation ran down her spine. "She's tough, aren't you, Katie?"

"Tough?" Her voice squeaked and Tim glanced down at the table, trying to hide his grin. "Why do I need to be tough?"

He just smiled, which sent her heart racing out of control. "Eat. You'll need your strength."

Caitlin stared at him silently wondering what he had in mind for her later. She knew he wouldn't do anything to hurt her, but for just a split second a little tremor of fear snaked down her flesh. Surprises, she decided, were highly overrated.

* * * * *

Caitlin tugged on the tie to her robe with anxious fingers. After breakfast, they'd cleaned the kitchen with a few stops occasionally to play around. Between the two of them, she'd been so turned on she could hardly breathe and begged them to fuck her right there in the kitchen.

But to her disappointment, Jonathan shook his head no. "I have other plans for you," he whispered and led her to the den.

With each step down into the basement den, her heart hammered harder. She had no idea what they had in mind, but she soon found out. Dangling from the ceiling was a pair of handcuffs. Her breath lodged in her throat. With trepidation, her gaze moved to the two brothers, who now stood before her completely naked, their cocks standing thick and proud. She swallowed just thinking of what those cocks could do to her.

"What is this?" she asked.

Tim smiled devilishly as he swung the leather fringe of a flogger before him. "You said you wanted to try everything."

"S & M?" She gulped.

"Trust me, Katie," Jonathan said as he held his hand out to her.

Squaring her shoulders, she took his outstretched hand. She did want to try it all. She could do this.

Jonathan smiled softly into her eyes as he untied her robe and pushed it down her shoulders. It fell to the floor in a soft puddle around her feet, leaving her bare and incredibly warm.

They'd put her before the fire and the heat of the flames was hot against her skin. Almost as hot as the smoldering heat of Jonathan's stare. Lowering his head, he placed a soft kiss against her lips while Tim lifted her hands and secured them in the cuffs.

Her heart pounded furiously at the click of the locks sliding into place, but not with fear. Something else swam through her veins. Something darker.

Jonathan's lips moved to her neck, sending currents of lust through her limbs. Tim still stood behind her, his palms skimming lightly over the flesh of her back and ass. His lips soon joined Jonathan's as they worked a path over her heated skin, leaving no part of her untouched or neglected. She squirmed, tugging at the cuffs that held her trapped, wanting desperately to touch them in return.

Palming her breasts, Tim squeezed them before lifting one and offering it to Jonathan. His lips covered her nipple and she moaned at the engulfing heat.

Tim moved away from her and cool air rushed across her back. She shivered just before the sting of the flogger caught her hip. She gasped in surprise, shocked at the ripple of pleasure that snaked down her spine. Again Tim flicked it, catching her across her thighs.

Jonathan placed one more kiss against her lips before joining Tim in their little game. Each flick of the soft leather against her flesh sent her soaring. She'd never imagined anything like this. One wrapped the flogger around her thighs, while the other caught her ribs, sending a stinging slap to the side of her breasts.

She groaned, her hands fisting and pulling at the bindings that held her immobile. They stopped and she whimpered for more, her pleas filling the quiet room. Their heat engulfed her as one stood in front and one behind, sandwiching her between them. "Please," she pleaded.

"Is this what you want, Katie?" Jonathan asked as he pushed two fingers into her throbbing pussy.

"Yes."

"Or this?" Tim whispered in her ear as he slid two lubricated fingers into the tight passage of her anus.

She moaned as the two of them moved their fingers in unison. Plunging in then out, over and over. Her head fell back as the pressure in her belly built.

"She's so fucking wet," Jonathan growled. Removing his fingers, he stared intently at her as he licked her juices from his knuckles.

Tim removed his fingers as well and replaced them with a dildo. It was cold and wet and she groaned as he slid it deep within her anus, stretching and filling her. Slowly he began to move it, pulling it almost out then plunging it back in. She was helpless and so close she could scream. Moving to his knees, Jonathan licked his tongue across her clit. She screamed as a shudder passed through her.

Lifting one of her legs, he placed his face more fully between her legs and fucked her with his tongue. She moaned in ecstasy as the two of them matched their rhythm exactly. Oh god. They were going to kill her with pleasure. She just knew it.

She couldn't take it anymore and sobbed. "Please, Jonathan. I need you. Both of you, fuck me."

Jonathan stood immediately and covered her mouth with his. She could taste herself on his lips and it only fueled her desire. Made her wilder. Placing his hands behind her thighs, he lifted her. In desperation, she wrapped her legs around his waist and welcomed the full invasion of his thick cock.

"Oh, yes," she sighed.

Tim continued to thrust the dildo in time with Jonathan's slow tempo, but she wanted more. She wanted both of their cocks inside her. "Tim, god, please. Take that damn thing out and fuck me."

With a growl, he removed the dildo and dropped it to the floor. Jonathan's movements stopped as he grabbed her ass and spread her wide in preparation. Tim slipped on a lubricated condom then positioned himself at the tight entrance to her anus and gently probed her opening. Jonathan pulled almost out then the two of them pushed in simultaneously, filling her beyond anything she'd ever felt before.

"Oh my god," she gulped, trying to capture the air that had escaped her lungs. She could hardly breathe as they pushed deeper, burying themselves balls-deep.

"Easy, baby," Jonathan crooned as they slowly began to move.

She closed her eyes, relaxing between them. Their lips each worked a side of her neck, nibbling and licking her sensitive skin. Tim's hands massaged her breasts, his fingers pinching her nipples. Every part of her body was caressed at once and she felt as though she'd die from the sheer pleasure.

Experimenting, she began to wiggle her hips, brushing her clit against Jonathan's stomach. She gasped and clenched her muscles around their cocks. Tim groaned as though in pain and Jonathan smiled. "Ah, that's it, baby. Come for us."

She moaned and wiggled her hips again, adding more pressure to the sensitive nub. Jonathan and Tim increased their rhythms, the head of their cocks brushing along a spot she never dreamed existed.

"Oh god," she groaned. "It feels so good. Don't stop."

"Ah, baby. I couldn't if I tried," Jonathan whispered. "You're so hot, Katie. So tight. And so fucking sexy."

Tim licked at her ear. "Hurry, darlin'. I'm not going to last much longer. Your tight ass feels too good."

Caitlin trembled at their naughty words and realized she liked it when they talked dirty. The first tremors of her release rippled through her muscles and she bit down on Jonathan's shoulder.

"Ah, Katie," Jonathan groaned as his tempo increased again.

Their thrusts became harder, deeper and she screamed as her body exploded into a white-hot mass of sensation. Her muscles clenched around them, milked them as her orgasm continued on for what seemed like forever. Every muscle in her body tensed and tingled, then relaxed only to tense and explode again in a pleasure so strong blackness engulfed her.

With a final thrust, Jonathan and Tim came together, their moans drowning out her quiet whimpers.

Jonathan looked down at her head on his shoulder and softly pushed the hair from her face. "Katie," he whispered. "Katie, baby. Answer me."

"I can't," she mumbled.

Jonathan grinned at Tim over her shoulder. "Let's get her in a warm bath. Let her relax."

Tim slowly slid from her body and she flinched in her sleep.

Jonathan was sure she would be sore and the warm water would help. He held her tight as Tim released her hands from the cuffs.

She was so beautiful, and he couldn't wait until later to tell her how he felt. She held his heart in the palm of her hand

and that scared the hell out of him. He'd been hurt more than once in his life. God help him if she didn't return his feelings.

Chapter Five

Caitlin awoke in the bed and glanced out the window. Snow clouds darkened the sky and she shivered beneath the covers, moving closer to the warmth next to her. What time was it? Glancing at the clock, she noticed it was almost time for supper. How long had they been asleep?

Vaguely, she remembered sitting in a warm tub, Tim and Jonathan washing her body. Wow, had she really had both of them at the same time? Begged for it even? She grinned and stared down at Jonathan. He looked so peaceful, sound asleep. Glancing behind her, she looked for Tim, but realized he was gone. Where was he?

With a frown, she grabbed her robe and headed downstairs. She found him in the kitchen, pouring coffee into a thermal mug. He wore jeans and a thick sweater, his leather jacket was slung over the back of a chair. "Are you leaving?" she asked.

He spun around to face her, a look of surprise on his face. "Hey, darlin'. Did I wake you?"

"No. I just woke up and noticed you were gone. Where are you going?"

"I'm bowing out," he said with a grin.

"Excuse me?"

"This was worked out before we came up here."

She shook her head, thoroughly confused. He wasn't making any sense. "What was worked out?"

"Caitlin, darlin'. Don't you see it?" Tim asked as he softly touched the side of her face. "He's in love with you."

"Who?" Her eyes widened in shock "Jonathan?"

Tim smiled. "Yes."

"But he's gay," she exclaimed.

Tim rolled his eyes and shot her an amused grin. "Jonathan has never been gay. He's as straight as they come. I, on the other hand, can go either way. Although I prefer men."

"He's straight?" She wasn't sure whether to clobber Jonathan or hug him. "Why would he let people think he's gay?"

Tim shrugged. "Ask him."

"I think I will," she snapped and headed back up the stairs to confront him, Tim's confession that Jonathan loved her momentarily forgotten in her haste to get answers to her other questions.

Why would he do this? It didn't make any sense.

Stepping back into the bedroom, she grabbed a pillow and hit him square in the chest. "Damn it, Jonathan Trelain. Wake up!" For good measure she hit him again.

He awoke with a start and stared at her warily. "What's wrong?"

"When the hell were you going to tell me you weren't gay?"

For a second he just stared at her in shock. "Are you just now figuring that out? What the hell took you so long?"

She gaped at him. What? "I didn't figure it out." She again hit him with the pillow. "Tim told me."

"He what?" Jonathan asked.

"Why, Jonathan? Why would you allow everyone to think that? Why would you allow me to think it?"

With a sigh, he patted the mattress next to him. "Sit down, Katie."

Pursing her lips, she watched him in uncertainty. Suddenly she felt as though she didn't know him. He stared up at her with pleading eyes, melting her resolve. They were puppy dog eyes, and she had to bite back a grin at how cute he looked. "All right," she finally relented with a sigh.

Instead of next to him, she chose to sit on the edge of the mattress facing him. Silently she waited while he sat up and rested his back against the headboard, the sheet crumpling around his waist. It was hard not to stare at his hard chest. How often did he work out to get so big?

"A few years ago," he started, and she turned her attention from his body to what he was saying. "I was in love with this girl. Tim didn't like her. Hated her, actually," he said with a grin. "Anyway, he was convinced she was up to no good. Of course I wouldn't listen, so Tim forced me to see her for what she really was. He found out about her boyfriend and set it up so that I would see them together."

"Oh, Jonathan," Caitlin began, but he held up his hand, stopping her.

"I was furious. And hurt. I confronted them and she very bluntly informed me she only wanted my money. Needless to say I had a hard time trusting women after that and my distrust only intensified when I ran into two more situations that were achingly similar."

"But how did the rumor get started?"

"Well, after money grubber number three Tim convinced me to go with him to a new bar that was opening up in Boston. I reluctantly agreed and we ran into a couple of coworkers. Since it was a gay bar, they just assumed I was gay." Jonathan shrugged. "And I never denied it. It actually worked out well. Women, for the most part, overlooked me. Some tried to convert me, but it was only the challenge they wanted and not the money. I felt much safer that way, so I let it continue. Until I met you." He smiled softly at her. "You stumbled into my office, literally."

The heat of a blush moved up her cheeks as she remembered that day. She'd tripped as she came into his office for her interview, falling flat on her face.

"You were so cute and so talented. I thought your portfolio was amazing and hired you right on the spot. As I got to know you, I..." Again he shrugged. "I found out you were in the middle of a relationship with...what's-his-name," he said with a sneer, making Caitlin grin. "So I left you alone."

"But he dumped me," she said quietly.

"Yes, he did and I wanted to kill him. I didn't come forward then because I didn't want you on the rebound. We were friends and I tried to be happy with that. Then Tim told me about this outlandish idea of yours. I thought, here's my chance. She'll realize I'm not gay and that she loves me and the two of us will go on to live happily ever after."

She licked at her lips nervously. "You love me?"

"Oh, yes, Katie," he said. "You hold my heart in the palm of your hand. It's up to you. You can either keep it, or crush it."

Her heart soared. He loved her. He really loved her. With a smile, she moved to straddle his thighs and cup his face between her hands. "I think I'll keep it, if it's all the same to you."

"It's yours forever, my Katie," he sighed into her kiss.

Wrapping his arms around her back, he flipped them, settling his body atop hers. His weight felt wonderful as it pushed her down into the soft mattress, and she deepened their kiss, hugging him closer to her.

Jonathan moaned and broke the kiss to stare at her. Brushing her bangs from her eyes, he placed a soft kiss on her forehead, then moved to her cheek and jaw. "Say you love me, Katie."

"You love me, Katie," she teased, then laughed as he buried his face in her neck and growled.

"I love you, Jonathan," she said once her laughter subsided.

He rewarded her with a kiss.

"I love you," she said again, and again he kissed her, this time letting his lips linger on hers just a little longer. They played the game a couple of more times, each kiss becoming longer until finally he slipped his tongue into her mouth, swallowing her moan of delight.

Gently, he feathered his hands along her flesh. He loved the feel of her beneath his hands. She was so soft and fit within his arms so perfectly. She was everything he'd ever wanted and the best thing about it was they'd started out as friends.

Not one inch of her body went untouched as he set out to explore and taste every part of her. She moaned and writhed beneath him, silently begging him for more. She was so passionate. How on earth could anyone think she wasn't?

Moving slightly to the side, he slid his hand up the inside of her thigh. Deliberately teasing, he bypassed her pussy and moved back down the other leg.

"Don't tease," she groaned, but he just smiled, enjoying watching her squirm.

"My beautiful Katie," he whispered against her skin as his lips worked a path down her stomach. He wanted to taste her. Needed it. He loved the taste of her along his tongue. She was sweet, like honey, and he couldn't get enough.

Spreading her thighs, he separated her labia with his fingers then blew hot breaths against her clit. She moaned and bucked her hips upward toward his waiting mouth.

"Mmm, so good, baby," he sighed as his tongue lapped at her cream. Gently, he pushed two fingers into her pussy, lubricating them, then moved to the tight hole of her anus.

She gasped as he pushed deep and began a slow, steady rhythm. He loved the feel of her hot walls as they gripped his fingers, clenching them tightly. He remembered how they had felt against his cock and strained to keep his control, to keep it slow.

With a patience he never knew he possessed, he leisurely licked at her pussy, the tip of his tongue teasingly circling her clit. He was driving her mad. He could tell by the shallow rise and fall of her breasts, the way the ring of her anus pulsed around his knuckles.

"Come for me, baby," he commanded and increased the pressure to her clit at the same time deepening the thrusts of his fingers.

She gasped, her hips rising from the bed to grind her pussy against his face. He growled, sliding his tongue deep within her hot, wet walls. She screamed and exploded around him, her juices flowing out to coat his chin.

Rising above her, he placed a kiss against her lips. Holding his face between her hands, she licked her juices from his chin and he smiled down at her lovingly. "You are such a hot little thing," he purred. "I know I'll never get bored."

She returned his smile and slid her foot up his leg seductively. "I love you so much, Katie."

Placing her palm along his cheek, she pulled his face down to hers. "Show me how much."

"Gladly, you wicked little witch."

She giggled, and he silenced her with a kiss, letting her know with his body how he felt about her. He kept it gentle and slow despite how badly he wanted to just thrust deep and bury himself inside her. He wanted it to be a night of making love, not just sex.

Settling above her, he kept his gaze locked on hers as he sheathed his cock within the wet walls of her vagina. Pushing deeper, he went balls-deep as her legs lifted and locked around his waist. She felt so good, like a hot glove encasing his length. It was perfect and he began to move, pulling out then thrusting back in, creating a friction he knew would drive them both over the edge.

She moaned into his kiss, his tongue mimicking his cock as he fucked her mouth just like his cock fucked her pussy. Over and over he plunged as her walls gripped and squeezed him, pulling him deeper still. Her vagina tightened and he thrust harder, his balls slapping against her ass.

It quickly went from slow to out of control as he pushed up on his hands and fucked her hard and fast. "Oh god, yes," she screamed. "Fuck me, Jonathan. Harder."

Repositioning himself, he went up on his knees. Throwing her legs over his shoulders then leaning forward, he rested his hands by her head. The position put him impossibly deep and she gasped, her tiny hands gripping his shoulders.

"Too much, baby?" he asked, afraid he'd hurt her.

"No." She shook her head and closed her eyes on a groan as he began to thrust in and out. "It feels…so…Jonathan," she gulped as her release hit her, making her pussy muscles quiver around his cock, and he fucked her harder, pumping into her over and over.

"Caitlin," he shouted as his own orgasm gripped him and he thrust hard one final time, spilling his seed deep inside her. "You're mine."

* * * * *

Two days later, on Christmas Eve, the log home was full of boisterous Trelains, all welcoming her with open arms. There was food and gifts everywhere, the closeness of the family was obvious as they all gathered around telling jokes and stories, each congratulating the others on accomplishments that had been achieved over the last year.

Jonathan had even flown her mother up so that she could meet him and the rest of the family. She'd never been happier or loved anyone more.

"Merry Christmas, Katie," Jonathan whispered as he handed her a package over her shoulder.

"What's this?" she asked as she took the small package from his hand.

"Open it."

With a smile, she tugged at the shiny red ribbon and lifted the gold lid. What she saw inside made her gasp and tears sprang to her eyes. A diamond engagement ring.

"When did you get this?" she asked in surprise as she lifted it from the box with shaking fingers. It was a beautiful square-cut diamond surrounded by a thin gold band.

"Actually, Friday morning before we came up here." He grinned. "I was optimistic."

She watched as he took the ring from her fingers and lowered himself to one knee right there in front of the soft glow of the Christmas tree lights and the anxious stares of their family. "I love you, Caitlin," he said. "Will you marry me?"

The room had gone silent as she looked down at him, tears of joy sliding down her cheeks. She didn't pay them any attention. The only thing she saw was Jonathan and the love shining in his eyes as he watched her expectantly.

"Yes," she laughed and the whole room burst with applause and shouts as Jonathan slid the ring on her finger. Dropping to her knees she wrapped her arms around his neck and hugged him tight. "I love you, Jonathan. I love you so much."

He smiled and kissed the tip of her nose. "Not as much as I love you—and I look forward to continuing this argument for the rest of our lives."

Tim came over and pulled her to her feet, engulfing her into his strong arms. "Welcome to the family, darlin'," he purred, then grinned. "I'm free February. I think we should go to the Caribbean for the honeymoon."

Jonathan snorted. "What makes you think you're going?"

"Hey. It was worth a shot, right?" Caitlin laughed and placed a kiss on his cheek.

What was she going to do with the two of them? A devilish smile crossed her features as she stared up at Jonathan.

"No," he growled. "That was a one-time thing."

She stuck her lower lip out playfully, teasing him. She really didn't need the two of them, Jonathan was plenty for her, but she couldn't resist toying with him.

"You, woman," Jonathan growled as he pulled her close to him, his eyes twinkling in laughter. "From this day forward are a one-man woman. Understand?"

She smiled. "I understand, and I couldn't be happier."

The End

Also by Trista Ann Michaels

Fantasy Bar
Fantasy Resort
Star Crossed

About the Author

Trista penned her first ghost story at the age of eight. She still has a love of ghosts, but her taste and writing style have leaned more to the sultry side. She started writing erotic romance two years ago and with the help of her critique partners was soon published and she's been running full steam ever since.

Raised an Air Force brat, Trista surprised her family by marrying a Navy man. But just as she knew he would, her husband won them over despite his military choice. Together they've had three children, and she attributes their successful marriage to the fact he's away flying a lot. Separation does make the heart grow fonder. After all, if he's not there, she can't kill him.

All joking aside, her family and writing partners are her biggest form of support and encouragement. Trista's a big believer in happily ever after and although she may put her characters through hell getting there, they will always achieve that goal.

Trista welcomes comments from readers. You can find her website and email address on her author bio page at www.ellorascave.com.

CHRISTMAS COWBOY

By Allyson James

Dedication

For my husband, the best hero ever.

Chapter One

In a large kitchen scented with Christmas baking, in the small town of Makeview, Texas, Mary Kincaid poured a quantity of rum into two eggnogs and set them on the table. "Look's like he's taken the bait," she said.

Her friend, Serena St. Clair, nodded. "Kelly's a sweet girl. When your grandson shows up, she'll let him in, and then…

"Nature will take its course?" Mary suggested over the rim of her mug.

The two women stared at each other, then, at the same time, shook their heads. "Nah," Serena said. "They're too young and stubborn."

"I don't know," Mary answered. "Your niece is a beautiful young woman, and Trey's a cutie. In my day, that's all it took."

"Young people are different now. All they think about is *work*." Serena grinned. "I think we're going to have to meddle."

Mary brightened. "Oh, goodie. After all, what's the holiday season without a little magic?"

"We shouldn't enchant people, you know," Serena pointed out. "That wouldn't be right." But her eyes twinkled.

"Well, we won't enchant *them*, exactly."

The two friends looked at each other and laughed. "Are you thinking what I'm thinking?" Mary asked.

"I sure am."

They shared another laugh, then Mary bustled around fetching candles, incense and crystals, and the two women went to work.

* * * * *

Knockity-knock-knock.

The knock was familiar, but Kelly, winding a towel around her wet hair and rushing down the cold stairs in her bright orange sweats, couldn't place it.

It wasn't her sister arriving unexpectedly from Hawaii, or her aunt coming to cheer her up, or worse, Kelly's ex-fiancé, John Hatton, the SOB who'd stormed out two weeks ago, coming back to haunt her.

John would *never* have a playful knock. In fact, he *never* knocked. He'd expect you to open the door as he came up the walk.

Something niggled at the back of her mind, something from the past…

'Twas the night before Christmas, and all through the house, not a creature was stirring, except Kenny Wayne Shepherd playing heavy blues on CD. Not Christmas blues either, because Christmas music would remind Kelly she was all alone.

That is, alone except for Mr. X, the new translucent blue vibrator her sister in Maui had sent her as an early Christmas gift. Kelly planned to put on something country, turn out the lights in her bedroom, and pretend Mr. X was Viggo Mortensen.

She'd even taken a long shower and scrubbed all over with scented bath gel just for him. Mango-coconut.

Smelling like a tropical drink, she scooted down the last couple stairs, across the living room, and flung open the door.

Standing on the doorstep in a sheepskin jacket, tight blue jeans, and cowboy hat was the most gorgeous cowboy she'd ever seen.

Kelly's eyes went wide, and something hot trickled between her legs. *Merry Christmas, who was he?*

He held one hand behind his back, like he was hiding something, and swept off his hat to show her unruly black hair that curled back from his face to the base of his neck.

His wide shoulders and chest filled out the sheepskin jacket and his jeans stretched over the best thighs that existed outside of a *Playgirl,* and probably inside it, too.

A sinful smile split his square, handsome face, and big, blue eyes twinkled under a slash of black brows.

"Hey, Kelly," he said.

Kelly blinked, aware that her hair was wrapped in a towel except for the two strands that dripped cold water into her eyes and that her sloppy orange sweats made her look like an oversized tangerine. She had no makeup on, and her mouth must be hanging wide open.

"You know me?" she blurted.

He lost his smile, but his face didn't look one bit less gorgeous. "Damn, I knew ya'll would forget about me. Serves me right for leaving home."

The voice was smooth and deep, and triggered memories. Kelly had a sudden vision of herself on a horse behind a long, lean young man, riding into a canyon to rescue a mare and foal. Kelly had been eighteen, he three years older.

She remembered wrapping her arms around his waist, feeling his tight ass against her thighs, breathing in his scent of sweat and fine male. She was the luckiest girl in Makeview, Texas, because she was out there riding behind—

"Trey Kincaid!" she gasped.

"Hey," he said again. "Now that you remember me, mind if I come in? It's fucking freezing out here."

Kelly backpedaled, opening the door wide in welcome. West Texas on Christmas day *could* be eighty degrees, but today a winter storm had blown through, dropping the temperature to a frigid twenty and killing all the geraniums Kelly had put out yesterday.

Trey waltzed in past her and did a little pivot on the polished floor, keeping hidden whatever was behind his back.

Trey Kincaid, the most wanted man in Makeview, who'd run off to UT Austin to get a degree in engineering ten years ago. He'd stayed there to set up his own business during the tech boom, and done well, according to his grandmother.

"A cowboy engineer," his grandmother, Mary Kincaid, proudly laughed. "A techie in a cowboy hat."

Dazed, Kelly pushed the door closed behind him. As soon as she did, a strange sensation shot through her, like a *click* in her brain, followed by very faint, gleeful laughter.

A second later, she reasoned she couldn't have heard anything of the kind. Kenny Wayne's guitar was wailing in the speakers, drowning out even the wind outside.

She turned the deadbolt and faced Trey, panting like she'd done a five-mile jog. "So, what are you doing here?"

"What?" Trey shouted over Kenny Wayne.

Kelly grabbed the remote and punched a button. Silence blanketed the room. "I said, what are you doing here?"

He grinned and brought his arm out from behind his back. He balanced three wrapped presents on his hand, the bows sad from the wind. "Delivering."

More memories flooded her. Trey Kincaid dancing with her at Hank's honky-tonk, a bottle of beer in one hand, his other on her hip.

Walking her out in the woods later, where he'd kissed her. His fingers, cold with the night, working inside her jeans, rubbing her pussy until she shimmied against him, her moans of pleasure silenced against his mouth.

She'd worked him, too, wrapping her fingers around his long, satiny cock. He'd squeezed his eyes shut tight, letting her stroke and stroke, until he shot into her hand.

They'd only played with each other that night, his fingers cold on her hot skin. It had been too muddy for either of them to go down on each other, and too cold and wet for complete sex.

He'd asked her out again, but she'd had to drive her sister back to college in El Paso the next day, and by the time she got back, he'd left for Austin, and that was that.

"You came all the way from Austin to give me presents?" Kelly asked. For some reason, she couldn't breathe right.

"No." He turned around, looked critically at her short Christmas tree in the living room, then waltzed over and laid the presents beneath it.

Jeans showed off a man's ass best, Kelly always said. Her eyes got glassy watching him bend over, his butt sticking out from under the sheepskin coat, the jeans hugging it tight.

He had long legs, thighs tight with muscle, and strong calves. Even the heels of his boots looked sexy.

He stood up again, then stopped, probably noticing her drool. She surreptitiously wiped her mouth.

"Were you looking at my ass?" he demanded, eyes twinkling.

"Um. Yes."

"Why?"

She licked her lips. "What do you mean, why? It's a nice ass."

Why had she just said that? She was totally off men, remember? Since John had walked out on her two weeks ago, after cheating on her and then telling her it was her fault, she'd decided, *no more men*.

Trey Kincaid shows up after ten years, and I'm drooling over his butt.

"All right," he said. "Now I get to see yours."

Kelly looked down at her bright orange sweat suit, which was *so* not sexy. Gathering her courage, she turned around, lifted up the tail of her sweatshirt and shook her butt in his direction.

He laughed. "Oh, yeah," he said appreciatively. "I'm staying."

She heard his boots click on the boards as he crossed to her, then his strong, gloved hands slid around her waist, and his body covered her from behind. "Don't stop wiggling it, baby. If I'd known this ass was here waiting for me, I'd have driven faster."

Kelly moved her hips back and forth, feeling his hard cock behind his zipper. Her juices started flowing, wetting her sweats.

What was she doing? Ten minutes ago, she'd been looking forward to Mr. X. She hadn't seen Trey in years, and it wasn't like they'd been dating, or in love, or waiting for each other. There had been that one playful night, then they'd gone their own directions.

"You couldn't have come back to Makeview to see me," she said.

"No." His breath was hot in her ear. "To see my grandmother. Your aunt was at her house, and she was worried she wouldn't get you your presents in time. So I offered to drive them over. I hadn't seen you in a while, so I thought, why not?"

"And you figured we'd pick up where we left off?" she asked.

Trey moved his cock against her backside, his hand sliding across the waistband of her orange pants. "No. I thought we'd talk, like old friends. You know, catch up. But I don't mind replaying that night at Hank's honky-tonk."

"Hank's burned down."

"Yeah, I heard. Too bad."

He gave her one last swipe of his hips, then he let her go. "We'll dance here, instead. Want to? Take a stroll down memory lane?"

Her heart was pounding, skin on fire. She pressed her hand to the towel on her head. "You want to dance with *me*? I look awful. I'm surprised you didn't scream and run when I opened the door."

Trey grinned, his handsome face sinful. "You look great."

Blushing, she dragged off the towel. Swaths of damp red hair fell around her face and down her back.

"Even better," he said, voice going dark.

She hugged the towel to her chest, suddenly shy. "Put on some music," she said hurriedly. "I'll be right back."

She ran for the stairs, wondering what she on earth she could slip into that was sexy and slinky and gorgeous.

"Don't change on my account," Trey called after her. "That orange thing is cute."

She looked down. He stood at the bottom of the stairs, grinning up at her, one arm resting on the stair rail, like Rhett Butler looking up at Scarlett.

He was to die for. Why hadn't she chased him to Austin all those years ago?

"You're crazy," she told him. Then she spun and ran up the stairs, knowing exactly what she was going to wear.

* * * * *

What the hell just happened?

Trey flicked through Kelly's CD collection, after discarding his sheepskin coat and gloves, looking for something danceable.

Shit, he'd come over here as a favor to Kelly's aunt Serena, not to jump Kelly's bones. But as soon as Kelly shut the door behind them, he'd wanted to have her and not be polite about it.

Kelly had always been cute, and he'd thought about her often when he was in Austin—about what might have been if he'd stayed in town a little longer. But he'd had girlfriends—hell, one lived with him for five years. They'd lost touch, him and Kelly. She was just a girl from back home.

But when she'd turned around and playfully wiggled her round, plump ass, he'd wanted to throw her to the floor, peel those baggy orange sweats off her and fuck her good.

He'd made himself back off and talk about the honky-tonk and dancing. Kelly didn't want some guy from way back when ripping off her clothes and screwing her senseless. Too crude.

He should go slow.

Trey lifted out a country CD and smiled at it. Some nice two-stepping, his arms around her, then he could slide his fingers into her pants, dipping into the crease and down toward her hole like he'd always wanted to.

He remembered like it was yesterday how her pussy had felt to his fingers, all hot and wet, her cum sliding all over him. He'd licked his fingers afterward, savoring her spicy taste.

He could skim her pants down to her ankles, make her spread her legs, and lick her clit, tasting her there. Hmm, he was wearing a belt. Maybe they could have some fun with that, too.

What the fuck was wrong with him?

Trey heard a step above him and looked up. His mouth dropped open, and he decided then and there, to hell with it. Whatever was going on, he was going to enjoy himself.

She wore a Christmas dress. It was a bright red knit and sleeveless, with a skirt that bared most of her thighs. A small white snowflake was embroidered right between her breasts.

Plain and simple, the dress outlined her body, her lush breasts that he'd always loved, and her sweet ass. She'd brushed out her gorgeous red hair that she hadn't cut short, thank God, and pulled it into a tail. She'd put on green earrings in the shape of Christmas trees.

Where most women would have donned a pair of spike-heeled shoes and lacy black stockings, Kelly had chosen to go barefoot.

That was erotic as hell, and he was willing to bet she wasn't wearing much of anything under the dress. Damn, this was worth driving five hours in Texas winter wind and icy rain for.

Trey held up the glittering disk of the CD and popped it in the slot. He didn't say anything, just let the strains of the music take over.

Kelly walked down the last few stairs and looked at him shyly. He was already harder than a steel girder, and that shy look sent him over the top.

He moved out into the middle of the nice big living room, holding his arms out, beckoning her. "Come on, baby. Dance with me."

Giving him a smile, she came to him.

"Woo-hoo!" he shouted as he grabbed her hand and her waist, and they started to heel-and-toe it around the room. She laughed. She had a great laugh and a wide, red-lipped mouth.

Why had he ever left home?

"I missed you, Kelly," he heard himself say. "That night outside Hank's, I wanted to fuck you so good."

She gave him that shy look again out of her big brown eyes. "Really? I wanted to fuck, too."

The naughty word on her cute lips made his cock dance. "Me and Kelly St. Clair, the hottest girl in Makeview."

She laughed at him. "I wasn't the hottest girl in Makeview."

"Yes you were, darlin'. You still are. When I was at UT, when class got boring, I'd imagine we'd gone all the way that night. I thought of peeling those jeans down your legs, bending you over the hood of my car and fucking you right there."

"Really?"

She didn't even look offended. More wistful.

"I had a lot of fantasies about you, Kelly. Some of them even make me blush."

She blushed. "I had fantasies about you, too."

"Oh, yeah?" His blood was pounding, his throat dry. "Like what?"

He thought she wouldn't tell him. Then she gave him a sexy look from under her long lashes and said, "I fantasized that, when you bent me over the hood of your car, you spanked me with your belt."

Chapter Two

Trey missed a step and staggered to a halt. He stared at her, his blue eyes wide. "You what?"

Kelly slapped her hand over her mouth, her face hotter than she'd ever felt it. "I don't know why I said that. I swear I don't know why."

His eyes darkened, the pupils widening to swallow the blue. "I hope you said it because you meant it."

"I did. But I've never, ever told a guy anything like that before."

Trey slid his hands around her hips, pulling her against him. He wore a tight, plain black sweatshirt that smelled like cotton and him. "I'm honored you said it to me. That I was the first one."

"And the last. The only one I'm ever going to say it to."

He dipped his head and skimmed his lips across her cheek. "I'm doubly honored."

She closed her eyes and whispered, "You spank me, and then you fuck me. Right under the lights of the parking lot. It feels so good."

Trey held her close, swaying back and forth, although the music's beat was still fiery fast. His thighs pressed hers, and she felt the rigid length of his cock against her abdomen.

"It's kind of cold for a parking lot tonight," he said.

Kelly drew a breath. "I guess a nice warm house will have to do."

"With a staircase."

She shivered. It had always felt safe to fantasize about Trey because she figured she'd never see him again. It was her version of an affair—a fantasy that no one knew about but her.

Trey looked like he was perfectly fine with being her fantasy man. He moved one hand between them, unhooking his belt buckle, then in one smooth move, he pulled the leather belt from his jeans.

Kelly twined her hands behind his neck, her legs shaking, wondering what he was going to do. Her pussy was roasting hot, already wet.

Trey slid the length of the belt around her butt, holding her against him with it. He kept swaying, dancing slow with her, rubbing the inch-wide leather up and down her ass.

At the same time, he kissed her.

She remembered the kiss from all those years ago, how his lips opened hers without asking permission, how she willingly gave it anyway. His tongue slid inside her mouth, rough and warm.

They kept on dancing slow, and then the music caught up to them, the next track a dark, languid tune, about how a woman could be sexy and hot. Trey sang along under his breath. Kelly closed her eyes and nuzzled his neck.

He moved her slowly over to the stairs. As the song went on about fires burning inside, he turned her around, still with the belt enclosing her, and swayed with her, his cock finding its way between her buttocks.

"You are so damn sexy," he whispered. "And I want you so bad."

Kelly traced the line of the belt, caressing it over her hips. "I want you, too."

He nipped the shell of her ear. "Bend over and hold onto the railing."

Shaking, Kelly leaned forward and grabbed hold of the polished post at the bottom of the stairs. She felt him slide his calloused palm up her bare thighs and push her tight skirt upward.

His fingers slid beneath the thin elastic strap of her panties. "Pretty," he said. "Black satin looks good on you." He chuckled. "Bet it looks even better off you."

With one hand, he pulled the panties down her legs. Air, dry and heated, touched her backside.

"Sure you want me to do this?" Trey asked, voice soft.

"Yes, I'm sure."

A bead of fluid trickled from her pussy to her thighs. She spread her legs slightly, wishing he'd rub the belt between them.

Instead, the belt came down, *slap,* on her bare ass.

He didn't hit very hard, only enough to sting. She made a soft noise, and he leaned over her, his jeans brushing her bare legs. "You okay?"

"Yes," she moaned. "Do it again."

She felt his chest rise with a sharp breath, then he backed away. She heard a swish of air then felt the strap, *slap!* A little harder this time.

"You have such a pretty ass," Trey said softly. "I want to fuck it."

Kelly gulped, her hands slick with sweat on the rail. "I've never done that."

"I'll teach you." *Slap, slap, slap.* Each stroke stung a little more, but at the same time, it felt damn good. Her hips moved, and she wanted him to shove his hand or his tongue or his cock between her thighs.

"Your ass is all red," he murmured. "I love it."

Trey held off on the strap and stepped into her line of sight to pull off his sweatshirt. He was breathing hard, his face damp with perspiration.

Her eyes widened as she looked him over. He was gorgeous enough dressed, but in only his jeans and boots, he was stunning. When she'd last seen him, he'd been twenty-one, lean and muscular, but still lanky with youth.

Ten years had filled him out into a hard specimen of man. His chest was sculpted with muscle, flat, pale nipples nestling in dark, curling hair. His shoulders were wide and tight—on the right one was a white, round scar left over from his rodeo days when he'd been the best calf cutter in Makeview county.

She'd seen him with his shirt off once, and had longed to trace the scar with her tongue. She still did.

Trey stroked his hand over her hair, then pressed a kiss to the top of her head. He moved around behind her again and laid the belt across her back. His two fingers skimmed down her buttocks, tracing the crease between them.

He sank to his knees, fingers feathering upward to find her quim. "You're soaking," he murmured.

"I know."

"Filled with honey for me." He licked the folds of her pussy. Her fingers tightened on the stair railing, wood cool on her palms. He pulled her panties all the way down, the elastic brushing her ankles.

He went on licking, hands spreading her thighs. He still clutched the belt, the leather stiff against her skin.

With his tongue, he did marvelous things. She twitched, swaying back and forth as he thoroughly licked her opening and thrust his tongue inside.

"Merry Christmas," she groaned.

He laughed, his breath hot on her quim. He blew softly, stirring the curls, then nibbled the petals of her skin. "Lean onto me," he said. "Let me have you."

She bent her legs, easing herself back to his mouth. He made a noise of appreciation, then he buried his tongue inside her. Hot and wet, his tongue sliced deep into her pussy, licking and stroking hard.

Then he withdrew his tongue and stroked it over her clit. The nub swelled, his tongue grating over it, fiery hot.

She felt her climax coming, and she didn't want it to. "No," she whispered. "Not yet."

Trey chuckled. He had her legs spread wide, the panties stretching around her feet. She could care less if they ripped, let them. His tongue danced from her clit to her cunt, teasing the nub, thrusting into the opening.

Mr. X would never, ever have been this good.

"Trey."

"I'm right here, sweet baby."

"*Fuck* me."

"Thought you'd never ask."

Did he stand up, rip off his jeans and thrust into her like she craved? No. He flicked his tongue faster, then nibbled on her hard clit. Tingles raced from her pussy down her legs and up her arms to her fingers and toes.

"Trey," she moaned again. She raised up on her toes, spasms pulsing through her. It wasn't a screaming, mindless orgasm, but it was pretty damn good.

Trey kept on licking, swallowing her cream, tongue lapping every fold. She twitched and rocked, moaning for more. He went on and on, licking and nipping her, suckling her clit until she thrust herself back, begging for his tongue.

He gave it to her. *Good, so damn good. Oh, Trey.*

She pulled away from him, kicking off the restraining panties, turned around and put the banister behind her. She gave him a wild-eyed look, her breasts rising with her ragged breath.

"I want to do that to you."

He looked up at her, hair tousled, mouth smiling. "You want to lick my cunt? I hate to disappoint you, but…"

"No, your cock, you pain in the butt." Of course he knew what she meant, he was just teasing her. "Get your pants down and sit on the stairs. I want your cock in my mouth right now."

Trey's grin widened, his mouth turning up in one corner. "Well…okay."

This had to be an erotic dream. Kelly couldn't really be standing here with nothing on under her tight red dress while Trey Kincaid slowly unzipped his fly and pushed his jeans and briefs down over his hips.

He sat down, jeans still hugging his thighs, then leaned back on his elbows on the stairs.

Kelly wanted to come just looking at him. His torso was dark where the sun would hit it, creamy white below the waistband. He didn't sunbathe in the nude. He was modest, and for some reason, that turned her on.

His jeans hugged the tight, well-muscled thighs she'd imagined, his skin bronzed below his hips. His cock stood straight up, tight and dark red, the tip smooth. His balls were high and full, rising from curls of black hair at the base.

She let her gaze run over him. His cock was long and tall, just like he was, firm and waiting for her. She could already imagine the taste in her mouth. She licked her lips.

He slanted her a smile filled with sin. "Like what you see?"

Kelly tilted her head, as though considering, one finger on her lips.

His grin vanished. "If you don't, don't tell me. But you know what? You look fucking adorable like that."

The lust in his eyes was plain to see. He was shaking, only a little bit, like he was holding himself back, waiting to see what she'd do. He still held the belt, folded once in his right hand, the leather dangling to the stair.

"Does this seem weird to you?" Kelly asked.

He blinked. "Weird?"

"We haven't seen each other in almost ten years, then you walk in, and we want to jump each other's bones."

"I don't think it's weird. You're beautiful."

He watched her, lying there naked with his jeans around thighs, his dark hair mussed from going down on her. Damn, he'd make a beautiful picture.

"Hang on a minute," she said. She whirled into the living room, snatched up the camera her mother had sent as an early Christmas present, flicked it on, and ran back to the stairway. Before Trey could say anything, she lifted the camera, focused and shot.

Flash.

Trey flinched, and his face turned bright red. "Hey, what are you doing?"

"Don't worry. It's digital."

"Yeah, but you could put that on the Internet." He stared at her in frozen horror, his embarrassment kind of cute.

"I'd never do that." Kelly held the camera at her side. "This is private."

He stared at her a few heartbeats, as though trying to decide if he could trust her. She asked him, "Did you ever tell anyone what happened that night behind Hank's honky-tonk?"

"No."

She smiled. "Neither did I. It was *my* memory to treasure."

"Mine too."

They looked at each other. Kelly's heart warmed.

"Here, how about this," Trey said. He turned over onto his front, his beautiful ass tight and smooth. His back tapered from broad shoulders to tight waist, then his jeans hugged his thighs, half on, half off. He gave her a wicked look over his shoulder.

"Perfect," Kelly breathed, and snapped a picture. "That'll make a great screensaver."

His eyes widened. "What?"

"I'm just kidding. I'll bury the pics in a computer file no one will ever see. Except me."

Trey put his hand over his eyes. "I swear I'm going to spank you again."

"I hope so. Turn over again. I want some more."

Trey complied. Kelly mounted the stairs, standing with her feet on either side of his legs, and aimed the camera straight down at his cock. *Click. Flash,* another beautiful photo.

He stuck out his tongue as she took another shot. She climbed up behind him and took a picture going down the stairs, while he held his cock up straight with his fingers.

He got into it, laughing and posing for her. He also didn't mind looking straight up her dress as she stood over him. "You're pussy is gorgeous," he said.

She blushed. Strange to be shy when she was taking pictures of his naked cock.

"I have an idea," she said. She scurried down the stairs again and held out her hand. "Take off your pants and come here."

"I thought you wanted to suck on me."

"I do. But I want to do something first. Come on."

Looking bemused, Trey stripped off his boots and socks, then shoved his jeans the rest of the way off. She got a shot of him doing that, too.

Her heart beating faster, she said, "Put the boots back on."

He gave her a *what*? look, but laughed. "All right." He pulled on his boots, then let her haul him to his feet.

A beautiful naked man in nothing but his cowboy boots. His body rippled with muscle, bronzed skin flowing like someone had dipped a perfect male statue into molten gold.

Except, of course for the pale skin of his ass, and his dark cock standing straight out.

He gave her a sexy look under his lashes, and Kelly stepped back, her cream flowing, and took another picture.

She seized his hand and led him over to the Christmas tree. "Sit down there," she said, pointing. Grinning, he did it. He sat in front of the tree, on the carpet, his knees bent, legs spread, his arms circling his knees. Another shot.

Kelly grabbed a roll of Christmas wrap she'd left on the floor and tore off a large sheet. She came to him and wrapped it around his middle, wadding it high over his still erect cock.

Trey started laughing. "Give me some bows."

She took fresh red, silver, and green bows from a plastic bag and handed them to him. He peeled of the backings and stuck one on his head, one at his navel, and one on the wrapping paper over his cock.

He leaned back on his elbows and spread his legs. "All ready for Christmas morning."

Kelly snapped pictures, her pussy hot and wet, her body shivering all over.

Trey posed for her, first lying on his back, legs apart, then on his hands and knees, his butt peeking through the paper, then lowering himself to his stomach, letting her stick bows all over his exposed ass.

He turned over again and Kelly ripped open the paper so that his stiff cock poked through. She took a picture of that, then put a bow on his tip. He laughed so hard, it kept falling off.

Finally, she dropped to her hands and knees and tore off the paper, opening her Christmas present.

His laughter died. He smoothed her hair, his hand shaking. She pushed his strong legs apart and lowered her mouth to fit it around his cock.

Chapter Three

Trey picked up the camera from where she'd laid it next to him, at the same time he felt Kelly's warm, wet mouth suck him in.

Damn, and I almost decided to spend Christmas in Austin, catching up on work.

He'd never really forgotten about Kelly, her red hair and big brown eyes and smile that could stop his heart. When she'd asked him to ride out with her that day ten years ago and find her father's mare and foal, she'd looked at him with sweet, troubled eyes, and he hadn't been able to say no.

Maybe she'd think he was brave and cool, helping her rescue the horses. Maybe she wouldn't mind if he grabbed her in his arms and planted a big kiss on her mouth. Maybe he could tell her he'd always thought she was hot.

But Trey had been shy, more comfortable around cutting horses than around women. Even in Austin, meeting women from all over the country, he could smile and nod, but not really talk to them. They all thought he was sexy, but that was just his good luck. The long, tall Texan who smiled and said *ma'am* became popular very fast.

He'd gotten up the courage to ask Kelly to dance at the honky-tonk that night after the horse ride, but she'd come there with her friends. He remembered standing at the bar watching her laugh and goof around with her girlfriends, wanting to go over to her, and not being able to.

He'd had to drink three beers before he could even walk to her table, and he'd only gone because her friends had trooped to the restroom, and she'd volunteered to stay and watch their stuff. She'd smiled up at him and said, sure, she'd dance with him, soon as her friends came back.

He'd almost scooted away, not wanting to be standing there, blushing, when the ladies returned. He remembered his face burning as they came back to the table, staring at him, smiles wide, and Kelly casually saying she was going to dance. Her friends had nudged each other, snickering, telling Kelly not to do anything they wouldn't.

Trey had almost dropped the idea, but once he had Kelly in his arms, and they were stepping around the floor, he forgot his shyness. She thanked him for helping her bring the horses back—Trey had carried the tiny foal across his lap all the way, while Kelly had held the mare's lead rein. It had taken them a long time to get back, and they'd spent it talking like they'd known each other forever.

On the dance floor, they couldn't talk much over the music, but Kelly smiled at him, so that was fine. They'd danced three dances, then Kelly said she was too hot, so they took a walk outside. Her friends watched them go with knowing grins.

Behind Hank's honky-tonk, a path led down through cottonwoods to the river below, a pretty walk on a summer day. It had been October, and a little nippy, but that meant the rattlesnakes were hiding, and they could walk under the moon without too much worry. Trey had started kissing her, unable to stop, and then she put her hands on his ass, and then he put his hands on hers, and things had gone from there.

When he asked to go out with her again, and she said she had to help her sister move back to UT El Paso, he figured she was letting him down easy. Sure, this was fun, but they would go their separate ways, and that would be that.

Every time he called home, he asked, casually, if his grandmother had heard anything about Kelly. His grandmother and her aunt were good friends, and usually, she volunteered the information.

"Oh, do you remember Kelly St. Clair? She got a degree in interior design and came back home to work with her aunt's decorating business. She's really good. All those millionaires retiring down by View Creek ask for her." And then, "Remember Kelly St. Clair? Well, she's getting married. One of those retiring millionaires has a son who inherited his dad's business. He took one look at Kelly, and that was it."

When Trey had come home tonight to find Kelly's aunt Serena at his grandmother's house, Serena had smiled like she knew a good secret, and then mentioned, ever-so casually, that Kelly's fiancé had dumped her. He'd had another girlfriend tucked away, Kelly found out, they had a fight and he walked out.

Fucking jerk, Trey had thought angrily.

But hey, lucky for Trey. Because Kelly had just started to suck *him,* not some stupid rich boy with a silver spoon in his mouth and a stick up his ass.

Kelly's mouth was all over him, her tongue flicking like a butterfly dancing. He dropped his head back and closed his eyes, feeling her lick and lick, her red hair falling like warm silk across his thighs.

He brought his head up, picked up the camera, and took a picture of her bent over him. Her ass was up in the air, hips tapering to a curved waist, the muscles of her arms working as she held herself up over him.

She jumped as the flash went off and nipped him.

"Mmm, yeah," he murmured. He lifted his hips, and her mouth slid over him again like a sheath.

Her tongue moved, not like she was practiced, but like she was having fun. She licked him hard, concentrating on the sensitive skin just under his tip.

He angled the camera to take in his cock and her lips on it and clicked the shutter. She jerked again, but didn't stop. He took another picture, this one from the other side.

When she backed off, he almost groaned in frustration, but she started licking his cock up and down, from tip to base and back again. He lifted his butt so she could get all the way down to his balls and beyond. He pointed the camera down there and kept his finger on the button.

She closed her eyes against the bright flash, but kept licking, *wonderful woman*.

He couldn't stop his finger clicking the camera. He took shot after shot of her slathering her tongue all over him, nuzzling his balls, her eyes shut, closing her teeth gently over one of his testicles.

She came up again and swallowed his cock into her mouth. He felt the climax building up in his balls, the seed wanting to burst out. Only his clenched muscles kept it in. He grimaced, the cords on his neck tightening as the pleasure went on and on.

"Oh no," he said. "I don't want it to stop."

She responded by sucking harder, lips and tongue encouraging him. She moved her hand to his balls, squeezing them lightly.

"Fuck," he whispered. The camera clicked once, twice, three times as his buttocks squeezed together, and he came.

Seed shot into her mouth and trickled out again over his cock. He laced his hand through her hair, loving it soft and warm all over him as she milked him with her mouth.

She licked and suckled until his throat ached with his groans. *Damn, you are so beautiful, why the hell didn't I grab onto you when I had the chance?*

He fell onto his back, spent, and Kelly lifted her head. She wiped her mouth on the back of her hand, and looked at him, shy but happy.

"I think you used up the card," she said, touching the camera.

Trey dropped the camera, sat up, and hauled her into his arms. He kissed her hard, tasting himself on her tongue, letting her taste herself in his mouth. She made noises in her throat and wrapped her arms around him, fingers pressing his back.

He kissed until his lips started to go numb. He smoothed her hair from her face and rested his forehead against hers. "That was good, that was *so* good."

She kissed his lips, softly this time. "Yeah, it was. Want some eggnog?"

* * * * *

Kelly poured eggnog from a carton into two highball glasses and handed one to Trey. He took it with a grin, not seeming to care that she hadn't made the eggnog from scratch. John had always expected her to be a gourmet cook.

Trey had taken off his boots, but put his jeans back on. They hugged his hips, reminding her he hadn't bothered with his underwear.

He looked good, and he tasted good, and he smiled at her good. When John had walked out, she'd thought this Christmas would be nothing but tears, and her trying to put on a happy face at her aunt's house.

And now…

They'd left the camera in the living room, because Kelly was right, they'd used up the card. She'd never dreamed she was the kind of girl to tell a guy to strip and then *take pictures* of him. And then let him take pictures of her sucking him off! She'd lost her mind.

If this is insanity, it sure is fun.

Trey rummaged through cupboards, muscles sliding under his bronzed skin, until he pulled out a bottle of Kentucky bourbon.

"A little for you," he said, unscrewing the bottle and dolloping some into her eggnog, then his. "And a little for me."

He screwed the bottle shut and picked up his spiked eggnog, leaning against the counter. He lifted his glass in front of his wide chest and said, "To Kelly, the most beautiful girl in Makeview."

Kelly's face heated. "I wasn't beautiful when I opened the door. I looked awful."

"Are you kidding? I knew you'd just gotten out of the shower, smelling all exotic with your fancy soap." He grinned, then suddenly his smile faltered. "Hey, were you prettying yourself up for someone? Do you have a date later, and I'm just the appetizer?"

She started laughing, and pressed her hand over her mouth. "Only Mr. X."

Trey's brows lifted. "Who the hell is that? Some wrestler? I work out, but I don't know if I could go against a guy who could lift me up and slam me onto the floor."

"Mr. X isn't a person. He's a…um."

"An 'um'? You can tell me anything, Kelly, I won't repeat it." He took a sip of eggnog around his grin.

If any other man had said that, Kelly would have been wary. But she believed Trey. She *knew* she could trust him, though she couldn't say why.

"He's a vibrator."

Trey choked on his eggnog. He set the glass down, coughing. "Oh, man."

"What's so funny? Women need release as much as men do."

Trey wiped his mouth and shook his head. "I'm not laughing. I was thinking maybe you should introduce me to him and show me exactly what you were going to do with him. Or, pretend I'm not there, and I'll just watch."

Kelly pressed her thighs tight together, imagining his steady blue gaze on her while she rubbed Mr. X all over her pussy.

"We should finish our eggnog first," she said hastily.

"Sure. You got any whipped cream?" He turned away and opened the refrigerator as he spoke, thoroughly at home. He found the can of whipped topping in the doorway and brought it out. "Great."

He squirted a glop on the top of his eggnog and held the can out to her. "Want some?"

"No, thanks." She watched, entranced, as he slowly swirled his tongue around the whipped cream on his drink. He snaked his tongue into his mouth, sucking up the cream, a white droplet clinging to the tip of his nose.

He caught her gaze, and his smile turned dark. "Kelly, take off your dress."

The juice between her thighs flowed faster. She touched her knit dress, knowing she had nothing on under it, having left her panties by the stairs.

She slowly inched the dress up her thighs, then pulled it up and off over her head. It was a little cold to be naked, and her nipples lifted, small and tight.

Trey put down his eggnog and strolled over to her, his bare feet whispering on the floor. "I was wrong about you being the most beautiful woman in Makeview. I have to say the most beautiful in the world."

She blushed. "You put too much bourbon in your eggnog."

"No, I didn't, baby. I remember dancing with you way back when, thinking you were so hot." His gaze raked her, resting on her plump breasts, the curve of her hips. "You've gotten hotter than ever. Damn." He shook his head, his eyes never leaving her. "I can't believe I haven't been with you all this time."

"You wanted to start your own life."

"I know. See what happens when you don't pay attention?"

Kelly didn't know quite what he meant, but she did understand the sly grin he gave her just before he squirted whipped cream all over her naked breasts.

She squealed. He bent her back over the counter, while she clutched her glass of eggnog and let him lick the cream off her breasts in slow strokes.

Her nipples tingled as he wiggled his tongue over each tip. He sucked off the cream and licked around the areolas, making her push herself into his mouth.

"You make a damn good sundae," he said.

She grabbed the whipped cream can from him and sloshed cream across his shoulders. She ate it off him, licking the round scar from his rodeo days, just like she always wanted to.

He snaked his arms around her waist as she cleaned him, feeling his hard cock rub her pussy through his jeans. She wriggled against him, letting the seam of his fly move like fire on her clit. The friction was good, almost as good as his hands or his tongue.

He caught her bare thighs in his hands and lifted her so her butt rested against the counter. Then he moved to her, pressing the hard denim bulge against her clit, holding her ass with firm fingers.

"I can't get enough of you," he whispered into her hair. "Can't get enough."

He ground his hips against her, spreading her legs wide. She moved with him, letting him fuck her through his jeans, getting the fabric all wet with her female juices. His cock, even behind his fly, was so much better than Mr. X could ever be.

She moved herself on him, the fabric burning on her clit, the heat feeling so good. She threw her head back, her long hair tickling her ass, so erotic, and pumped against him. "Ohhh," she said. "I'm going to come."

"Do it," he whispered. "Come for me."

Kelly didn't want to, not so soon. She wanted to savor the hot feel of his pants on her cunt, his cock pressing so tight against the seam she was surprised the zipper didn't break.

A blackness came over her mind, edges tinged in white fire, and her whole body jerked. "Trey," she babbled. She bucked against him, and he slammed his ridge into her, holding her tight, sliding on her. Noises escaped her mouth and then all-out screams.

Suddenly, the beautiful bulge left her, and she nearly cried. Trey lifted her around the waist, carried her two feet, and deposited her on a kitchen chair. "I don't want to come in my pants," he said, sounding desperate.

He ripped open his zipper, thrust his jeans down and off, then straddled her and started rubbing his hard, hot cock between her breasts.

Still frantic from her climax, Kelly thrust her own fingers against her clit. She moaned with delayed release, and clutched his smooth cock, letting him fuck between her breasts and fingers at the same time.

Trey closed his eyes and moaned, and then his seed squirted out and spilled all over her. He held himself against her, pumping against her breasts. Ropes of cum shot out, and she caught them in her hand, liking the silky texture and the feel against her bare skin.

He held himself against her, cock snug between her breasts, for a long time. Then he opened his eyes, dropped to his knees, spread her legs apart and licked her swollen clit and pussy until she screamed her release again.

* * * * *

A short while later, Trey sat naked on the chair, holding an equally naked Kelly on his lap.

Kelly smelled good, a mix of coconut soap and his cum and hers, kind of like they'd made love on a tropical beach.

She was a warm and soft lapful, her head resting on his shoulder, her red hair flowing down to his lap.

The clock over the door said eleven, the night outside was black, and winter wind howled around the windows. He kissed her cheek. "Kelly, sweetheart, I have a problem."

She lifted her head, brows puckering. "You have to go to the bathroom?"

He stared at her in surprise, then burst out laughing. "Oh, man, no wonder I'm in love with you. No. I want to take you up to your bedroom and fuck you the rest of the night, but I don't have any condoms."

"What?" She sounded amused, but something watchful entered her brown eyes. "The gorgeous Trey Kincaid wasn't prepared to get laid?"

He shook his head. "I came home to Makeview figuring I'd visit with my grandmother and uncle and nephews. Not exactly a reason to pack condoms."

"Oh," she said. "I guess not."

"You don't have any lying around, do you?"

"No. I don't have anyone to buy them for." She sounded a little wistful. But Trey was here to change all that.

"Well, then." Trey eased her from his lap, and then held her hands while she stood in front of him. Damn, she had the most beautiful body he'd ever seen. "I'll drive to the convenience store up on the freeway. It's open twenty-four hours, even on Christmas."

Kelly looked shy again—while standing stark naked in front of him. She was so damn cute. "If you go up there and buy condoms, everyone in town will know," she said.

"I know." He stood up, skimming his hands up her arms and locking his fingers behind her neck. "But I'll have to risk it." He kissed her lightly on the lips. "I want to make love to you, Kelly. I'm going to. All right?"

She kissed him, her lips warm and smooth. "Fine by me."

Trey released her, but held her hand as they walked back to the living room. "It's too much to hope that they have lube up there, too, isn't it?"

She squeezed his hand. "Now that, I do have." When he glanced at her in surprise, she said, "To smooth the way for Mr. X."

Trey laughed softly. "I am so looking forward to playing with your friend. He and I are going to teach you a thing or two."

He loved how she shivered in excitement. He imagined her moaning for him as he massaged her clit with the vibrator and his hands. His cock went rock-hard.

She noticed. "Are you sure you can get into your pants?"

"I don't know, but I have to try."

Back in the living room, Trey picked up his underwear and put it on, stuffing his needy cock away. He pulled on his jeans, zipped them with some struggle, and reached for his sweatshirt.

Kelly watched him, looking disappointed that he was hiding his body away. Well, when he returned, he'd do a slow striptease for her. He'd like her watching him undress, her eyes all eager.

He threaded his belt through the loops again and buckled it, remembering what fun it was to spank Kelly's ass with it. Another thing he'd be sure to do some more tonight.

He pulled on his socks and boots, then picked up his sheepskin coat and his hat. She hung onto the newel post at the bottom of the stairs and gave him a wistful look, like she thought he was going out for condoms and not coming back.

Fat chance. He bent over her and gave her a slow, loving kiss. "You stay warm, now."

She nodded. "I will."

It was hard to turn around and walk away. Trey made himself do it, reasoning that the faster he left, the faster he'd get back, and then they could make love all night and all the way up to time for him to show up at the Christmas dinner table.

He undid the deadbolt, then reached for the doorknob. It wouldn't turn. He tried again, but the thing didn't budge under his hand.

"Is this locked?" he asked.

Kelly came forward, bare feet whispering on the board floor. "I only have the dead bolt." She reached around him for the knob, her naked body brushing his.

If they were together, like a married couple, he wouldn't need to rush out for condoms. He'd be able to strip off again, lay her down on the floor, and go for it. He suddenly wanted that with all his might. Kelly, *his* and his alone.

She was still messing with the knob. "I guess it's stuck. You'll have to go out the back door."

But when they got to the back door, that knob wouldn't work either. Trey rattled it and pushed and pulled the door.

"This is weird," Kelly said. "Maybe the door swelled with the storm. I can call a locksmith, see what he thinks."

"At eleven p.m. on Christmas Eve?" Trey asked. Standing here fully dressed with her stark naked was making his cock throb harder than ever. He didn't want a locksmith bothering them just now.

She nibbled her thumb. "Hmm, this is starting to remind me of a horror movie."

Trey chuckled, suddenly understanding what was going on. He took off his hat and rubbed his hand through his hair.

"No. I know exactly what this is. It's your Aunt Serena and my grandmother. They decided I should stay here tonight. And believe me, honey, when they're scheming, they're scarier than any horror movie you ever saw."

Chapter Four

Upstairs, sitting on Kelly's dresser, in plain sight, was an unopened box of condoms.

Kelly, clutching the dress she'd picked up on the way out of the kitchen against her cold skin, stared at it in surprise. "How did that get here?"

Trey cut her a glance. "You tell me."

She approached the box and looked at it. Magnums, unopened. "I don't know. I didn't buy it."

Trey put his hands on his hips, looking sexy, even fully dressed. "Maybe your fiancé left it behind?"

Kelly snorted. "Not magnums."

Trey's look turned thoughtful. He picked up the box, not pissed off or suspicious, just curious. "I guess they thought of everything."

"They who? And what were you talking about downstairs—your grandmother and my Aunt Serena?"

Trey dropped the box on the nightstand and sat down on the bed. He took Kelly's hands and pulled her down to sit next to him. The quilts felt cool under her butt.

"Have you ever heard of witches, Kelly?"

She considered. "You mean Wicca? That kind of thing?"

"That kind of thing. Well, my grandmother is a witch. So is your aunt. They kind of keep it under wraps, but I've always known. My grandmother does all kinds of tarot readings for me. How do you think I make all my business decisions?"

"I'm finding this hard to believe." Kelly wound her arms around his chest, liking the warmth of his sweatshirt and his hard body beneath. "I knew aunt Serena was into incense and charms, but I didn't think it was real *magic*."

"Think about it. Doesn't your aunt always know things before everyone else? Don't things always happen the way she wants?"

"I thought that was just her personality."

"It is. She's like my grandmother. My grandmother wants something to happen, and the universe arranges for it to happen."

Come to think of it Aunt Serena *did* have an uncanny way of deciding what the future would bring. She was never wrong. And she did like to dish out advice. If you didn't take her advice, you usually regretted it.

"You're saying that the two of them want us to get together?" Kelly asked slowly.

Trey nodded. "That's why we looked at each other and all the sudden wanted each other. That's why the doors won't open, but *poof,* here's a convenient box of condoms. We're supposed to stay in the house and have all kinds of sex and fall in love."

Kelly met his beautiful blue gaze. "Of all the nerve."

"Yep."

"Like we aren't grownups who can make our own decisions."

"Like we can't figure out what we want," he agreed.

Kelly's ire rose. "I'm calling them right now and telling them what I think."

She crawled across the bed, Trey appreciatively watching her breasts sway. She picked up the phone and started to punch her aunt's number, then she stopped. "The phone is dead."

"Yep." Trey leaned back, his hands around one knee. "Figured as much."

Kelly slammed down the receiver. "I have a cell phone."

"So do I. How much you want to bet we can't get a signal?"

"They can't do this to us," Kelly fumed.

"They're doing it."

She turned around, kneeling on the bed, her arms folded. "We should just play cards the rest of the night, to show them who they can push around."

"We could." Trey laid down across the bed, resting his warm hands on Kelly's thigh. "But I don't really want to."

Kelly didn't really want to, either. Trey was to die for, and a card game would be a waste of time. Unless they could turn it into strip poker…

"I guess we'll have to make the best of it," she said softly.

"Guess so." His voice was equally as soft.

He dipped his hand between her thighs and parted her legs. "We could play with Mr. X a little," he said. "Or you could just have me."

Kelly tangled her fingers in his black, thick hair. "I'll choose you."

"Thank you."

She grinned suddenly. "We'll save Mr. X for later."

He looked up at her, his eyes dark. "Oh, you're asking for it, sweetheart."

He dragged her down the bed, flipped her over, and slapped her ass with his hand. Kelly squealed, loving it.

She never thought she'd want a man to spank her—she'd never, ever have asked her ex—but she liked it with Trey. It stung and it tickled and it turned her on.

"On your back, baby."

She rolled over again, lying full length, parting her legs a little, so he would see how wet her pussy was for him. He looked and licked his lips. His tight jeans showed his cock rigid and hard again, a huge bulge, and he didn't bother to hide it.

"Hands above your head."

He slid his belt off. Shivering, Kelly raised her hands and rested them on the pillows above her.

Trey crawled over her, his sweatshirt brushing her breasts, grabbed her wrists, and wrapped the leather belt around them. He looped the end of the belt around a post in her decorative iron headboard and tied it in a makeshift knot.

"There," he said. "You're mine."

Kelly laid still, her hands over her head, arms stretched. She could probably get away if she really wanted to, but she didn't really want to.

His clothes rubbing her body made her shiver with excitement. He kissed her face, then her neck and throat, tickling his tongue over her skin. She lifted herself toward him, wanting more.

He licked his way down to her breasts, then spent time suckling and lapping her nipples. He closed hard fingers around the globe of one breast and lifted it into his mouth.

She dropped her head back, loving the feel of his tongue and teeth. She should be more worried, being trapped in the house, the phone dead, and him binding her to the bed, but she wasn't.

She loved it. She was locked in a box with Trey Kincaid, the most gorgeous man in Makeview. At twenty-one he'd been plenty cute—at thirty, he was stunning.

She wished she could run her hands all through his hair as he suckled her, but her wrists were tied to the bedstead, gloriously bound. She wriggled, as though trying to get free, and he bit her playfully.

"You wind me up any harder, baby, and I'll explode," he said.

She smiled, feeling wild and wicked. *She* could wind him up, *she* could get him hard. Her, plain old Kelly St. Clair.

He moved his tongue down to her navel, giving it a few licks, then he went to work on her pussy. Like before, he really knew what he was doing. He licked her clit, moving it back and forth under its tiny sheath. He pressed his tongue onto her hood, stroking hard, while dark tingles raced through her body.

He nipped her and sucked her clit, then delved his tongue into her opening. "Trey," she whispered, lifting her hips.

He backed off then, and she cried out in disappointment. But he replaced his tongue with his fingers, pushing deep inside her pussy. He planted his thumb on her clit and moved it back and forth, back and forth.

"Fuck," she said hoarsely.

She was going to come. Way too soon. *Please not yet, not yet,* she begged her body.

Trey rubbed her, his thumb a point of fire, his fingers inside her widening and opening her. She was so wet, she could feel her juices pouring over his hand.

"Please, not yet," she gasped.

"Well, all right." Trey slowly withdrew his fingers. She whimpered in disappointment, then forgot about it when he began to strip.

Kneeling over her, he slid off his sweatshirt and tossed it away, his hard-muscled torso a feast for her eyes. He'd already kicked off his boots, and now he popped the button of his jeans and unzipped them.

His cock tumbled out, thick and engorged, the shaft red from base to head. She ran an eye over it, knowing it was bigger and harder and longer than any vibrator could be. She wanted it in her mouth, she wanted it in her hands, she wanted it in her pussy.

"Kelly," he said. He shoved the jeans all the way off and dropped them on the floor. "I really want to fuck you."

"Fine by me." She spread her legs wider, wanting to pull him in.

He grinned at her, then went through the process of opening the box of condoms, selecting one, peeling back the wrapper, and pinching the end. He made each movement slow and deliberate, like he was putting on a show for her.

He rubbed his cock with his thumb and forefinger, then slid the end of the condom on it, unrolling it slowly. It fit him tight, making his cock shiny.

She wanted him in her bare, but this might be a one-night stand. A Christmas Eve stand. The thought made her wistful, but at the same time, she was determined to enjoy every second of it.

"Lift your hips a little," he murmured.

He leaned down and kissed her mouth, his lips warm and seductive, then he positioned himself between her legs, resting the tip of his cock against her opening.

"Ready?" he asked.

Kelly strained at her bonds, wanting to grab him and pull him inside but not able to. "Ready," she said, a little breathlessly.

Slowly, stretching her, making her ache and love it at the same time, he pushed his cock all the way in.

* * * * *

Why the hell did I ever leave Makeview?

Trey moaned. Career, college, financial success, it was *nothing* compared to the feel of Kelly closing snug around him. She was tight, she was oh-so tight, and she squeezed every inch of him.

Home, he thought, *I've come home*. Then he began to move.

Kelly squirmed and squealed under him, her body covered with a sheen of sweat, her pussy full of honey. She'd almost climaxed under the assault of his tongue, then his fingers, and now she was rocking and wriggling, straining against the belt that held her to the bed.

He slid all the way in, right to his balls, feeling her ass against his hard testicles. He held himself up with his rigid arms, fists sinking into the mattress on either side of her. She turned her head and licked his forearm, tongue strong and wet.

His cock pulsed, the seed building, wanting to escape. He lowered himself onto her, still braced to not hurt her with his weight, and she lifted eager lips to his.

They kissed and kissed, tongues sliding over each other as they tried to taste as much of each other as possible.

Trey's balls lifted hard and tight, pressing him forward. He shoved into her with strong thrusts, feeling her curls of hair around his base, feeling his balls banging her ass.

Kelly lifted to meet him, her pelvis hard against his, pushing herself onto him as far as she could. The walls of her cunt pulsed around him, the sweetest, hottest feeling he'd ever had.

When she'd asked him downstairs to bend her over and spank her, he thought he'd die. Who knew that sweet, shy Kelly liked it a little hot? She liked being tied with his belt, too, if the expression of rapture on her face was any indication.

Love it, love it, love it, he thought with each thrust. *Love you.*

Did he love her?

You'd better believe it.

"Kelly," he panted. "I'm gonna come."

She ran her bare feet up his calves, lifting her hips, swallowing him inside her. Spasms fluttered behind his balls, sending his seed up, and then he was coming and coming, squirting deep in mindless thrusts.

He shoved his fingers between them, his thumb pressing her clit, and she let out a moan. "Trey. Yes, *ohhhh*."

"Baby, *thank you.*"

He kept coming, kept pumping into her, his cock not ready to give up yet. She squeezed him hard, drawing every last bit out of him, squealing with her own pleasure.

Trey stroked and felt her as long as he could, riding it out hard and fast. Black dots swam across his vision, and he thought he'd pass out. Manfully, he kept his eyes open and his breathing going while he fucked her until the very last minute.

Finally, he collapsed beside her, then, with his fingers and his tongue, brought her to climax twice more. She strained and screamed, nearly breaking the belt and the headboard itself.

By the time her cries died down to breathy sighs, he was hard as a rock again, and he rolled over her and fucked her again. And then again.

At last, when they were both drooping with tiredness, Trey loosened the belt and let her hands go.

"Merry Christmas, baby," he whispered as he kissed her lips. He dragged the now messed up quilt over the top of them and snuggled down with her into a warm nest. "I love you."

She stared at him, brown eyes wide, lashes thick against her cheeks. "Trey…"

"Shh." He put his fingers against her lips to stop her saying something like, *That's sweet, but I just want to be friends.*

Kelly watched him a moment longer, then her mouth relaxed into a smile. "Merry Christmas, Trey," she said, then closed her lovely eyes and drifted off to sleep. Trey followed her not long after that, utterly exhausted and loving what had made him that way.

* * * * *

"So, honey, you think it worked?" Across town, Serena swept the salt circle from the table and plopped tiredly into a chair.

"I sure hope so," Mary answered. She'd put on a flamboyant Christmas sweater with a hunky elf who looked like Orlando Bloom on it. "Trey is too damn stubborn to see what's under his nose."

Serena nodded. "I thought for sure those two would get together years ago. I couldn't believe Kelly didn't even *call* Trey, or try to see him again."

Mary shook her head. "She was young. At that age, you figure you have your whole life to sort out that stuff. But it goes by so fast."

"Trey will figure out what we did, you know. He's a smart boy."

Mary shrugged and sat down at the table. "Doesn't matter. He loves Kelly, and maybe this will make him get up the gumption to tell her."

"And Kelly loves him."

Mary scowled. "Damn kids. That little bit of lock magic wore me out. Not to mention popping that box of condoms from the convenience store to her bedroom. Remind me to drop some money by for that."

Serena grinned and got to her feet. "I know what we need." She dug out a bottle of champagne she'd been saving for Christmas dinner. She knew were Mary kept the glasses and brought some to the table. She popped the cork, let the foam gush, and laughed.

"Here's to us," she said, pouring the champagne into glasses. "The smartest women in Makeview."

"They're gonna *yell* at us," Mary said, grinning. Serena sat down, and they clinked glasses.

"You bet," Serena said, and they drank.

Chapter Five

Kelly woke Christmas morning feeling both sore and relaxed. For a few minutes, she couldn't decide why she felt so warm and happy, then she remembered Trey coming to the door, Trey coming inside, Trey *spanking* her.

The night's activities swept through her mind in a rush, and she blushed. She remembered him tying her up with the belt, and her loving it, which made her blush more.

The only problem now was, both Trey and the belt were gone.

Kelly sat up straight, her hair crackling as it came off the quilt. Trey's clothes were gone, and he was nowhere in sight.

A cold feeling formed in the pit of her stomach. He wouldn't leave without a word, would he? Without a goodbye, without a kiss, without even a *Merry Christmas*?

Then again, maybe he would. Kelly scrambled up from the bed, grabbed her discarded orange sweats and put them on. There was no sign of Trey in the upstairs hall, in the guestroom, or in the bathroom, although the wet shower curtain and a towel on the counter told her he'd been there.

When she was halfway down the stairs, she realized that the smell of brewing coffee permeated the house. She relaxed, holding onto the banisters. When John had lived here with her, he'd always gotten up early and made the coffee. She'd gotten so used to the smell she hadn't noticed it.

Then again, Trey could have started the coffeemaker for her and departed. But why would he?

"Trey?" she called softly.

"Down here."

She nearly collapsed in relief. Last night, when he'd looked down at her and said, *I love you,* her whole world had spun around. She hadn't been able to say anything back around the lump in her throat.

She stepped off the stairs and glided into the living room, then stopped, her heart thumping.

Trey was under the tree. He'd stripped off again—or maybe he'd never gotten dressed. He had wrapping paper around his middle, his cowboy boots on, and his hat on his head, pushed back so he could see her.

"Mornin'," he said.

Kelly touched her fingers to her lips. He looked delectable with his tanned and muscular chest, his legs tight and bare and laced with wiry black hair. The paper pulled away a little at his right hip, revealing the curve of a pale buttock pressed into the carpet.

And here she was, once more in her bright orange sweats with her hair a complete mess.

"Oh," she said, her heart beating faster. "I didn't get you anything."

"Yes you did." He nodded, his hat slipping. "You sure did, sweetheart. I loved every minute of it."

She flushed, remembering how she'd eagerly taken off her clothes for him and let him squirt whipped cream all over her in the kitchen.

He gave her a slow smile, telling her he remembered that and possibly wanted to do it some more. "So," he said, his Texas drawl slow. "Are ya'll gonna unwrap me?"

Kelly bit her lip, then dashed to him, slammed to her knees under the tree, and tore the paper off the best Christmas present she ever had.

He was naked underneath, his cock standing up, all satiny and warm, the tip moist. Kelly thrust off her ugly sweats, vowing never to wear them again. She took his cock in her hand, loving the smooth feel of it, loving how the bead of moisture on the tip moved slick under her thumb.

She leaned down and licked him, inhaling his smell, sucking the cock into her mouth. He moved, hips rising, and she saw his hands ball to fists on the carpet.

"Kelly, fuck me," he said softly. "Ride me."

Kelly ignored him a few minutes, driving him crazy licking him and running her fingers lightly up and down his shaft. Then she slanted him a smile, straddled him on the floor, and lowered herself down on top of him.

He closed his eyes, his head dropping back. His cock went all the way up inside her, straight and tall, like a flagpole. She moved her hips, gripping the base of the cock with the folds of her pussy.

Then, slowly at first, she began to rock back and forth on him.

Someone had once told her that to sit the canter on a horse, a woman should think of how she moved when she was on top of a man. The same thing worked in reverse. The little scoop movement she made when letting her horse lope across the dry valleys worked wonders on Trey.

He clenched his teeth and his fists, and moved his hips in time with hers. "Hot damn," he groaned.

He went up and in, grinding over and over, Kelly's pussy widening and so slick that he almost slid out. She sat down harder. He gripped her hands and they rode together, scooping and pumping.

And then he came, squirting high up into her.

Kelly moaned her own release, climaxing hard and fast.

A moment later, the doorbell rang.

Kelly jumped about a foot. Trey grabbed her, and slowly eased her off his cock.

"It's probably your aunt, come to gloat," Trey said. "You get the door, I'll dress in the kitchen."

Kelly pulled on the hated sweats again, then stopped to watch Trey walk in nothing but his boots and cowboy hat toward the kitchen. His ass was nice, tight and small and beckoning her tongue. She watched in a daze, until he disappeared.

Whoever it was pushed hard on the bell again.

She opened the door easily, like it had never been hexed shut. But it wasn't Aunt Serena or Trey's grandmother on the doorstep, it was John Hatton.

"Kelly," he said.

John looked slim and shaved and neat, his black hair combed and slick as always, even though it was eight o'clock on Christmas morning.

Kelly stared, her heart thumping with anger, happiness and hard, hot sex. "John," she said, not knowing whether to laugh or scream. "To what do I owe this pleasure?"

He spoke evenly, as though he'd rehearsed a speech. "You know, I thought about it, and I felt bad about leaving you alone on Christmas. So I thought, 'I should go see Kelly. It's not fair to make her lonely on this day of all days'."

Kelly leaned against the doorframe, arms folded. She felt herself smiling. *What a jerk.*

She wondered what would have happened if Trey hadn't popped up last night, carrying an armload of gifts, looking sexy as hell and giving her the best Christmas Eve of her life. Would Kelly now be desperately dragging John inside to stave off the Christmas blues?

Maybe. Or maybe she'd have shown him the door, like she was going to do now. He'd cheated on her; why should she do him any favors?

"Why do you assume I'm lonely?" she asked.

John looked surprised. "Well, I know you have your aunt. But you said your mother wasn't coming down this year, and I thought…"

Her smile widened. "You thought I'd be dying for you. You thought you'd come over here and get an easy lay."

"Kelly," John said, shocked. He looked behind her. "Can I come in? It's freezing out here."

Trey had said the same thing last night, but Kelly's answer was different. "No."

"Thanks…wait, what did you say?"

"I said no." Kelly idly traced the doorframe. "I'm busy. I have to make the biscuits for my aunt's Christmas dinner."

"Just for a little while. I—"

John broke off with a gulp, and his face turned a strange shade of green. Kelly didn't have to turn around to know what he looked at. She heard Trey's boots on the board floor and then felt his warm presence behind her.

"Hey," Trey said in his friendly voice.

"John, did you ever meet Trey Kincaid?"

John didn't say one way or the other, but his brows slammed down. "Were you sleeping with him?" he demanded of Kelly. He switched his gaze to Trey. "She's my *fiancée.*"

"Ex-fiancée," Kelly corrected him.

Trey slid his arm around Kelly. "I heard the story, how you had yourself a girlfriend, then got mad at Kelly when she found out. Her aunt told me. I should punch your lights out for that."

John looked him up and down, Trey all hard muscle and cowboy strength. John took a step back, but sneered, "So you caught her on the rebound and slept with her."

Trey gathered Kelly close. "Let's just say we took the opportunity to tell each other how we felt. Congratulate us. We're getting married."

* * * * *

Kelly was quiet after her ex-fiancé left in a huff. Trey walked past her where she stood in the middle of the living room, in her cute orange sweats that he was not going to let her throw away, and went over to the computer he'd booted up before he'd made the coffee.

She looked stunned. Well, sure, he was stunned too. Not stunned that he wanted to marry her, but stunned that he'd waited this long to ask her. He planned to ream out his grandmother and her aunt for playing a dirty trick on them, but he had to admit the result was worth it.

If he could get Kelly to say yes.

"I uploaded those photos we took last night," he said. He sat down at the computer desk and brought up the program.

Kelly walked to him very slowly. When she stopped beside him, he wrapped his arm around her hip, liking how she smelled. He clicked to start the slide show.

"Oh my God," Kelly breathed.

First were pictures of him lying on the stairs, his jeans around his hips, his cock stiff and hungry for her.

Kelly gazed in rapture at the pictures as they flashed up, one by one, first of him and his cock, then him lying facedown, his ass bare, him looking over his shoulder at her. She snaked her hand down to rest on his, her body relaxing and warming.

Next were the pics of him on the floor under the tree, with the paper around his middle ripped to show his cock with the bow on it. She made a little noise in her throat and reached toward the screen.

His arm tightened around her, and he kissed her hipbone. She liked him, that was for sure.

And then came the pictures he'd snapped of Kelly taking his cock. There were many of those, some blurry, but there she was, gazing at him in rapt concentration, her red lips against his cock.

He'd snapped pictures of her nuzzling his cock, licking it, nibbling it, tasting it, her red hair tangling around the black hair at his balls. He'd taken a picture of her ass up in the air as she leaned over him—a pretty, sweet ass covered in a red knit dress.

And then there was the picture snapped just as he'd come, his hips leaving the carpet and his cock hard in Kelly's mouth.

The slide show came to an end, and the screen returned to the photo software's innocuous menu.

"Wow," Kelly said.

"You know," Trey answered wrapping his other arm around her, and nuzzling her hip. "I never liked porn. Too impersonal. But dirty pictures of you and me, on the other hand..." He guided her fingers to the hard thing in his pants, his balls lifting and tightening. "It gets me going."

Kelly ran her hand along his length inside his jeans, pressing just enough to make his whole cock tingle. She said softly, "If you uploaded the pictures, that means we can use the card again."

His heart beat faster, wondering what she had in mind. "Yep."

"I want more pictures, then. Of you, just like you were under the tree when I came down this morning."

He pretended to consider. "All right, you talked me into it."

He got off the chair, ready to throw off his clothes, but her hand on his arm stopped him. "Trey."

"Yeah, baby?"

Her serious look made him nervous. Was this the speech, then? *We'll have this pleasure today, enjoy our Christmas, then it's back to our own lives.*

She looked up at him, her red lips parted. "Why did you tell John we were getting married?"

Trey stopped. "I didn't like what he did to you. I wanted to rub his face in something, so I told him I was going to marry you." He smoothed a lock of hair from her face, liking her hair messy with lovemaking. "We really can, you know. Make it true."

Her eyes widened, just like they had last night when he'd told her he loved her. "You want to marry me?"

"Sure do."

"Why?"

He cupped her shoulders, pulling her body the length of his. "Because I love you, Kelly. I always have. I was just too shy to say it, and then life split us apart. But I have the chance now, so I'm saying it. I love you, and I want us to be married."

"Oh."

He swallowed, his pulse quickening. "You about to break my heart? If you are, will you wait until after you take the pictures? Or else I'll be crying and look really stupid."

Kelly grabbed him, her fingers sinking into his biceps. "Break your heart? You're an idiot, Trey. I love you." She shook her head, red hair flying. "I want to marry you, and fuck you, and have you show me how to take you in my ass, like you said last night. I want to suck you off and have you spank me and tie me up with your belt. I want you to take pictures of my bare ass that's all red where you've strapped me, and I want you to take pictures of me tied up and waiting for you. I want all that."

"Sounds good." His heart slammed in his chest, his cock dancing as it rejoiced that his girl liked it hot and nasty. "Which one first?"

She let him go and snatched up the camera where he'd left it on the desk. "First, I want your naked ass under my Christmas tree. I want you wrapped up like a Christmas gift—my Christmas cowboy."

"You got it, babe." His eyes were wet with happiness. *You're crying, you big sap.*

But he didn't care. It was Christmas, he was in love, and the girl he'd wanted all his life just said she'd marry him. And that she wanted him to fuck her and tie her up and spank her…

Trey kissed her hard, savoring it, then he stepped back and pulled off his sweatshirt.

He sauntered back to the tree, knowing that she was watching his ass in his tight jeans. Then, for about the fifth time since he'd walked in last night, he pulled down his pants.

Kelly waited, still in the sweats, one hip canted, while he kicked out of the jeans and arranged the paper around his huge, stiff, naked cock.

He picked up his Stetson from where he'd dropped it earlier, and planted it on his head.

"Ready, ma'am," he drawled.

"Good." Kelly raised the camera. He saw the damp patch on her sweats where her cream was already flowing hot and heavy for him.

His cock danced. This was sure going to be a great Christmas.

"Say cheese," Kelly said, and snapped the first picture.

Also by Allyson James

Double Trouble

Ellora's Cavemen: Dreams of the Oasis I *(anthology)*

Tales of the Shareem: Maia and Rylan

Tales of the Shareem: Rees

Tales of the Shareem: Rio

About the Author

Allyson James is yet one more name for a woman who has racked up four pseudonyms in the first two years of her career. She often cannot remember what her real name is and has to be tapped on the shoulder when spoken to.

Allyson began writing at age eight (a five-page story that actually contained goal, motivation, and conflict). She learned the trick of standing her math book up on her desk so she could write stories behind it. She wrote love stories before she knew what romances were, dreaming of the day when her books would appear at libraries and bookstores. At age thirty, she decided to stop dreaming and do it for real. She published the first short story she ever submitted in a national print magazine, which gave her the false illusion that getting published was easy.

After a long struggle and inevitable rejections, she at last sold a romance novel, then, to her surprise, sold several mystery novels, more romances, and then Romantica™ to Ellora's Cave. She has been nominated for two Romantic Times Reviewer's Choice awards and has had starred reviews in *Booklist* and Top Pick reviews in *Romantic Times*.

Allyson met her soulmate in fencing class (the kind with swords, not posts-and-rails). She looked down the length of his long, throbbing rapier and fell madly in love.

Allyson welcomes comments from readers. You can find her website and email address on her author bio page at www.ellorascave.com.

SANTA'S LAP

By Lani Aames

Chapter One

"Is that a candy cane in your pocket or are you just happy to see me?" Tasha Elliot whispered in Santa's ear, wiggling her butt over the hard bulge in the front of his red velvet suit. She had hitched up her skirt and straddled his lap, facing him, but couldn't see much of his face around the curly white beard and froth of white fur trimming the Santa cap.

She planned to teach her best bud Rob Sinclair a thing or two about teasing her. Just because she was in between boyfriends as well as jobs was no reason to send her an invitation requesting her to sit on Santa's lap and tell him all about how naughty she'd been this year—after the store had closed and everyone else had gone home.

The expensive note card had been signed with a large scrawled letter "R". Who else but Rob? He'd filled in as Santa because the man who usually wore the suit had called in sick that morning.

The long hard object expanded beneath her rump, confirming that it wasn't a candy cane at all. The size of his cock impressed her but she considered it TMI—too much information—about her friend.

What the hell did Rob think he was doing? He knew she had never considered him in that way, and she would have sworn he'd never thought of her like that either. They'd known each other forever, but there'd never been a hint of anything other than friendship between them. He also knew she'd had the hots for his older brother Reed for as long as she'd known what "the hots" were.

If Rob had no problem continuing the game, she might as well play along too. He'd be the one to end up with a raging case of blue balls, not her, because she had no desire whatsoever to sleep with Rob Sinclair. She pushed the fake whiskers aside and licked the curve of Santa's ear—a couple of wet, sloppy swipes—then she breathed heavily.

He shuddered and his cock jumped. It felt like it had grown another two inches in length *and* diameter. That had to be the imaginative product of her overactive libido, of course, because it had been months since she'd last slept with anyone. Santa's cock hadn't really enlarged quite that much, but it still felt bigger than any she'd ever had before.

If Rob was built like a horse, couldn't Reed be even bigger? The brothers looked enough alike that they could pass for twins to someone who didn't know them well. Both were tall and well-built with deep brown hair. There were differences, of course. Reed's eyes were blue while Rob's were brown. Reed was a little taller and a little broader, and the Sinclair cut-granite features of his face wore the five years he had on his brother in rugged experience and maturity.

She knew the breadth of the man didn't have a thing to do with the dimensions of his cock. Wasn't it the size of his feet or hands? Reed had large hands and huge feet. A little moan escaped her lips. Blowing more air into Santa's ear, she fantasized about the scope of Reed's cock.

Santa's hand, enclosed in a red velvet mitt with white fur trim, glided up her leg, under her mid-calf skirt. A little curl of heat started in the pit of her belly and spread deliciously. It had to be a joke, but how far would he go? Oh, Rob was going to pay dearly for this.

Reed had been away the past three years, managing an upscale department store in the city. When he came back home to manage Sinclair's after the death of their uncle had left the store to the two brothers, Tasha knew it was her chance. After being downsized from her last job, she had begged Rob—who just happened to be the personnel manager—to hire her during the Christmas rush.

The soft velvet mitt slid up her thigh and her clit started to throb. She wanted to spread her legs wider and squirm on that candy cane of a cock, but she couldn't let Santa know how much she was affected.

Tasha needed the job to get her through until she started her new position as manager of a health food store opening in mid-January. Even though she invariably bought a lottery ticket twice a week, the state lottery that had just started last spring hadn't made her a millionaire yet. She also wanted Rob to give her a job so she could be close to Reed.

She should stop this right now, but everything felt too wonderful…the hard cock prodding her butt and the velvet mitt exploring her leg. Santa knew how to use that cane, and that mitt.

Rob had hesitated about hiring her because they'd already taken on all the extra employees they needed for the season. But after thinking about it, he'd agreed—if she'd help him in return. Expensive items had been disappearing at an escalating rate since Thanksgiving.

After questioning all the employees, they'd received no leads. Even with surveillance cameras turned on day and night, they'd been unable to catch anyone in the act. Although they had a security guard making regular rounds during the hours when the store was closed, nothing had been seen.

Santa's mitt brushed farther up her thigh and another moan sounded deep in her throat. She needed to stop this. Now. Right now. But the velvet felt so good against her skin she forgot to tell him to stop.

She didn't mind playing detective if it placed her close to Reed. She had agreed to keep her eyes and ears open and let Rob know if she saw or heard anything suspicious from the other employees. Rob had even consented to look the other way when she flirted with Reed, though it was against store policy for employees and management to fraternize.

Tasha didn't want to fraternize with Reed, she wanted to fuck him. Fast and hard. Slow and deep. Any which way he wanted and she could imagine. Thoughts of doing the nasty with Reed set her body on fire. After this little tease with Santa, she'd have to go home and break out the toys she hadn't touched in weeks—after picking up a jumbo pack of batteries on her way out.

So Tasha had agreed, but Rob had stashed her back in Auto Maintenance, the least busy department during the Christmas season except for de-icer, snow scrapers and antifreeze. But Tasha didn't care. Being in the store every day put her in close proximity to the elder Sinclair brother.

And it worked! She'd come into daily contact with Reed the past few weeks. She sat with him at lunch in the break room nearly every day. He'd come to her department to help shelve stock with her the few times they'd been shorthanded. She was impressed that he'd get down and dirty, with a smile on his face.

She'd like to get down and dirty with him in another way, and the resulting perma-grin would *never* leave his face.

She and Reed had talked and laughed, but he'd never asked her out. She didn't have the nerve to ask him because if he turned her down, her heart would simply break in two.

When Santa's other mitt covered her breast, his thumb and forefinger easily finding the hard, sensitive peak through the layers of red velvet, her knit sweater and lacey bra. It was time to bring the game to an end.

She knew Rob hadn't had a date in a while either. Just the day before they'd exchanged horror stories about how long it had been, each trying to outdo the other with increasingly worse scenarios. Did he think because they were both desperate they could become fuck buddies? No way! She could never screw Rob just to get her rocks off then sleep with Reed if the chance arose. She just couldn't!

Maybe it was time to call his bluff and watch him backpedal. She rocked against his cock, giving him—and her—a last little thrill, then twirled one finger in the luxurious white beard.

"Tasha's been a very naughty girl this year, Santa." She kept her voice low and breathy which wasn't hard to do because she was already turned on. "She couldn't help herself. Being naughty is a lot more fun than being nice. Don't you think?"

Santa nodded as she twirled her finger deeper into the beard.

"Can you think of some way to punish Tasha for being such a naughty girl?"

When Santa nodded again, he pinched her nipple. Hard. Pain mixed with pleasure shot through her. She winced, but the sensation wasn't unpleasant at all. Then his hands slid down and grasped her hips.

Apparently, Rob wasn't going to call an end to it. She pushed the cap off his forehead and looked into baby blue eyes. She grabbed a fistful of beard to yank it down and—

Tasha froze. *Baby blues.* Rob had brown eyes. *Reed* had blue eyes. She jerked down the beard and looked into the handsome, chiseled face of Reed Sinclair.

Snapping her hips forward so that her thighs spread wider, he ground his candy cane against her pussy, and Tasha thought she would die. From embarrassment or pleasure, she didn't know. Heat flushed her cheeks, but it could very well have been from the sensations flooding her body as the underside of Reed's cock rubbed her pussy.

Reed. She'd said and done all those silly things to Reed!

His mouth covered hers, and it was all she'd ever dreamed about and more. His tongue probed between one set of her lips while his cock prodded the other. Her hips began a rhythmic undulation, stroking her clit against his cock. It had been so long since she'd even bothered to self-pleasure that her body had gone into some kind of dormant state.

What a way to wake it up!

She slid her arms around Reed's neck and her tongue clashed with his. She was so close to orgasm, her pelvis moved on its own and she could barely breathe. One of his hands moved from her hip and slid under her sweater and bra. He'd removed the mitt and his warm fingers and thumb found the hard pebble of her nipple.

When he squeezed, she exploded, her back arching as icy fire rocketed along every nerve. Her hips moved in a frenzy, rubbing her clit against him to make the pleasure last as long as possible. When the last of it moved through her, her body relaxed against his, her pussy resting on his still stiff cock.

"Oh, Reed," she whispered and buried her face where his neck met his brawny shoulder.

He removed his hand from her hip and stroked her hair while his other gently tweaked her nipple, keeping it hard and sensitive. His cock rubbed her pussy in a slow rhythm. Small currents flowed through her, stoking the heat within. If he continued to play with her breast and tease her clit with his cock, she could easily come again.

"Santa knows what Tasha wants for Christmas," he murmured, his voice thick and husky.

"More of that would be nice." She raised her head, making sure she didn't pull her breast away from his hand or her clit from his cock.

"I think that would be considered naughty as well as nice."

Tasha laughed, slipping her hand between their bodies until she found the hard length of his cock. "How did I ever mistake that for a candy cane? I've never held one that big."

Reed groaned as she massaged up and down his erection. "Do you mean candy cane or cock?"

"Both."

She unzipped Santa's trousers and then undid Reed's slacks. His cock popped free, tall and straight and hard as the sweet treat she'd compared him to. She ran her fingers over the hot, velvety skin, thick with veins. The engorged head seeped clear lubricant.

"Hmm. Sinclair's carries candy canes this big." He drove his cock hard through her caressing fingers. "And the Sinclair men are equally well equipped."

"All of them?"

"So I've been told. We don't measure them and keep a record, if that's what you're wondering."

They both laughed, and Tasha quickened her strokes on his cock. "I think you're getting delirious."

"Maybe. Damn, Tasha, you're driving me crazy."

She put both hands on him, but he stopped her.

"I have a better idea if you're willing."

"I'm listening."

"There's the display in Bed and Bath. We could put the bed to good use."

"Here? Now?"

"Sure. The store is closed, and I've had this fantasy of fucking you in every department in the store." His dark brows knitted together. "But if you'd rather not, we can finish this at my place. Or yours. Whatever you want, Tasha. It's *your* Christmas wish Santa wants to fulfill."

She placed her hands on his tall erection again, amazed that it took both hands to wrap around it completely. "Your cock will be very fulfilling, and I'm too impatient to go somewhere else. Besides, we might as well take care of both our fantasies while we're at it."

He pushed her sweater and bra up farther and leaned forward. His mouth sealed over a nipple, his tongue raking the hard point. Tasha let her head fall back and moved her hips until she could press his cock against the soaked panties that covered her clit. She trembled as the heat built up again.

He moved to her other nipple and gave it the same attention. When she didn't think she could take much more, he pulled free. His hands still held up her sweater and he thumbed both damp nipples.

"Let me get you something from lingerie. Then you can change and we'll meet at the display bed in Bed and Bath. We've got all night, Tasha, and we'll make it a night to remember. I want to fuck you over and over again."

"Oh, yes, sounds like a plan," she whispered.

Reed pinched both nipples, and she squirmed from the pleasure darting through her.

"Santa wants to see just how naughty Tasha can be."

Chapter Two

In the lady's room, Tasha washed up at the sink. She scrubbed her face clean and put on fresh makeup. She stripped off all her clothes and used a handful of wet paper towels to spot bathe, then spritzed with a small bottle of body spray she kept in her purse. Looking at the nightie, panties and robe in a lovely shade of lavender, she approved of Reed's choice in lingerie.

She picked up the panties that would cover only a little more than a thong. She was glad she'd gone to the trouble of shaving her legs that morning. She pulled on the panties. The thin straps hugged her hipbones, and the triangle of material barely covered her patch of dark curls.

She dropped the nightie over her head and adjusted her breasts in the cups. Her erect nipples poked the silk, and she rubbed them experimentally. Closing her eyes, she imagined it was Reed's hands on her.

Her pussy grew wet, dampening the panties, and one of her hands automatically caressed between her thighs.

Quivering, she opened her eyes. Why was she standing here fondling herself when Reed waited for her and wanted to do the fondling? She didn't have to imagine or daydream any longer. Tasha smiled in the mirror over the sink. She'd received the best Christmas present ever—Reed.

Putting on the matching robe, Tasha stepped into the slippers. She tied the belt in a pluckable knot and took a last glance at her reflection. She smoothed a few strands of her short auburn hair that had ruffled from changing clothes then left the restroom.

When she reached Bed and Bath, Reed was now dressed in midnight blue silk pajama bottoms and loosely tied robe. He stood beside an intimately small, linen-covered table she recognized from Kitchen and Appliances decorated with an array of tapers, pillars, and votives from Candles and Scents. Dishes and utensils pilfered from Housewares were stacked amid boxes and tins from Gourmet Foods. A bottle protruded from a bucket, also from Housewares, filled with ice probably taken from the break room.

She spied one large candy cane. This one was straight, but it was about a foot long and maybe an inch and a half in diameter. Her eyes widened and she wondered what Reed had planned for that stick of candy. Then she noticed a box of chocolate-covered cherries and knew exactly what she could do with them later.

The puffy comforter on the display bed was turned down on one side. A radio from Electronics sat on one bedside table, and a slow romantic instrumental played softly.

"Oh, wow. Was I gone that long?"

Reed grinned and began lighting the candles with an electronic lighter. "I work fast when I'm motivated. Since we don't carry alcoholic beverages, I brought sparkling white grape juice and club soda. Are you hungry?"

He meant food, but all she really had an appetite for was Reed. She sighed and nodded to please him because he'd gone to the trouble of setting it all up. All she wanted to do was jump his bones. She wanted Reed's cock inside of her, and the thought made her burn with desire.

He poured the sparkling juice as she sat in one of the chairs. His robe was open and the front of his pajama bottoms bulged suggestively. He still had his hard-on. Of course, anticipation was as much fun as actual fucking, but for some reason she wanted to bypass all the foreplay and get to the main event.

She took a glass and sipped a bit of the juice. It bubbled in her mouth like champagne.

"All of this is impromptu. I'd hoped you would, but I didn't expect you to take the invitation to sit in Santa's lap literally."

Tasha nearly choked on the juice. If he only knew *why* she'd taken the invitation literally, he'd probably throw her out on her ear. How embarrassing if he ever found out she'd thought his brother was under all that red velvet and white fur, and she'd sat in his lap to teach him a lesson. She wondered what she would have done if she'd known it was Reed? Would she have still sat in his lap and teased him mercilessly?

She didn't think so. She had always been too self-conscious around Reed. Perhaps it was best she hadn't known. They wouldn't be here now, on the verge of jumping into bed and doing the horizontal tango.

He opened crackers and a vacuum-sealed package of soft cheese. She spread the cheese on a cracker and took a bite, washing it down with a swallow of juice.

"I see you brought one of the Sinclair candy canes."

He picked it up. "You said you'd never seen one this large."

"I guess I'd never noticed them before. Now it takes on a whole new meaning."

"Yes, it does." His blue eyes had darkened, and his cock bounced a little behind the midnight blue silk.

She set down the remainder of the cheese and cracker and glass of juice. She didn't want food. She wanted Reed. She reached out and placed her hand on that bulge. The silk radiated his heat and almost burned her hand. Reed set his glass aside and caught her hand, pulling her to her feet.

He kissed her, his lips sliding over hers as their bodies picked up the rhythm of the music playing on the radio. Silk glided over silk, their bodies rubbing together. They swayed until he simply scooped her up and carried her to the bed.

Reed still had the foot-long candy cane in his hand and tossed it on the bed. Tasha sat up and pulled off her robe while he shed his robe and pajama bottoms. He had to stretch the waistband out over his jutting erection. She had started to remove her nightie but was mesmerized by the size and rigidity of his cock.

Reed got on the bed on his knees, straddling Tasha's outstretched legs. She wrapped her hands around his hot length and massaged from the bulging tip to where it nestled in a bed of coarse curls. He placed his hands on her back and gathered the nightie, drawing it over her head. Tasha released him long enough to pull her arms through the straps then replaced one hand on his cock. She teased his balls with her other hand.

The nightie dropped into a puddle of silk on the bed. His back arched, and he groaned, a guttural sound that came from deep inside his chest. Tasha's fingers played over his sac, and his hips pushed his cock in and out of her other hand until he finally put his hands on her shoulders and pulled free of her touch.

He blew out a deep breath. "Better hold it, Tasha."

He was ready, and she had been ready for some time. She lay back and hooked her fingers in the straps of her panties. But, again, Reed stopped her.

"I want to do that," he said and bent over her.

Tasha stretched her arms over her head and closed her eyes. He grasped her panties by the straps and slid them over her hips. The triangle of silk peeled away from her wetness. He spread her bent legs as far as they would go and touched her gently around her labia. She gasped, her hips raising her pussy into his caress.

His fingers swirled over the folds and creases, dipping in and out again, teasing her. Her clit burned and tingled, and when he touched it, warmth spiraled out. Her body squirmed restlessly, ready for the burst of pleasure that was soon to come.

She heard the crinkle of plastic and her eyes barely opened to see Reed with a condom pack between his teeth. He ripped it open in one yank and pulled out the rolled-up rubber. She closed her eyes again. They hadn't discussed taking precautions. She was on the patch and disease free. But she was happy he had the forethought to grab condoms while setting up for their romantic interlude.

She expected him to crawl between her legs any second and drive into her with a force that would send her skyrocketing into orbit. Instead, she felt the bed shift and his fingers on her pussy again. He spread open her lips and something big and hard entered her.

She opened her eyes and raised her head. He grinned up at her. "It doesn't hurt, does it?"

She shook her head. "What are you doing?

She rose to a sitting position and saw he had put a condom on the stick of candy and was inserting it inside her.

"Oh, wow."

"Have you ever been fucked with a candy cane before?"

She shook her head.

"How does it feel?" He pushed it in a little farther.

"Good." She lay back again and closed her eyes to enjoy the ride.

By tilting her pelvis, she guided him as he inched the cane in farther and farther. When she was filled completely, Reed fucked her with the candy cane, moving it in and out, and his thumb stimulated her clit. Her hips met the rhythm and moved faster as she neared orgasm. Whimpers and moans escaped her lips, and her hands clenched the sheets. When the pleasure burst and washed over her, she cried out and ground her clit against the pad of his thumb.

As she spiraled down and her body relaxed, Reed eased the candy cane free. His fingers caressed her pussy, sending little tingles and shocks throughout her body. Now he crawled between her legs, propping on his elbows on each side of her.

She looked up at him lazily. Her body was drained of energy. He smiled and kissed her.

"That felt wonderful," she murmured.

He moved down a little and kissed the taut tip of one breast then the other. He shifted to one elbow and his free hand surrounded her breast as his lips suckled, his tongue raking the hard peak.

After coming twice, Tasha didn't think she would react, but his lips and tongue stirred her again. He kissed a trail from her breasts, over her ribs and belly to where her curls began. A line of fire followed behind. Then he straightened up.

Tasha sat up and put her hands on his rigid cock. "My turn. Now, lie down."

He did as he was told as she scooted off the bed. She found what she wanted from the table and crawled back on the bed, between his legs. She opened the box of chocolate-covered cherries and picked one out.

He had folded his arms behind his head and watched her intently. Tasha took a bite out of the confection and savored it, licking the drop of liquid that dripped over the open edge. Then she stretched out on her belly between his thighs. She wrapped one hand around his cock and held the piece of candy over it with the other.

Slowly, she tilted it until the thick, gooey liquid drizzled over the head. When the last drop streamed out, she popped the rest of it into her mouth and started massaging him, spreading the liquid all over his hard length.

Reed groaned, pumping his cock into her hands. His movements were short and hard and she knew he was nearing his release. She pressed her thumbs against the underside so when he drew back, they touched the soft, sensitive spot just under the head. Within a few more strokes, his body stiffened and he exploded. He grunted, the sound coming from the back of his throat as semen jetted into the air, sprinkling his belly and her hands. She milked his cock with slow rubs until no more white fluid seeped from his slit.

Tasha watched his body relax. She had pleased him as well as he'd pleased her. He lay with his eyes closed, his breathing becoming more even. She left the bed and went to the table. She dampened a cloth napkin with the club soda and washed off the sticky candy goo and Reed's semen from her hands. She poured on more club soda and returned to the bed, carefully cleaning the stickiness from him. When she finished, she crawled up beside him, and he gathered in her in his arms. She snuggled close to him.

"Where'd you pick up that trick?"

She shrugged. "It just came to me when I saw the box of chocolate-covered cherries."

"I'll never be able to look at chocolate-covered cherries the same way again."

Tasha laughed. "I feel the same way about candy canes."

She closed her eyes and felt herself drifting into sleep. Her last thought was that they'd pleasured each other, but they still hadn't actually fucked.

Chapter Three

Someone shaking her, gently but firmly, woke Tasha. She didn't want to leave the wonderful dream where Reed had dressed in a red velvet Santa suit and fucked her till her eyes crossed. She didn't want the fantasy to end, so she pushed the insistent hand aside and muttered, "Go away."

"Tasha, it's Reed." The hand jiggled her shoulder again. "You have to get up now. I just thought of something."

Reed... It hadn't been a dream! Tasha blinked her eyes open and turned over to look up into Reed's devastatingly handsome face. His dark hair was tousled, and he looked like he'd just had a good fucking. Which was sort of what had happened before she'd fallen asleep. He looked like he needed it again, and she was more than happy to oblige.

Her hand stole under the comforter toward Reed. When her fingers met his cock, she seized the moment. "I just thought of something too," she murmured and proceeded to massage the part of Reed that grew longer and harder the more she rubbed.

He groaned but put his hand under the comforter to stop her. "I was thinking of that, but I meant there's something else we need to consider."

Tasha maneuvered her hand past his, and she continued what she'd been doing when he interrupted her. "What could possibly be more important than *this*?"

"That." Reed pointed.

Tasha's gaze followed the line of his finger up to where the nearest wall met the ceiling. Next to a dimly lit light fixture a camera, small red light aglow, stared back down at them. Tasha snatched her hand away from Reed's cock and pulled the comforter—suddenly not much of a comfort at all—over her bare breasts. "Uh-oh."

"Uh-oh is right. Stu's had an eyeful tonight."

Tasha cringed. Stu Denison, the security guard, was in his fifties and had worked in security for decades. She had heard him remark that he could afford to retire, but he continued working because he couldn't imagine *not* working the rest of his life.

Reed slipped out of bed and pulled on his slacks and shirt. "I'd better get in there and try to explain. Damn, I can't believe I didn't think about the cameras—and Stu—before this. I'll have to erase tonight's recording, too."

"I'll go with you." Tasha couldn't imagine waiting in front of the camera for Reed to return, knowing that Stu might still be watching. She started to get up but glanced at the camera. "Will you throw me the robe?"

Reed handed her the silk robe, and she managed to wriggle into it while under the comforter. She stepped into the slippers as she got out of bed. Thankfully the robe reached her knees and covered everything adequately.

Reed grasped her by the arm and pulled her up close. "I should have remembered the cameras and Stu, but you drive me crazy, Tasha, and make me forget everything when I'm with you."

"Me too," she murmured.

Reed leaned in close to her ear. "We can play the recording and watch ourselves."

Heat rose in her cheeks, but she was curious. How would it feel to watch all the things they'd done that evening? It surprised her just how much thinking about it turned her on.

"How about it?" he asked, his hand slipping between their bodies and caressing her breast. Fortunately, her back was to the camera and blocked his actions.

Tasha nodded. "Sounds like fun."

"Hmmm, the thought of watching me fucking you with a candy cane while fucking you is exciting."

"What about Stu?"

"He can watch too, if he likes."

Tasha gasped. "Reed!"

He laughed. "I'm joking. I'll send him on an extended break."

"That sounds better."

They walked hand-in-hand through the dimly lit store to where the offices were located. Tasha stayed out of sight, clutching the edges of the silk robe together, while Reed opened the door to the security office.

"Mr. Sinclair!" She recognized Stu's voice. He sounded truly surprised to see Reed. "I didn't know you'd stayed late tonight."

She saw Reed smile. "I told you to call me Reed."

"Yes, sir."

Stu was the type to stand on formality with his superiors no matter how much older he was. He would never call Reed by his first name.

But she couldn't understand why Stu was surprised to see him. Reed and she had fucked and played in front of several cameras. No way could he have missed seeing their wanton behavior unless he'd dozed off or just wasn't paying attention to the monitor like he was supposed to. Tasha couldn't imagine conscientious Stu doing either.

Reed glanced at her and shrugged minutely. The same thought must have run through his mind. "I'd like to take a look at tonight's recordings. You can take a long break, if you don't mind. I'll give you a call when I'm through in here."

"I'm not supposed to leave the office other than to make my rounds, and I take my breaks during rounds. Mr. Greene made it clear I'd be fired if I didn't do exactly as he said."

This time Reed frowned. "I appreciate you taking your duties seriously, but Paul Greene works for me. I think it's all right if you do as I ask. I'll be sure to speak to Paul about it."

Tasha heard the creak of the chair as Stu got up. "You're the boss."

Reed looked at her and motioned for her to come to him. She shook her head. She wasn't ashamed of what they'd done, but it would be simply embarrassing—for her as well as Stu—to face him after what he'd witnessed on the monitors. Stu might well be able to keep a poker face with Reed about what he'd seen, but there'd be no denying it with her in a robe. Reed beckoned her again.

"A friend is with me," he told Stu.

Reed had made it impossible for her to continue hiding. She was going to kill him! Her hand tightened on the silk lapels until her knuckles brushed her throat, and she scurried to Reed's side.

Reed put his arm around her. "Tasha and I were—um, testing some of the merchandise."

Stu's eyes widened and his mouth fell open in absolute shock, but he recovered quickly. His jaw snapped shut, and he blinked until his eyes were normal sized again. There wasn't anything he could do about the red creeping into his face.

"Hi, Stu," Tasha greeted him as if she saw him every day wearing nothing but a robe.

"G-good e-evening, Tasha," he stammered. He edged by them and out the door. "I-I'll make rounds early and be in the break room when you're done. I've got a walkie-talkie with me. The other one is on the desk. Just call me when you're ready for me."

"Thanks, Stu," Reed said, but Stu had already disappeared down the hall.

Tasha punched him in the ribs. "That was embarrassing and humiliating for both of us. Why did you do that?"

Reed rubbed his side. "I'm sorry, Tasha. I didn't plan for Stu to see you at all. When he didn't act like he'd noticed anything unusual on the monitor, I wondered how he'd react to you."

"He didn't see anything, did he?" She frowned. "Do you think he's getting senile? I can't believe he's slacking on the job."

"Me either. I've known Stu Denison most of my life, and I've never seen him try to get by with anything. He's always been hard-working and reliable." Reed glanced at the shelf of recorders and electronics beside the desk. "Something might be wrong with the equipment."

But Reed shut the door instead of giving the equipment a closer inspection. He sat in the chair at the desk that held the computer. Tasha watched the monitor.

Twelve cameras had been placed around the store. Four of them covered the exits, and the other eight were discreetly placed in various departments. The monitor showed a split screen divided into quarters. The four doorways showed for a few seconds, then the screen changed to scenes from four of the departments, then it changed to the last four areas with cameras. The next screen change started the loop over again.

Each screen stayed on long enough to detect movement within the view of the camera but not long enough to study details. Still, Stu should have noticed them making out in Santa's chair and on the bed.

"Come here." Reed caught her wrist and pulled her into his lap. His cock had grown long and hard again, and she could feel its heat through the material of his trousers and the thin silk robe she wore. She squirmed on top of it while Reed spread the lapels of her robe open without untying the belt.

One of his hands went to the back of her neck and the other covered one of her breasts, his thumb and forefinger lightly pinching her already hard nipple. His lips clamped to her other nipple, and his tongue made quick circular strokes around it. Sensation tumbled through her, settling in a rhythmic throb in her clit. She spread her legs and shifted, seeking the head of his cock with her damp pussy.

"Hmm, I never knew sitting in Santa's lap could be so much fun," she murmured as she rubbed against his cock.

Reed humped his pelvis against her, then his lips popped free of her nipple. "You never did tell me how naughty you'd been."

She giggled but it turned into a sigh when he licked her nipple over and over again, intensifying the burn in her clit. "Before tonight I'd only been nice. Now you know exactly how naughty I can be."

"Oh, Tasha, you're nicest when you're naughty."

Reed slid his hands to her waist and set her on her feet. Her back was to him and her legs straddled his. She looked over her shoulder to find him unfastening his slacks. When his beautiful cock sprang free, she reached for it, but he stopped her.

"I thought we were going to watch ourselves," she reminded him.

"Later. Right now, I want your pussy, Tasha," he said in a low, husky voice. "I'm going to fuck you hard. No candy cane this time."

Heat flashed from her clit through her pussy at his words. Her womb clenched, released and clenched again, anticipating the explosion he would detonate within her. He raised her robe to the small of her back, exposing her rear cheeks, and laid his hot hands on them. Branding her with his touch, his fingers kneaded her flesh in deep, deliberate strokes.

He moved lower and spread her labia. "Oh, Tasha, you're so wet and hot. I have to taste you first."

Weakened by his ministrations, Tasha leaned over, resting her arms on the desk, her face only inches from the monitor. She watched the scenes changing one after the other. Something was different…but then he licked her from clit to perineum and back again, and she closed her eyes to enjoy the sensation without being distracted. Her hips undulated, matching his rhythm, and her breathing deepened. Just before Tasha reached paradise, he stopped, and a mournful moan escaped her throat.

"I want to be inside you."

She heard the rip of a condom package, and a few seconds later his hands were at her hips, pulling her back toward him. She lowered with his guidance, and when the tip of his cock touched her she moaned again. He pulled her down quickly until his length was completely inside her. Breath escaped her lips in a rush. The candy cane had been nice, but this was heaven.

Reed rocked the swivel chair, and Tasha bounced to keep up with his pace. Her clit bumped his balls, and she twisted when she hit to increase her pleasure. When the explosion careened through her, her back bowed and she cried out her release.

At the same time, Reed's hands tightened on her hips and his body stiffened. His sounds mingled with hers as their bodies wrung every bit of ecstasy from the other.

When the last tremors dissipated, Tasha collapsed in Reed's lap, leaning back against him. Reed's hands roamed her body, from the tips of her breasts, across her ribs and stomach, to the patch of curls between her thighs. He stroked her skin with a gentle, lover's touch as he slowly rocked the chair back and forth.

Tasha sighed, her lids half-closed, her body completely relaxed. She'd never experienced anything like this night with Reed. There had been several men in her life, but none of them had ever treated her to a night of fantasy.

The security monitor continued to change screens, the tempo almost lulling her to sleep again. The four exits. The first four departments—Jewelry, Bed and Bath, Gourmet Foods and Kitchen and Small Appliances. The next four departments—Toys and Games, Auto Maintenance, Santa's Corner and Women's Lingerie. Back to the exits.

They'd played in Santa's Corner then played in Bed and Bath. Now they'd fucked in the security office. Bed and Bath popped up again. The display bed dominated that quarter of the screen. Fun and games with a candy cane and chocolate-covered cherries. Food could be incredibly sexy and not just by eating it.

The bed showed again, and Tasha bolted upright, staring at the screen.

"Something wrong?" Reed asked, but his hands didn't stop. His fingers delved into her wetness, his thumb brushing her clit and bringing on an aftershock of pleasure that rippled through her. Her hips tilted to rub her clit against his thumb again.

No, she had to concentrate. Something was wrong with the picture on the monitor. The bed. Yes, that was it. They'd left the bed in a mess, but the bed on the screen was still perfectly made up, not even a pillow out of place.

Chapter Four

"Look at the bed." Tasha tapped the monitor screen.

Reed pulled his fingers free and shifted her to the side so he could see the monitor. He watched as the screens cycled through.

"The bed," he murmured. "We didn't clean up before we left and came here to the security office."

"No, we didn't," Tasha agreed. "The bedding should be all jumbled up, the comforter and pillows strewn all over. We should be able to see the table you set up too."

"What the—" Reed didn't finish. He pushed Tasha up as he stood. After examining the equipment, he straightened. A puzzled frown creased his face. "I didn't notice before, but there's a DVD player here, and it shouldn't be. Guess what? It's running."

Tasha shook her head. "I don't get it."

"This system digitally records everything to the hard drive, then it's burned to a DVD and stored short-term. If nothing happens that night, there's really no reason to even view the recording or keep it for any length of time." He pointed to the bottom shelf and the row of jewel cases. "We only store the past two months of disks."

Tasha looked at the equipment, but she still didn't understand. "Why would the thief bring in a player? The computer has that capability, doesn't it?"

"Yes, that's how the DVDs are burned from the hard drive. It has an internal player-recorder. But..." He thought a moment. "Stu knows which computer lights should be on. If he saw the DVD player on the computer lit up, he would report it as a malfunction. He knows very little about the other equipment, and he'd never notice a small external DVD player hidden in the back."

Tasha's eyes widened. "Smart thief."

"Yeah, someone went to a lot of trouble to cover his—or her—tracks." Reed bent over the equipment again, pointing as he talked. "The DVD player is hooked up between the cameras and the monitor. At some point, the DVD player was switched on and overrode the camera feeds. What we're seeing was probably recorded earlier this week."

"You're right." Tasha pointed to the screen. "Santa's Corner is still intact with the tree and the fake snow drift full of merchandise."

Reed tapped in a key sequence. The cycle stopped on the screen with Santa's Corner.

"Most of the display was moved into the big window this afternoon…or yesterday afternoon now since it's well after midnight." He looked at Tasha and grinned. "The chair and a few of the candy cane poles were left so the children who came late yesterday would still get to see Santa."

Tasha smiled back. "I'm sure they appreciated it. I know I appreciated being able to sit in Santa's lap."

"So did Santa." Reed kissed her—a warm, solid kiss—then turned his attention back to the equipment. He moved the coax cables, connecting the computer directly to the cameras again. He sat at the desk and keyed until the screen blinked. This time, the cycle of screens showed the departments exactly as they were. The bed was covered in a disarray of linen and pillows with the table nearby, and most of the Santa display had disappeared.

Tasha chewed her lip. She was losing her heart to this man, but now wasn't the time to revel in the newfound emotion. They had to figure out what was happening. She focused her attention on the monitor.

"So if someone broke into the store, Stu wouldn't know it. He's watching an old recording where nothing happens." She shook her head. "Who would have access to the equipment to be able to do something like that?"

"And the knowledge. Stu has access to the equipment but doesn't have the know-how. Paul and I had to teach him how to operate the computer as well as how to use the system." He let out a rush of air. "Rob and I have both."

"You obviously didn't do it. And Rob wouldn't do it—You're not thinking Rob did it, are you?"

He shook his head emphatically. "No, I certainly don't suspect Rob. I trust him implicitly, and I'm confident he feels the same about me. There are only five years between us. It was just enough for us to avoid any rivalry and hard feelings when we were teenagers, but we're close enough in age to still have things in common and be friends."

"I'm glad. I don't have any brothers or sisters, but I've always thought it's great that you and Rob get along so well. I trust Rob, too. He's been my best friend since grade school. So, who else?"

"Paul Greene, our security consultant. Security was the main source of tension between Uncle Roger and me. He believed in running Sinclair's the old-fashioned way. I could go along with most of it. After all, the store had been run that way since the early seventies when Dad and Uncle Roger established it. But I thought we should upgrade to a modern, state-of-the-art security system."

"And your uncle didn't agree."

"He hated computers. Said they were going to be the end of civilization as we know it. In a way, he was right. Computers have changed everything." Reed sighed and leaned back in the chair. "He thought I was trying to completely take over running the store, but I wasn't. I only wanted what was best for Sinclair's. I thought installing a computerized security system would bring us all peace of mind."

"But he didn't see it that way." Tasha laid her hand on his knee and squeezed. "And Rob agreed with you."

"Yes. We didn't want both of us to alienate Uncle Roger. We agreed that I would push, in case his mind could be changed, and Rob would pretend to go along with him. It was a good thing too. When Uncle Roger and I had that last big argument, he threw me out." Reed propped his elbow on the arm of the chair and rested his head on his fist. "I was glad Rob was here for him. I didn't even try to talk my way back in. I got a job at a department store in the city, thinking I could learn the most efficient way to modernize Sinclair's. And maybe one day, I'd get the chance to explain it all to Uncle Roger so he would understand."

Reed fell silent.

Tasha perched on the edge of the desk and let him brood. She had heard most of the story from Rob, but she let Reed tell her as much as he wanted.

He drew in a deep breath. "We never expected him to die of a heart attack at fifty-five. Barring accidents, like the car crash that killed our parents when Rob was barely out of high school, the Sinclairs usually live to be in their eighties."

"I'm sorry," she said softly. "I know you and Rob were close to your uncle."

"Until the argument, yes, we were. But Uncle Roger could be unreasonable where the store was concerned. Anyway, because Uncle Roger had no children, Rob and I inherited it all. We decided to modernize everything, including the security system…even though we knew Uncle Roger wouldn't approve."

She wished she knew the right words to make him feel better. "You have to do what you feel is best for Sinclair's. Surely, he would approve of that."

Reed turned his eyes up at her and smiled. "I keep telling myself that. Rob and I both feel we're betraying his memory every time we get rid of the old and bring in the new. We know it's working because sales are up and, financially, the store is doing better than it has in two decades."

"Then you're doing the right thing."

"I know." He nodded. "But it still feels wrong. Maybe one day Rob and I will feel the store is really ours instead of feeling like we're just taking care of it for Uncle Roger."

"It takes time to adjust. It's only been…what? Six months?"

"Almost." He raised his head and motioned for her to come to him. She sat in his lap once again and nestled in his arms. "I'm sorry. I'm rambling like the ungrateful, pompous ass my uncle called me."

"No, you're not." Tasha reached up and stroked his cheek. "You sound like you haven't finished grieving for a man who was like a father to you and your brother. You'll have to come to terms with the fact that you and your uncle weren't at the best place in your relationship when he died."

"You're right about that. I was about ready to do anything I had to do to come back to Sinclair's, even grovel, when he died. I wish I'd had the chance to tell him how much I respected and loved him."

"He knows." She put a comforting arm around him.

He sighed. "I hope so."

He sounded so sad. Tasha knew it was time to move the conversation back to the security breech. "Who else besides you and Rob would know how to rig the equipment and have access to it?"

"Miss Monroe, my secretary. But she's in her seventies and has been with the store since the day it opened. She is incredibly computer savvy for someone her age, and she has been talking about retirement. But I can't imagine her planning and executing a scheme like this. Besides, Uncle Roger's will left her enough to live comfortably for the rest of her life."

"Anybody else?"

"Chelsea Lowell, Rob's secretary." Reed shook his head. "The girl is an airhead, but Rob likes her. I assume she has some computer knowledge, but her keying skills leave a lot to be desired. I can't imagine Chelsea plotting to break into Sinclair's either."

"You, Rob, Paul, Miss Monroe and Chelsea. That it?"

Reed nodded. "The only ones who have access to the keys to the security office. Only Rob, Paul and I—and to a certain extent Stu—know how to run the system."

Tasha ticked them off on her fingers. "But Miss Monroe is a computer whiz, so she might be able to figure out how to run the system. You said you can't see Miss Monroe doing something like this, and frankly, neither can I. Chelsea's probably been exposed to computers most of her life, but I agree that she's ditzy—unless she's a good actress. Stu doesn't really understand how the equipment works—unless he's playing dumber than he is too—but he wouldn't need to bring in the DVD player in the first place. Unless he was using the DVD to throw off suspicion in case someone came in unexpectedly and would notice the extra light on the computer. So those three are possibles. That leaves you, Rob and Paul. It's not you or Rob, so that narrows it down to—"

"Paul!"

"Right." Tasha scratched her head. "But I can't see Paul Greene doing it either. His company is the only security consulting firm in three counties. Most of the businesses use him. And I've always heard he's a wealthy man."

"No, Tasha. Look."

Reed was pointing at the monitor. When the four doors flashed onscreen, Tasha saw Paul Greene disappearing out of the shot of one of the back doors. From the glimpse she got of him, it looked like he was carrying two suitcases.

Once again, Reed pushed Tasha out of his lap. He scooted the chair up close to the desk, and they watched the monitor until the screens had cycled through a few times.

"There he is," Tasha said as Reed started keying to halt the loop.

Paul Greene, only a few years older than Reed, was a tall, burly man with crisp red hair and pale, freckled skin. He was dressed in dark clothing and black gloves. He had gone directly to the jewelry department and started loading the more expensive rings, bracelets and necklaces. By the time he'd reached the pricey watches, Reed had dialed 911 and the police were on their way.

Reed snatched up the walkie-talkie. After explaining to Stu, he told the guard to wait for the police at the front door and bring them to the jewelry department.

"You stay here, Tasha. I'm going to make sure Paul doesn't leave the store."

"Reed, no. He might be armed."

"I doubt it." He got up and headed for the door. "He didn't expect any problems tonight. He thought he had the system fixed and knew Stu would never notice the extra piece of equipment or that it was wired differently."

"I wish you'd stay here and wait for the police." But she put her arms around his neck and kissed him thoroughly. "Be careful. Paul Greene may not seem like a threat, but if you corner him—"

"I know, Tasha. I won't take any chances. I just want to keep him talking until the police get here."

Then he was gone, shutting the door behind him.

Tasha sat in the chair and watched Paul clean out the good jewelry. Sinclair's carried merchandise in all price ranges to appeal to the widest customer base. Paul knew what he was doing. He ignored the low-quality items.

Suddenly, Paul froze and his head snapped up. His eyes opened wide as he looked at something—or someone—out of camera range. Unfortunately, the system didn't have sound. If there was a way to turn on the audio, Tasha didn't know how to do it, and she was afraid to try to figure it out. She didn't want to inadvertently erase the evidence.

Reed moved into view, and Tasha could see he was talking. Paul listened then his face contorted angrily and he started shouting, his mouth working furiously. Without warning, Paul charged around the display case toward Reed.

Tasha gasped, but Reed was ready. He stepped out of the way so that Paul missed him. When Paul turned around and swung, Reed ducked. As he came up, he plowed his right into Paul's midsection. The security consultant grabbed his stomach and went down to his knees. Then Reed clipped his chin with a left hook. Paul fell down face first.

Reed looked up at the security camera and gave her the a-okay sign.

A few minutes later, just as Paul started to move, Stu and two police officers crowded into the scene. Tasha watched as they listened to Reed and handcuffed Paul. The cops hauled Paul to his feet and took him away. Reed spoke a few words to Stu then they both disappeared out of view.

Tasha wrapped her robe up tight in case Stu came back to the office, but Reed entered alone.

"I sent Stu back to the break room for a few minutes."

"Good. You know, what you did to Paul was impressive."

He shrugged. "I did a little boxing in college. And I've had a few fist fights over the years."

"It's nice to know you can protect me if I ever need it."

"You can count on it. Now, give me a few minutes. I want to burn the recording of Paul to DVD."

"Did he say why he was stealing from the store?"

Reed nodded. "Paul owns a successful business that would have given him a comfortable retirement, but—believe it or not—he's spent every dime on lottery tickets. He embezzled from his own company, trying to win back what he'd lost. Then he started stealing from the store to fence the goods and buy more lottery tickets."

"How sad. He had everything, a thriving business and financial security, but wasn't satisfied." Tasha thought about the two bucks she spent on tickets weekly. Spending hundreds or thousands of dollars every week was beyond her comprehension.

When Reed finished, he stood and pulled her into his arms. "Where were we?"

"Anywhere you want to be," she said suggestively.

"I wish we could go back to bed, but with the system now working properly, Stu would see everything."

Tasha looked up into his blue eyes, deep enough to drown in. "I guess our time together is over. It's been wonderful."

Reed drew in a deep breath. "Well, we knew tonight would have to end."

Tasha waited, hoping he would say anything to let her know he was interested in seeing her again. What if all he'd wanted was one night of fun and games? Did he expect everything to go back to the way it had been now that the night was almost over?

He said nothing more to her but called Stu on the walkie-talkie, telling him it was all right to return to his post. Reed opened the door and they left the office.

Chapter Five

"I have only a few hours to clean this place up," Reed commented as he glanced at his watch after they'd returned to the display bed.

The bedding was all tangled, and most of the pillows were on the floor. The remains of their late-night snack littered the table. It had been a night of dreams coming true for Tasha, but now it was over. She had to face the reality that Reed might not be interested in anything more permanent.

"Yeah, Rob will be here at seven sharp," she said quietly. "I'll help you."

"No, I'll drive you home then come back."

"I have my car, but I'll stay until we get things set right again. By the time we're done, nobody will ever know what happened here tonight." Tasha started to pick up a pillow, but Reed caught her and swung her around.

"What kind of date is that if I let you help clean up?" He brushed back the short hair that had flown into her face and looked deeply into her eyes. "I want more dates with you, a lot more. A lifetime of dates."

Tasha's heart skipped a beat. This is what she wanted to hear from him. "I want that too, Reed."

"Did you know that I've been half in love with you for a long time now?"

Startled, she shook her head. "Why didn't you ever say anything?"

"You were too young."

She laughed. "You're only five years older than me."

"Now it doesn't matter, but back then when I was nineteen and you were fourteen, you were jailbait."

Tasha laughed. "Yeah, I guess you're right."

"I went away to college, and on my visits home watched you change from a girl into a woman. You were my little brother's friend, and sometimes I thought there was more than just friendship between you two. By the time I realized you would never be anything more than buddies, Uncle Roger and I had our big argument. When I took that job in the city, I hoped you'd still be here when I came back."

"Oh, Reed. I never knew." For some reason, tears burned her eyes, and she blinked. She didn't cry but she wanted to. "I had a crush on you back then, but I never dreamed you thought of me in any way other than Rob's pesky friend."

"You were never a pest."

"You were always telling us to get lost," she protested.

"Rob was the pest." Reed grinned. "You just happened to be with him."

Tasha shook her head. "It's probably a good thing I didn't know. I would have been even more awkward and self-conscious than I was."

"I didn't see you that way. I saw a very pretty girl who would—and did—grow up to be a beautiful, sexy woman."

Warmth seeped into her cheeks. "Thank you, Reed."

"But that was the past. We have the future ahead of us, Tasha. I want to share it with you."

"Me too," she murmured breathlessly.

It was enough for now. Love would come. She could feel it blossoming in her heart, the teenage crush changing into real feelings for this man. And she could see it shining in Reed's eyes when he looked at her. Love would grow between them in their future together. She was so happy she had decided to sit on Santa's lap.

Tasha stared at the mess they'd made. "Before we start cleaning this up, I'd like to see you in the red velvet suit one more time."

Reed threw back his head and laughed. "So you can sit in my lap again?"

She looked up at him, fluttering her eyelashes. "Maybe."

They made their way to the front of the store where Reed had left the Santa costume. He picked up the pile of red velvet. "I'll have to send this to the cleaners as soon as they're open."

She searched around the chair. "Isn't there an elf costume somewhere?"

Reed nodded. "It's on a mannequin in the window with the rest of the display."

Tasha moved aside the red curtain and went up the steps into the window. The whole area had been transformed into a winter wonderland. The floor was covered in a white cloth over thick padding to simulate snow, and the corners of the window had been sprayed to appear ice-frosted. Tinsel, garland and strings of lights were draped along the walls and around the edge of the window.

The decorated tree sat in one back corner. The waist-high snow drift was next to the opposite wall. Huge candy cane poles tied with big green bows sat on the drift among toys and small appliances which were there to suggest gifts potential customers might want to get those hard-to-buy-for people on their lists. The mannequin, dressed in a red velvet elf suit that matched Santa's, stood behind the drift.

She peered out the window. Everything was quiet and still. This early, no one was stirring, not even a mouse. No cars passed by and no pedestrians braved the cold. Tasha eyed the mannequin again. The elf suit should fit...

Reed joined her in the window. Behind the snowdrift, he changed into the Santa suit and Tasha donned the elf suit, complete with the pointy ears she'd found in the makeup kit sitting on the floor. The flared skirt fit well enough and went halfway to her knees, but the top was a little snug. Her breasts threatened to spill over the stretchy neckline trimmed in white fur if she breathed too hard or bent over.

"Come here, my little elfling," Reed growled in a husky Santa voice behind the frothy white beard.

She went into his arms and his mouth covered hers, the whiskers tickling but not enough to distract her from Reed's lips and tongue as they moved over hers. He rolled her to the white-covered floor, the padding beneath cushioning her shoulder blades and hips as she stretched out beneath him. He settled between her legs and she felt his cock, candy cane hard once again, nudge her.

When their lips parted, Reed gasped for air. Her hand searched between them for his cock.

He hadn't zipped the Santa trousers, and she closed her fingers around his hard shaft with a sigh. His cock was hot and a finer smoothness than the velvet they wore. She moved her hand up and down over the hard length, from the nest of coarse curls to the bulging tip.

Reed groaned, sitting back on his heels, and Tasha rose, propping herself on one elbow while still caressing his cock. His mittened hands lifted the hem of the skirt to her waist. He smiled at finding she hadn't put on the brief shorts that went with the suit.

Red velvet touched her wet pussy. He rubbed her labia and clit, sending shock waves of pleasure through her, and she squirmed, her hips writhing to match his movements. The night had been a fantasy come true for her too, but the reality fueled her passion. Her body responded easily to Reed and his touch.

He brought out a condom pack and ripped it open with his teeth. He rolled it down over his cock then leaned forward, resting a hand on each side of her. She wrapped her legs around his waist, and he drove into her.

Their bodies pumped together, and each thrust brought her closer to the edge of orgasm. Their hips became a frenzy of movement until every nerve ending ruptured with pleasure. She cried out, and Reed leaned forward, his mouth covering hers and catching the sound.

Then Reed groaned his release as his hips screwed against hers. When his cock slithered out of her, he rolled over to his side, and she went into his arms, her backside against him. She looked up at the string of lights twinkling around the window. They had shifted beyond the snow drift and were partly in sight of the window.

"Oh, Reed," she cried out. "Anyone could have come along and seen us."

"If they did, I hope they enjoyed the show as much as I did," he growled into her ear.

"Too bad we didn't catch this time on camera either."

Reed rifled in his pocket and brought out a DVD. "The camera actually recorded us earlier. While I was making the copy of Paul, I made a copy of us playing in Santa's chair and on the bed then erased them from the hard drive. We can watch this to celebrate New Year's."

Tasha giggled. "That sounds lovely."

They lay still for a while, basking in the afterglow of their lovemaking and enjoying being in each other's arms.

Then Reed kissed her cheek. "Tonight is like a fantasy come true."

"You've fantasized about fucking an elf?"

He laughed. "That too, especially if the elf is as sexy as you. But I meant fucking you in every department in the store."

She grinned. "We missed a few."

Reed's hand dipped into her red velvet bodice and caressed her breast. "We can take care of that next Christmas."

"And will I get to sit in Santa's lap?" Tasha closed her eyes, melting at Reed's touch.

"You can sit in my lap," Reed promised, "any time during the year, for many years to come."

Also by Lani Aames

Desperate Hearts
Ellora's Cavemen: Tales from the Temple I (*anthology*)
Enchanted Rogues (*anthology*)
Eternal Passion
Lusty Charms: Invictus
Statuesque

About the Author

Lani welcomes comments from readers. You can find her website and email address on her author bio page at www.ellorascave.com.

SCARLET STOCKINGS

By Mary Wine

Chapter One

Silver Peak, California 1874

A person really could hear their heart stop beating.

Bethany Wilton stood looking out the second-story window of her home as her entire world froze and everything that mattered to her was sneaking into one of the upper rooms at the saloon across the street.

Her heart was simply frozen as she watched Gabriel hand over three dollars to a feminine hand before the woman stepped out of the doorway and he dashed inside. The door closed shut as Bethany sucked in a huge gasp of air. Her temper exploded right at the same time her eyes filled with tears. She couldn't seem to decide just what to do and her mouth opened and then closed as she spun around to turn her back on the saloon.

In her hand was a forgotten box of Christmas decorations that she'd left her first-story shop to come and pull from its shelf above the kitchen sink. The joy that had filled her heart for the impending holiday was now a mere vapor.

Her eyes fell on the bed and those tears threatened to break through her temper. Bethany stomped her foot onto the floor and forced herself to turn back around to look at the saloon. She would not stand there and cry over her empty bed! She dropped the box on the kitchen table and wiped a hand over her eyes.

No sir! Not her. Bethany moved towards the window to see if she could catch a glimpse of her husband in that upper floor bedroom. Oh, she knew full well what went on, on that second floor of the saloon.

Sex. It was bartered and sold right there by women who made the journey west to earn a fortune on their backs. It was the shameful truth that most of the madams across the way wore finer clothing than she did.

What Bethany wanted to know was just why her husband was paying three dollars a throw when she was his wife. Her temper boiled so hot, it was a wonder steam didn't rise from her ears. What on God's green earth could that woman possibly know that was worth three dollars an hour?

Bracing her hands on the window frame, Bethany leaned out to look at the saloon. It had a railing that ran the entire length of the second story. On Saturday night, the madams would hook one of their legs over that wooden railing and show off their ankles and calves to the men drinking below them.

Bethany had always been taught to turn a blind eye to the "sin" being practiced in front of her home. After all, those same miners were in her store the next morning keeping her small tailoring shop open. Women were still rather hard to come by in the new state of California. The harsh conditions accounted for the lack of feminine population and that fact also allowed both her business and the saloon to flourish. If a man didn't have a wife to make his shirts, he had to lay down his money in her shop.

There appeared to be two things that men needed and would always manage to find the money for. Clothing and sex.

Oh…but that didn't explain why her husband was paying for what she would willingly give him at home. Bethany felt her face burn for another reason now. It was the honest truth that she would eagerly follow Gabe upstairs for an afternoon marriage chore. Yes, she knew she was wicked. Good girls didn't long for any more of their husband's attention than needed, but she did.

Bethany suddenly stood up. Well, obviously Gabe hungered for something that he wasn't getting either. She set her teeth into her lower lip as she tried to think of just what a man did with a madam. Half the good ladies in town would have fainted at that idea but Bethany wanted to know. In fact, she was almost certain she needed to understand what Gabe was doing right now that he had not received in their bed.

If that colored her scarlet with shame, so be it, but there was no way she was going to let another woman take her husband before their first anniversary had even passed.

The corners of her lips rose into a smug grin as she remembered one little detail that she'd noticed about the saloon girls. Turning around, Bethany pulled her bonnet off its holding peg and quickly tied the bow on the right side of her face. She picked up her shopping basket and took the stairs two at a time on her way down. She only stopped as she flipped the sign on the front window over so that it read "closed".

She had a bit of shopping to do before her husband came home.

Three blocks behind the saloon and rows of mercantile shops was where the Chinese lived. Bethany held her head high as she stepped right up onto the boardwalk that was teeming with men who had long braids hanging down their backs.

Gabe wouldn't be very happy to hear she was walking alone but that felt rather fair to her way of thinking. She might be a good girl but she still had ears and knew where the madams got their fancy silk dresses. They came here to the Chinese to get their garments made because the proper businesses on the main street of town wouldn't have them in their shops.

Bethany found the dress shops rather quickly. Bright silk was displayed in the windows and a cage crinoline hung over the door. She looked at the silk lovingly. It was plum and shiny but ever so unpractical. For one tiny moment she was actually envious of the saloon girls. They had a reason to dress up and look pretty. The church social was the only event worthy of fancy dressing in her life and silk would be quite misplaced among the calico and white lace.

Bethany froze in shock for the second time that day as she walked a little further into the shop. Right there was a corset made of another silk. In all her dreams she had never considered owning an undergarment that was so decadent. She moved closer to it and ran a single finger over the scarlet corset.

"You like pretty corset, lady? It make your husband happy man."

Her face flamed red but her lips curled back up into that smug smile. Did she dare? Who would have thought that women wore silk undergarments!

Bethany felt her smile fade as she noticed a stack of colorful stockings. She pointed at them and the shopkeeper instantly moved them onto the counter. This was the thing that had sent her into the Chinese shops. When the saloon girls hooked their legs over the railing, you could see the scarlet stockings on their legs and the shop on the main street in town would never sell the colorful underwear. Bethany looked back at the silk corset—it would appear those girls did not stop at fancy hosiery.

Well, that felt like a good place to begin. It might all erupt in her face but that was a chance she was willing to take. Gabe's face swam across her thoughts as she felt her nipples tighten. Her body always shivered when she saw her husband. He was covered in thick muscle that made her belly twist. The way he looked at her made her blood race through her veins.

Bethany stepped back into the sunlight with her basket loaded and a bread cloth carefully tucked over the scarlet stockings and silk corset. Her body tingled as she hurried back towards her shop. She was suddenly so hot that she hated her dress. Just the idea of putting on the scandalous underpinnings made her passage ache.

She couldn't quite feel guilty about it. Gabe was her husband. Was it so wrong to think about having sex with him? Or in this case—to plan his seduction?

Bethany did not know, but she was very certain that she would not be standing by turning a blind eye while her husband took his body to the saloon.

* * * * *

Honey sighed as she watched the one thing that she had never had walk out her bedroom door. Gabe Wilton was a man worth trying to keep but he just cleared his throat and tipped his hat before he left.

Honey stroked the three dollars he'd paid her and giggled at what the man had demanded from her in return. For a woman who made her living at men's demands, Gabe's still slightly astonished her. He had wanted to know what pleased her.

The other girls would fall over with laughter if they knew a man had paid her to tell him...bluntly...what she enjoyed while on her back.

Well, Honey did have to admit that there were a whole lot of men out there who could benefit from a few lessons like the ones she had just given Gabe. Most of the males in California thought stuffing their cocks into a woman was the complete beginning and end to sexual enjoyment.

Oh, but there was so much more, if you took the time to linger over your lover's body. Honey smiled as she folded the money and hid it away until she could get to the bank. It was rare but she had known a few lovers in her time. Men who demanded more than spread thighs from her. A shiver crossed her skin at the image of the things they had her yield to them and the pleasure that they applied to her body.

Gabe Wilton was that kind of man. The sort who could make a woman scream and beg him for more. His only problem was his ideas that good ladies didn't have all the same parts as a madam did.

His wife was in for a rather interesting surprise when she got into her bed tonight. Gabe Wilton was about to toss off his respectable image and show her what kind of man lurked beneath the polished suitor who'd won her hand.

* * * * *

Gabe wasn't a drinking man but he was looking at the scotch rather fondly as he walked in front of the bar. The liquor wouldn't cure the ache in his cock though. He cast his vision across the street at the little "tailor" sign and growled.

Bethany was rustling around in her shop, just as sweet at the day he'd first laid eyes on her and watched his heart land smack at her feet. His brother had always threatened him with the fact that a woman could do that, but until a man faced the reality…well, there was no way to truly understand the level it reduced a man to.

Their wedding night had scared the hell out of him. Gabe considered the shop again as he recognized that three months later, he still hadn't managed to muster the courage to show his wife what kind of man her husband was.

Bethany had just looked so damn angelic when he pulled back the bedding that first time. He was so sick with love that the idea of frightening her with his darker cravings actually scared him. There wasn't a man walking the face of the planet whom Gabe feared. Somehow, he'd ended up with a virgin in bed with him and it was still rattling his chain.

But it didn't change the hunger growing in his cock. The craving for more than gentle intercourse was keeping him awake at night. The scent of his wife's body helped to push his control to snapping point and let the harder side free. He wanted more than the controlled penetration he'd forced his cock to limit itself to. Maybe that was blunt, but so was he.

His visit to the madam's room hung in his thoughts. Sure, he'd had a lot of women before meeting Bethany. Worldly females who understood the harder needs of a man like himself. Honey was one of those kind, which explained why she'd been the woman to give him what he needed today.

Knowledge. Fucking a woman and understanding just why she enjoyed it were two vastly different things. He'd taken partners to the edge of sanity but never really known exactly why they flung their bodies against his and cried out for more.

Christ! Gabe needed to hear Bethany demand that of him. His control was in tattered strips now. Another night of soft penetration wasn't going to satisfy him.

But thanks to Honey, he had a few more clues as to just how to open Bethany's eyes and senses to the darker shadows of lust.

Chapter Two

Gabe was silent when he got home. They lived above her shop because he was an official working on the railroad. He hadn't had a home until meeting her and it was almost funny sometimes to see his huge frame in her tiny kitchen.

Bethany held onto her courage as she served up supper and flashed her husband a saucy smile.

At least she hoped it was a "saucy" look. His eyes closed slightly as Gabe stopped chewing but she turned around to hide her pleasure at having gained that much of a response from him. Her husband was a man of action and he didn't waste time on conversation. It was something about him that had made her follow him out of a church dance to investigate. His dark silence drew her to him, somehow it hit her as solid strength, the sort that no words could explain.

Gabe's fork clattered to his plate and his chair went sailing into the wall. He shook out his body as Bethany turned around to face a man she was not certain she knew.

"What are you wearing, Bethany?" Gabe knew her inch by inch and a peek of scarlet on her ankles as she turned grabbed his complete attention. His cock sprang to instant attention as he watched his sweet wife lift an eyebrow, and then grab a handful of her skirt and petticoat and pull it to her knee. It was the most forward thing he'd ever seen her do.

"Do you like them?"

Gabe felt his mouth go dry and his cock harden painfully. The scarlet stocking was more than his control could bear. But the fact that Bethany had something so scandalous on gave him one startling clue.

"You saw me going into Honey's room." He cussed under his breath but relief slammed into his head as well. There was no longer any reason to hold back his needs.

"If you like scarlet stockings, Gabe, you should have just told me so. I'm all the woman you need." It was a bold statement, one Bethany wasn't too sure she knew how to back up, but she was not yielding her husband to Honey.

Gabe's face lit with something she did not understand but she felt it hit her like a wave of heat. Every nerve ending she had tightened as hunger burned in her husband's eyes. Bethany stood straight as Gabe lowered his eyes to her exposed calf. Something…raw…crossed his face and she felt her mouth go dry.

"God, I hope so." His voice was dark and husky as he raised his gaze to hers again. Something flickered in those eyes that shot straight into her belly making her passage twist with heat. It was pure reaction, the thing that happened to her whenever Gabe was near her. It was a good thing the man had offered to marry her, because the stark truth was, he could strip her of any self-control just by looking at her…like he was right now.

Gabe lifted one hand and curled a single finger at her. "Come here." His tone demanded immediate obedience. Bethany had heard him use that voice on his men but never between them. A shiver worked its way through her belly as her passage twisted yet again. She was suddenly wondering just what else he might order her to do.

The hunger in her eyes made his mouth water. Gabe watched the skirt drop back over her leg as she moved towards him. Need burned painfully through his body as his wife moved towards him with a firm expression on her face. There wasn't a hint of fear anywhere in her dark eyes and the need to get between her thighs doubled as he witnessed her strength. She had made some kind of firm resolution and was determined to stick to it.

Damn, he loved her spunk.

Gabe cupped her face between his hands and her body jerked in response. Her breath got stuck in her throat as he hovered over her mouth a moment before lowering his lips to hers. His mouth slid over hers just once before he pushed her lips apart and took a deep taste of her. His tongue swept into her mouth where it stroked her tongue. Bethany listened to her own moan as she twisted with surprise. Gabe hooked an arm around her waist to pull her against his body as one hand moved from her cheek to the back of her head to hold her in place for his kiss.

It was a hard branding of possession. His tongue thrust deeply and then stroked hers, teasing her to return the touch. Bethany twisted in his embrace once more, only this time her body was trying to get closer to Gabe's. Her hands landed on his shoulders as the fingertips lamented the layer of cotton denying her his skin.

Gabe pulled her head away from his with the hand that gripped the back of her head. Bethany had never felt so completely helpless in his embrace before. She should have, Gabe was large for a man and twice her size. Yet he had always managed to hide it and trick her into thinking that she was in control during their lovemaking.

Tonight she recognized the fact that Gabe had been cleverly masking his actions to keep her calm. She shivered again as she stared into the hard hunger pulling his face tight. His jaw was clenched as he looked at her mouth. His gaze returned to hers and Bethany was sure that she saw smug approval for the fact that she was helpless against his superior strength. There was something deep inside her husband that enjoyed capturing her.

What surprised her most was the answering twist of excitement that traveled through her. Her passage actually cramped in its quest to be filled by her captor. A harsh male grunt hit her ears before Gabe spun her loose. Her skirts flared out from her feet as she turned in a circle before stopping next to the kitchen wall. Bethany watched her husband with wide eyes because she had no idea what to expect of this *primal* form of Gabe.

"Take your dress off." His fingers clenched tight into twin fists as his teeth clicked against each other. Bethany looked at the doorway into the bedroom and the dressing screen that she always used to disrobe behind. Not even wives displayed their bare bodies to their husbands. It simply wasn't done.

"Right here, I want to watch you." That wasn't completely true. Gabe wanted to rip that damn calico off her body and shove her back against the wall so that he could fuck her. It amazed him to see the flash of excitement in her eyes. Uncertainty moved over her face also but she wasn't scared of the harsher side of lust. That bit of knowledge made it more impossible than ever to hold back his needs. In a whole lot of ways, it was still their wedding night. Easing her into his embrace was his job to handle right so that she wasn't scared off sex for the rest of her days. Society did a fine job of convincing girls that passion was dirty.

Watch her? Oh, what a wicked idea! Bethany forgot to breathe as she looked at Gabe. The man had touched her bare body but only in the dark. His words rang with hard authority making her tremble as she faced submission to his whim.

"Do it, Bethany, and don't turn the wick down." Gabe was testing her now. Seeing just how much she had meant those words about being woman enough for him. Did the madam parade her naked body in front of her customers? The gossips in town said so. Bethany reached for the top button on her dress as her temper restored her composure. Well, if a bit of bare skin was what prompted her husband to seek another woman, she would just make sure he saw all he wanted right here at home.

It was amazing the way it felt to undress for a man. Well, for Gabe. Excitement raged through her body as the buttons on her dress parted. Gabe's eyes followed the progress of her hands like slaves. It was an odd reversal of power—he commanded but she captured his complete attention.

Her dress slipped over her shoulders as Bethany reached for the button holding her petticoat closed around her waist. One little twist and it slid down her thighs. Undressing was rather simple because her clothing was designed for her to get into and out of without help. Back-closing underpinnings were for women who had maids.

"God, you're beautiful, Bethany, Do you want to know what I did with Honey this afternoon?"

His wife snorted at him. Gabe lifted a single finger in the face of her temper. "If I had any idea that you would act like this, I would have gone to see Honey weeks ago."

Bethany stepped out of her pooled skirts and propped her hands onto her hips. The posture thrust her breasts forward with her new corset helping to make sure they were high and proud. Gabe sucked his breath in as her scarlet-clad legs came into full sight. "Does that mean you're planning on going back?"

Gabe chuckled, the tone of her voice said he'd better think twice before telling her he was taking his time to another woman. "I got everything I needed from Honey today. The whole point was to learn what I needed to make you scream."

Chapter Three

That twist of excitement gripped her once again. Make her scream? Fear edged the emotion but all that did was make it more intense. Fluid eased down the walls of her passage as her eyes dropped to the fly on her husband's pants. Bethany just couldn't help it. Need was pulsing through her body and she knew that what she craved was the hard contact of his cock pressed into her.

"That's right. I didn't lay a finger on her but I needed a woman who would tell me exactly what part of your body to stroke."

"You asked a woman about me?" Bethany's face burned with fire. People did not just ask about…well…about sex!

"Sex is like a whole lot of things in life. Details matter." Gabe considered the blush on her face. "Take your corset off. It's too damn pretty for me to tear."

There it was again, that hint of primitive behavior. Bethany fumbled the first metal hook on the front busk as she saw the proof of her husband's deteriorating control flicker across his eyes. She felt like cornered prey that didn't have a prayer of escaping. If she bolted, he'd spring at her fleeing form.

But Bethany had never shown Gabe her bare breasts. She held the edges of her corset over her body as she tried to find the courage to expose herself to his keen stare. Gabe had cupped her breasts in his hands as they made love, but he had never seen them in full light.

"Show me, Bethany, and then I'm going to show you exactly what Honey told me about today."

Bethany let the corset go and Gabe hissed through his teeth. His eyes lingered over her nipples as the tender crowns tightened into little hard buttons. He was moving towards her before he thought about it. The distance suddenly too much to tolerate when she stood there displaying her breasts for him. The only thought crossing his mind was the fact that he had the right to touch her. Stroke those globes of creamy flesh and actually taste her little brown nipples. Bethany had granted him her body and only him. Right then his blood surged with the need to prove to her that she had chosen wisely.

Gabe's hands slid around her torso and flattened on her back. He lifted her slightly forward as he loomed over her. Her breasts ended up thrust high as he lowered his mouth and took one between his lips. Bethany cried out as his mouth sucked on the sensitive tip, sending a bolt of need spearing into her passage. Her hips actually jerked towards Gabe, lifting and offering her body for his possession. His mouth was almost too hot but pleasure spiked through her breast as he pulled her nipple deeper and she felt the tip of his tongue flicker over the little button.

Bethany listened to her own whimper as Gabe gave her nipple a final lick and then he took her opposite one into his mouth. It was the most exquisite torment. Pleasure swept through her as his tongue lapped over her nipple but her body was burning with the need to be stretched with his length. Her fingers curled into his forearms, and the fabric of his shirt made her angry.

Gabe chuckled low and deep as he lifted his head from her nipple. "No one ever told me that talking to a madam could be better than using her but I admit that marriage has changed my view on the subject."

Bethany was caught between the need to giggle and the urge to hit Gabe. It just couldn't be right to agree in any form to her husband spending time with a madam. But the little ripples of pleasure still moving through her breasts made a liar out of any temper she might display. It was the plain truth that she liked having her nipples sucked, even if Honey was the one who told her husband to do it.

That giggle did escape as she considered that Gabe was doing what Honey had said. What a strange picture that was as she stood bent back over his arms. One dark eyebrow rose on her husband's face.

"Ah, sweet Bethany, are you amused at my expense? I might have to take you in hand—wife." Gabe frowned at her but there was a sparkle of mischief in his eyes as his hand found her knickers and gave a twist. The button on the waistband popped off sending the button against the wall. That fast she was reminded of how much strength lived in her husband's body. He had always touched her with such tender control. Tonight Bethany was beginning to understand that letting the man inside that polished exterior touch her at his whim might just be more exciting than remaining a delicate flower while the window shades were pulled down.

Gabe drew the last bit of clothing off her body and caught the full scent of her arousal. His cock gave a twitch as it sent up a hard demand to get inside her. Gabe forced his control into place. A gentle mating wasn't what he craved and he needed trust for Bethany to enjoy the harder side of his lust.

"Scarlet stockings. How did you know I want some for Christmas?"

Bethany giggled again as Gabe stood up. He cupped her chin and lowered his mouth to hers again. The kiss was full of hard possession and it made her skin tingle with hope that he would back up that promise.

"If you go to Chinatown without me again, I'm going to spank your fanny."

Despite the fact that she'd expected just that type of reaction to her shopping trip, Gabe's attitude rubbed at her pride. She had managed quite nicely on her own and didn't need him to hold her hand along the way. "I think I just might be shopping there a bit more often."

Gabe frowned at her before his eyes dropped to her scarlet stockings and then moved back up her body. One dark eyebrow rose. "Now Bethany, maybe you should just wait until after Christmas for that shopping. I might have a few surprises hidden away."

Bethany snorted at him. She propped her hands on her hips and raised one of her eyebrows. "The ones you'll be shopping for tomorrow, you mean?"

A huge grin split her husband's face but his eyes didn't stay on her face for very long. Her bare breasts drew his attention and any hint of joking fell aside as she caught the raw look of hunger that reentered his eyes when he was looking at her nipples once more.

"Take my clothes off."

"What?"

Gabe stepped forward to cup her chin and repeated his order. "Undress me, Bethany."

Oh, she did like the sound of that! Her fingers were already reaching for the middle button on his shirt. The top two were open and tips of black hair curled through the opening. The lamp still burned, bathing them in yellow light as she worked those buttons open. Her fingertips stole little strokes as she moved downward. The skin-to-skin contact fed her need to get closer to him.

"The pants, too."

Bethany froze on his belt. She had never seen what was hiding under his fly. She had felt it enter her body but never actually seen what her husband's cock looked like.

A desire to do just that raced through her blood as she pulled the first button free.

"That's a good girl." Gabe sat in one of the kitchen chairs and offered her one booted foot. Leaning over meant letting her bare breasts hang in his line of vision. It was an odd sort of submission. One that required her to be obedient, but his eyes would become obsessed with her body. Grasping the boot, she pulled it free and then waited for the second one to be presented.

Gabe stood up and shrugged out of his open shirt. Bethany sighed as his skin came into view with its ridges of hard muscle and crisp dark hair. His chest was wide and it tapered into a lean waist. His pants hung on his hips as his eyes considered her study of him. Gabe hooked his hands into the waistband and pushed the pants down.

His cock thrust out at her with nothing to bar her view. The rod was thick and crowned with a ruby head that had a little slit on top. Bethany found herself wondering exactly how it had all fit into her body. Two sacs hung beneath it and she felt her body shiver because that staff had filled her passage and she had enjoyed it.

"Touch me, Bethany."

Gabe had stepped free of his pants and stood completely bare. His body was a feast for her eyes and she wasn't entirely sure what part of him she wanted to stroke first. She placed her hands flat over his male nipples and smiled at the warm skin pressing back against hers. She spread her hands up to his shoulders and down over the muscles on his upper arms.

"Now touch my cock." Gabe said it in a hushed whisper, almost like he needed her to follow his instructions. Her palm itched to feel that one part of him that had always been so forbidden. The attention he'd lavished on her bare breasts was also rejected by polite society.

But it had felt so incredible. Her hands smoothed down his body until she found the longer hair that grew around his cock. She traced her fingers through it and then hesitated at the first contact. Gabe's breath hissed through clenched teeth, making her watch his face in wonder. The simple touch of her hand was the center of his attention and it put her in control.

Bethany stroked the length of his cock and listened to the second hiss of his breath. She curled her hand around the staff and rubbed her thumb over the slit on its crown.

"Jesus, Bethany! I can't hold back when you do that." Gabe jerked away and opened frustrated eyes at her.

"Hold what back?"

His face darkened. "I want to get up inside you so bad it hurts, but not soft and controlled. I want to use you hard and I just can't ignore it any longer." As far as confessions went it was blunt, a lot like him. Maybe that was why he loved her so much it hurt—Bethany was all smooth and polished and she made a place a home just by being there.

"So you went to Honey?"

Gabe snorted at her. "I did not fuck her, Bethany. She's a workingwoman who knows a thing or two about what a female likes when a man is between her thighs. I needed blunt answers and figured Honey was the best place to get them fast. I'm interested in fucking you and making damn sure you enjoy it as much as I do."

It might have been the oddest sounding declaration of love but that was exactly what Gabe was telling her. Bethany felt it hit her straight in the heart because his eyes told her he meant each word more than anything he had ever said to her. The harder words just intensified the way she felt as she stared at the raw hunger blazing from her husband's eyes. Bethany was quite sure that every member of the town church would have fainted at the word "fuck", but men used it rather regularly when they figured there were no ladies about to overhear them. Hearing it bounce off the wall behind her told her Gabe was being bluntly honest with her.

And that transmitted more emotion than "I love you" could ever do. Sure, Gabe had said those words to her and meant them, but there was a hard side to him that she glimpsed from time to time that frightened her almost as much as it enticed her.

"So what else did Honey tell you about?"

Oh hell.

Whisky might be able to cut through a man's resolve quick but not nearly as fast as the excitement flickering across his wife's face. She stood there proudly as the lamplight bathed her body in soft yellow and it was the damnedest thing Gabe had ever witnessed. Her nipples were still tight and he could smell how wet she was as his cock gave an insistent demand to find out firsthand how ready she was for his possession.

Her words stopped him as he considered one more little thing that Honey had mentioned.

Gabe placed his hands on her waist and her feet left the ground. A wicked smile curling his lips up as he sat her right on the kitchen table. He grabbed his half-eaten dinner and shoved the plate off onto the sink counter.

"Put your hands on the table behind you." Complying caused her breasts to be thrust forward and Bethany pulled her hands back a second later.

"Do it," Gabe growled at her as he placed a hand on each of her thighs and spread them wide. Bethany gasped as her body was exposed so completely. She felt so vulnerable and putting her hands behind her would be complete surrender. Like a captive on the auction block in some Persian market. Her hands landed softly on the cold wood as excitement made her tremble. The temptation to sample what else Gabe intended was too great to resist due to her sense of right versus wrong.

Here there was only a man and woman and the way they used their bodies to make the other feel.

Gabe cupped her breasts and his thighs held her wide as his thumbs brushed over her nipples. He leaned down to suck one and then the other very slowly, his tongue lapping each peak before he raised his head. "Don't move."

He knelt a second later and his face ended up right between her spread thighs. Bethany gasped and jumped but

Gabe slapped his hands over the top of each thigh to hold them apart.

"Put those hands back on the table."

"What are you doing?" His face was right in front of her…um…sex. She actually felt the warm brush of his breath hit the opening of her passage and pleasure spike up into her from it. Gabe chuckled as he raised one hand and placed it on her bare belly. He pushed her back while holding onto her thigh and she put her hands behind her to keep from landing on the tabletop.

"Good girl." His hand returned to her thigh and gently stroked the top. His breath hit her open sex again and that same curl of pleasure went into her passage once more. A little moan made its way past her lips and Gabe looked up her body at her.

"Honey told me about one more place that a woman likes to be sucked besides her nipples." Bethany was frozen in shock as his hand smoothed over her pubic hair and then pulled the lips of her sex further apart.

"Hidden right here is the center of a woman's pleasure. It's what my cock slides against when I'm inside you." One thick finger penetrated her passage and she cried out. The need to climax was building to an unbearable level. The walls of her body tried to clamp around that finger and hold it. Gabe pulled it free and slid it up her open slit to the top where he centered his fingertip on a little button that throbbed with delight as he rubbed it.

Her hips bucked up off the tabletop to press harder against his finger as a deep moan left her throat. Bethany wasn't thinking about anything except the rapture that little bundle of nerves was promising her aching body.

"Honey called it a clit."

A second later, Gabe sucked that button right into his mouth. It was searing and her hips bucked frantically as she cried out. Climax was instant. There was no controlling the timing, one flick of Gabe's tongue and she twisted as pleasure tore into her body and wrung her like a dishtowel.

She screamed and it tore the last bit of resolve from him. Gabe pushed to his feet as he caught Bethany's body before it collapsed to the tabletop. His cock pressed into her body in the same motion. She was so wet, he penetrated her in one hard thrust and his growl mingled with her moan.

Her hips rose to offer her body to his in the most primitive of unions. Gabe slid his hands down to her hips as her arms took her weight once more and he clamped his fingers around each curve. His hips drove his cock hard. The slap of their bodies meeting made him growl as Bethany kept pace with him. He clamped his teeth together as he refused to let his cock erupt inside her. He wanted to fuck. Hard, fast and long.

She did not want him to stop. Bethany felt her lungs attempting to draw enough air to keep up with their frantic rhythm but she did not care if she died because they failed. Nothing mattered but the hard motion of Gabe's mating. She suddenly recognized that this was what had been missing in their bed. This hard thrusting that shook her as her husband slammed his cock deeply into her. The way his hands held her hips in place for that possession. The way she was crying for more.

Her bare breasts were bouncing as Gabe continued his hard rhythm and everything felt so right. Like she had been yearning for Gabe to take her exactly like he was using her body now. Controlling her hips so that his cock could penetrate hard and deep, over and over. He was refusing to climax. Bethany saw it in his eyes as he snarled softly and rammed his cock harder into her body.

The minutes fell away as time meant nothing compared to the hard thrusting between her thighs. That clit at the top of her slit throbbed, sending out a new rush of pleasure. Her hips tried to rise to meet each thrust as need clawed at her for another climax.

"That's right, baby, I'm going to hear you scream again."

Gabe let her hips go and then he was leaning right over her, pressing her back until her back was against the tabletop, her thighs clamped around his hips as he continued to thrust hard into her passage. His hands captured hers and pulled her arms above her head as he held each of her hands captive. The hair on his chest brushed her bare breasts and nipples, making her sob as the sensation added to the growing insanity.

His cock now slid over her clit with each and every thrust. Gabe pressed her flat against the table, making her take him. She wanted to move but his weight held her down as his snarl of delight hit her ear. Their skin was slick with sweat and nothing mattered as Gabe kept driving his cock into her. She actually felt his cock swelling bigger inside her, could feel the impending eruption of his seed, her passage began to contract around his length as her body demanded proof of his pleasure.

Climax ripped into them both, catapulting them into a spinning vortex where there was nothing but each other. His seed hit her passage and her hips surged up from the table to deepen the penetration. Gabe's hands tightened around hers as his grunt hit her ears and his cock filled her belly with his seed. Pleasure washed over them like the tide coming in, it was obedient to nothing but its own whim and they were carried away by the current like driftwood. Bethany screamed because she had to let the rapture escape. Her husband snarled as his hips gave a last few thrusts that rubbed along her clit.

And then his body shook. Bethany felt her breath catch on a sob as the powerful chest imprisoning her shuddered. Gabe cupped her face as his lips dropped little kisses along her checks and lips. Their breath still came in pants as she smoothed her hands over his hard biceps. Her thighs were still clasped around his hips as she slid her hands over his shoulders. Her fingertips marveling at the strength and the contrasting tremor that rippled through those muscles.

"I love you, Bethany. God above only understands how much."

A moment later, Gabe lifted her body like a child's from the table. He cradled her against his chest and hesitated for only a moment as he turned down the lamp wick. Darkness surrounded them like a kindred sprit, encasing them together where no one would interrupt their intimacy. The ropes holding the mattress in the box frame creaked as Gabe laid her among the bedding. He rolled back onto the mattress and pulled her over his body. One hand pressed her head onto his chest as his knee rose slightly to part her thighs and make one of her legs lift and drape between his.

Bethany giggled as she felt the brush of her stockings against his bare skin. She still wore the indecent hosiery and it was very possible she might never go to bed without a pair on again!

"So I guess you approve of my new stockings."

The wide chest rumbled under her ear as one of her husband's hands slid down her back and slapped her bare bottom. "Best Christmas I ever celebrated."

Bethany lifted her head from his chest to consider the man lying there with her. Christmas was still another day away. She was going to have to do some thinking on just what to do to top tonight.

The best Christmas presents were always the ones you kept a secret and tonight had proven one thing to her beyond a single doubt.

A woman needed to plan her revelations wisely!

Chapter Four

Bethany spent an hour scrubbing the pots she'd left on the stove. It was a huge mess but one she just couldn't seem to get mad about. The coals had baked the remaining food into a thick coating of burnt food that she was forced to chip away at with a fork.

And Bethany giggled all the way through the chore. She was so lucky it was Saturday and she didn't need to open the shop until noon. The town didn't begin to thrive on Saturday until midday because the men who would be spending money in her shop would be staying well past sunset to lay down more of their weekly earnings at the saloon.

Honey would be busy tonight. Bethany stopped for a moment and looked across the room to the window. How many times had she noticed the lamp burning in those rooms and thought harshly of the women selling their favors? The truth was, she had quite a nerve judging anyone. She was far from perfect and knew it, but it was more than that.

She enjoyed sex. Even further than that idea was the firm knowledge that she craved it. Like the women who got addicted to the cocaine painkiller sold in the pharmacy. Her body was sore this morning but it was a pleasant ache that told her she had met her husband's needs and fed hers at the same time.

A little frown wrinkled her forehead. But had she really done everything that Gabe had desired? He was a man who had walked a whole lot of miles in his day and until yesterday had hidden his darker longings from her. What else was there lurking in those saloon rooms that men saved their money for?

Well, there was only one way to find out. Bethany opened her little tin of salt that sat on the back shelf and dug her fingers into it to pull out the little cloth bag that she kept money in that was hidden beneath the rock crystal. The west was untamed and it was wise to keep your money in a few different places besides the town bank. She tucked three dollars into the top of one glove and turned to leave.

Honey was going to have one caller today that the madam wasn't expecting.

* * * * *

"I don't service women." Bethany jumped as the madam swept into the room with a graceful sweep of her ruched skirts. Honey frowned slightly at her before she looked at the three dollar bills lying on the table. She stiffened slightly before fingering one of the tassels hanging from her brocade jacket.

"Cherry will take your money but I only take male customers. No women."

"A woman and a woman?" Bethany heard the shock in her own voice and marveled that she could still find something to make her blush after last night. She was standing in a madam's boudoir—one would think that she was quite past blushing at this point.

Honey considered her face and smiled slightly. She looked back at the money and then raised a gloved hand towards Bethany. "Yes, there are women who enjoy a female's touch more than a man's. It will cost you triple that amount though. Challenging biblical taboos isn't done for the same price."

Bethany giggled. The sound broke through her lips as she thought about what, exactly, two women might do with each other. Last night sprang to mind and the intense pleasure that Gabe had wrung from her with his mouth. Her cheeks flooded with heat as she considered women doing that to each other. She shuddered as she decided it was definitely not for her!

Honey smiled and raised a dark eyebrow. "It is a rather unique taste. Not one I enjoy either. So just why are you here, Mrs. Wilton?"

Bethany tore her thoughts away from what Gabe had done to her last night. But her body still clung to the idea, her passage slowly heating as she felt the first soft throbs from her clit. Hunger began to twist in her belly for Gabe and the hard command that he had used on her.

Yet her pride reared its head as she looked at the madam. Right there was the answer and she was just going to have to find the spine to ask. They were both women who understood what happened between men and women, so there was no reason to feel ashamed. Like Gabe had said, Honey was the woman to see when you were looking for blunt information.

"I want to know if there is more that you do to a man than let him between your thighs."

Honey smiled wide enough to show her teeth. "So you enjoyed it? How very surprising."

Bethany raised her own eyebrow in return. It was rather odd to find Honey someone that she enjoyed conversing with. Because she had been taught to look down on women who sold their flesh, she had never considered that they might be very much like herself.

"I envy you, Mrs. Wilton. Someday, I wish to have a husband as devoted to me." Honey's smile faded as she sighed and reached for the money. She aimed her dark eyes at Bethany as the money disappeared into the top of her glove. "Someday, not so far from now, Honey will disappear forever and I will find a house to buy where I can wear calico and search for a husband like your Gabe. By next Christmas, I will be sitting in the church when the bell rings for the faithful to praise the Lord."

"Then why did you ever become a madam?" The longing burning in the woman's eyes tore that question from Bethany.

Honey offered one of her controlled smiles to Bethany. "My father got me a job in a textile mill in the north. The overseer would take me out back twice a day to have his way with me and my sire found nothing wrong with that arrangement. So, when I met a man looking for women to come west and work in his saloon...I went. If my body is for sale, then the price will be high enough to set me free someday." Honey suddenly offered Bethany a naughty look. "Did you like being sucked off?"

Although Bethany knew Honey had told Gabe to do that to her, it was still a little blunt to hear it out loud. "Um…yes. I want to know…um…can a woman do other things to a man? I mean, other than let him ride her?"

"Suck his cock, men crave that almost as much fucking."

Bethany fluttered her eyelashes as that blunt remark hit her ears. It was so simple, she should have thought of it as Gabe was doing the same to her. She suddenly looked at Honey. "Exactly how do I do that?"

Honey raised an eyebrow once again. "Are you sure you want to know?"

"Well, I'm standing here in your room, aren't I?" Bethany propped her hand onto her hip and shook off the last of her nervousness. Now was not the time for backsliding into girlish uncertainty. She was going to be woman enough to hold her man's attention if she had to blush for three days straight! "For three dollars, I sure hope to learn something valuable."

"Well, I always give my costumers what they pay for."

The madam gave her a naughty smile as she pointed to a velvet-covered chair. Bethany sat down as she leaned forward to listen to the feminine secret being reveled. But Honey stood up and pulled a cord hanging discreetly in the corner by the bed. It was a bell cord, something you'd find alongside a lady's bed in a house with maids who listened in the kitchen for the little bells that told them their mistress was awake and ready for their assistance. Honey smiled at Bethany as she began to unbutton her gloves.

"A man's cock is the best place for a woman to control him." Honey laid her glove aside and opened the other one. "Never doubt that there is a certain part of every man that will guide him back to the woman who handled his cock just the right way. They may declare on the church steps that a proper girl is all they ever think about but trust me, I could identify most of the town fathers by their cocks."

Bethany giggled, she just could not help herself. The idea of her friends' husbands being lined up, fly open and feed sacks over their heads, was too wicked to ignore. The inner door to Honey's room shook with a hard knock before it opened. Bethany's amusement died instantly.

"Relax, Mrs. Wilton, this is JinLu, he works here." The man stepped right into the room and grinned at Honey. She lifted her hand and motioned him forward. He was a Chinaman and it really wasn't that odd to find him at the saloon. Chinese were inexpensive labor for most of the businesses in town. Honey looked at the man and popped one of her fingers into her mouth. She pulled it free almost to the tip and then pushed it back into her mouth. JinLu grinned wide enough to show his teeth but looked at Bethany first. Honey nodded her head and the man began to open his fly.

"JinLu doesn't speak English." Honey turned to look at Bethany. "So, I believe he's perfect for our lesson today. You can't suck a cock correctly unless you've seen it done."

Bethany couldn't decide whether to giggle again or gasp as JinLu reached into his open pants to pull his cock out. Never once had she ever considered being in such a situation. Exactly how did you behave while looking at a cock that did not belong to your husband? Honey walked over to JinLu and curled her fingers around his cock. Bethany watched the way the woman handled the flesh. There was no hint of hesitation as Honey pulled her clasped hand to the end of JinLu's cock and the man sucked in a harsh gasp of air.

That reaction pleased Honey as she moved her palm over the head of the cock and then firmly pressed her hand back to the base of his staff. "Play a little with it first. A firm grip but not hard and always run your thumb through the slit on the head."

Bethany's eyes were glued to her lesson. Now she knew she was headed for a fiery end but that didn't matter just then. She was fascinated by the look on JinLu's face. Pure enjoyment was sitting there as Honey moved her hand up and down his cock. The madam bent to her knees and held his cock with one hand as she opened her mouth and licked the little slit on the head of that cock. JinLu jerked and his breath hissed between his clenched teeth. Honey moved her eyes to look at Bethany. "See what I mean? Play with the cock a bit before taking it completely into your mouth. Men love having their cocks handled by a woman."

It certainly looked that way! Bethany was barely breathing as she waited to see Honey actually suck that cock. Excitement raced through her bloodstream even as she felt heat pooling in her passage. She wanted to do this to Gabe. The idea was firmly rooted in her brain and she didn't give a hoot what anyone thought about it...only that Gabe looked at her bent head like JinLu was looking at Honey. Pure devotion was flickering in his eyes and the harsh rasp of his breathing told Bethany the man was completely at Honey's command right then. The madam returned her attention to the cock in her hands and she leaned forward and took the head of the organ into her mouth. Her lips closed around the head as she slid her hand down the length that wasn't in her mouth.

JinLu's body bucked as his hips thrust towards her mouth like he was fucking her. Honey gripped his length and opened her mouth wider to take more of the cock into her mouth. Bethany listened to the little wet sounds that came from JinLu thrusting into Honey's mouth and the rasps of JinLu's breath as it increased. Honey worked her hand as JinLu's hips thrust his cock deeper into her mouth.

JinLu muttered something in his own language as his body went rigid. Honey tightened her hand around his cock as she sucked on the part inside her mouth. The man jerked a few times and then groaned low and deep. When Honey released his cock it was going limp and his face wore a satisfied smile.

"Just make sure to use your tongue on the little spot right under the ridge that runs around the head of the cock. It will make your husband come."

Excitement surged through her as Bethany absorbed the little details that would allow her to turn the tables on her husband. Marriage might work well as a team effort but there was nothing better than a good battle of wills to keep the relationship spicy.

* * * * *

Bethany burned dinner that night. She looked at the mess and worked up a batch of gravy to cover it with. Her mind wasn't on food. Oh no, now that she'd opened her mind to wickedness, she was falling headfirst into a pit of continuous hunger.

Her body was twisting with need already. She knew Gabe would be home soon and her skin tingled with just the idea of him being in the room with her. It had always been that way between them, the difference was that now she knew what it was she wanted.

Everything. Bethany wanted to give as much pleasure as she got and everyone else's opinion could go straight to Satan. They were married and, to her way of thinking, there was nothing wrong with enjoying the bodies that their creator had gifted them with.

The window rattled telling her Gabe had opened the back door. Every nerve in her body was suddenly alert and waiting for the night to commence. That idea sent her into a fit of giggles that Gabe raised an eyebrow at as he entered the kitchen.

Right there was the main reason he loved her. Gabe caught the slight tinge of burnt battered steak and Bethany was laughing. It was strange how a man could find solace in something as common as cooking supper. He could stand there and watch Bethany scrub the pots and a grin would turn up his lips every time. It was the way she twisted her lips when she was mad and the soft scent of her skin and the rustle of her skirt as she moved. All of those things that made her a woman who welcomed him home and into her bed.

That was where his smile melted into an expression that was much more intense. His cock was already swelling as he looked at the table and saw Bethany's nude body stretched out over its polished wood surface. Bethany stopped laughing as she looked at his face. She brandished a wooden spoon at him in warning.

"You can just eat this supper first, Gabriel Wilton. The pot will not be left on the coals all night making me a mess to clean."

"Yes, ma'am." His duster was hung on the coat rack as he passed her on the way to the sink to wash up. A hard smack landed on her bottom making her yelp.

"Gabriel!"

The water splashed as Gabe turned a smirk at her. "Yes, wife?"

"I believe I'm much too old to be swatted like a child."

Gabe wiped his hand on a towel and placed his hands on his hips for a moment. His eyes considered her as some kind of decision formed in his brain. He reached right past her and hooked the handle of the black pot and slid it over to the kitchen cutting board. A second later he hooked that arm around her waist and pulled her against his body.

"I'm really hungry, Bethany, but not for food." His mouth landed on hers and pressed her lips apart. The wooden spoon clattered to the floor as his tongue thrust into her mouth and found her tongue. He stroked her tongue with his as his lips moved over hers in a hard kiss. Hunger spread to life instantly now that she understood exactly what her body craved. Her clit was heating as her passage began to grow wet.

Gabe lifted his head and grinned at her. A second later he turned her around and pushed her body down over the table once again. Bethany gasped as her skirt was pulled right up and tossed over her back. Gabe twisted the waistband of her knickers and the button went popping off once again.

"A few smacks on a woman's fanny means a different thing than they do on a child's bottom. Some women say it makes them hot for a fucking."

Bethany was sure her eyes were as wide as a child's about to be chastised. Gabe swept her knickers down her legs and tossed them over a chair. The cool night air brushed her bare bottom and she shivered at the pure submission of her position. Gabe granted her no mercy as he used one foot to separate her feet even further.

"I'm not going to fuck you until we're in bed tonight, baby." Gabe leaned down to nip the top of her ear with his teeth. "No matter how much you beg me to."

"Oh really, Gabe." Bethany snorted but there was a little tremble to her words that made a liar out of her bravado. Her passage was already hot for the return of the hard attention she'd received last night. Knowing Gabe could open his fly and sink his cock into her at any second somehow made everything more intense. She couldn't see him and that doubled her excitement because she had no idea what he was doing.

Gabe chuckled and smoothed a hand over one cheek of her bottom. He moved to the opposite side and rubbed that mound too. A second later a hard smack landed on her right flank and she cried out at the unexpected pain. Gabe pressed a hand onto her lower back to hold her over the table as he smacked her other cheek and then delivered a few more to her bare bottom.

She whimpered but it wasn't in pain. The sharp sting from his smacks was traveling straight into her clit. More fluid poured down from her passage to wet the top of her thighs as Gabe spanked her some more.

"I can smell your pussy getting wetter." Gabe smacked her bottom and then a single finger moved through her wet slit. "Oh yes, babe, I'm going to have to spank you more often." His fingertip found her clit and rubbed the little button as Bethany whimpered with sheer need. Her passage demanded to be filled.

"Gabe…"

He smacked her bottom twice more and then rubbed her burning flanks. All that heat bled right into her passage where it twisted for the cock she knew was right behind her. Gabe's finger slid through her slit once more and rubbed over her clit.

"Gabe, please!"

Oh, she did not care if she was begging! But the truth was she wanted to scream at him and demand that he finish what he'd started. Her body was shivering as her bottom burned and actually lifted to offer her passage up for his penetration. The hand on her back lifted and Bethany pushed her body up off the table. She turned around and growled at Gabe.

He chuckled at her temper and cupped her chin in one hand. His mouth landed on hers in a hard kiss as a moan rose from her body. She was roasting alive in the flames of the fire he'd set with his spanking. Maybe it was the first hint of the inferno of damnation but Bethany intended to help this fire spread so that she wouldn't be the only one desperate for release.

She reached for Gabe's waistband and heard another chuckle, but that amusement ended in a harsh grunt as she pulled the buttons open and boldly slid her hand right into his pants to clasp his cock. The thing jumped in her grasp and she curled her fingers around it and pressed her hand down his length before pulling her hand back up to the head of his cock.

"You're a dreadful tease, Gabriel, and I do believe it is time to even up the score."

Bethany dropped to her knees and pulled his cock from the open fly. She looked at the ruby head with its slit, and leaned forward to let the tip of her tongue run over just the crown of it.

Gabe cussed and jumped away from her. Bethany stood up and began to open her dress. "You can just come right back here, Gabriel."

Holy Hell!

His wife had licked his cock! Gabe stared at her sweet face and tried to understand just where she might have got the notion to do a thing like that to him.

"Bethany Marie, did you go to that saloon today?"

A huge smile split her lips as she shucked her dress and petticoat. Gabe couldn't keep his eyes on her face as she stood there in a red corset and scarlet stockings. They were pulled up to her thighs and he decided she was the sexist thing he'd ever set eyes on. There was no awkward shiver or stance tonight despite the fact that her pussy was on display because he'd taken her knickers off. She even trailed one of her fingers over the swells of her breasts above the top of her corset.

Gabe felt his throat go dry.

"Why, yes I did, Gabe, and I must confess it was a very interesting conversation. You did tell me not to go to the China shop again. Honey has some very interesting bits of knowledge that she kindly shared with me." Right then they could hear the first shouts of the evening as men began to gather in the street below the madam's rooms. Bethany suddenly lifted one of her legs and placed her foot on one of the kitchen chairs. She curled a single finger at him exactly like the madams did. "Want to relax with me, sugar?"

His feet were moving before his brain formed a single thought. This was a saucy side of his sweet Bethany that gave her even more appeal. She had gone to a madam for him. Now some men in town might have fallen over and died from shock but Gabe savored the burn of excitement that rushed through his veins as he got close enough for her hand to clasp his cock once again.

Bethany took her foot off the chair and knelt once again in front of her husband. Oh, how was it possible to feel so empowered while on your knees? She shook her head as she worked her hand down to the base of his staff and back up once more. Gabe sucked in his breath and she grinned. Yes, she was in control now. Her husband would be the one driven to the edge of control instead of her.

But she would reap the benefits when his control snapped. Bethany sobered as she leaned forward and licked the slit on top of his cock once again. There was a tiny drop of fluid that tasted salty and she sent her tongue back through the slit a few times. It wasn't an unpleasant duty. Her tongue moved around the ridge that crowned his cock before she opened her mouth and took the head between her lips.

Gabe cussed. A harsh phrase that burned her ears but it also polished her ego. She used her fingers to stroke the length of staff not in her mouth and his hips jerked forward, driving more of his cock into her mouth. She heard his breath rasping between his clenched teeth and worked her tongue over the cock head inside her mouth.

A second later, Gabe held her head with one hand threaded through her hair and pulled his cock away from her lips. His eyes flickered with burning need as he hooked a hand under her arm and lifted her from her knees. Gabe caught her waist and lifted her feet right off the floor. He turned and pressed her body up against the wall. His hips spread her thighs wide as the head of his cock probed her wet slit for the entrance to her body.

"Wrap your arms around my shoulders." Gabe growled the command a second before his cock thrust up into her. One of his hands had slipped beneath her bottom to help hold her up and the other slipped between their bodies to her slit where he gently moved the folds covering her clit open. His cock slid right against her clit a moment later when he began to fuck her.

His hips drove his length deep into her body with hard thrusts that made her whimper each time his cock rubbed against her clit. His hands grasped her bottom as his chest pressed her against the wall and his hips continued to thrust that cock into her body. Gabe snarled next to her ear as she felt his cock swelling inside her. He bucked between her thighs and shoved deep into her body as his seed began to hit her insides.

Her clit twisted with pleasure so mind-numbing, Bethany had no idea if she screamed or not. Her fingers turned into claws that dug into the shoulders pressing her back against the wall. Gabe's chest rose and fell with huge motions that proved exactly how emotional he was at that moment too. Bethany smoothed her hands over his shoulder and unbuttoned the first button still holding his shirt closed.

Gabe lifted his head from the wall and smiled at her. It was a tiny lifting of his lips that said far more than words could. Contentment wasn't explained with flowery speeches, it was communicated in the deep rhythm of a heartbeat that she could feel through her corset.

Dinner was only lukewarm but neither of them cared. Gabe served it up after tossing his clothing over a chair. Bethany kept her stockings on but unhooked her corset as Gabe turned the wick in the lamp down. The coals in the stove cast a ruby glow over them as they laughed like children and dined listening to the mischief brewing across the street at the saloon.

Gabe pressed her back into the bed as he cupped her face and lingered over a deep kiss. There was no rushing hurry this time. The heat was still burning in their blood but it wasn't a frantic fire. This was the type that radiated through the body, touching each and every bit of skin.

Gabe thrust deep into her and made his hips control the possession this time. His hands captured hers as he stretched her arms above her on the mattress. The pleasure built by slow degrees as Bethany enjoyed the ride as much as the climax.

His cock wanted to leave more seed inside her. Her pussy was clutching at his cock as he rode her. Her thighs clamping around his hips as she lifted for each thrust and took his length deeply into her. It was dark and primitive but right then, all Gabe thought about was fucking her. Not just driving his cock into a willing female body, he was thinking about fucking Bethany. It was her pussy that he wanted to push his member into, her little whimpers that he needed to hear when his cock pressed against her womb. Releasing his seed had always been a matter of relief but tonight it was more. Tonight it felt like completion as he felt his balls tighten and his seed begin to erupt from his cock. His hips slammed forward to bury his full length in her body, making sure his seed was trapped as deeply as possible inside her body.

Bethany's fingernails bit into his hands as she cried out beneath him. The ultrafeminine sound made him snarl softly as he held her on her back for endless moments while he just enjoyed the contractions of her pussy around his cock. He was a beast but she was his mate right then as he listened to the way she struggled to slow her breathing back down to a more composed rhythm.

"God alone knows how much I love you, Bethany."

His words were thick but they sounded so perfect to her. Knowing he wasn't any more relaxed than she completed the moment. His hands still imprisoned hers and she looked up to see Gabe watching her, almost like he was waiting for her to acknowledge that she was still his captive. That was the little hint of his dark side, his desire to know she understood his strength even though she could feel his seed inside her. A tiny shiver shook her as the night air hit her skin. Her hands were free a second later as Gabe slid out of her body.

Gabe rolled over and took his wife with him. Her body was draped over his as the night covered them, sealing them together for a few stolen hours of intimacy. It was the purest form of affection, the way her head lay on top of his chest. Words could be twisted to suit a person's design but the way a woman embraced a man did not lie. Love sometimes was best expressed by two hands clasped together long after passion had been satisfied.

"I have something for you." Gabe moved in the dark and caught her hand. He moved over each finger until he found her third one. She felt the cold slide of metal as he pushed some kind of ring onto her hand.

Bethany sat up and tried to see what kind of ring he'd put on her hand. In the dark she caught just a tiny glint of light reflection from a stone set into the gold.

"It's a topaz because the jeweler said that was your birthstone."

Bethany stared at the ring and then back at her husband. They had agreed to do without wedding rings because they wanted to build a house and every penny went into their savings. Spending the money on the stockings had been a shocking disobedience to that agreement.

"You make sure you wear that. I believe I need to know every man who sees you understands you're a married woman." Gabe tried to sound harsh but amusement lurked in his voice as he pulled her back into his embrace. "Or should I just say Merry Christmas?"

A little feminine sigh was the only sound Bethany managed to make. There was no jeweler in Silver Peak. Gabe must have bought the ring when he was in Stanton last month.

Maybe it was just a ring but it felt like it was warming her heart from all the way down there on her hand.

Merry Christmas? Well, it was certainly one that they would both be remembering for a good long time!

* * * * *

Two months later, Honey left Silver Peak.

Most of the good townsfolk pretended they didn't see the madam standing next to her trunk as she waited for the noon stagecoach. Bethany hurried to pack up some fresh baked bread and cut off a chunk of cheese. She wrapped it all in a cloth and took the steps two at a time as she went to say goodbye. Across the street, Tom Filk sputtered in outrage as Gabe turned the dock corner.

"What is your wife doing with that whore?"

Gabe pushed his hat brim up and looked across the street to see Bethany smile as she handed a willow basket up into the stagecoach.

"I believe Bethany is being neighborly, and right Christian of her, too." Gabe shot a hard look at Tom's disapproval. "My wife doesn't judge others. I believe that's what the good pastor was talking about last week." Gabe raised a dark eyebrow. "Wasn't it?"

Tom found something better to do as Gabe crossed the street to stand next to Bethany as the stage pulled away. Honey raised a gloved hand to cover her smile as she looked at the two of them through the back window.

"Now there goes someone I think I will miss." Gabe raised an eyebrow at her and Bethany winked at him in response. "Students should always remember their mentors, Gabe, don't you agree?"

Her husband laughed and Bethany hooked her arm over his forearm as they strolled back to their home. Life was about balances, the sweet and the spicy, the gentle and the strong.

But it was the combinations that were turning out to her favorite. If she was lucky, her husband would never stop surprising her and she was going to do her best to return the favor in kind.

Also by Mary Wine

A Wish, A Kiss, A Dream (*anthology*)
Alcandian Quest
Alcandian Rage
Beyond Boundaries
Beyond Lust
Dream Shadow
Dream Specter
Dream Surrender
Ellora's Cavemen: Tales from the Temple III (*anthology*)
Tortoise Tango

About the Author

I write to reassure myself that reality really is survivable. Between traffic jams and children's sporting schedules, there is romance lurking for anyone with the imagination to find it.

I spend my days making corsets and petticoats as a historical costumer. If you send me an invitation marked formal dress, you'd better give a date or I just might show up wearing my bustle.

I love to read a good romance and with the completion of my first novel, I've discovered I am addicted to writing these stories as well.

Dream big or you might never get beyond your front yard.

Mary welcomes comments from readers. You can find her website and email address on her author bio page at www.ellorascave.com.

A VERY FAERIE CHRISTMAS

Mackenzie McKade

Trademarks Acknowledgement

The author acknowledges the trademarked status and trademark owners of the following wordmarks mentioned in this work of fiction:

Q-tip: Unilever Supply Chain, Inc.

Velcro: Velcro Industries

Venus Butterfly: California Exotic Novelties

Chapter One

Who would have thought that in the blink of an eye Candice Lowry's life would change so drastically? It all started with the purchase of a five-foot Christmas tree from the local tree lot in Chandler, Arizona. Well, it wasn't the tree, but the faery within. A wood faery, to be exact.

Three inches in height, he sat on her dashboard casually picking at the hem of his vest—which looked as if it were made from tree bark embroidered with wilted leaves and vines. He wore tights and slippers a deeper brown than his dark skin tone. The warm smell of soil and nature surrounded him. His appearance was rugged, as if he could melt into the earth itself and disappear.

He glanced at her through narrowed eyes. "You shouldn't have ignored me."

Her face flushed with heat. "You made me look like a fool." Unconsciously, her foot pressed harder on the gas.

He feigned surprise. "Me? You're the one who leaned on the tree." Then he pulled his knees to his chest and began to laugh all over again. "Did you see that lot attendant's expression when all the trees fell like the parting of the Red Sea?"

Candice cringed. The trees had fallen in different directions, in a domino effect, one right after another. The crash was loud enough to be heard a mile down the street. Everyone nearby witnessed her humiliation.

Embarrassed and dismayed, all she'd wanted to do was leave. She chose the only tree left standing, which had held a certain faery named Hector within its branches.

"I thought your hissing was a rattlesnake," she said innocently. How was she to know all he had wanted was her attention?

The little man rolled onto his back, holding his stomach, his tiny legs kicking in the air. "I know. I know. You should have seen how quickly you moved. It looked like you were standing on a bed of hot coals the way you danced about."

"Ha. Ha." She pressed the brake a little too quickly at the oncoming red light. Her tires squealed, the car slid a short distance.

Hector's eyes opened wide as he rolled across the surface of the dashboard. He hit the window and then rolled back before falling off. Midair, his translucent wings appeared, fluttering madly. When he rose into the air a shower of dark green faery dust wafted around him.

His smile was gone. "You're killing me, Candice. Work with me here."

She glanced at him and then the stoplight. "Okay, tell me again why you're here."

Unbelievable. She was talking to a faery. Or was it her imagination? She *had* drunk two eggnogs before she'd shut down her accounting office for the holidays.

He situated himself on the beaded necklace hanging from her rearview mirror as if it were a swing. Holding on, he kicked his feet and set it into a slow, swaying motion.

"Girl," he paused, "you're in need of a serious makeover."

The light turned green. Candice eased her foot onto the gas pedal as her gaze shot to Hector. "Makeover?"

"On the lonely meter you're registering a nine point three out of ten." He leaned back and forth on the necklace, making it move faster, higher. "You look like a cranky librarian. How old are you anyway?"

Just her luck—a faery with an attitude.

She focused her attention on the road. Did he have to remind her that she would be spending another Christmas alone? "Twenty-six." *But I feel like eighty.* "And you don't need to get nasty."

When she pulled to a halt in front of her apartment complex, she switched the car off. The engine whined, coughed and shuddered before dying. She opened her door and Hector zipped by her so quickly that she felt a brush of air across her face. His wings were a blur as he darted around, taking everything in.

From a distance he looked like a hummingbird. Still, she had no idea how she was going to get him past the lobby attendant. Then he dove into the tree atop her car, burrowing in the branches.

A sigh slipped from her mouth. Yes. She wanted to get into the Christmas spirit, but how the hell was she going to get this monstrosity off her car and into her apartment? Remembering her fingernail clippers, she dug through her shoulder bag and retrieved them.

With a snip here and there, Candice used the clippers to cut through two of the four pieces of twine holding the tree securely in place. *Snip.* The tension in the line loosened. Only one more to go.

When the last cord snapped, the tree tumbled down. She didn't have time to move as it whacked her chest, branches slapping her face.

"Watch out," a small voice burst from within the tree.

So much for not getting tree sap on her outfit.

"Sorry," she muttered, trying to find a comfortable way to hold on.

Six inches taller than the five-foot tree, she still felt like the darn thing engulfed her. It was everywhere. The needles poked into her and the bark was sticky as she inched her way toward the entrance of the complex.

"Left. Go left," Hector yelled as she approached a toy car that some kid must have dropped.

"Shush. Someone is going to hear you," she warned.

If she hadn't been so uncomfortable she would have laughed. From the front she probably looked like a possessed Christmas tree wandering aimlessly. The only visible parts of her were her feet. There was just enough space between the branches so that she could see where she was going, but barely.

The lobby attendant, a young man dressed in brown slacks and a tan shirt, opened the glass doors. "Merry Christmas, ma'am," he said. "I'd assist you, but I can't leave the doors unattended."

"Thank you. I can manage," Candice grunted. If you could call what she was doing managing—moving at the speed of a geisha, using tiny steps that were more of a shuffle. When she approached the elevators, she braced the tree against the wall and pressed the button. The doors parted and she heaved the tree into her arms and stepped inside. As the doors closed, a hand shot in, stopping them.

* * * * *

A delicious burn developed in Gordon Nash's midsection as he finished his last sit-up. His abdominal muscles felt tight and alive. Tension that was present in his neck and shoulders was beginning to fade. This was just what he needed to curb his frustration.

He hated to disappoint his family, but business called. With Japanese associates in town and negotiations for their new communications systems not yet completed, there was no way he could make it to Boston for Christmas. There was no telling how much time he would have to put in at the office the remainder of this week.

At least he had been lucky on the apartment-hunting front.

It was a find to locate an apartment with a health club and other amenities across the street. He grabbed his towel off the floor and wiped the perspiration from his forehead as he headed for the free weights.

He picked up a dumbbell, straddled a nearby bench and bent his right elbow, performing arm curls. *One, two, three…*

Negotiations would be completed just before December twenty-fourth, but he wasn't crazy enough to try to make it home. Perhaps next month he'd fly home to see his parents and brother and sisters who still lived nearby.

He focused inward. Breathing deeply, releasing slowly. A drop of sweat rolled from his forehead and disappeared into his eye. *Fuck.* It burned, but he kept focused on how his arm muscles strained against the iron in his hand. Tendons running across his biceps flexed and relaxed, bulging as they pressed tightly against his hot, moist skin.

He had never missed one of his mother's homemade pumpkin pies, not in all his thirty years. She made one especially for him each Thanksgiving and Christmas. The memory of the spicy scent filled his nose. He could almost taste the whipped cream as his mouth began to water. His stomach even growled.

He focused again on his breathing, slowly raising and lowering his arm, feeling the sting, relishing the burn.

One thing he wouldn't miss was his family chastising him about getting married and having children.

It seemed everyone around him was married or getting married. His boss had even said that he should find a woman and settle down. His thoughts turned to his neighbor down the hall from his new apartment.

On the surface she appeared to be a meek, mild thing, but when she looked at him he saw something different in her eyes. She gave him the impression of a trapped bird wanting to be released, wanting to spread her wings.

The endorphin high he was on and the image of the woman in his mind made his cock harden. She wore too many clothes, one layer over the other. Her hair was always held captive on top of her head, so tight her eyes had a slant to them. She wore no makeup and she hid behind her glasses.

But those eyes… She had the most unusual violet eyes he had ever seen.

He couldn't really tell what lay beneath all those clothes, but her body language definitely said, *Stay away. I'm not interested.* On the other hand, her eyes screamed, *I'm yours. Do anything you want to me.* His business experience had taught him a lot about reading people, and this woman was *all* woman. She just needed a little help discovering herself.

As he dabbed the towel against his forehead, he placed the dumbbell back on the rack and then strolled to the bench press. He added fifty additional pounds per side and took a seat. Sliding onto his back, his chest centered beneath the weights, he placed his palms against the cool iron bar.

He paused in reflection.

The brunette was like a block of clay waiting to be formed. He wiggled his fingers, stretching and working the tightness out of them, then folded them firmly around the bar again. And he had just the right hands to mold her.

An ache squeezed his balls at the thought. He could almost envision the shock on her face as his handcuffs clicked shut around her wrists, the wild and curious look in her beautiful eyes as he gently stroked her body with his flogger. His cock jerked with excitement. He imagined the way her eyes would close, her head lolling, the soft cry of ecstasy she'd make as he marked her body.

Inhaling deeply, he lifted the bar with a grunt. The weight fought against his hands. His mind focused on the iron above him as he raised it higher and higher. When his elbows locked a quiver raced through his arms. He held the three hundred pounds suspended before slowly easing the bar down. The strain against body and mind was a sweet sensation. When the iron was a breath away from his heaving chest he lifted the weight once more until it was high above him. He repeated the exercise a few more times, then settled the weight in its cradle. In silence, he lay there—slowing his heart rate, controlling his breathing—and smiled.

Oh yeah. Her silky skin would be a soft pink all over. He would dominate her—and she would enjoy every minute of it.

He couldn't help reaching down to adjust himself. He was rock-hard just thinking about her. He hadn't noticed another name on her mailbox. Perhaps if things worked out just right he wouldn't be alone for Christmas.

He gathered up his towel and made his way to the door. Outside, the air smelled fresh from the recent rain. Gray clouds littered the sky, but looked like they were finally moving on.

He waited for three cars to pass, then crossed the road to his apartment complex. The doorman nodded his greetings just as Gordon saw a Christmas tree disappear into the elevator. Heavy steps carried him to the closing doors, which he halted, wedging himself inside.

To his surprise and delight it was the brunette who had filled his thoughts.

* * * * *

Candice felt her blood pressure soar. It was Mr. Tall, Dark and Handsome, the man who had just moved in two doors down from her on the third floor. Each time she saw him her imagination took a leap. It seemed to be doing that more often these days, she thought, as she remembered the little faery hidden within her tree.

There was something about her new neighbor that stirred a fire within her, a slow burn that made her hot and bothered.

"Candice, your pulse is racing," Hector informed her.

"Shush," she whispered. Damn. How would she justify talking to a tree?

Every night for the past week her dreams had included wild, passionate sex with the man standing before her. Even now her breasts felt heavy. Her nipples tightened and it wasn't just because the Christmas tree rubbed against them.

"Psst." Hector continued to be annoying.

Please be quiet, she prayed.

Candice pulled the tree closer to her and peered through the branches at the fine collection of muscles packaged into a six-foot-three frame of solid male. From the perspiration dampening the neckline of his t-shirt, she knew he was a jogger or into some type of exercise or sport. Even the male scent warring against his light woodsy aftershave and the Christmas tree aroma kicked her libido into high gear.

"Hi." His tone was deep and sexy, releasing a flood of desire between her thighs.

Sure that she looked stupid hiding behind the tree, she let it lean forward. Her tongue wet her lips. "Hi." Her voice was a squeak as she tried to rein in her emotions.

Hot damn. He was gorgeous. His smile was like hot chocolate on a winter's night, it warmed her through and through. His sky blue eyes sparkled as if they held a secret.

When she reached up to smooth her hair, she almost died. Without looking, she knew the rain had done a job on it, and there were pine needles sticking all through the bun that was now leaning to the side of her head.

As if things couldn't get worse, the tree slipped from her hand, fell, and slapped the man against his chest before she could catch it.

"Ooof." Both Hector and the man said in unison. She knew the needles must be burrowing into his skin.

"Oh my God, I'm so sorry," she cried, as she hurried to retrieve the tree.

His laughter was light as he easily took control of the situation. "No problem. Why don't I carry it to your apartment? You're only a couple doors down from my place."

She was speechless. He knew where she lived? When she could speak again, she said, "Really? I mean…that would be great, if you don't mind."

Again, he graced her with a bright smile that made her toes curl and a delightful knot form low in her belly. "Not at all. I'm Gordon Nash." He held out his hand and clasped her sticky one to his.

Shit. She grimaced. Their hands stuck together. "Sorry." She slowly withdrew. "Candice Lowry."

His brows rose and his smile grew into a sexy grin. "Candice." He paused as if he were trying it on for size. "I like that." His tone dropped an octave, smoothing over her like a warm summer breeze.

His penetrating blue eyes remained on her, making her skin feel a little too tight. Hell. Even her loose clothing felt too tight. She resisted the urge to pull at her neckline or to pluck the needles from her hair.

When the elevator doors opened, he stood aside, held them and allowed her to exit. He heaved the tree into his arms like it was nothing and followed her.

Hector was blessedly silent.

Fumbling in her purse, Candice retrieved her keys and opened her apartment door, jamming her foot against it to keep it open as he passed through.

When he was in the middle of her living room he halted.

Was it just her imagination, or did the man fit perfectly in her apartment? She considered shutting the door and locking it tight. Possession was nine-tenths of the law. Legally, he would be hers—wouldn't he? Instead, she pulled it closed and drifted further into the room.

Her meager belongings—a loveseat, chair, coffee table and entertainment center—looked so much better with him standing before them. Her eyes darted toward the bedroom and she wondered if it would be too presumptuous to ask, *coffee, tea or me*?

Just the thought of having him between the sheets heated her cheeks. Her palms itched to touch him, to feel his rippling muscles beneath her fingertips. She looked at his large hands and could only imagine what hid beneath those shorts. Her mouth watered.

What would he do if she knelt and took his cock into her mouth?

He looked around the room. "Where would you like it?"

Bedroom, kitchen table, couch, floor, it didn't matter. She'd make love to him anywhere. "Anywhere you do," she answered dreamily.

His forehead furrowed. "What?"

She felt her eyes jerk wide. *Ohmygod.* He was talking about the tree. "Uh…I said anywhere will do." Heat raced up her throat and burst across her face.

When he turned away, she released the breath she held. He was gorgeous even in his workout clothes. She sighed, wishing his shorts were tighter.

"This looks like a good place. Close to the window so when the lights are lit everyone can enjoy it with you." He chose an empty space and leaned the tree against the wall. "If you need help getting it in its stand, let me know." His tongue slid across his lips and his eyes seemed to darken. Candice's own tongue darted across her bottom lip as if tasting him.

Man, her imagination was working overtime. The man wasn't coming on to her. Men who looked like he did weren't attracted to women like her. His help with the tree was only the neighborly thing to do, she told herself.

She forced her mouth into a smile. "Thanks, but you've already done so much."

He headed for the door, opened it, and then paused. "If you change your mind," something flickered in his eyes, "you know where to find me." He stood for a brief second, then disappeared, closing the door behind him.

Candice gazed wistfully at the spot where he once stood.

When Hector fluttered from out of the tree she turned to him and sighed. "He's my wish. I want him for Christmas."

Chapter Two

Boink. Boink.

Candice was barely aware of the repetitive jabs to the tip of her nose. Tired. So tired. She cracked her eyes open to the sound of fluttering wings and the sight of last night's apparition suspended above her.

"Rise and shine." Hector zipped back and forth in front of her face leaving a trail of sparkles. Softly, he landed on her pillow, tucking his wings against his back. He took a step toward her. "You look like shit."

Wonderful. Not only was this not a dream, but she was saddled with a three-inch faery more than willing to point out the flaws in her appearance.

He plucked a pine needle from her hair and leaned on it as if it were a cane, crossing his legs at the ankle. With a critical eye he took in her disheveled appearance. "What you need is a makeover. Hair, makeup, clothes—and we have to do something about those glasses."

Now that was something she could get into. She'd seen miraculous makeovers on television. She pushed herself into a sitting position. Since her imagination refused to release this whimsical daydream, what would it hurt to go along with it? "Really? You can do that?"

"Oh ye of little faith." He straightened to his full height and whacked the pillow with the pine needle. "Now get up and let's go to the mall."

Her eyes widened. "What?" Surely she hadn't heard him correctly.

"You know, the place where people congregate to buy and sell items."

Her brows pulled together. "I know what a mall is. Can't you just wave your wand or hands and—*poof!*—change me?"

He chuckled, tucking the pine needle beneath his arm. "Magic should only be used in dire cases. You, my dear, have a decent package to work with." His vision lit on her breasts. The twinkle in his eyes was pure male appreciation. "Guidance is what you need—and a credit card."

Candice couldn't believe her ears. She was just about to protest when he blew a handful of faery dust into her face causing her vision to blur. The itch of a sneeze tickled the back of her nose. As her sight cleared, an image of Gordon Nash flashed in her head.

Her heart stuttered.

Shit. She was desperate enough to try anything and Hector knew it. This Christmas she would not be alone, even if it meant listening to a wood faery.

Hector made big movements with his arms. "With my help the butterfly will emerge." Somehow his words weren't comforting.

* * * * *

Candice's gaze flickered to her rearview mirror. Staring back was a stranger. It was amazing that a beautician, makeup artist, optometrist and fashion coordinator could turn her into a sexy and attractive woman in only five hours. She had gone from a plain Jane to a modern version of Cleopatra. Heads had turned and more than one man whistled…actually whistled!

She even wore three-inch stilettos with her short black leather skirt. The shoes had taken several hours to get used to. A soft white cashmere sweater lay softly on her shoulders. Her dull brunette hair now had red and gold woven through it as it brushed the top of her hips. Makeup lined her eyes, not heavy—just enough to bring attention to them. It was amazing how a little lipstick could make a woman's lips look so full and luscious.

A horn blared and she jerked the steering wheel and her attention back to the road. The fact she'd almost run into another vehicle wasn't funny, but watching Hector ping-pong off the dashboard and ceiling brought a giggle to her lips.

"Funny? You think that's funny?" A cloud of red mist formed around him. "Turn in here."

She did as she was told and parked the car. "Uh, Hector, this is an adult store. I can't go in there."

He buzzed his frustration, his wings fluttering as he landed on the dashboard. "Sure you can. Get out of the car and move one foot in front of the other until you're inside." He made a scooting motion with his palms. "Now get."

Smart-ass. Her pulse sped up. "But I've never been inside a place like this." Her voice sounded small, lost and scared.

"And that's the reason we're here. Educational purposes, of course. You can attract a man, but do you know what makes him tick?" Hector's tone turned serious, little lines creasing his forehead. "Candice, do you know what a man likes a woman to do to him? What he enjoys? How to keep him happy?"

Hector's words echoed her fear as well. She wasn't a virgin, but there had definitely been something missing with her previous experiences. But could she really go through with it?

You can do this. The car door squeaked as she opened it, the sound creating a shiver that raced down her spine. Her heart pounded. "Hector." His name came out tight and high-pitched.

In a flash, he was in flight. The impact as he landed just above her left breast made her take a step backwards. "I'm here for you, babe."

"But you're in plain sight for everyone to see."

He tucked his wings away and bent an arm, resting one hand on his hip. "I'm a stick pin." His expression went blank. He held perfectly still.

An uneasy laugh spilled from her lips. A really ugly stick pin, but she wouldn't tell him. His rugged looks and earth tones weren't exactly what a woman would wear, yet it would have to do.

As she walked inside she was greeted by two young women behind the cash register. Candice's smile was forced, but she managed a "hi" as she moved on.

"What now?" Candice asked softly.

"Books," Hector murmured, his lips barely moving.

Candice was surprised to see rows and rows of books. The titles of some of them made her jaw drop. Among them were instructions on masturbation, bondage and something called the Venus Butterfly.

"That one." Hector pointed to a book entitled *101 BDSM Tips for Dummies*. He lost his grip and slid down her chest, until he rested on the swell of her breast.

"Hi, can I be of assistance?" asked a young woman with so many piercings that Candice couldn't help but stare. There was one in her eyebrow, nose, lip and six earrings in her right ear alone.

Candice shook her head. "No. But thank you."

"Interesting pin." Cherry, as her name tag identified her, leaned closer and looked at Hector whose hand was now held high. "Where'd you get it?"

Shit. Candice stumbled for an answer. "Ah…the mall. You know that little novelty store? I forget its name."

"It almost looks real." Cherry drew back. "If you need anything just ask." She took one last look at Hector and then strolled away.

"Bah. 'Almost looks real'," Hector growled, moving so that his feet poked into Candice's breast. "What would a pinhead like her know about real?"

Cherry glanced over her shoulder.

Candice turned away. "Shush. You're drawing attention."

"Grab that book, one on oral sex and the one on female pleasures. You need to know what makes you tick, too."

"Shush," she repeated as she gathered the books, her hands shaking. Arms full, she moved away, out of Cherry's line of sight.

Candice was amazed, strolling down the aisles. Rubber cocks so large they almost made her cringe. Butt plugs, clit stimulators, lotions and lubricants, anything you needed to enhance your sex life. She was ready to try anything, including the little leather ensemble and a couple of other toys that Hector insisted she just had to have.

After an hour they were ready to go.

With her bag of goodies beside her on the car seat, her new look and her faery godfather swinging once again on the necklace, a wave of confidence rushed through her.

She was ready.

* * * * *

Gordon nearly tripped over his jaw as Candice breezed into the elevator. Was this the same woman? He couldn't help the slow caress his gaze made up her long, slender legs. He could almost imagine them locked around his waist as he parted her folds and plunged into her warmth.

"Oh. Hi." Even her voice seemed sexier as it slid across him like silk. She wore no glasses and her violet eyes were mesmerizing. He found himself drowning in them.

"Hi." His response was a rasp, sandpaper against metal.

Fuck. She was hot. He had been attracted to her before, but now the woman was a knockout. She simply took his breath away. Not to mention the rush of blood that filled his cock. He dragged his briefcase in front of him to hide the hardening evidence. The ache behind his slacks was becoming uncomfortable as he adjusted his hips, seeking relief.

Within twenty-four hours Candice had gone from a mild, meek girl to a full-blown woman. What was responsible for the transformation or, more importantly, who?

Was he too late?

"Do you like Chinese food?" The impulsive words spilled from his mouth. Strangely, his pulse raced. He wanted this woman.

"What?" Her brows pulled together. She looked nervous as she shuffled her bags from one arm to the next.

The corners of his lips tugged into a smile. This time when he spoke he felt more in control. Slowly, he said, "Would you like to go to dinner tonight?"

The way she paused, mouth parting, he could tell he'd taken her by surprise. Her mouth didn't move, but he swore he heard, "No."

She glanced at the ugly brooch she wore on her chest. "Shush..." Her gaze rose meeting his. A shy smile caressed her lips. "Yes. Yes. I'd love to."

Her reaction and response were odd, but Gordon wasn't willing to pass up the opportunity to get to know her better—all of her.

Then, as if her packages had been torn from her arms, they fell. She lunged, but was too late as the contents scattered on the floor. Both stooped at the same time to retrieve her merchandise. She moved frantically to retrieve the items and he could see why.

Among clothes and shoes and array of other things were several risqué items. His timid little mouse had purchased a vibrator and a sexy little black leather ensemble. But when he picked up her BDSM book, he knew they were made for each other. She was curious and he was just the man to quench her thirst for knowledge.

"Oh God." A wisp of desperation crept into her voice. Humiliation brightened her eyes as spots of embarrassment appeared on her cheeks. Her chest rose and fell quickly. Her gaze darted around the elevator as if the walls were moving in on her.

His fingers circled her slender wrist. "Candice." Her throat tightened as she swallowed. "Honey, there's nothing to be embarrassed about." Her eyes were unblinking. He deepened his smile. "In fact, I'm pleased to see where your interests lie." His palm slid up her arm to her elbow, touching the softness of her cashmere sweater. A finger dipped beneath the material and moved back and forth. The bell rang, announcing they had reached their floor.

Gordon gathered her packages. Then he helped her to rise. He knew she was feeling vulnerable as he led her from the elevator to her door. He moved closer to her so that their lips were a breath away and the pin on her chest poked him. He ignored the pain and softly pressed his lips to hers. Then the brooch dislodged, a needle driving beneath his skin. He jerked back and both their gazes fell to the ugly thing.

"I think it's broken," he said rubbing his chest and wondering why she would wear such a weird object. It looked like a conglomeration of sticks and leaves molded into a little man. She cupped it gently, almost cherishingly. Her innocent eyes rose to meet his.

Then she began to fumble with her purse, extracting her keys. In minutes they were inside her apartment. He lay her packages down on the couch and then moved toward her. She still hadn't said a word since the elevator. Her teeth worried her bottom lip.

He slipped his fingertips beneath her chin and leaned in for another kiss. This time he stayed away from her brooch, but the desire to feel her breasts pressed to his chest was strong. His hands itched to really hold her. He was dying to strip her of her clothing and unveil her secrets. There was so much he could teach her about herself.

Cheek pressed to hers, he whispered, "I'll pick you up in three hours. I suggest you check out the bondage book. Skim through it and we'll talk about it at dinner. Perhaps I can help you with any questions you may have or research you may want to explore." He felt the tremor that shook her, whether from fear or excitement, he couldn't tell.

As they drew apart, she forced a smile that didn't show in her eyes. How slow would he have to take it with her? His cock was beyond hard. The ache made it difficult to move as he headed for the door.

It looked like Christmas might prove promising after all. With a little luck he wouldn't be spending the holiday alone.

Chapter Three

The knock on the door ripped Candice off the couch. The book in her lap fell, the sound muffled by the carpet. As she stood and retrieved the book, the thrum of wings grew louder as Hector darted from her bedroom. The little devil was nosy. After berating her for accepting Gordon's invitation to dinner, he had pouted and then began to rummage through her things.

They had argued for over thirty minutes. She wanted this night to herself, insisting that Hector remain behind. The wood faery was adamant that he would attend.

"He's here." She couldn't believe how her heart beat, the rapid pulse echoing like drums in her ears. Hands trembling, she glanced down at the book she set on the coffee table. Just the subject matter brought heat to her face. Could she go through with what it recommended? The thought of giving her body and soul to someone who would dominate her was exciting. Even the idea of being tied up sent a thrill through her.

Hector frowned. "This is not a good idea." His wings were a blur as he hovered a foot away from her nose.

She ducked around him. "Why do you dislike Gordon?" Her stilettos were silent against the carpet as she moved to the door.

A steady buzz followed her throughout the room. "It's not that I disapprove of the man, I just believe that you need more time to learn about yourself and your own sexuality."

She pivoted and faced the faery. "I want this." Emotion bubbled up from out of nowhere, choking her. "I-I *need* this, Hector." The desperation in her voice softened the faery's stern expression. Her eyes widened to force back tears that threatened to fall. She took a deep breath and released it slowly. "Now. How do I look?" She slipped her palms down her dress. It was cool beneath her touch.

Hector had insisted she wear her old clothes, saying things were moving too quickly. But she had chosen a silky red dress that clung to her curves. She wanted Gordon to want her. The strapless bra and tiny thong made her feel as if she wore nothing at all. She felt sexy. But the confidence she had earlier was gone as if blown away by a heavy breeze.

"Candice, you're breathtaking." He smiled, but his eyes held a touch of concern. His little Adam's apple dipped as his features drew tight. Then in a single gust of air, he said, "Remember—keep your distance. Keep the conversation light and away from sex." He sucked in a breath as his wings released a light cloud of dark green faery dust.

She shook her head. His anxiety wasn't helping her. Still, she was determined to show Hector and prove to herself that she was ready for anything—including Gordon Nash.

As she opened the door, Hector gathered a lock of her hair and plastered himself against it like a barrette. It was too late to argue with the faery—Gordon stood before her.

When his gaze swept across her, Candice forgot about the faery pinned to her hair. Raw hunger burned in his eyes and it was all for her. She choked, realizing she'd held her breath. For some reason she wanted to please him.

"Damn, you're gorgeous," Gordon groaned. He inhaled deeply and she knew he caught the light scent of the citrus perfume she had chosen with him in mind.

He smelled good, too. She loved the spicy fragrance that rose from his red polo shirt. Her gaze followed the veins that slid across his tanned arms. To finish off his neat appearance were navy blue slacks that had a freshly pressed seam down the middle and brown loafers. He had a brown leather jacket in the bend of his arm. She loved the scent of leather.

"And you smell good enough to eat." His words stirred a memory from the book about oral sex. She had never experienced a man going down on her, but damn, she was ready. Ready to experience what she had been missing all these years. And she wanted that experience to be with this man.

He swept a hand into her hair.

Hector grumbled.

"Hungry?" Gordon asked as he released her and his gaze lit upon her belly.

Oh thank you, she sent her gratitude to the Big Guy upstairs. Gordon had thought it was her stomach growling. If he only knew. "Famished." She placed her palm on her stomach.

Please, Hector, behave.

"The restaurant is just across the street, so I thought we'd walk. Will you be warm enough?" Gordon asked. Again she felt the heat of his gaze across her skin.

"I have a wrap." Candice disappeared into her bedroom. Addressing Hector, she asked softly, "Are you going to behave?" She grabbed the thin, transparent wrap from the bed.

He didn't speak until she reached for him. "Yes. Yes. I'm just worried about you, Candice. Do you think he can make you happy?"

Oh yeah. Gordon Nash could make her very happy. "It's just dinner, Hector." She tried to reassure him, even though she would give anything for it to be much more.

As she drifted back into the living room, Gordon said, "Ready?" and opened the door.

Candice picked up her purse from the kitchen table. "Yes."

Ready as I'll ever be.

It was amazing how good Candice felt against his body as Gordon slipped his arm around her shoulders. She didn't pull away, instead she graced him with an innocent smile as they crossed the street.

The clouds had disappeared. The night was lit with a thousand stars, and a crescent moon hung in the sky. Aromas from different restaurants across the street filled the air. The most dominant was a barbeque restaurant, the heavy aroma of mesquite overpowering.

"Did you get a chance to look at the bondage book?" he asked and she stiffened beneath his arm.

"Yes." Her voice was timid and small.

He drew her closer to the heat of his body. "Is it something that interests you?"

She refused to meet his gaze as they crossed the parking lot. Still she answered, "Yes."

Excitement raced through him. "Have you ever thought of being dominated by a man?" He didn't wait for her to respond. "It's a deeply erotic experience, a thrill and intensity that can't be reached with vanilla sex." Her shoulders rose and fell rapidly beneath his arm. His cock jerked with her reaction. "Have you dreamed of being tied up or spanked, Candice?"

He slowly turned her in his arms and held her close. "Let me introduce you to my world," he whispered, then pressed his mouth to hers.

Candice's head was spinning. His kiss was gentle, yet firm and commanding, as his tongue slid along the crease of her lips, then pushed between them to taste her. She had never been kissed like this. There was control and strength and passion that stole her breath. She found her fingers gripping his shirt. Her body trembled with desire and need, making her breasts feel heavy. They swelled, burrowing into his chest. A rush of moisture dampened her panties. Her legs felt weak.

She doubted her ability to stand, much less walk, at the moment.

A tickle against her ear made her aware that they stood in the middle of a parking lot, a multitude of people strolling to and from the strip mall. Again the titillating itch against her ear appeared.

"*Psst.*" Candice had forgotten about Hector. "Too fast. Slow it down," he warned as the kiss ended.

But she didn't want to slow it down. She wanted to feel the thrill and intensity Gordon spoke of.

The gentle way he stroked her hair. The lust in his blue eyes—for her—sent her body into meltdown. She wanted to please him like the book said. She wanted to feel his hands roam across her heated skin, to feel that moment when their bodies came together as one.

She wanted it all.

Tremor after tremor shook her and she didn't know how to stop them. Her skin felt too tight. The silk of her bra was tormenting her taut nipples. The string of material wedged between the cheeks of her ass—the patch of cloth now damp with her arousal—needed to be replaced by his hand, his mouth, his cock.

A moan slipped from her trembling lips. "Gordon," she whimpered.

"Do you want me to touch you?" Deep and sexy, his voice teased her with the wicked question. "Touch you in front of all these people?"

Yes. She was a breath away from screaming the word. *Yes.*

Instead she heard the word "No". It didn't come from her mouth, but Gordon certainly thought it did, as he released her and took a step backward.

Damn Hector. That wood faery was interfering again. Making out in a parking lot probably wasn't wise. But she was *this* close to holding a man who apparently wanted her as much as she wanted him. Couldn't Hector understand what that felt like? Moisture touched her eyes and she fought to hide it from Gordon as she focused on her purse.

He reached for her and she let him take her into his arms, burying her face into his chest. "I'm sorry, Candice. Did I push too fast?"

"No!" she answered quickly, before Hector could throw his voice again. "I want to experience everything you described."

When he held her at arm's length, he placed a kiss upon her nose. "Tonight? Now?"

She nodded. This was what she wanted.

"We'll start slow. But you'll have to promise to follow my orders without hesitation. Do you have a safe word?"

She had read about this part. "Yes."

The gentleness disappeared from his voice as he guided her between two cars. "Yes, Master. You must call me Master when we're at play."

"Yes, Master."

He placed a finger beneath her chin, raising her gaze to meet his. "Your word?"

"I choose faery. Um, Master."

"Take your panties off." He held out his hand. "Place them in my palm."

She froze. Her pulse leapt. *Without hesitation*, he'd said. As she reached beneath her dress her gaze darted around the parking lot. *You want this, Candice. You want to experience something new – different.*

Hector grumbled, but she ignored him. Stepping out of her panties, she placed them in Gordon's hand. A gust of cool air swept up her dress. She trembled.

He rewarded her with a smile as he slipped her panties into his pocket.

There was no mistaking Gordon's intentions. Tonight he would dominate her and make all her dreams come true.

Taking her hand, they closed the distance to the restaurant. It felt sexy and naughty to be walking into the restaurant with no underwear on.

They were seated immediately. Gordon took charge, ordering for them both. As the soup was delivered, he quietly explained her role. All she had to do was obey and pleasure him. The waiter dumped sizzling hot fried rice into the broth, dished out the soup and then promptly left.

With a spoon to his mouth, Gordon said, "Spread your legs."

Her face grew hot. She took a breath of courage and parted her thighs.

He must have read her uneasy expression. "I won't do anything to embarrass you. Your sweet pussy is hidden by the tablecloth." He sipped his tea. "How does it feel to be bare and exposed?"

"Wicked," she breathed the single word. That's exactly how she felt. And it was wonderful.

"Good."

She absently brushed back her hair and discovered Hector was gone. God, she hoped he wasn't up to something.

Dinner was served and they began to eat. There was small chitchat as Gordon asked her about her business, where she was born and other questions. The night went on as if nothing out of the ordinary existed.

All too soon the check arrived. Two fortune cookies lay beside it.

Gordon chose a cookie, then handed one to her. She broke off a piece, dropping it when a little hand waved at her from inside. Damned if Hector hadn't infiltrated her dessert. How he managed to fit in the small space, she had no idea. She snatched the cookie off the table, receiving a baffled look from Gordon. She chuckled, tossing the cookie into her purse. "I'll save it for later. Uh, if that's okay with you, Master."

While Gordon paid the bill, Candice requested permission to use the bathroom. The minute the door closed, Hector sprang from her purse. He was a blur as he flew from one end of the restroom to the other. He stopped in front of her, his wings throwing off a spray of faery dust.

"Do *not* go home with that man." His hands perched on his hips.

"Oh, shut up. Why don't you go look for a bug zapper?" He flinched and she softened her tone. "I'm sorry, Hector, but this is what I want. Gordon is what I want."

"Then you don't need me." In a puff, Hector vanished.

Candice knew that wasn't so. Her wood faery had done more for her than he would ever realize. He had given her confidence, even his nagging had given her the encouragement to step out of her shell and to reach for what she wanted. And tonight she wanted Gordon.

Chapter Four

Gordon reached inside his apartment and turned the light switch on, illuminating the room. Very little difference existed between his apartment and Candice's, although his was furnished in darker, masculine colors, and his furniture was mostly leather. His kitchen table was glass, his briefcase open upon it.

Her steps were hesitant as she moved further into his living room. But that wouldn't last long. She was so responsive. He had never had a woman who trembled at his mere touch. It did something to him—made him feel that much more a man.

With a brush of his hands he slipped her wrap from around her shoulders. As she turned, innocence brightened her eyes. He ran his knuckles across her cheek and she leaned into his hand, closing her eyes.

"Do you want me to touch you?" he asked.

"Yes, Master," she whispered as if it were a plea.

Featherlight, he drew a path along her scooped neckline, down a collarbone and across the swell of a breast, pausing at her cleavage before continuing on. "Keep your eyes closed. Strip for me." At his words her breathing became more pronounced.

With a swipe of her tongue, she wet her lips, making them glossy and drawing his attention. He wanted to kiss her, take her down on the floor, fuck her hard and fast. Yet he would wait—wait until she was writhing with need, screaming his name.

Palms resting on the couch before her, she slipped from her shoes, her feet burrowing in the soft carpet. Her hands shook as she reached for the hem of her dress. In a sharp, quick motion, she pulled the dress over her head. The minute the swirl of air from the fan above stroked her body hundreds of tiny goose bumps rose across her skin. She trembled before tossing the dress aside.

Gordon cupped himself, sucking in a breath. She was beautiful standing before him in a red strapless bra and no panties. Even before her transformation, he'd known she was special. On an exhale her breath rattled, and she nibbled on her bottom lip. Her long brown hair draped down her back. Her lashes were crescents upon her flushed cheeks. She radiated an undeniable naiveté. Yet he knew she craved knowledge, hungered to learn about pleasures of the flesh.

And she had chosen him to instruct her.

Eyes still closed, she reached for the clasp of her bra, releasing her full breasts. Gordon went weak in the knees. His grip on his cock tightened. A throb pulsated through his balls. He needed to be naked and to feel his skin against hers, part her thighs and thrust into her hot, wet heat. Instead, his gaze stroked her.

The silence was an element of seduction. He wielded it like a weapon to keep her tense, on the edge of excitement. Still, he couldn't resist the groan that surfaced. The curly patch of dark hair shadowing her sex drew him to her side.

"Master," her whisper was almost inaudible.

"You are not to speak unless I give permission." He inched closer so that she could feel his warm breath against her skin. Lightly, he blew a warm stream across her neck and chest until he reached a breast. Her nipple puckered, drawing tighter when his tongue stroked across the nub. He blew again. Tiny bumps formed around her rosy areola. He did the same to her other breast, savoring her responsiveness.

"Spread your legs." Her hand blindly reached out and clutched the arm of the couch as he spoke. She didn't move.

"Now, or you'll be punished." He hardened his voice. A soft whimper left her lips as she complied with his demand.

Gordon wanted to grasp her thighs, splay her wide and taste the sweet nectar of her pussy. Instead he knelt and breathed warm air against her slit, watching her glisten with arousal. The soft scent of woman caressed him and he felt his nostrils flare.

As he rose, he took her hands and placed them at his waist. "Undress me." Her eyelashes flickered. "Keep your eyes closed or I will punish you—drape you over my lap and spank you like a naughty little girl."

She swallowed hard, her tongue again wetting her lips. Her unsteady hands tugged at his shirt. When her palms touched the skin above his waistband a tremor shook him. Her fingertips were chilly sliding across his body, pushing the material up his chest, over his head. She laid it upon the couch.

A knowing grin pulled at his mouth. Before long the woman would be warm—real warm. He would stoke her body from a low simmering burn to a raging wildfire.

Without sight she struggled unfastening his belt, then undoing the button of his pants. A hiss of the zipper and his cock burst from its restraints. His jaws clenched. Shit. This was pure agony. He threw back his head, suppressing the groan that lingered on his tongue.

As his pants slipped down his thighs, he watched her gently sink to her knees. God, she was every man's dream. She was so eager, so willing. First she pulled his shoes off, one at a time. When his pants pooled around his ankles, he stepped out of them and kicked them aside. Candice made to rise, but he placed a hand at her shoulder, staying her.

"Touch me." His voice was deep and scratchy. He was holding on by a thread. He needed to feel her soft hands on his cock.

Her touch was tentative, smoothing across his thighs. His legs inched wider, he braced himself for the moment of contact. A gasp of surprise slipped from her lips as her fingers brushed his cock. He was rock-hard. His balls were drawn tight against his body. He ached to feel her hands grip and squeeze him.

And then something happened that shook him. He wasn't expecting it—wasn't prepared as she slipped her hot, wet mouth over his erection. A breath caught in his throat. He couldn't speak as her tongue slid up and down, taking him to the back of her throat, working her muscles, creating a tantalizing suction. Somehow she had ripped control from him. His hands gathered fistfuls of her hair, drawing her closer. His hips automatically moved with the sway of her head. He should stop her—regain control, but he was too close to orgasm. He wanted this—wanted her down on her knees in sweet surrender. The bob of her head, his cock slipping in and out of her mouth, it was too much.

Gordon threw back his head and released a groan he felt from head to toe. The rush swept down his cock as his seed burst into her mouth. She choked, struggling to breathe as she continued to milk him. Her fingertips dug into his thighs. Unsure and awkward, her rhythm slowed. A sparkle of moisture dampened her eyelashes. Clearly she had never taken oral sex to this level. He was proud of her. She worked her mouth, her throat, swallowing until his cock lay quiet. Then he slipped from between her lips.

Her shoulders rose and fell rapidly as he helped her to her feet, took her into his arms and kissed her.

Candice felt the Earth move beneath her feet. She didn't know what had possessed her. Maybe it was the book she had skimmed through. Whatever it was, Gordon's reaction was more than positive, at least, until the kiss ended.

"You sucked my cock without permission. You've earned a punishment." His voice was formidable, sending a chill down her spine. Hadn't he liked what she'd done? As if he could sense her apprehension, his tone softened. "You must ask permission, learn to obey and earn the right of pleasure. Trust me and you'll be rewarded. Open your eyes."

Her eyes were mere slits, the bright light stinging and bringing tears to them. Then they widened with appreciation. Gordon was a combination of rippling muscle and sex appeal. His thick cock was impressive, even semi-hard as it was at the moment.

A squeal of surprise pushed from her mouth as he grasped her wrist and pulled her to him. His body was warm against her chilled one. "How shall I punish you?" His eyes were dark, but it was his lips that she watched. "Do you want me to spank you?"

Her pulse sped. Did she? "Whatever will please you, Master."

A tic teased the corner of his mouth. His eyes shone with pride. "You did read the book."

She nodded, unblinking.

His gaze searched her face. "You want to play?"

She nodded again.

"Excellent." His palms brushed up and down her arms. "Then a spanking it will be."

Nervous yet excited, Candice swallowed hard. She couldn't wait to see what Gordon did next.

Grasping her hand, he led her into his bedroom. She took in the differences between her room and his. There wasn't a feminine thing about it, including the large four-poster bed that he sat upon. With a yank, he brought her across his lap, his now hard erection pressed into her belly.

He parted her thighs and a slice of fear shook her. She tensed, drawing her butt cheeks together. She thought she heard him chuckle, but her head was clouded, her pulse moving to thrum in her throat. Then his large palm smoothed across her skin and she swallowed the breath she held.

The first swat was nothing, just a little sting. The surface of her ass warmed beneath his touch. The next swat made her flinch, not necessarily from the pain, but the sound of flesh slapping flesh. A couple more, a little harder each time, then he placed a strong hand at her back pinning her down. His strength was heady. A wave of desire released between her thighs—this was turning her on. Then his palm landed with a smack that echoed the power beneath his touch.

Fuck! That one stung.

It was over. He released her, helping her to a standing position. Her ass smarted as he guided her in front of his mirrored closet doors. He turned her so that her back was to the glass, then had her turn her head so she could see over her shoulder.

"Look at my mark." He was breathing as hard as she was. Her ass was a light pink with one red handprint that reflected from the mirror. His cock jutted out before him rigid and proud. "You're beautiful."

Within a heartbeat she was back in his arms. His lips moved tenderly over her neck. He nibbled lightly on her earlobe, before burning a path to her lips. Then he took her mouth in a searing kiss. There was nothing gentle in his caress. Teeth meshed and tongues dueled as his hands moved over her body. She clung to him like he was an anchor, the only thing that kept her from floating away. When his arm swept beneath her knees, she wrapped her arms around his neck.

His heavy footsteps moved toward the bed. Gently he settled her upon the soft comforter and gazed at her. From one corner of the footboard he extracted a piece of Velcro that he fastened to her ankle. His blue eyes darkened as he moved around the bed to bind her other ankle.

Candice couldn't hide her trepidation. Her body shook. Her chest heaved. Was this what she really wanted?

Their eyes met. His Adam's apple dipped as he swallowed. "Do you want me to fuck you or would you rather use your safe word?" He was asking permission to continue. Something she hadn't expected. There was a hint of concern, almost as if he thought she might decline his offer.

She licked her lips. No way was he going to stop now. Not when her body burned for him. "Yes."

His expression grew firm. "Yes, what?"

"Yes, Master, I want you to fuck me." Within seconds her wrists were bound together, high above her head, connected to the headboard. She was helpless, spread wide for his delight.

Her chest filled with nervous excitement. What would he do next?

A squeak sounded as he slid the drawer of his nightstand open. She couldn't see what he was doing. But she almost laughed when he approached with a feather in hand. His other hand was tucked behind him as he climbed upon the bed.

The exquisite tickle that chased down her side as he dragged the feather across her body made her jerk against her bindings. Her nipples drew into taut beads. His eyes were pinned on her breasts as he circled them. She couldn't believe the way her body reacted, releasing its juices. Then the quill lightly caressed her folds, teasing her clit. The sensation made her pussy spasm, sending white-hot rays of sensation through her body.

"Ahhh…" Her cry brought a chuckle of male satisfaction from him.

Then Gordon reached behind him and retrieved a small flogger, no more than eight inches long. The elastic thongs were cool as he dragged them across her stomach. When he flicked his wrist there was a delightful sting. Then with a steady rhythm he began to softly whip her arms, her legs, until her skin felt alive. As the flogger landed on a breast, the ache between her thighs doubled. She needed him to fill her. To stoke the fire that simmered and to release the desire that sat like a coiled spring in her belly. She closed her eyes briefly.

When she opened them Gordon was between her thighs, a condom already in place.

This was the moment she had been waiting for.

He leaned forward, catching a nipple in his mouth. Hot and moist, the sensation was so intense that her back arched. She jerked against her bindings, needing to touch him. His other hand slid down her hip to the apex of her thighs. When a single finger caressed her slit and slipped inside, a soft whimper pushed from between her lips.

"Master." Her breaths came in small pants. She was going to die if he didn't take her. Her pulse felt like it would leap from her throat. She felt fevered and chilled at the same time. Her body shook uncontrollably.

She couldn't think as he rose between her thighs. His eyes were dark with desire, a look that made her brace against her bindings. In one quick thrust he penetrated her, filling Candice like no other man had. She struggled to breathe, fought to grasp control, but she shattered like glass. Her climax moved through her like a tidal wave, washing away her emptiness and replacing it with such a beautiful sense of fulfillment, she couldn't speak. Ripple after ripple filtered through her body like the aftershocks of an earthquake. She didn't think they would ever stop—didn't want the moment to end.

Gordon drove into her again and again, with a force that wrenched a cry from her trembling lips. It was pleasure-pain, as his orgasm moved through him. Unbelievably, it felt as if he grew larger, firmer—spreading her wide. His expression was intense, his eyes closed. After a few more pumps of his hips, he collapsed atop her.

Chest to chest, his heart beat against hers. It felt so intimate that she shivered with his nearness. She had never experienced anything like this before. When he silently rose and began to release her bindings, she wondered what was next. Would he kiss her goodnight and send her on her way?

Their eyes met and for a moment she wondered if her night of bliss was over. Instead he smiled. "That was wonderful." Then he crawled into the bed, dragging her to him so that he spooned her back. Without another word he fell fast asleep.

Tears filled her eyes. Would her wish come true this year?

Chapter Five

Waking up with Candice in his arms this morning had been invigorating. Gordon felt good, really good, as he stretched his arms wide. A smile teased the corner of his mouth as he grabbed the desktop and scooted his chair forward. His gaze quickly skimmed across the contract laying in front of him. He started to read, pleased with the changes. On an inhale a light feminine scent rose to caress his senses. Memories of last night's delights surfaced, causing the words on the paper to blur and his thoughts to drift. Work was the last thing on his mind. A certain brunette kept invading his thoughts. Her soft moans and cries of excitement played over and over again in his head, until his cock stirred to life.

He couldn't believe how responsive she was to being bound and flogged. She had gone wild when he'd tied her thighs together and teased her clit. The need to spread her legs, to touch him, drove her mad with desire. Her outburst had ended with a punishment. A tingle tightened his balls as he remembered the look of ecstasy on her face. In fact, it was quite possible that, for her, nipple clamps were far more pleasure than pain. Her nipples had been delightfully sensitive after that.

It was amazing how comfortable he felt around her. She was eager to please him, always willing to make love. After a couple of hours of sleep, he had awakened to her warm body beside him.

He couldn't help it—he just had to have her again. Then they'd been forced to go their separate ways. She back to her apartment and he to work.

A smile crept across his face as he looked around his office. He had a meeting scheduled in ten minutes. Already, he was eager for the day to end. He had explained exactly how he wanted Candice dressed and what he wanted her to do when he arrived at her apartment. He grew harder just thinking about it.

If it weren't for missing his family, this would be a great Christmas. Which reminded him, he needed to call his parents to wish them a Merry Christmas. He grabbed his cell and punched in the number.

"Hello, Nash residence." It was his older brother, John.

Gordon glanced at his watch. "Hey, bro. Mom and Dad there?"

"No, they went shopping."

Damn. He should have known they'd be out wrapping up the last of the shopping today. "I just called to wish all of you a Merry Christmas."

"Ohhh…not good. Ma's going to be upset that she missed your call." John's playful tone made Gordon long to be home.

"I'll try calling after my meeting this morning."

"Are you sure it isn't a woman keeping you there?" John asked. Gordon paused a little too long. His brother chuckled. "Just what I thought. Ma might go easier on you missing Christmas if she knows a woman is involved."

"It's business, but maybe I'll bring Candice home in January." Now where did that come from? He didn't even know her that well yet.

"Sure gonna miss you." Gordon heard the sadness in his brother's voice. They were a close family. But it couldn't be helped.

"You too. Did you get the presents I sent?"

"Yeah, they came yesterday." In the background Gordon heard John's kids begin to argue. "Cutting it a little close—

Johnny. Carol. Stop that. Take care, Gordy, Merry Christmas. I'll tell Ma and Dad you called."

"Merry Christmas." Gordon punched the off button on his phone.

Damn. This would be the first family Christmas he'd miss. But he didn't have time to mope. He had work to do and a night to spend in a Christmas angel's arms.

* * * * *

Candice burst into laughter. Hector couldn't be left alone for a minute. While she'd been shopping for holiday dinner and a present for Gordon, the faery had gotten into her face cream and destroyed everything in her bathroom. Standing before her, drenched in cream, he looked like a bad rendition of Frosty the Snowman.

He stretched his wings out, looking at them with disgust. "How do you get this stuff off?"

"Very carefully." She laughed, standing before the bathroom counter and the wayward faery. Baby powder was spilled on the floor. Cotton balls were strewn around the sink. "Come here." Q-tip in hand, she began to gently clean him up.

"You know, you're not a bad human." Hector looked at his lotion-free wing and gave it a flutter. "Good as new."

"And you're not a bad wood faery. Well…most of the time," she added, looking around at the mess.

"Funny," he grumbled, trying out his other wing. Then he looked at her as she began to wipe his cheek. "Happy?"

Heat flooded her face. Her decadent night was a delicious ache between her thighs. She had forgone a bra today because her nipples were so sensitive.

Candice nodded. She was happy. Yes, so far it was only sex. No one could fall in love in one day, but she definitely felt the beginnings of a relationship—something she had never had—something to look forward to.

"Gordon asked me to spend Christmas Eve and Day with him." She wouldn't be alone this year. Tomorrow morning she would wake in his arms.

Hector took flight, darting around the room. Then he halted in midair, his wings a blur. "Then you'd better get ready. Your Christmas wish should be here soon."

She nibbled on her bottom lip wondering how to ask Hector to become scarce. As if he heard her thoughts, he said, "Don't worry, I'm not sticking around."

Then in a puff of green faery dust, Hector vanished.

Candice didn't have much time to spare, now that she had to clean the bathroom as well.

* * * * *

Soft candlelight lit Candice's living room as Gordon entered, using the key she'd given him that morning, then shut the door behind him. Low music hummed in the background as the delicious scent of lasagna wafted through the apartment. He set his briefcase down and eased out of his jacket. The atmosphere was right for seduction, the stirring in his pants confirmed it.

But where was Candice?

The Christmas tree was in its stand. There were several boxes of decorations tucked in the corner. The table was set. He glanced into the kitchen, no Candice. Then she emerged from the bedroom.

His heart stopped.

She leaned in the doorway wearing a black leather bustier, thong and garter belt that held up her silk stockings, along with heels and a Santa hat. Shadows and light flickered across her face. The timid, shy woman he had first met was gone, before him stood a temptress.

The small smile on her face was sexy. The slink of her hips as she moved toward him was sensuous. A light citrus scent rose as she drew closer.

Christmas was apparently early, because Candice was a hell of a gift.

He reached for her and she came willingly. As he had instructed, she silently began to undress him. His tie and shirt were the first to go. When she laid her warm palms against his bare chest, Gordon knew she could feel his rapid heartbeat. Taking his hand she led him to the couch, eased him down, then drifted to her knees to remove his socks and shoes.

She was so fucking hot that his cock jerked against its confinement. He knew what was coming, but it still excited him. She had arranged the room and was performing the scene as he had demanded. It wasn't long before she had his pants undone and he was naked.

Fingernails scraped across his sensitive skin as she dragged them from his ankle to his thighs. Her touch was gentle when she cupped his sac and began to knead gently. His gaze was riveted on her. Candlelight flickered across her violet eyes making them look like velvet pools. He grew harder, longer. Her smile was soft.

Then she took him into her hands and began to stroke, long, smooth motions from the base to the tip. His balls tightened with the feel of silk moving up and down his erection.

She leaned forward and her warm breath teased him. His hips rose, but she kept just the right distance between them so that he could feel her presence, but never her touch. He'd wanted her to tease him, drive him crazy, but he was holding on by a thread.

"Ahhh…" Forget what he'd said before, he wanted her to take him into her mouth, suck and lick him.

When he gripped her head, fisting his fingers in her hair, she didn't fight him. Instead her lips parted. He thrust forward, delving into her wet warmth. It felt so fucking good, a throb started in his balls, and then shot down his cock. She circled the base with her thumb and index finger and squeezed, following the up and down rhythm of her mouth.

God, he couldn't take any more. Watching his cock slide in and out of her lips made his toes curl into the carpet. He tensed. Jaws clenched. He fought to hold back the inevitable climax, wanting to linger on the edge as long as possible. Just as he felt the pinnacle approach, she released him.

"Fuck." He groaned deep and low as he struggled to restrain himself. It was so intense it was painful. His fists were clenched. He couldn't breathe.

She eased back on her haunches. The question of whether she had made a mistake shadowed her eyes.

It was exactly what he'd wanted and expected. His body burned. The knowledge that she'd done everything he'd instructed—down to the condom on the coffee table—thrilled him.

Pushing from the couch, he rose, gripped her wrist and brought her up with him. He trembled with the need to take her. "Sheathe me."

Immediately, she complied.

When their bodies touched, he lost control. He wanted her naked. He wanted to be inside her. And he wanted it right now.

Her hands were everywhere on his body as he fumbled with the lacings of her bustier. The more frustrated he became, the more desperate he was to have her. Where had his control gone?

Step by step, he guided her closer and closer to the bedroom.

"Fuck the corset." In a single pull he ripped the laces, revealing her tender breasts. He was dying to have her. His erection was aching to the point of pain as he drove her against the wall. She released a sharp breath at the impact. Her arms snaked around his neck. Hands cupping her ass, he lifted her so she could wrap her legs around his waist. Bracing her against the wall, he reached between her thighs, moved the little scrap of material, then with a single thrust, buried himself inside her.

It was a primitive act that excited him beyond belief.

Relief came in a groan that shook him. He took her hard and fast. She was wild in his arms. Her need was as great as his. Instead of soft whimpers, cries filled the air.

"Come for me, Candice."

Her scream of ecstasy met his groan as he exploded, his seed ripping down his shaft like steam from an engine. Her pussy gripped him, then contracted, pulsing and squeezing the last bit of energy from him.

Candice's couldn't breathe. What an unbelievable experience. The passion and fire was uncontrollable. She felt wild and free. Her chest filled with emotion. She fought back the tears filling her eyes. No. She wouldn't cry—not even tears of joy.

His lips were soft, nuzzling her neck. The scent of sex, his spicy cologne, garlic and tomato sauce teased her nose. Oh no. She'd forgotten about supper. "Master, the lasagna."

He laughed. "You weren't dinner?" As she tried to escape his arms, he grasped a handful of hair, stopping her. He pulled her back into his arms and his hot gaze slipped down her body. His lips barely touched hers. His mouth moved across hers so gently. The moment was so tender, so soft that she struggled to swallow her happiness. Then he took her in a masterful kiss that left no doubt he was back in control.

The blare of the oven timer drove them apart. "Saved by the bell." His eyes were still dark with passion. "Dessert in bed?"

A few quick nods were her answer. "Shall I dress, Master?"

"No." His palm cupped a breast, his fingers pinching and rolling her nipple into a taut nub. "I want to be able to touch and watch you throughout dinner. You look so sexy in those stockings." He stroked her with his voice.

Having him naked was also a benefit. She loved to watch his muscles flex, especially the one between his thighs.

It seemed awkward walking around with her breasts exposed, but each time he gazed at her with hunger in his eyes, she found the courage. Within minutes, dinner was on the table and they began to eat.

A large bite of lasagna disappeared in Gordon's mouth. He chewed. "Playtime is over for the moment, Candice. Let's just talk." He broke a breadstick in two and continued to eat and talk at the same time. "I'm really going to miss spending Christmas with my family. But I'm glad I'm here with you." He reached over and tweaked her nipple, making her squeal. He kissed her softly. Then he drew back laughing. "My nieces and nephews are a handful." Another bite disappeared. "My two sisters have five children between them. Counting my brother John's kids, that makes nine total."

Warmth as thick as a coat embraced Candice. An only child of a single mother, she had never experienced anything like what he was describing. His eyes sparkled when he talked about his mom and dad, siblings, nieces and nephews. It was a life she'd dreamed of, one simply out of her reach.

When they finished eating, he stood and gathered his dishes. Together they cleared the table and began to clean up. Her mother had been sick for so long, she couldn't remember the last time someone had helped her in the kitchen. Gordon looked so comfortable in his nudity, not to mention with household chores. When he wrapped his arms around her waist and cuddled up to her back, she released a sigh of contentment. He was hard, the evidence pressed against her back.

This is how life should be lived.

"Let's forgo decorating the Christmas tree and go straight to bed. I need to be inside you." His deep, sensual voice slipped around her like a glove.

She turned in his arms and whispered, "Yes, Master."

With a quick sweep of his arms beneath her knees, Gordon cradled Candice against his chest. He nipped the tip of her nose as he moved toward the bedroom, but not before switching off the light. In the dark he made it to the bed, softly laying her down upon it.

Tonight Gordon wanted to please Candice. He was proud of how quickly she'd learned. She was an excellent submissive, but she was more than that to him. His life felt like it was shifting. His desires and needs too. He not only wanted to dominate her, but to pleasure her and simply talk with her. She was so easy to be with.

He held her leg high and slipped her shoe off, snapping the clasp of her garter to release the silky nylon. Her skin was like satin as he rolled the stocking over her thigh, her knee, slipping it free of her foot. Then he repeated the same thing with her other leg. "Did I tell you how incredible you look tonight?"

Her answer was a breathy, "No, Master."

He smiled in the dark, dragging her garter and thong down at once. His palms stroked her legs before he parted them wide. She trembled as he moved close to her sex. With a single finger he caressed her slit.

"What do you want, Candice?" The finger delved between her folds. She was warm and wet and ready. "Do you want me to fuck you with my cock or tongue?" Another tremor shook her. "You've never felt a man's tongue slide across your pussy, have you?"

"Master. Please." It was a breathy plea that made his erection impossibly harder. The soft sounds she made drove him crazy.

He reached for a condom off the nightstand. The ripping sound echoed through the room. It was cold against his warmth as he slipped it over his engorged cock.

"You haven't. I knew it." He raised her legs, bending her knees so she was held open to him, then pushed his finger back inside her. "First I'm going to fuck you with my tongue. Then I'll fuck you with my cock." While one finger pumped in and out of her pussy, he reached down with his other hand and folded his fingers around his erection. He gripped himself tighter, moving up and down several times, relishing the pulling sensation and pressure building behind his balls. "Would you enjoy that, Candice?"

She whimpered again, her hips writhing beneath his touch. Her desire for him was incredible. It stroked his ego, made him proud to be her man.

Grasping the insides of her thighs, he slid down and pressed his mouth to her sweet folds.

She gasped. Her legs jerked as if to close, but he held her wide. The fitful way she moved beneath his assault made him want her more. As his tongue slid across her slit, she cried out. "*Master*!" It was a high-pitched squeal.

But he wanted to hear his name on her lips. "Gordon. For tonight call me Gordon."

"*Gordon*," she breathed. The sweet sound of her voice filled him with warmth.

The knowledge that he was the first to taste her and pleasure her in this way made his blood simmer through his veins.

Mine.

This was proving to be his best Christmas ever.

He sucked, licked and nibbled until he felt her muscles convulse. Then he released her thighs and moved atop her. The darkness stole his sight, but he heard her raspy breathing, felt her hands grabbing and pulling him into her embrace. For a moment he held himself suspended. Grasping his cock, he ran the crown of it across her wet folds, loving the feel as she slid along the tip of his member. Inch by inch, he pushed into her body. Slowly, he drew each sensation out until he was fully seated in her. Then he began to move, thrusting his hips, taking his time to build the heat inside her once again.

Fingernails bit into his back. Sudden pain flared, then a pleasure so intense that his orgasm hit without warning. His hips slammed into her once, twice and then fire raced down his cock. Stars exploded behind his eyelids. His legs braced against the bed, tightening until his toes dug into the mattress. A deep satisfying groan was wrenched from him.

Candice's body jerked beneath him. A soft cry caressed his ear as she climaxed. Her breathing came in small, fast pants. Although spent, he thrust again and again, hard, riding out her climax. The head of his cock was ultrasensitive. His arms quivered beneath his weight. He strained to show her the same pleasure she had given him. A final moan and she writhed as the last ripples of her orgasm died.

Gordon collapsed, rolling to his side. He took a moment to clean up, using a tissue and disposing of his condom.

"Master—uh, Gordon, may I use the restroom?" Candice asked.

"Yes. And we're through playing for the night."

She rose and headed to the bathroom. The bed was warm from their body heat as he lay upon his back, his hands folded behind his head. When she moved back into the doorway, the light behind her illuminating her silhouette, she looked like an angel.

His angel.

Then the light went out. The bed squeaked as she crawled upon it. Within seconds he was wrapped in her arms. She snuggled close and then drifted off into peaceful slumber.

The alarm clock on her dresser flashed midnight in fluorescent green.

It was Christmas.

Chapter Six

Candice woke to the emerging dawn of Christmas morning and Hector perched upon her pillow. He pressed a finger to his lips. "It's time for me to go," he said in hushed tones.

A knot formed in her throat. The scent of soil and earth that was uniquely his surrounded her. For a moment she couldn't speak. Then her head rose from the pillow. "Hector, don't go. I *need* you."

Did he have any idea how much he meant to her? He had opened the door to a new and promising world, given her so much.

A crooked grin touched his mouth. "You never really needed me." A caring note rose in his soft voice. "The magic was inside you all the time. You just needed to believe in yourself." Mischief sparkled in his eyes. "Of course, those books you bought may have helped some."

She chuckled, knowing she would miss his teasing. "Will I ever see you again?"

He shook his head. But there wasn't an expression of sadness on his face, just one of joy.

Gordon moaned, shifted, and then pulled her back into his arms. His warm body pressed close to hers. She snuggled back into his embrace.

"Be happy, Candice," Hector mouthed. Then, in a puff of glittering light, Hector vanished.

Tears clogged her throat. She was going to miss him.

Teeth nipping at her earlobe drew her attention. "Merry Christmas." Gordon's voice was rough from sleep. She turned in his arms and he kissed her gently.

Crash. Bang. The sudden disturbance startled them both into a sitting position. They glanced at each other.

"What the hell?" Gordon grumbled, throwing back the covers. He reached for his robe and slipped it on, covering all that wonderful flesh.

Bright laughter came from the hall beyond the apartment door. The damn walls were so thin. Candice rose, donning her robe, too.

Together they walked into the living room and jerked to a stop. The Christmas tree was decorated, its lights twinkling like stars in the heavens.

It was beautiful. *Magical.* White icicles hung neatly off the branches, colorful bulbs sparkled.

"How? Who?" Gordon asked as the noise in the hall grew louder.

Hector. Candice smiled, gazing at the wooden faery atop the tree. It was an exact replica of her little faery, something to remember him by. Goose bumps slid across her skin. He had made her wish come true.

The pounding of a fist against the door stole Gordon's attention, heavy footsteps carried him toward the sound. As he opened the door, Candice heard a youthful voice yell, "Uncle Gordy. I thought you lived in 305, not 307."

Abruptly, all hell broke loose. It sounded like an invading army as everyone began to speak at once. Within seconds, Candice's apartment was filled with strangers, big and small. Hugging and kissing and talking. All she could do was stand speechless, until Gordon drew her to his side.

His face was flushed. "Apparently my family decided to surprise me." His tone was cautious. A little blonde girl hung on his leg, gazing up at him with a grin and big blue eyes.

Candice inhaled and released it slowly. "I can see that."

"So this is Candice." A woman around Candice's size and shape, but more than twice her age, approached. "Are you the reason my son was willing to forego Christmas with his family?"

Candice froze. The pit of her stomach twisted.

Then the gray-haired woman smiled, drawing Candice into her embrace. "I'm kidding, sweetie. We just couldn't have Christmas without our Gordon. I hope we're not imposing. Harry," she waved frantically to Gordon's father, "come meet Candice."

For about ten minutes total chaos reigned. Candice was passed from one person to the next for introductions and hugs. Gordon tossed the little girl who had been wrapped around his legs high into the air and then released her to join the other children.

Then all the women present descended upon her kitchen. Brown paper sacks lined her kitchen table and counters, while behind her children laughed, placing presents beneath her tree.

"Gordon, why don't you and Candice get dressed while we start breakfast and Christmas dinner," his mother, Mary instructed, reminding Candice of her nudity beneath her silk robe. "Honey, where is your roasting pan?" she asked Candice.

"But, Mom—" His mother's brow rose. Candice almost laughed as Gordon's mouth snapped shut.

"Beneath the microwave," Candice responded.

Gordon clasped her hand in his, then pulled her toward the bedroom. Once inside, with the door closed, he drew her into his embrace. "I'm so sorry. I never expected this to happen." But the glow on his face told Candice that he was happy it had.

She cupped his face and kissed him lightly. "I think it's wonderful."

"You do?" Surprise lifted his voice.

The muscles in her neck and jaws tightened as she fought her emotion. "Yes." It was what she'd dreamed of for years. A real family. But would he share them with her?

Gordon took Candice into his arms. "It'll be fun. I promise." He hugged her tightly. Behind him Hector suddenly materialized, his wings a blur as he dangled just beyond Gordon's shoulder. Softly, he whispered, "Merry Christmas, Candice."

"Did you hear that?" Gordon turned, but Hector was already gone.

Her life was fuller now.

She had hope.

And her Christmas wish had come true.

Also by Mackenzie McKade

A Tall Dark Cowboy

Ecstasy: Forbidden Fruit

Ecstasy: The Game

Return to Wonderland: Kalina's Discovery with Cheyenne McCray

Return to Wonderland: Lord Kir of Oz with Cheyenne McCray

The Charade

About the Author

A taste of the erotic, a measure of daring and a hint of laughter describes Mackenzie McKade's novels. She sizzles the pages with scorching sex, fantasy and deep emotion that will touch you and keep you immersed until the end. Whether her stories are contemporaries, futuristics or fantasies, this Arizona native thrives on giving you the ultimate erotic adventure.

When not traveling through her vivid imagination, she's spending time with three beautiful daughters, a devilishly handsome grandson, and the man of her dreams. She loves to write, enjoys reading, and can't wait 'til summer. Boating and jet skiing are top on her list of activities. Add to that laughter and if mischief is in order — Mackenzie's your gal!

Mackenzie welcomes comments from readers. You can find her website and email address on her author bio page at www.ellorascave.com.

A TASTE OF HONEY

By Michele Bardsley

Trademarks Acknowledgement

The author acknowledges the trademarked status and trademark owners of the following wordmarks mentioned in this work of fiction:

Formica: Formica Corporation

F150: Ford Motor Company

Honda: Honda Giken Kogyo Kabushiki Kaisha (Honda Motor Co., Ltd.)

Chapter One

New Year's Eve

Jarod McClure stumbled out of the warm, cinnamon-scented house owned by Roger and Cindy Morrison. Behind him, Clay Aiken's "What Are You Doing New Year's Eve?" spilled into the cold night air. Thanks to ol' Clay, what had been a loud and raucous party morphed into a lovey-dovey-kissey-wissey affair. *Blech.* The partygoers had split into slow-dancing couples and made him all too aware that he wasn't part of a twosome or threesome or anysome. And he hadn't been for a long, long time.

Shit. He'd left open the front door but wasn't sure he had enough motor control to turn around and shut it. Before he could attempt what might be a life-threatening turn, he heard the door slam, immediately muting the sounds of the New Year's Eve party.

It sucked that he was leaving before midnight. Even without a steady girl to smooch on, chances were good he could've found *someone* to lock lips with at midnight. Oh well. It was a long walk to his house and he needed to get there before his Great Dane, Marvin, got impatient and started peeing on furniture.

He managed the three steps off the porch. He weaved right…weaved left…and fell face-first into the double-D chest of an X-rated snowwoman. *Oh yeah.* Roger had jokingly made the Snowie the Slut and Cindy retaliated by creating Snowjohn the Stud.

Laughing, Jarod sucked a lungful of snow, and the stupidity of doing *that* made him laugh harder. He extracted himself from the icy breasts—the purple lace bra clutched in a triumphant fist—and…fell ass-first into the snow-blanketed front yard.

"I give you points if you did that clasp one-handed," said a melodic female voice.

Blinking away the buzz gained by a mere two glasses of eggnog so potent people were getting drunk just *smelling* it, Jarod looked up and saw a beautiful blonde angel.

She smiled. "You had the eggnog too, eh?"

Jarod held up two fingers and she chuckled. "I had one," she admitted. "And I've been seeing double ever since."

She extended her hand and he grabbed it, attempting to pull himself up. Instead, she was thrown forward, on top of him. Delighted with this turn of events, he wrapped his arms around her. "Angel," he muttered.

From the house, a cheer went up. Then Jarod recognized the tune of "Auld Lang Syne".

"Midnight," he said. "Happy New Year!"

"Whoa, sugar. What are you—"

His lips took hers in a gentle caress. Her mouth was so cherry-hot he found himself unable to stop lip-locking her. She didn't protest…so he kissed her until the snow melted around them.

Finally, reluctantly, he let go of her lips to explore the shell of her ear. Such a delicate, pretty ear. Like a butterfly's wing. "We're sorta inebriated," she managed.

Nuzzling under her turtleneck, he said, "Uh-huh."

Oh God. She smelled like honeysuckle and tasted like soft bread. She was warm and wiggly and *holy shit* he really wanted to see what was under that parka that hid her body from him.

"It's probably unwise to think about continuing this…fun somewhere less cold," she said.

"Definitely unwise," he said. "But I'm sure we can find an unlocked car."

"You're such a romantic," she said with a laugh.

They rose on unsteady legs. She held onto his arm and he to her waist and just as they decided to move forward, they fell into a heap all over again.

"This isn't going to work," she said.

"Eggnog and the fates are against us," he said. "Give me your number. Your name. Your zip code. We'll have a New Year's Day brunch…in bed."

"Tell you what," she said. "You meet me here tomorrow night—" she handed him a white business card "—and we'll see what happens."

He peered at the card. "The Sex Club?"

"What's the matter, sugar? You afraid of a little challenge?" She leaned forward and kissed his throat. "I want to play with you. Eight p.m. Ask for H."

"H."

"Yeah." She patted his cheek and sauntered away, leaving him alone in knee-deep snow contemplating the strange card.

And the beautiful woman.

Chapter Two

"Mrs. Conroy, please reconsider. We can discount our services—what?" Jarod rolled his eyes. "No, I won't ask my employees to do that. Our men are skilled professionals, not strippers. I'm sorry too, Mrs. Conroy. If it doesn't work out, just give us a call."

Jarod dropped the phone receiver into its cradle. "That's the third customer this week." He picked up the pencil and tapped it against the papers littering the check-in counter. "Our services are unmatched and we get the job, any job done. There hasn't been a complaint yet. Sheesh. Where else can you call to get your car fixed, your pipes looked at, and your roof patched?"

"Honey Do," answered Ian drolly. "And you're preaching to the choir over here."

"Yeah, I know." The small office was located in a shopping center, crammed between the dry cleaners and the grocery store. ProCare's first office had been a garage, the only employees himself and his brother, Ian. They'd spent the last five years carefully building a solid, profitable business.

Truth be told, his thoughts weren't on business but on pleasure. He and his brother Ian always worked a full day on New Year's. Hell, they worked every holiday because they promised twenty-four-hour care no matter what. And, well, they had no lives. No girlfriends, no wives and no prospects of either one.

I want to play with you. 8 p.m. Ask for H. The card given to him by the blonde angel last night was in his front jeans pocket. It had become a talisman. Even without an eggnog-clogged mind, he remembered her scent. Her smile. The feel of her curves. Oh man. He really wanted to explore those curves again. Just a few hours more and his hands would be stroking her skin. He swallowed his groan.

"We haven't gotten a new customer since Honey Do opened two months ago and they're kicking our ass. I can't believe the shallowness of women. They want to ogle half-naked men." Jarod looked out the floor-to-ceiling windows and watched the cars dart in and out of the parking lot. "They could care less if the job gets done right."

Silence met his outrage. He glanced over his shoulder at the desk across the room. His brother, who looked like a grown-up Harry Potter, worked on the computer. He typed fast—the tap-tap of the keys sounded like a machine gun report.

"We're losing business," said Ian. "Our profits are down for the first time in two years."

"Are we in the red?"

"No. But it's a real possibility." Ian stopped typing and adjusted his glasses. "Honey Do poses a big threat. It's not like Clement Falls is a huge city. We have one of everything in this town. Remember when Harry Johnson's big-shot son came up from Tulsa and opened one of his chain dry cleaners here? Nan's dry cleaning service closed within six months. She'd been in business for thirty years." He shook his head. "We're in trouble."

Jarod dropped the pencil on the counter and turned to face his brother. "Do you know anything about Honey Sinclair?"

"She's the granddaughter of Odemina Wilson."

"Well, shit. Are you sure she's related to Odie?"

"Yeah."

A moment of terrified silence passed. Seventy-eight-year-old Odemina was sharp as a tack and mean as a hornet. Clement Falls elected a mayor every two years, but the truth was that Odie was the Queen of Everything. Her family had founded the small Oklahoma town one-hundred and twenty-seven years ago and she never let a soul forget it.

"Since Odie blessed the Earth with only one child...I take it that Honey is the daughter of He Who Must Not Be Named."

"According to the gossip at Sammy Jo's Dinerette, she is the result of Odie's disinherited son and the stripper he ran off with."

Jarod snorted in disgust. "Well, that explains her tendencies to encourage her employees to take off their clothes."

"Heard they were killed in a car accident a couple of years ago," said Ian. "Must've been hard on Miss Odie."

"Maybe that's why she invited Honey to live in Clement Falls. That girl's her only kin now." He frowned. "It's got to be illegal to require a man to disrobe as part of his job. Discrimination. Sexual harassment. Something." Jarod stroked his chin, an idea percolating. "I bet she wouldn't hire Ernie. He's a great worker, but I don't think his *wife* likes to see him with his shirt off."

Ian laughed and shook his head. "Poor Ernie."

"What if I could prove sexual harassment?"

"You're dreaming. There's no way you're going to be able to implicate Odie's kin in anything nefarious." Ian frowned. "I know that look. It's the same look you had when you talked me into sneaking onto old man Tyler's hen house. I nearly got pecked to death."

"It was a character-building experience."

"It was a painful experience. What are you planning?"

"I'm going to prove Honey Sinclair is doing something nefarious."

* * * * *

"Hubba, hubba," exclaimed the pink-haired female as Jarod entered the small, windowless office. Jarod blinked as the woman gave him a slow once-over that left him with the impression she was imagining him naked.

"Hi ya, sweet cakes," she said, waggling her eyebrows. She wore an amazing shade of gold eyeshadow and her fake lashes were glittery. She walked from behind the tall white Formica counter and Jarod stepped back. She was sheathed in a plastic pink dress that should have, by all rights, disabled her ability to breathe.

Behind the counter, a door opened. "Margo, where are the—"

A petite blonde dressed in white jeans and a yellow half-top stopped and looked at him. "Hubba, hubba."

"Are you referring to me?" he asked.

She lifted a thin eyebrow. "Wow, he's articulate. Where'd you find him, Margo?"

"He found us. Unless Santa Claus forgot to deliver one of my presents."

What the hell had he gotten himself into? No one had ever referred to him like a—like a thing before.

He leaned against the counter, directing his gaze to the blonde who seemed to be in charge. At least, he hoped so. He didn't know if he wanted to deal with the pink demon perusing the front of his jeans a little too avidly.

"Don't you worry about sexual harassment suits?" he asked.

"Nope," the woman answered. "If you can't take the heat, stay out of the kitchen."

"You advocate sexual harassment in the work place?"

"No. But I need to know our employees can deal with the…enthusiastic behavior of some of our clients." She smiled and revealed a dimple at the left corner of her mouth.

Jarod felt zapped in the pit of his stomach. Whoa. He hadn't counted on being attracted to her. *Get a grip, man.* His thoughts leapt to where he'd like to grip Honey—she had really nice…*no, no, don't go there*.. He took a fortifying breath to calm his racing pulse. If he didn't figure out a way to put Honey Do out of business, then ProCare was toast—and that meant a lot of good men would be jobless. His workers didn't have the muscles or the youth to work for Honey Do.

The bell above the door jingled and he turned to see who'd arrived. A young man in a wheelchair rolled through, popped a wheelie and skidded to Honey. He grinned, a flop of brown hair covering his right eye. "Hiya, toots."

"Charlie, you big show-off. How'd the job for Mrs. Firman go?"

He withdrew a folded paper from his pocket. "The check's stapled to the Job Completion Order." He flashed a twenty-dollar bill. "And she tipped me."

"Twenty bucks? What did you do?"

"I stripped down to my shorty shorts with no shirt and flirted my ass off. It was a simple leak too. I think Mrs. Firman likes me."

"You're a slut."

"I know." He grinned again. "Got anything new, boss?"

Jarod slipped out of the office and walked to his car. His theories about Honey Do were way off. The owner wasn't a sleazy, money-mongering exploiter of men. She was vaguely familiar. Had he met her before? A fuzzy memory flitted…then faded. Oh well. What did it matter? The truth was that Honey Sinclair was nice and pretty and kind.

Damn it.

* * * * *

"He didn't recognize me," said Honey Sinclair as she and Margo shut down the office. "We shared a mind-numbing kiss at a party. It was magical. He might've followed me. And I waited for him. Then stupid Roger came out and dragged him off to a taxi. Sheesh. Despite all that, I still figured out he was Jarod McClure, rival and expert kisser."

"Give the guy a break, babe. It was dark and he was sloshed."

"*Magical*," stressed Honey. "And apparently one-sided."

"Doubtful. Maybe he didn't remember a drunken New Year's kiss, but I saw the way he was looking at you." Margo shut off the computer and straightened the files scattered on the desk.

"If you say so. Are you going with me to the New Year's party?"

"The one at the *sex* club? I don't think so. Besides, aren't you worried Jarod will recognize you?"

"If he didn't recognize me in a face-to-face, then he'll be less likely to recognize me with a mask." Honey locked the deadbolt and chained the front door. Then she turned around and looked at a bemused Margo. "Now, there's only one question."

Margo shouldered her purse and followed Honey out the back door. "Yeah, toots? What's that?"

"What ever shall I wear?"

* * * * *

"Does it say 'I'm a slutty snowflake'?" asked Honey.

"Short and stout," sang Margo, her pink head popping up next to Honey's shoulder. "Here is your handle...and whoa, look at that spout!"

"You're a pervert." Honey assessed her barely-there negligee in the floor-length mirror attached to her closet door. Hmmm. She could live with the way her breasts were showcased, held up by the flimsiest of lace bras. And the thong was okay too. Hell, she didn't even mind wearing the mask.

The thigh-high white boots were the real problem.

"Maybe I should switch to high heels."

"No way!" said Margo. "The boots scream 'Fuck me, big boy'."

Honey grinned. "I like what they're saying. I just don't think I'm tall enough to do 'em justice. Do you think dressing in all white suggests 'virgin bride'? Because marriage is so not what I'm looking for."

Margo cackled, nearly falling over on Honey's bed as her laughter pealed. "Anyone who knows you wouldn't use *virgin* or *bride* to describe you."

"Gee, thanks." Honey grabbed a fringed pillow and threw it at Margo who dodged it easily.

"Do you have a decent jacket?" asked Margo. "Otherwise you'll freeze to death on the way there. On the up side you'll be the sexiest dead body ever found."

Honey rolled her eyes. "Yes, mommy dearest, I have a coat. What I don't have is a friend going with me. I can't believe you're gonna stay home with your new boyfriend and drink champagne."

"Don't forget the part where we fuck like bunnies all night."

"TMI, Margo."

She grinned unrepentantly. "Stop worrying, doll."

"I'm not worried." *I'm freaking the fuck out.* Panic fluttered in Honey's stomach. *I'm going to a party so I can have hot sex with Jarod McClure.* Wait a minute. What was the bad part again?

Honey stared at the sexy image reflected in the mirror. Yeah. She'd dressed for the dark-haired man with the blue, blue eyes who called her an angel and kissed until she forgot her own name.

Jarod had made her knees quake and her body sing. With his lips and his words, he'd made her want, made her need…

And she couldn't wait to finish what they'd started.

*****

Jarod McClure sat at the long black-and-chrome bar sipping a beer and looking over the crowd.

The Sex Club was Clement Falls' best kept secret—that everybody knew about. Sure, he'd heard about it and had friends who frequented it, but this was the first time Jarod had stepped foot into the place—and only been able to do so because of H's little card. The invitation-only club partied in a converted barn located on a member-owned farm more than twenty-five miles out of town, away from the prying eyes and wagging tongues of local gossips.

Roger and Cindy, longtime members, had gleefully imparted Club guidelines when he'd dropped by their house and admitted he'd been invited to "play".. The rules were simple and based on anonymity and safety. Wear a mask and never take it off. Always use a condom. Bring your own toys. Use initials, not names. Establish a safe word or gesture and if used, stop immediately.

The bar was located in the Meet-and-Greet Room. According to Cindy, this area was the only sex-free zone in the building. Some participants liked to watch, others liked to go at it in front of anyone willing to watch, but quite a few liked the private rooms.

Jarod was an open-minded guy, but he wanted a private room. He just hoped H felt the same way. He wasn't sure he could drop his pants and do her against a convenient wall while other Club members watched. Hell, he'd passed two such couples on the way into the bar.

Kind of a turn-on. Huh.

A tall, lithe woman dressed in head-to-toe black leather approached him. Her mask was a black leather cat, complete with ears and whiskers. She held a whip in one hand and a champagne flute in the other. "My, my, my…aren't you yummy? Wanna play?"

Jarod's lips lifted into a regretful smile. "I'm not your guy, hon."

"Gay?"

"Not a sub…or a dom, for that matter."

"You didn't smell like vanilla. Too bad, so sad." She toasted him with her glass and moved on to other prospects.

"What are you into?"

Jarod turned and found a short, stacked blonde sitting next to him. Her brown eyes twinkled behind her simple white mask. Her white-lace teddy offered a view of mouthwatering cleavage and the hem showed the luscious curve of her ass. But it was the white thigh-high boots with three-inch heels that caught his attention. An image of this little morsel naked underneath him, those boots wrapped around his waist as he fucked her…his heart stuttered as desire roared through him. *Jesus, God.* Please, please, please let this woman be H.

"The strong, silent type, huh?"

He blinked. Then grinned. His mask was simple and black, his outfit merely a black T-shirt with well-worn jeans and his most comfortable black boots. "Sorry. You were saying?"

"What are you into?"

"I'd like to be in you."

Smiling, she leaned forward, a slim, pale hand toying with his wrist. "And why would a sweet, innocent girl like me go anywhere with a big, bad man like you?"

"I'm not bad," he said, his fingers stroking her silky blonde hair. "I'm just drawn that way."

She laughed. "Isn't that my line?"

"I'd rather be Jessica than Roger Rabbit."

Her brows rose.

"I'm not a cross-dresser, either. Though I will admit that at the tender age of six, I did run around in my mother's heels, but only because my brother dared me."

"Ah." Her smile drifted into a seductive curl. "So you're not into men, BDSM or women's clothing. You do sound a little vanilla there. What is your kink?"

He pretended to think about it. "I like to fuck."

"Okay. So anal, vaginal, oral?"

"All three, sweetheart." He cupped her face in his hands and gazed into her melting-chocolate eyes. "I love everything about fucking. The feel of a woman wiggling against me, her soft flesh scraping mine. The smell of perfumed skin, the sweep of silky hair, the heat of mouths, the moans of pleasure."

Her breath hitched. "And what would you do to me?"

"I'd like to strip you naked and play with those gorgeous breasts. I'd start by kissing those perfect mounds—kissing every inch of flesh. I'd save your nipples for last. God, I'd love to suck those nipples, make them hard and aching. You'd be squirming then, wouldn't you?"

"Maybe." Her voice was reedy, her eyes glazed with interest. "What else would you do?"

"Would you like to find out?"

Chapter Three

The gorgeous blonde slid off the chair and offered her hand. "I'm glad you showed up. You know I'm H. And you are?"

"J." He took her hand, placed the palm against his lips and watched her shudder. *Oh yeah, baby. You're mine, all right.*

He paid the bar tab and grasped her hand again. She led him up two flights of stairs to a private room. Woo-hoo! Relieved he wouldn't have to show off his manly moves in front of an audience just yet, he spent an excellent thirty seconds studying H's ass as she unlocked a door.

"I pay to have my own special play place," she said as they entered the room. "It has everything we need to have fun."

She locked the door and flicked the lights on low. The walls were purple. The king-sized bed was sheathed in purple silk. The bed and the two nightstands on either side of it were pink. The carpet was pink too.

"Interesting color scheme. Very Austin Powers," Jarod said as he drifted around the room. He studied a couple of purple beanbags tossed carelessly near the pink mini-fridge then looked at a pink door. "Dare I ask what's inside door number one?"

"You can ask," she said, "but that doesn't mean I'll tell." She crossed to the fridge and opened it. "By the way, door number two is the bathroom. So…beer, wine, coolers, spring water and juice pops."

Jarod's lips hitched into a grin. "Juice pops?"

"I love juice pops," she said. He watched as she took out a yellow one and unwrapped it. The mini-fridge door snicked shut as she rose and ambled toward him. "Hmmm. I love the lemon ones."

She licked the pop from tip to base. "So good," she murmured. She stroked the lemon ice with her tongue with such…expert enthusiasm, Jarod felt his cock get hard and needy. When she took the entire pop into her mouth, he thought he might pass out.

He closed the space between them and plucked the icy treat from her hand.

"I suppose now is a good time to establish a safe word," she said.

"Angel."

"Angel it is. Now what do you have planned for that lemon-sicle?" Her gaze was challenging…almost mocking. No, almost as if she *dared* him to pleasure her. His cock hardened as he thought about all the things he would do to this little ice princess. She wasn't skittish. He liked that.

"Take off your panties," he demanded.

"If you want them off," she said, spreading apart her legs and planting her booted heels firmly into the carpet, "then you do it."

Her insolence sucker-punched him and made hot lust flare in his belly. The only thing he loved better than a woman who gave him what he wanted…was a woman who made him work for it.

With his free hand, he slipped three fingers under the wispy lace of her thong. She looked down at his hooked fingers then up at his face. "You've got to be kidding. That will never—"

With one quick yank the material ripped and before she could finish her sentence, he dangled the shredded panties from his forefinger. Her stunned expression made him chuckle. "You were saying?"

"Been practicing that move, have you?"

"Maybe." He knelt at her feet, oddly feeling like her captor *and* her slave, and leaned forward to scent her shaved pussy. The feminine spice of her sex was like ambrosia to him. He loved the taste and smell of woman's pussy. He loved to put his lips and tongue on her tender flesh to suck and to kiss and to plunge until she came on his face. Just thinking about H's cum dripping into his mouth made his hard cock tremble. *Whoa, boy. Slow down or you'll go off before you get inside her.*

Still holding the lemon pop, he leaned forward and kissed the spot just above the crease of her sweet cunt. He dragged his tongue down the slender line, sighing in ecstasy as he nibbled the plump flesh. His lazy exploration continued until her thighs quivered and her hands fisted into his hair. Though he intended to make her crazy, his actions only served to stoke his own lust to an agonizing peak.

Finally…slowly…he traced her cunt with the melting lemon pop. She gasped but didn't protest. As the yellow juice pearled on her skin, he licked off the drops. Using one hand, he pushed apart her vulva. With his other, he slid the pop inside her cunt.

"That's cold," she murmured. He looked up and noted with satisfaction that her eyes were closed and her face was flushed.

As he established a slow rhythm with the lemon ice, which was melting too fast, damn it, he suckled H's clit mercilessly. *Come for me, princess. Come* on *me.*

"You feel good," she said, moaning. "Your tongue…oh hell! What a glorious, talented tongue."

She tensed…then rammed his face into her pussy. He dropped the lemon pop and held onto her ass with both hands. He took the assault of her clawing fingers and pumping cunt. He drank the lemon-tinged cum until she broke free of his grasp and stumbled backwards.

Jarod was on his feet in two seconds flat. He withdrew a condom from his front pocket then unzipped his jeans and pushed them and the black-silk boxers off his hips. She watched him roll on the condom, her wide gaze not quite as confident as before, and yelped when he picked her up and slammed her against the wall. "I want to fuck you," he whispered into her ear. "God, baby, I want to fuck you hard and fast until I come in that beautiful pussy."

Her erratic breathing told him she was either scared or turned on. He sucked in a breath, trying to gain some control, but all he could feel was the sensual press of her body against his. His heart pounded furiously and his blood raged. *God.* The tang of her sex was still in his mouth tormenting him as he waited for her decision. Would she say the safe word? Or give him permission?

Her arms wrapped around his shoulders and her legs tightened around his waist. Almost too softly to hear, she said, "Please…fuck me."

He was too far gone to play nice. He plunged his cock into her pussy and nearly died from the tight, warm feel of her flesh around his. Shit, shit, shit. Sucking in a steadying breath, he pinned her to the wall, his fingers digging into her thighs, and took her again and again. He wanted to make it last, but damn it, he was too turned on and she felt too good.

"I'm going to—"*Oh God!* Jarod moaned loudly as the orgasm shuddered through him. He held onto H tightly as his seed spurted, meeting the resistance of the condom. A minute later, he slumped forward, pinning his blonde prize to the wall. "I'm sorry. It's been a really long time."

"We have a lot of time to play, sugar," she murmured, her fingers dancing along his shoulders. "Don't you worry."

The hard points of her nipples pierced his chest, and he groaned in erotic anguish. He had plans for those beautiful breasts. Hell, he had plans for this beautiful woman. She smelled like honeysuckle and her skin was as soft as flower petals. A memory of last night skittered…soft laughter…hot mouth…cold snow.

He wanted to know his partner's name. Would she tell him? Should he tell her his identity? Maybe exchanging personal information was against the Club's rules.

"My turn," said H.

Jarod managed raise his head. "Your turn to what?"

"To come again." She grinned. "Me. You. Me again."

"I'll need some recovery time," he said.

"Hmmm."

Not sure what "hmmm" meant, Jarod released H who wandered toward the bed. He went into the bathroom to dispose of the condom, clean himself off and undress. He left the mask on, but he hoped by night's end, he and H would reveal their identities to each other.

When he reentered the playroom, he stumbled to a stop.

H was spread-eagled on the bed, a long pink vibrator thrusting in and out of her pussy. She had shed everything but her mask and those incredibly sexy white boots. Her eyes were closed and her mouth was opened in a silent "O".

His gaze lingered on her breasts. God, they were beautiful. The most gorgeous pair he'd ever seen. Big as grapefruits with nipples pink and juicy, he watched 'em jiggle as H's enthusiasm for the vibrator gained momentum.

Without waiting for an invitation, he crawled onto the bed and whispered, "Need some help with that?"

"My nipples," H said. "Play with them!"

Jarod moved so that he kneeled at the top of her head. While she fucked herself with the big vibrator, he leaned down and lavished attention her breasts. The huge, fleshy mounds turned him on. God, did they ever. He was a breast man, through and through, and H's tits were luscious. Eagerly, Jarod kissed the puckered flesh around her nipples, tracing the crinkles with his tongue.

"More," she begged. "Suck them. God almighty, *suck* them!"

Jarod scraped his teeth along one nub then he lightly nipped the other peak. A low moan escaped H's throat. That erotic sound sent lust zinging straight to his balls. *Oh yeah.* He gave up his playful torture in favor of an all-out sensual assault on H's gorgeous breasts. As he suckled and pinched and squeezed, he got hotter and hornier. And he kept sucking and pinching and squeezing until H screamed, "I'm coming. *Ooohhh!*"

Her hips arched as she plunged the vibrator into her pussy. Her nipples went hard and tight, he tugged them as she gave herself over to the orgasm. As she went loose and limp, sweat rolled down her stomach, pearling in her belly button.

He smelled her cum, the musky scent of it, and felt his mouth go all slobbery. Crawling over her, he placed his knees on either side of her head, his hands on either side of her thighs, and flicked a tongue over her sex. He wanted to drink her cream. Again.

"I love your taste," he said hoarsely. He licked her slit clean then pushed his tongue into her vaginal opening.

He felt her move, adjust herself, but caught up in the taste and scent of her pussy, he merely adjusted with her.

Then he felt her mouth on his cock.

"Whoa. Wow. Uh…" Jarod's eyes rolled back into his head. He heaved a breath.

"What's wrong?" she asked. Her tongue flicked the tip of his dick. "Don't you like blowjobs?"

"*Yah-uh,*" he managed, "but I'm losing my focus on your beautiful, and may I add very tasty, pussy."

"We'll just have to make the best of it," she said, laughing. She kissed his cock, nibbling its ridges, and licked it repeatedly. *I've died and gone to heaven. And I have my own personal angel…*

Her hot mouth worshipped his penis until *he* was crying "Amen!" Her soft hands cupped his balls, squeezing gently. Frissons of heat skittered through him as she sucked his cock. And just when he thought he might explode, H took all of him. He felt the warm slide down her throat…and he dove into her pussy with renewed vigor.

She came before he did, and as he licked away the juice that dribbled from her pulsating cunt, the low moan that vibrated on his cock sent him shooting to the stars. She drank from him too, swallowing his seed with a gratifying purr.

A few moments later he flopped onto the bed and watched her wiggle off the white boots. When she was done, he said, "C'mere." And opened his arms.

"What's this? Snuggling?" She sounded amused and, if he wasn't mistaken, a little surprised.

"What's wrong with snuggling?"

"Hmmm. I just thought it broke some kind of man code."

"I'll demand dinner and a foot rub later. I'll also call you 'woman' to an annoying degree and growl a lot."

H laughed. Then she wrapped one leg around his, her arm sliding along his waist. Relaxed and happy, they both drifted into sleep.

* * * * *

When Honey awoke from the short nap, she looked at the digital clock on the nightstand. 12:30 a.m. Her gaze coasted down the still sleeping form next to her.

She had expected great sex. Their attraction was nigh-on combustible. And truthfully, she had expected that she would like Jarod McClure. He was funny and sexy and looked damned good naked.

But she hadn't expected the gooey, sweet emotion warming her like a just-baked batch of chocolate-chip cookies. She'd felt this way once or twice in her life but never this quickly. And with a man she had, well, lied to…not that he'd cared to ask who she was before he bedded her.

Usually, at least here in this place of sexual safety and satiety, not knowing a man's name didn't bother her. Honey loved sex. She loved the male body. She loved her play place here at the Sex Club.

Maybe she didn't exactly like going home alone every night. Or not having someone to snuggle with. Yeah. That's what did it, all right. Jarod, He-Man of ProCare, liked to snuggle after sex.

Damnation. She was a goner.

What would he do once he found out about her identity? That she was Honey Sinclair, owner and operator of Honey Do, his only competitor? And she was kicking his ass too. She knew it.

Guilt swirled. She hadn't expected to feel guilty for her duplicity. She just wanted to have some fun with Jarod. After all, he'd been the one to topple her into the snow and kiss her.

Maybe he'd never talk to her again once she told him the truth. And she'd live with his choice. But for now…

Honey rose onto her side. Leaning forward, she kissed his naked chest. His skin was taut, all muscled curves and ridges. She feasted on his pectorals, peppering kisses on every centimeter of flesh. She laved his tiny brown nipples into hardness then flicked her tongue across each nub until a soft, low groan issued. Glancing up at his face, she saw his eyes were open.

"Hello," he said in a whiskey voice.

"Hi." She licked the space between his pecs, tasting the faint musk of his skin. Moving upward to his neck, she traced patterns from collarbone to ear. "You taste good."

"Better than lemon juice pops?"

She grinned. As she explored his body with fingers and lips, his hands were restless on her back, her shoulders, her buttocks.

Her engine got revved all over again. And, apparently, so had Jarod's. Before she could take her next breath, Jarod looped his hands under her arms and pulled her forward so his mouth could ravage her breasts.

Zings traveled from nipples to pussy as he tugged one peak then the other between his teeth and flicked his tongue rapidly against the turgid points. The need built, an ache that bloomed between her thighs, a heat that engulfed her whole body.

When he let her go, she scooted down and rubbed her nipples over his chest. His hand snaked around her neck and brought her down so he could nibble on her throat. As he occupied himself with teasing the sensitive spot behind her ear, Honey's hand drifted down his thigh and snuck between their bodies.

She squeezed his hard-on then caressed it. She loved the stone-wrapped-in-silk feel of his cock. His moan zapped the pit of her stomach.

"I want to taste you," she murmured.

He released her and she crawled between his legs, her hands coasting up his rock-hard thighs. Honey wanted to feel that big, thick cock slide inside her again. Soon, very soon, she'd take him and ride him. But for now…she spent several glorious minutes fondling his balls and rubbing his cock.

Jarod's hands fisted in the bedcovers and his hips thrust, a silent begging for her mouth. She ignored that plea, stroking him rough then soft. Finally, he begged in a whisper, "*Please*."

Only then did she put her lips against his flesh. She savored that gorgeous penis, kissing it from base to head before taking the tip into her mouth and sucking it. Torturing him with endless tongue swirls and long licks, she took all of him.

His hands dove into her hair and held her captive. Not content with her gentle worshipping, he fucked her mouth.

She held on to his thighs and took his strokes, her tongue teasing the cock pumping between her lips.

With a persecuted groan, Jarod released her, gasping and panting. Honey saw pre-cum pearl the tip of his penis and she sucked it away.

Jarod looked at her, his eyes glazed. "I want to come inside you."

"That's very good news." She rose to her knees then planted herself on either side of his hips. She slid her hand between her legs and pinched her clit. Pre-orgasm shivers racked her. "That feels so good." Her gaze held his. She rubbed her slick inner folds then spread them apart and showed him her succulent cunt.

"That *looks* good."

Honey pressed down and slicked her cunt across his cock.

Jarod's eyes went blind and his hands fisted in the covers.

In a hurry, she leaned over and opened the nightstand drawer. Grabbing the box of condoms, she opened it and dumped a shower of condoms on the bed. Reaching down, Honey rolled on the protection then finally—*oh finally*—guided Jarod's cock inside her pussy.

Their breathing was harsh, shallow. Their gazes held, mirroring passion. Then Jarod's fingernails dug into her hips. He thrust upward and she followed his eager movements. His calculated strokes drove her mad. An ache stole across her, made her belly tight with need, made her core spiral with pleasure.

He released her hips and played with her breasts, pulling on her sensitive nipples, bringing her closer and closer to orgasm.

Then she felt his thumb stroking her clit and she squeezed her vaginal muscles as she fucked him, over and over, until he stiffened and shoved his cock deep inside. As he came, his stroking thumb never stopped.

The bliss sparked, trembled…then…oh *then*…

She shattered into a million sharp pieces that shredded her ability to think. For an endless moment she was only light and sound and feeling.

When she was able to breathe again, Honey collapsed against Jarod, her tongue flicking out to taste the sweat beading his skin. Her heart pounded a trillion miles a minute and she still felt that gooey warmth. Jarod wrapped his arms around her and spent the next few minutes doing some expert snuggling.

"H?"

"Hmmm?"

"How would you feel about exchanging names?"

"Names?" Panic fluttered, but she swallowed the knot of dread lodged in her throat and rose up a little to look into his eyes.

"No," he said, uncertainty ringing in his voice. "I don't want just your name. I want to unmask you."

Chapter Four

Honey hesitated too long. Even through his mask, she could see that Jarod's gaze reflected disappointment at her perceived rejection. Damn. If they took off their masks, the fun would be over. And selfish though it was, she wanted more time with him. Once he discovered that he'd been fucking his competition…well, it could go one of two ways. He'd laugh and snuggle with her. Or he'd yell at her and leave. Since men had as much pride as they had testosterone, she was guessing he'd go with Option B.

"Tell you what," she said, stroking his tense jaw. "If you can give me three more orgasms…we'll take off the masks."

His lips curved into naughty smile. "A very erotic version of truth or dare?"

"Yeah."

The smile went wider, naughtier. "Just three, huh?"

"Not a big enough challenge?"

"I guess we'll find out."

Jarod's fingers drifted across her arm, down her side, to her hip. "Your skin is so soft." He stroked her buttock, cupping it and kneading it. Then his hand moved leisurely to her thigh. "You smell good too. Like honeysuckle."

Ah. If only he knew…

"You're very distracting," she murmured, stretching against him.

He chuckled as he rolled her onto her back and covered her, his hardening cock nestled against her pussy. "I like making you come."

"Ooooh. And I like coming."

He kissed her shoulder and the soft press of his lips made her shudder. He tasted her collarbone, moved up her neck and peppered kisses along her jaw. His eyes were glazed with desire, his breath harsh against her lips.

Jarod stretched her arms above her head. Her back arched slightly, pushing her breasts into his chest. Her nipples pebbled against his warm flesh. "Do you have anything that might help me tie you up?"

"You mean like ropes or leather or…silk strands?"

"Where?"

Her hand felt to the edge of the bed and pulled out the attached tie that had been tucked between the mattresses. "There are four."

"I need only two."

He moved off her only long enough to attach the silk strands. When he finished binding her wrists, she tested the material. Her arms had some movement, and she had no doubt Jarod would release her if asked, but she still felt a little vulnerable.

Lowering himself onto her body until his mouth hovered above hers, he kissed her. It was a slow melding of the lips that made her breath hitch and heart pound. His tongue slipped into her mouth and danced with hers. He tasted like mints and like need. He released her mouth then licked the seam of her mouth. Her pulse leapt at the unexpected eroticism of such an act.

"You have the most beautiful breasts," he said.

"And here I thought you liked me for my keen intelligence and acerbic wit."

He grinned, obviously unrepentant about his love of boobs. Just to mess with him, she wiggled her chest.

Jarod took that as an invitation and cupped her breasts. The feel of his strong, warm fingers against her aching flesh made her squirm. He pinched the nipples into hardness and she felt the buds tighten almost painfully. He kept pulling and tugging and she kept moaning and squirming. It was like he'd plucked a string that connected her nipples to her pussy. She shivered with liquid desire. "I like it when you suck on my nipples."

"Do you?"

"Yes. A lot."

"What a coincidence. I like it when I suck on your nipples too."

His mouth surrounded one tight bud and his tongue flicked the peak. Pleasure jolted through her, spearing her at the core. He laved her nipple, suckling one while his hand tormented the other. Then he switched mouth and hand and she went up in flames, wiggling some more against him. His penis bumped her clit and she cried out at the tortuous contact.

Crawling down her body, hot fingers dragged sensuously down her skin as his mouth trailed a wet line to her navel. His tongue encircled her stomach before sliding oh so slowly to her thigh. He pushed apart her legs and kissed the flesh on either side of her cunt. He parted the folds to taste her.

Honey tugged at the silk holding her hostage and bucked her hips, wanting Jarod's mouth on her, desperately. His tongue flicked her clit, teasing the hard nub before sliding down and tasting her again.

God almighty. His kisses drove her wild.

His tongue delved into her slit, licked the juice pearling there, then his mouth settled on her clit and sucked it, hard. The orgasm swelled, waves of pleasure threatening, then burst, sensation after joyous sensation rolling over her. She moaned and bucked, her cunt pulsating as she came.

"One," he murmured, and damned if he didn't sound smug. She didn't know if she should feel amused or annoyed.

From somewhere in the bedding, he produced a condom. She watched as he rolled it onto his erection.

Jarod pushed her legs up and forward until her heels rested on his shoulders. She panted, still shuddering from Orgasm One, when he lifted her hips and, without so much as a by-your-leave, plunged his cock inside her. He impaled her to the womb, stretching her and filling her in a way that made her shudder all over again.

His hands slid under her ass and adjusted the angle. She felt his dick slid along her G-spot and a rush of breath left her. She clawed at the silk, her back arching. "Oh my God. Do it again."

He not only did it again, he did it just right. His hands were sweaty on her thighs as he held onto her legs and pumped into her again and again. The rocking of their bodies singed her to the core. She heard the erotic slap of flesh as their bodies met. And she saw the glazed look of lust in his eyes that surely reflected her own.

Then there was that thick, delicious cock piercing her over and over and over.

She felt the rise of another orgasm. Her body strained toward bliss as her mind reeled with the implication that Jarod might very well do as he promised.

His thumb rubbed her clit and he fucked her harder, his cock pistoning into her pussy. She pulled on the silk bonds and closed her eyes, matching his movements, her heart pounding, sweat slickening her skin. His low moans brought her closer to another orgasm…

"I love how you feel," he said, "So warm and wet and tight."

She plunged over the edge into bliss. As stars exploded behind her eyes, she vaguely realized that Jarod was groaning, plunging deeply…coming inside her pussy. She convulsed around his cock, mini-waves of pleasure undulating from her core.

"Two," he said with a grin.

Honey was too satisfied to berate him for arrogance.

He slipped out of her then left the bed to dispose of the condom. When he returned, he kneeled between her legs and massaged her quivering thighs, leaning down to kiss her knees. He spent an inordinate amount of time on her legs, kissing and stroking. It wasn't so much a seduction as a way to relax her.

Slowly, her body gave way to his gentle touches and before long, she sank into the mattress, drowsy and sated.

Her eyes had drifted closed and she faded into a half-awake state. Jarod had fucked the energy right out of her. She felt deliciously mellow.

When she felt Jarod's mouth on her nipple, sucking it into hardness, she smiled and murmured encouragement. Lust stirred anew. She'd never had such an eager, willing, tender partner. Then she felt something looped around her left nipple. Her eyes slitted open. She looked at the tiny black leather nipple clamp. Jarod pushed the tightener up until her nipple tingled with pleasurable pain. Then he paid exquisite attention to her right nipple. With its tightener pushed until the bud pulsed and ached, Jarod turned his attention to a third item.

"You've rummaged my drawers," she said in a lazy voice.

He chuckled. "You have quite a stash of goodies. I liked this one in particular."

He held a clitoris clamp, which reminded her of an oversized silver bobby pin. She watched him trace the object with his forefinger. "I can't wait to put this on you."

"Then don't wait."

Her body had pulsed to life, no longer feeling languorous or tired. How he'd managed to rev her up so many times in so short a period still wowed her.

His fingers parted her pussy and he carefully pushed the clamp onto her clit. The nub reacted to the constriction with pleasurable tingling. "Going for number three, then?"

"Damn right."

The vibrator whirred on and Honey watched as Jarod placed the pink tip onto her tormented clitoris. As he rubbed her clit gently with the toy, nearly unbearable sensations rocketed through her.

She gasped then panted then lost breath.

He moved the vibrator across her swollen flesh and circled her entrance. "You're so wet," he said, his voice low and harsh. "You have a beautiful pussy. I love watching you. Love doing this to you."

"Do it to me some more."

He rewarded her for that sassy comment. The pulsating toy pressed inside and Jarod maneuvered it up just a little. With small, quick strokes, he fucked her with the vibrator.

Orgasm Three nearly melted her bones.

All the pleasure points triangulated into one big explosion.

Her hips surged off the bed. A sob caught in her throat. She screamed his name.

Then she was floating softly, softly back to Earth.

Jarod removed the nipple cuffs and clit clamp, loosed her numb wrists and gathered her into his arms. She snuggled into his embrace. Wow-oh-wow. She felt so incredibly wonderful. Safe. Happy. Well-loved.

Then Jarod leaned down and whispered, "How did you know my name?"

Heart pounding, Honey splayed her fingers on his chest. "I know who you are," she admitted. "I made some inquiries after that kiss at the Morrisons' party."

"Isn't that breaking the rules of the Sex Club?" he asked. He sounded playful, not angry.

"You could've done the same," she accused. She bit her lip. Stupid to sound that way. Like she had a right to be petulant about his behavior. "I guess that kiss wasn't as…memorable for you."

"I wouldn't have showed up if that kiss hadn't boiled me alive." His fingers edged along her mask. "I didn't think you wanted to be known. And that's the reason I asked to unmask you. I want to know your name. I want to see your face. I want to know your favorite color and if you like baseball and if you prefer chocolate or flowers on a first date."

Honey felt her heart plummet to her toes. He sounded so romantic. So eager to take steps beyond being just bed partners. And oh, how she wanted it. Wanted it badly.

The mask shifted and, coward that she was, she closed her eyes as he lifted away the lace-edged plastic. For a long, terrible moment, she heard nothing.

Then he inhaled sharply and said, "*You.*"

The word was pure heat. Pure accusation. With nervousness clawing at her stomach, Honey opened her eyes and met his gaze. He looked shocked. And betrayed.

"What did you hope to gain from this…this charade?" he asked. Already he was rolling away from her and off the bed. He searched for his clothes, pulling on the jeans he found first. "You've already put the squeeze on ProCare. This your way of making sure we go under? You like your men naked, don't you, Honey?"

"Damn right I do," she said. She let him verbally flog her. Let him be pissed off. She deserved it for not revealing herself to him before they'd played together. "This wasn't about business. It was about pleasure."

"You got cameras in here? Am I going to see myself in the *Clement Falls Tribune* buck-naked? Good thing it wasn't me in those bonds."

That insult cut her like jagged glass scraped across her chest. But the image of him being tied up and at her mercy also sent a wave of lust through her. Lord, what fun it would be to take him…big, strong Jarod McClure…take him until he begged for her mercy.

She sat up and glared at him. "You don't know me. Or what kind of woman I am. But I would never hurt you like that. And I would never do something to betray the Club."

He tugged on his shirt and found his socks and boots. "Whatever you say, sweetheart."

"You're upset. You have a right to be. But I just wanted…you. I'm sorry I hurt you by not telling you who I was. But c'mon, Jarod. I saw the stars with you. You've got me twisted into knots. No other man's done that. Not like you. We have something that we can build on."

"Lies and mistrust?" His gaze burned into hers and she felt tears prick at her eyes. "I don't cotton to that, Miss Sinclair. You can't build anything on that kind of flimsy foundation."

"Would you have taken me?" she asked softly. "If I had introduced myself as Honey Sinclair, would you have met me and done the same beautiful, wicked things?"

He was dressed now. He ran agitated fingers through his hair. He smiled grimly at her. "Guess we'll never know, will we?"

Jarod turned and strode to the door, unlocked it and left.

She swallowed the knot in her throat then fell back onto the bed. Shoot. That had not gone well. She cried, feeling the pain of losing something she hadn't quite had in the first place. How could you miss what had never really been yours?

Best thing she could do was give herself a nice pity-party then suck it up and move on. She would find a way to apologize to Jarod. Maybe he'd accept it, maybe he'd tell her to go screw herself. But at least he'd know she was truly, deeply sorry about her lie of omission.

But she'd never be sorry that she'd spent New Year's night with him. Would never, ever regret the hours that she'd had him all to herself. Maybe, when he got over being mad, he'd realize the same thing she already knew.

"Magical," she whispered into to the empty, lonely room. "It was magical."

Chapter Five

One week later…

Jarod drove his F150 up the imposing driveway that had already been cleared from last night's snowfall. The three-story Victorian was in near perfect condition, as gorgeous now as it had been in its heyday. It was also a shade of pink that made him shudder in masculine terror. It looked like a gingerbread house surrounded by mounds of white frosting.

He followed the circular drive halfway then parked. It took him a moment to gather the courage to get out of the truck and walk up the three wooden steps to the porch.

As he crossed to the etched glass door, it swung open. A slight girl with gray eyes and blonde hair beckoned him forward. "Come in, Mr. McClure. I'm Mettie Jamison, Miss Odie's assistant."

He had to admit, he was terrified to cross into the domain ruled absolutely by Odemina Wilson. He nodded to the girl then stepped inside. She took his coat and gloves then led him to the left and gestured for him to enter a big parlor. For just a second, he felt as if he'd gone back a hundred years in time.

"All original furnishings," said Mettie. "And as far as I can tell, still sitting in the same locations Miss Odie's great-great-grandmother arranged them." With a flourish of her hand, she indicated he should sit down on a red-velvet couch with fancy wood scrollwork along its top. Though he felt like a fool, he did so.

"Would you enjoy a cup of tea?" she asked.

"No, thank you. But if you had a shot of tequila, I might well say yes."

She grinned then slipped from the room, her job done.

Odemina made him wait fifteen minutes in the room filled with antiques and smelling like lemon wood polish. When she finally deigned to join him, she walked in leaning heavily on a silver-tipped cane. Regally, slowly, she made her way to a wingback placed opposite of the love seat. Separating the seating arrangement was a large cherrywood table filled with ceramic bric-a-brac.

Miss Odie was a small, thin woman, as white as paper and just as sharp-edged. She was dressed in a simple black dress with a single strand of pearls dangling from her neck. Her gray hair was done up in a double-bun and pearls shone at ears. She wore black hose and black shoes. Miss Odie never wore any other color—not since the death of her husband, Jeremiah Wilson, ten years before.

"Mettie tells me you turned down tea in favor of spirits," said Odemina. She said *spirits* in the same way a preacher might say *Satan*.

Her brown gaze sparkled with ire and intelligence, pinning him like a carnivore that had just discovered a tasty bit of meat.

Jarod's mouth opened then closed. Good Lord, it was a blow to his manhood to realize how much awe and fear he held in reserve for Miss Odie. She was a formidable woman. Finally, he said, "Yes, I did, ma'am. In jest."

"You have a peculiar sense of humor, Mr. McClure."

"If you say so, ma'am."

She narrowed her gaze at him, taking his measure. Or maybe she was supposed to wear glasses and pride kept her from correcting her vision in such an obvious way. His own grandmother refused to go to the eye doctor until she plowed through the garage door with her Honda. The remote control hadn't worked and she was so vision-impaired she hadn't realized the door never rolled up.

"You know my granddaughter, Honey Sinclair Wilson."

Boy, did he ever. He wondered why Honey didn't use Wilson. As if Odie were reading her thoughts, she said, "She doesn't want to bank on the family name. She's got gumption. Like me."

He didn't know how to respond so he merely nodded.

"I would like you to stay away from her, Mr. McClure. And I'm willing to pay you to do it." Her pink lips thinned.

Flummoxed by this firmly delivered edict, Jarod stared at her. Miss Odie was used to verbally walloping people in conversation. She met his gaze head-on without apology.

"I heard tell her little business is putting a hurt on yours."

"Competition is a healthy thing," he said, though he barely managed to maintain his respectful tone. A week away from Honey had cooled his ire. He hadn't been able to stop thinking about her, in particular the look on her face as he let his pride dictate his final words to her. He'd hurt her.

Now that his mind was less clogged with testosterone-fueled grievances, he could admit they'd enjoyed each other. He'd told himself plenty of times that the mind-blowing sex had been enough. He'd also told himself that she wanted nothing more than to blackmail him to cement her business in Clement Falls.

But he hadn't heard a word about Honey…or from her…and he'd been left in a swirl of guilt and anger ever since.

"Pride is a terrible thing," said Miss Odie. "Pride lost me a son, Mr. McClure. And it might very well have lost me a granddaughter if she hadn't had the heart to forgive an old woman. She's patient, that one. Sweet too."

As much as he didn't want to think about Honey having decent qualities, he knew Miss Odie's reputation well enough to be impressed. She wasn't one to heap compliments on anyone—not even relations.

Damn it. He hated thinking that he might very well have told Honey no if she'd revealed her identity after that snowy kiss. What a shameful thing to know about himself—that he would judge her motives instantly without getting to know her.

Miss Odie seemed to be waiting for him to respond. So he said, "I'm sure you're right about your granddaughter."

"What kind of man takes a woman's body and rejects the rest of her?"

Jarod felt the blood drain out of his face. Did Odemina Wilson know about the Sex Club? About the night he and her granddaughter had shared? He wanted lightning to strike him or Mettie Jamison to smack him unconscious with a tequila bottle. He'd take any abuse or punishment to avoid hearing that the town matriarch knew he'd fucked her only heir.

Miss Odie wasn't looking at him though. Her eyes looked distant, as if she were remembering something that pained her. After a moment, her face cleared and her eyes found his again. "That's what my son said to me when he ran off with Honey's mother. I couldn't abide it, Mr. McClure. Couldn't give up my pride to accept my son and the wife he'd chosen. And it's too late to take back my words or my actions."

"I'm sorry, Miss Odie," Jarod said gently. He was sorry too. It had to hurt a mother deeply to not only outlive her child but know that the wounds between them would never be healed.

"Thank you for your kindness," she said. After a pause, she added, "How much, Mr. McClure?"

"Pardon me?"

"Boy, you're not deaf or dumb. How much money do you want to keep away from my granddaughter?"

"Seems to me, Miss Odie, you're about to make the same mistake twice."

She straightened in her chair and smacked the cane on the floor. Her gaze sparked with her infamous temper. "*Mind your tone.* Honey has been moping around town for a whole week. Won't tell me why." Miss Odie sniffed, her regal head tilted up. "Doesn't want to upset me or get my dander up. But I make it my business to know what goes on in my town."

Her gaze let him know what *business* she knew and Jarod felt embarrassment heat his neck. *Oh my God.* Odemina Wilson not only knew about the Sex Club but that he'd spent New Year's night with her granddaughter in one of its private rooms.

"You've already made up your mind about my granddaughter," said Miss Odie. "I'm just helping you to keep it made up."

"I won't take your money," said Jarod. "And I won't stay away from Honey. I like her." The moment the words popped out of his mouth, he realized it was true. He did like her. Well, then. What the hell was he doing here jawing with her grandmother?

"I'm a powerful woman, Mr. McClure. Powerful and wealthy. Only a fool defies my will."

"Then I guess I'm a fool." That said, he rose to his feet, nodded goodbye and left the parlor. Mettie waited in the foyer with his coat and gloves. He put them on and went through the door she opened.

Once he got into his truck and turned it on to warm the engine, he put his shaking hands on the wheel and squeezed until his heart stopped trying to leap out of his chest. He'd just told Odemina Wilson to stuff it. There'd be consequences. He shuddered to think how she might retaliate.

Let the old biddy do her worst. He had something more important to worry about. He started the truck and headed toward town.

* * * * *

Inside the Wilson house, Odemina sat in her chair, staring into the distance, thinking about the past and the present. When Mettie entered, a smile playing on her lips, the old woman heaved herself out of the wingback. "Well? What's he doing?"

"Got in his truck and took off," she said, wrapping her arm around the fussy old woman to lead her out of the parlor. "You think he'll go to Honey?"

Odemina gave a rusty chuckle. "Oh now, Mettie. Only a fool defies my will."

* * * * *

"Mind if we talk?" asked a familiar male voice.

Honey dropped the paperwork in her hand, not caring that it missed the desk and scattered onto the floor. She whirled around and cried, "Jarod!"

He lounged against the doorway, his fists clenched by his side. He looked at her for a long time...so long it felt like a year passed. Then he said, "I'm sorry I hurt you."

His apology was unexpected. Her heart tripped over in her chest. "I've been trying to figure out how to apologize to you. I should've told you who I was, even if that meant you walked away."

"Ian told me, Honey. I called him on my cell to tell him I was coming to see you. He said you called ProCare today to tell us you were shutting down."

"It was the only way to—"

"To reward a foolish, prideful man?"

Oh wow. He was so tender-hearted. Stubborn, yes. But so was she. "It just makes me wild when you say things like that," she admitted.

"I don't want you to shut down your business just to say you're sorry. Please, don't do that."

"Okay," she said, relieved that he felt that way. She liked Honey Do. Liked running her own business and keeping townspeople employed. And she knew Jarod felt the same way about ProCare. They could come to some understanding, she was sure.

"What now?" she asked. It was a loaded question. Filled with risk and with possibility. She wasn't going to shrink away from her feelings or pretend they didn't exist. "I think I could fall for you, Jarod."

He crossed the space between them and gathered her into his arms. "I do believe you've already fallen for me."

The laugh caught in her throat. In his eyes glimmered what they might one day call love. And she sure felt the same way. But for now…

"You think we could go back to the Club tonight? Try out those silk ties on you?"

He shook his head. "I was thinking you might like to go to dinner. Maybe a movie. *Casablanca* is playing at the Wilson Theatre."

"Don't you think we're past the courting stage?" She was thrilled that he wanted to spend time with her in and out of the bedroom. Though maybe she'd give him a surprise in the theater.. She seemed to recall that it was very, very dark in there. "You thinkin' we should start over?"

"I'm thinkin' we can start wherever we want," said Jarod. As his lips lowered toward hers, he whispered, "So I'll start with a taste of Honey."

The End

Also by Michele Bardsley

ꝏ

1-800-SEX4YOU *with Chris Tanglen*
Life Without Raine
Lighthearted Lust (*anthology)*
Redial 1-800-SEX4YOU *with Chris Tanglen*
Shadows Present
Two Men and a Lady (*anthology)*

About the Author

ꝏ

Michele Bardsley put pen to paper in junior high in the form of angst-filled poetry, angst-filled journals, and angst-filled short stories. She wanted to be a journalist, but after getting associates degree in liberal arts – otherwise known as the degree of the perpetual student – she ended up majoring in marriage and motherhood whereupon she failed housework, plant care, and staying calm in the face of big owies.

Multi-published in several genres, Michele is a bestselling author in electronic and print. She is also an admitted contest slut. Her works have won the Grand Prize in the 72nd Annual Writer's Digest Writing Competition, Best Published Romance Novel in the Royal Palm Literary Awards, Best Fiction Book from the Oklahoma Writer's Federation, Inc., an EPPIE for Best Romantic Suspense, and numerous other honors from publications and organizations.

Michele welcomes comments from readers. You can find her website and email address on her author bio page at www.ellorascave.com.

Why an electronic book?

We live in the Information Age—an exciting time in the history of human civilization, in which technology rules supreme and continues to progress in leaps and bounds every minute of every day. For a multitude of reasons, more and more avid literary fans are opting to purchase e-books instead of paper books. The question from those not yet initiated into the world of electronic reading is simply: *Why?*

1. ***Price.*** An electronic title at Ellora's Cave Publishing and Cerridwen Press runs anywhere from 40% to 75% less than the cover price of the exact same title in paperback format. Why? Basic mathematics and cost. It is less expensive to publish an e-book (no paper and printing, no warehousing and shipping) than it is to publish a paperback, so the savings are passed along to the consumer.
2. ***Space.*** Running out of room in your house for your books? That is one worry you will never have with electronic books. For a low one-time cost, you can purchase a handheld device specifically designed for e-reading. Many e-readers have large, convenient screens for viewing. Better yet, hundreds of titles can be stored within your new library—on a single microchip. There are a variety of e-readers from different manufacturers. You can also read e-books on your PC or laptop computer. (Please note that Ellora's Cave does not endorse any specific brands.

You can check our websites at www.ellorascave.com or www.cerridwenpress.com for information we make available to new consumers.)

3. ***Mobility.*** Because your new e-library consists of only a microchip within a small, easily transportable e-reader, your entire cache of books can be taken with you wherever you go.
4. ***Personal Viewing Preferences.*** Are the words you are currently reading too small? Too large? Too... ANNOYING? Paperback books cannot be modified according to personal preferences, but e-books can.
5. ***Instant Gratification.*** Is it the middle of the night and all the bookstores near you are closed? Are you tired of waiting days, sometimes weeks, for bookstores to ship the novels you bought? Ellora's Cave Publishing sells instantaneous downloads twenty-four hours a day, seven days a week, every day of the year. Our webstore is never closed. Our e-book delivery system is 100% automated, meaning your order is filled as soon as you pay for it.

Those are a few of the top reasons why electronic books are replacing paperbacks for many avid readers.

As always, Ellora's Cave and Cerridwen Press welcome your questions and comments. We invite you to email us at Comments@ellorascave.com or write to us directly at Ellora's Cave Publishing Inc., 1056 Home Avenue, Akron, OH 44310-3502.

LaVergne, TN USA
05 January 2010
168926LV00001B/64/P
9 781419 956003